Nola's Worlds #1

changing moon

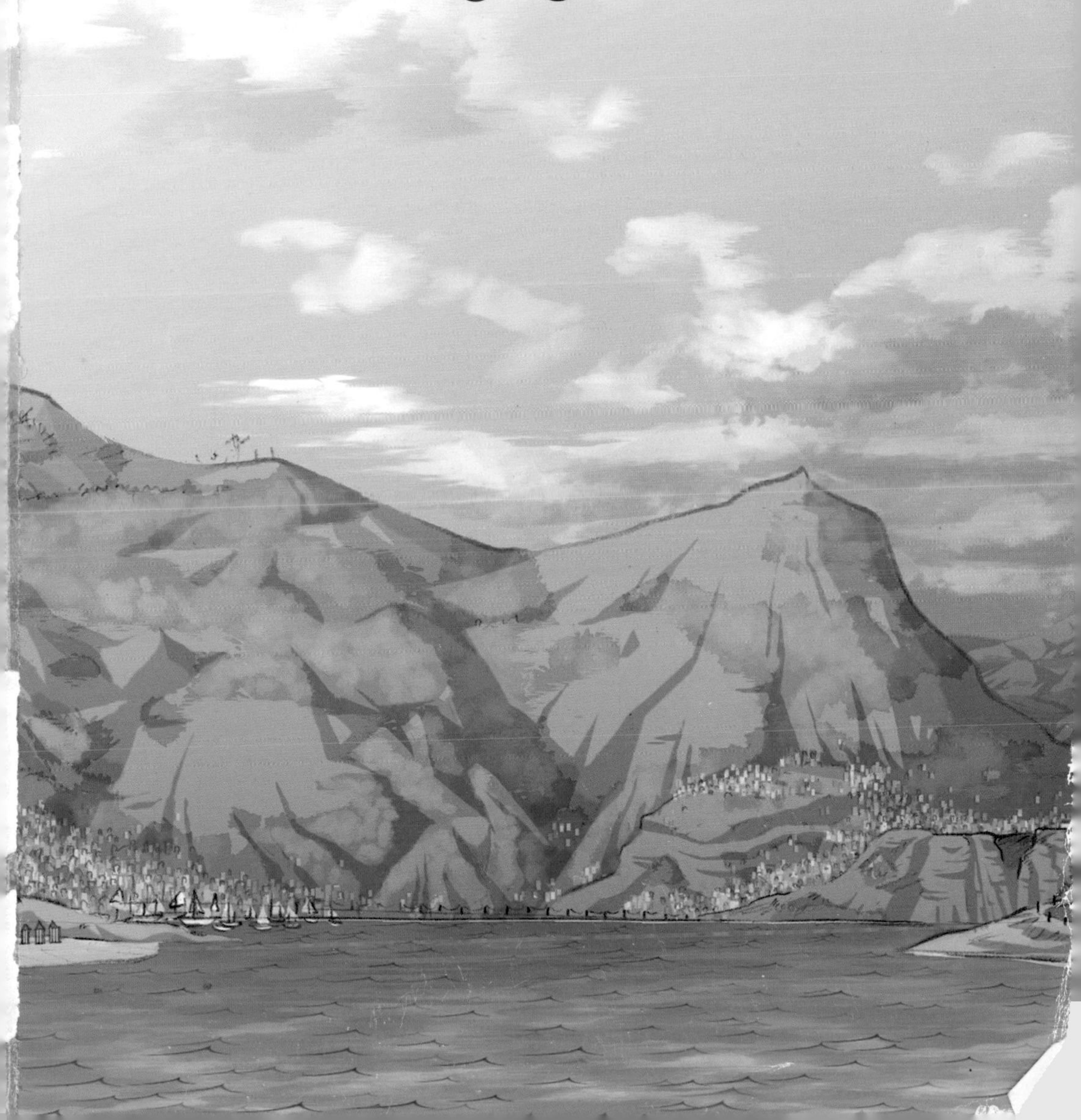

THANK YOU TO KiM and POP FOR THE TRUST, THE TALENT, and THE PERSEVERANCE!
AND FOR THEIR SUPPORT and THEIR LAUGHTER EVERY DAY, THANKS TO ALICIA and GAËL.

THANKS, MATHIEU, FOR THIS BEAUTIFUL STORY.
THANKS, MÉLANIE, FOR YOUR PRESENCE, YOUR SUPPORT, and YOUR PRICELESS ADVICE.
WITHOUT YOU, ALTA DONNA WOULD NOT HAVE THIS FABULOUSLY LEMONY EYE-WATERING FLAVOR!

IN ADDITION TO COLORING, I LIKE WRITING BIG BLOCKS OF TEXT, SO THANK YOU...
...TO KiM and MATTHEW FOR TAKING ME ON BOARD FOR THIS ADVENTURE and CONSIDERING
ME a CO-CREATOR... TO MAGNUS, IRWIN, VÉRONIQUE, KARINE, TARTUFF, and GATE FOR
HELPING ME PREPARE BOARDS... TO GATE and MINIKIM FOR THEIR DAILY SUPPORT... TO
JAMES FOR NIGHTTIME CHATS... TO LÔ FOR BETA-READING... TO GATE and MAGICFRED
THEIR NON-BETA-READING (BEATING iT TO DEATH ^.^)... TO HK FOR THE WINK TO NOLA ON
CROQUEMONSTER (WWW.CROQUEMONSTER.COM)... TO KiM FOR THE BIG WINK TO OOWARD
(WWW.KAOCOCO.COM)... TO MINIKIM FOR HER PATIENCE. AND THANK YOU TO EVERYONE NEAR
and FAR WHO FOLLOWED ALTA DONNA ONLINE... TO MY PARENTS WHO WILL FILL AN ENTIRE
SHELF WITH COPIES OF THIS BOOK... TO GATE FOR HIS UNCONDITIONAL LOVE OF LITTLE ME...
TO CAMILLE FOR INVITING US TO THE 2007 LYON COMICS FESTIVAL BEFORE THE BOOK WAS
EVEN OUT... and THANK YOU iN ADVANCE TO ALL THE BOOKSELLERS and ALL THE FESTIVALS
OF FRANCE, NAVARRE, and QUEBEC (YAY ^.^)! FINALLY, THANK YOU AGAIN TO GATE, BECAUSE
HE'S WELL WORTH iT?

(GATE, MY DEAR, DON'T FORGET I'VE JUST MENTIONED YOU 5 TIMES—6, NOW—SO I'VE
EARNED a GIFT? ^.^)

STORY BY MATHIEU MARIOLLE
ART BY MINIKIM
COLORS BY POP
TRANSLATION BY ERICA OLSON JEFFREY and CAROL KLIO BURRELL

First American edition published in 2010 by Graphic Universe™.
Published by arrangement with MEDIATOON LICENSING — France.

Alta Donna 1 - *Changement de lune*
© DARGAUD BENELUX (DARGAUD-LOMBARD S.A.) 2009, by Mariolle,
   MiniKim, Pop.
www.dargaud.com
All rights reserved

English translation copyright © 2010 by Lerner Publishing Group, Inc.

Graphic Universe™ is a trademark of Lerner Publishing Group, Inc.

Graphic Universe™
A division of Lerner Publishing Group, Inc.
241 First Avenue North
Minneapolis, MN 55401 U.S.A.
Website address: www.lernerbooks.com

Library of Congress Cataloging-in-Publication Data

Mariolle, Mathieu.
   Changing moon / by Mathieu Mariolle ; illustrated by MiniKim
and Pop. – 1st American ed.
       p. cm. – (Nola's worlds ; #1)
   Summary: Nola's teacher and friends little realize that Nola's
stories, often an extension of her dreams, may hint at something
strange going on underneath their perfect and boring town of Alta
Donna, especially after two unusual new students enroll in school.
   ISBN: 978-0-7613-6502-0 (lib. bdg. : alk. paper)
   1. Graphic novels. [1. Graphic novels. 2. Dreams—Fiction.
3. Schools—Fiction. 4. Supernatural—Fiction.] I. Minikim, ill. II. Pop,
1978- ill. III. Title. IV. Title: Number one changing moon. V. Title:
Changing moon.
PZ7.7.M34Ch 2010
741.5'944—dc22   2010005718

Manufactured in the United States of America
2 – DP – 1/1/11

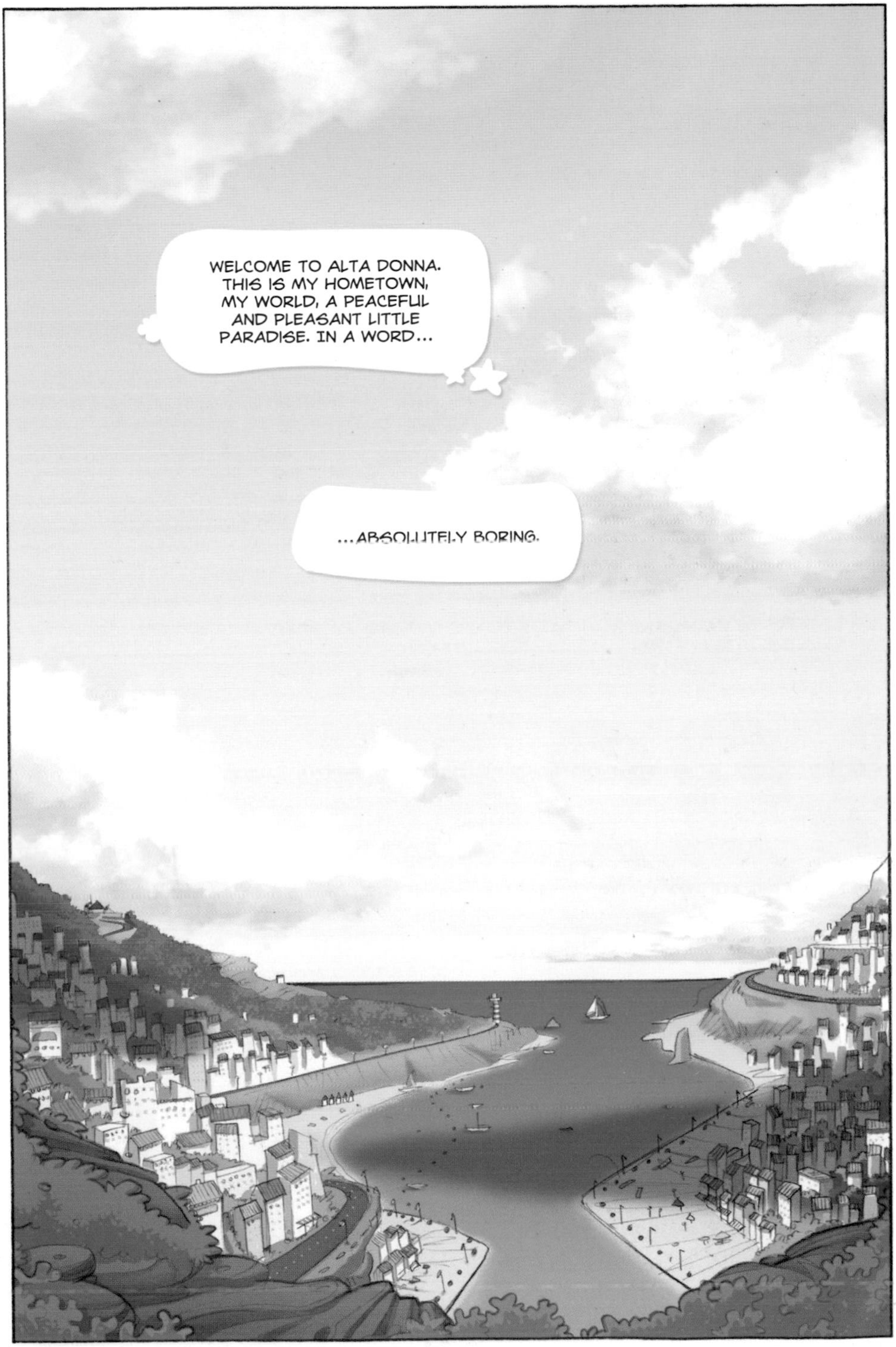
WELCOME TO ALTA DONNA. THIS IS MY HOMETOWN, MY WORLD, A PEACEFUL AND PLEASANT LITTLE PARADISE. IN A WORD...
...ABSOLUTELY BORING.

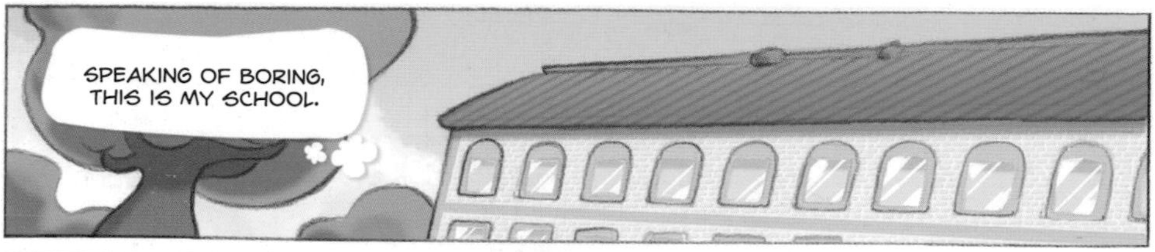
SPEAKING OF BORING, THIS IS MY SCHOOL.

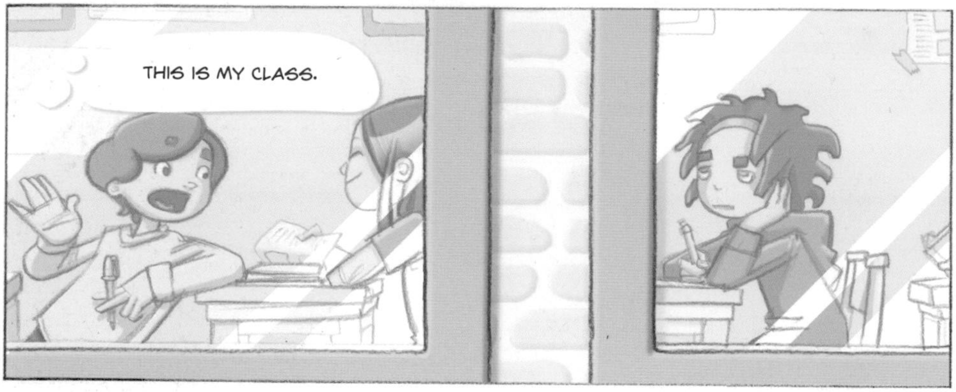
THIS IS MY CLASS.

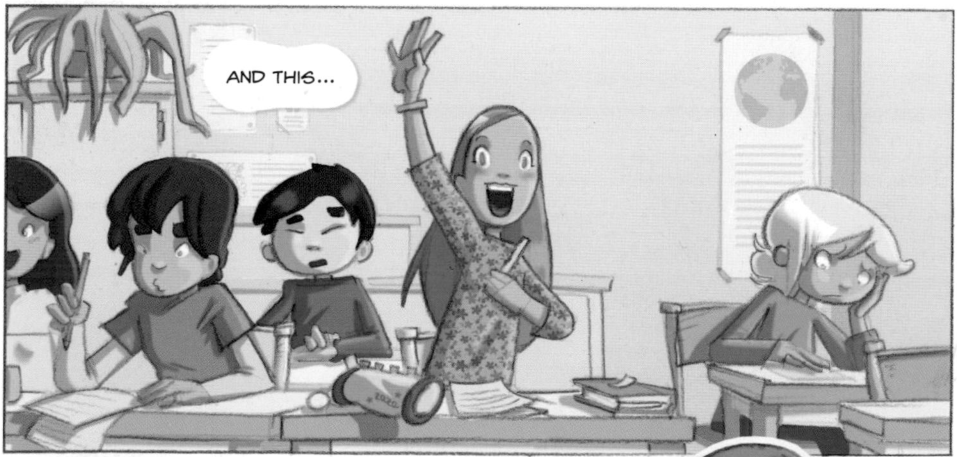
AND THIS...

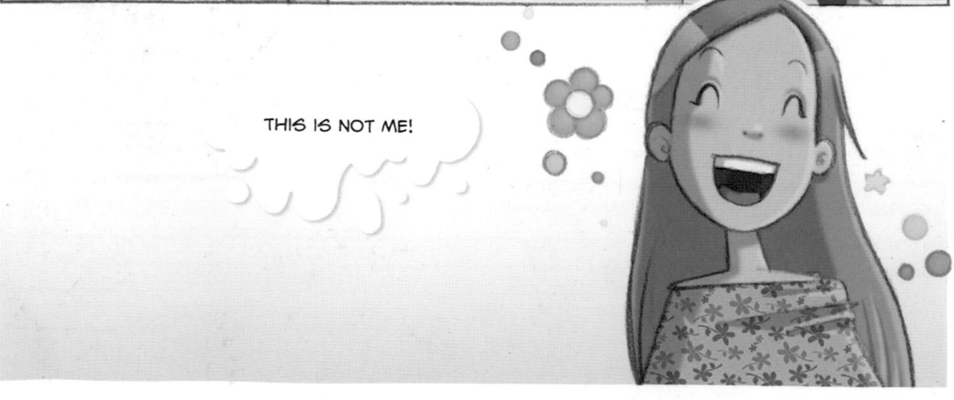
THIS IS NOT ME!

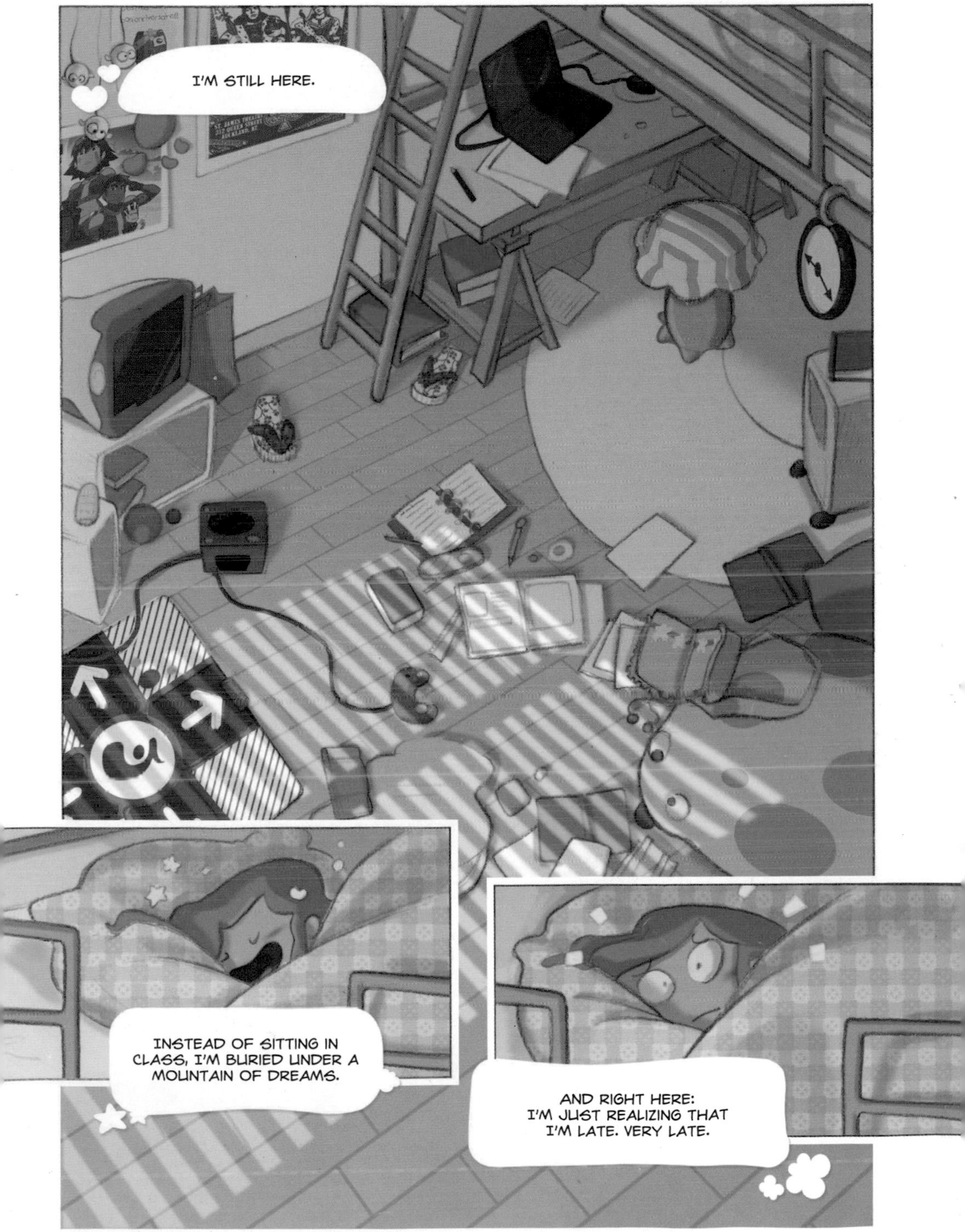
I'M STILL HERE.
INSTEAD OF SITTING IN CLASS, I'M BURIED UNDER A MOUNTAIN OF DREAMS.
AND RIGHT HERE: I'M JUST REALIZING THAT I'M LATE. VERY LATE.

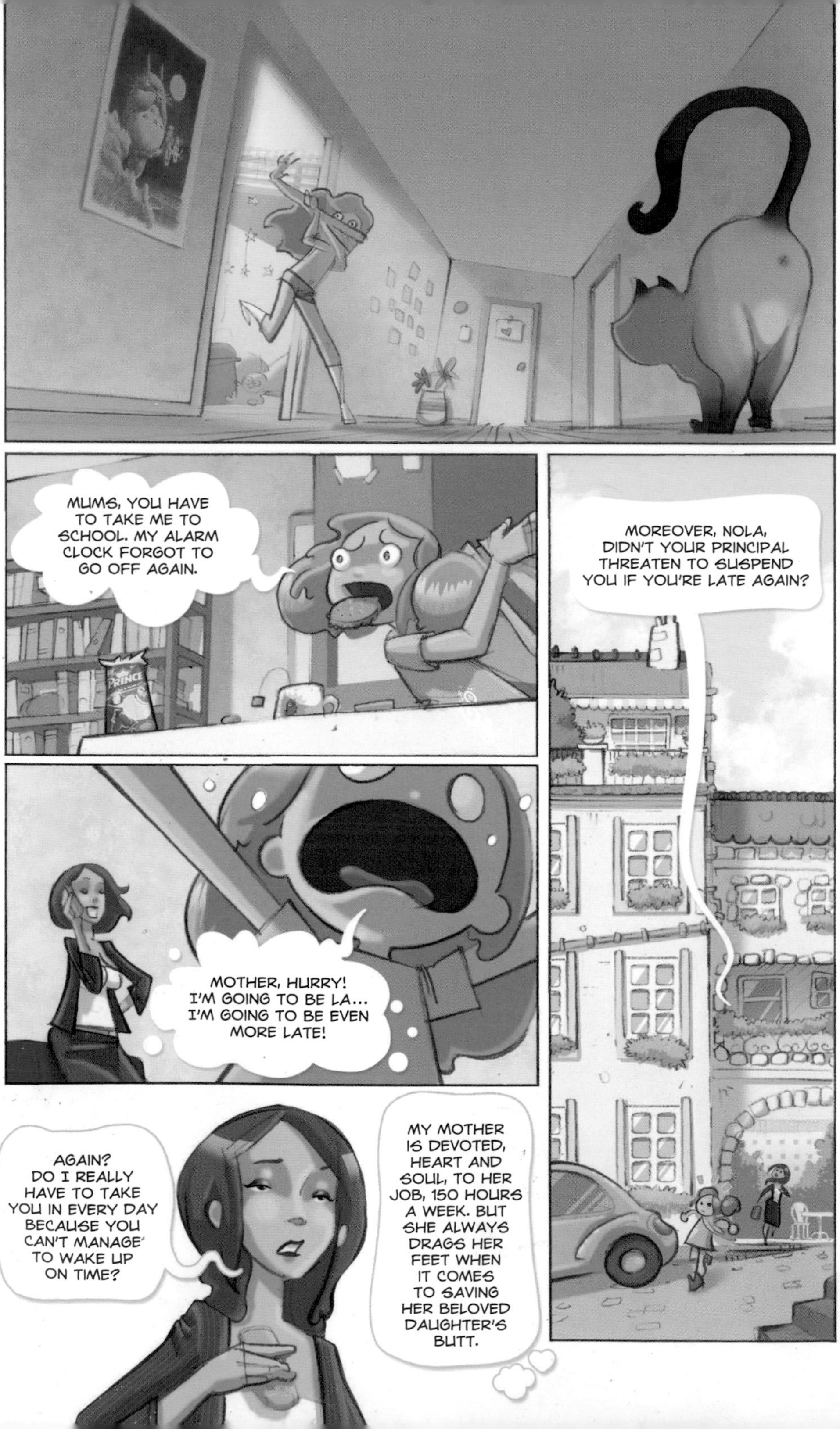
MUMS, YOU HAVE TO TAKE ME TO SCHOOL. MY ALARM CLOCK FORGOT TO GO OFF AGAIN.
MOREOVER, NOLA, DIDN'T YOUR PRINCIPAL THREATEN TO SUSPEND YOU IF YOU'RE LATE AGAIN?
MOTHER, HURRY! I'M GOING TO BE LA... I'M GOING TO BE EVEN MORE LATE!
AGAIN? DO I REALLY HAVE TO TAKE YOU IN EVERY DAY BECAUSE YOU CAN'T MANAGE TO WAKE UP ON TIME?
MY MOTHER IS DEVOTED, HEART AND SOUL, TO HER JOB, 150 HOURS A WEEK. BUT SHE ALWAYS DRAGS HER FEET WHEN IT COMES TO SAVING HER BELOVED DAUGHTER'S BUTT.
PRINCE

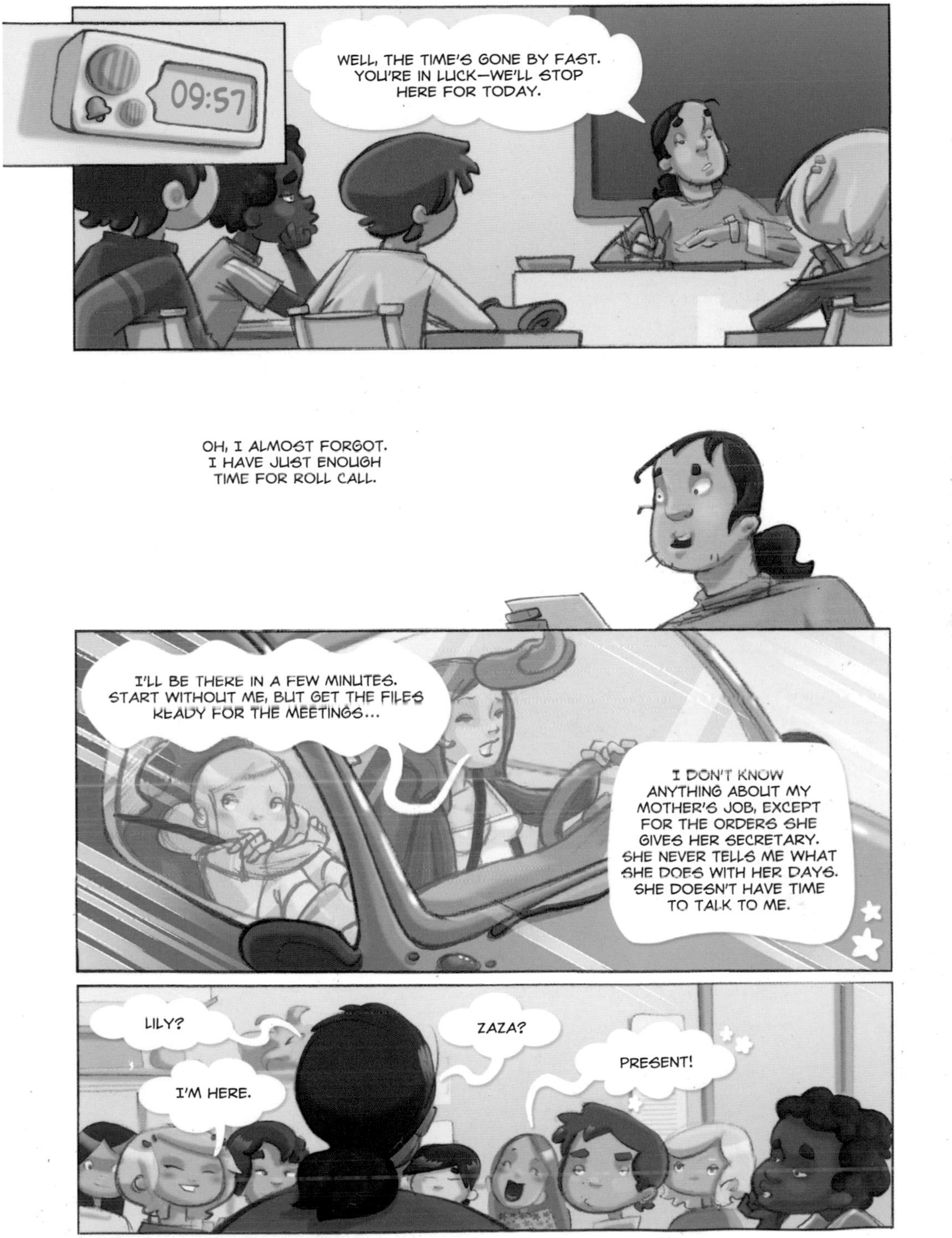
09:57
WELL, THE TIME'S GONE BY FAST. YOU'RE IN LUCK—WE'LL STOP HERE FOR TODAY.
OH, I ALMOST FORGOT. I HAVE JUST ENOUGH TIME FOR ROLL CALL.
I'LL BE THERE IN A FEW MINUTES. START WITHOUT ME, BUT GET THE FILES READY FOR THE MEETINGS...
I DON'T KNOW ANYTHING ABOUT MY MOTHER'S JOB, EXCEPT FOR THE ORDERS SHE GIVES HER SECRETARY. SHE NEVER TELLS ME WHAT SHE DOES WITH HER DAYS. SHE DOESN'T HAVE TIME TO TALK TO ME.
LILY?
I'M HERE.
ZAZA?
PRESENT!

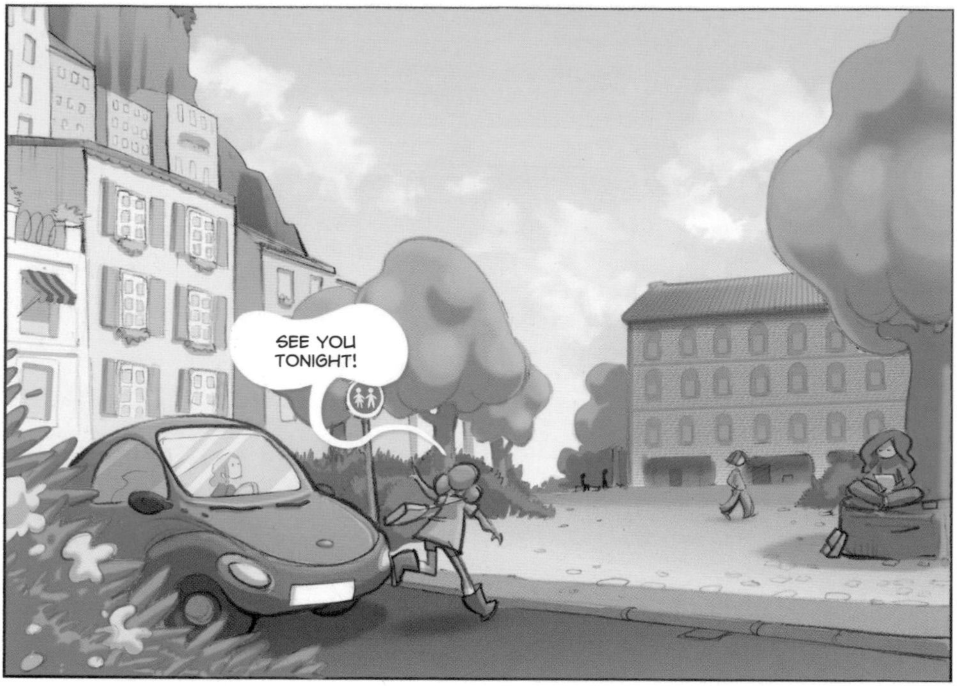
SEE YOU TONIGHT!

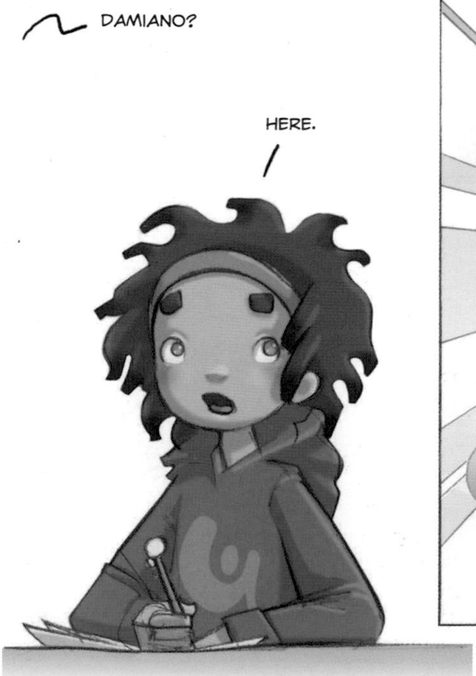
DAMIANO?
HERE.

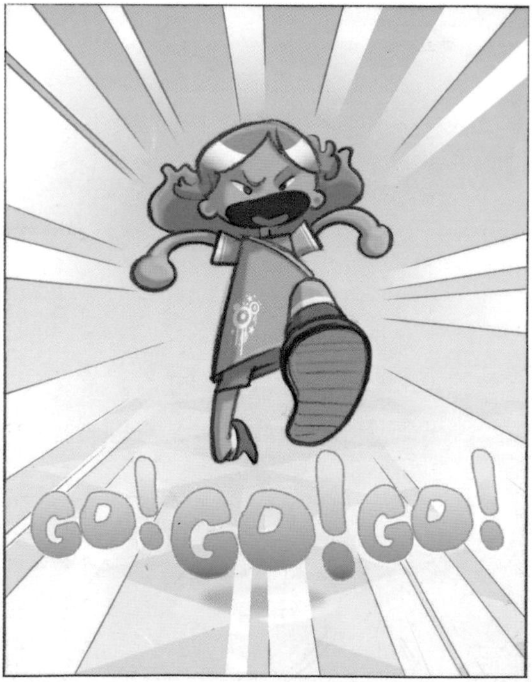
GO! GO! GO!

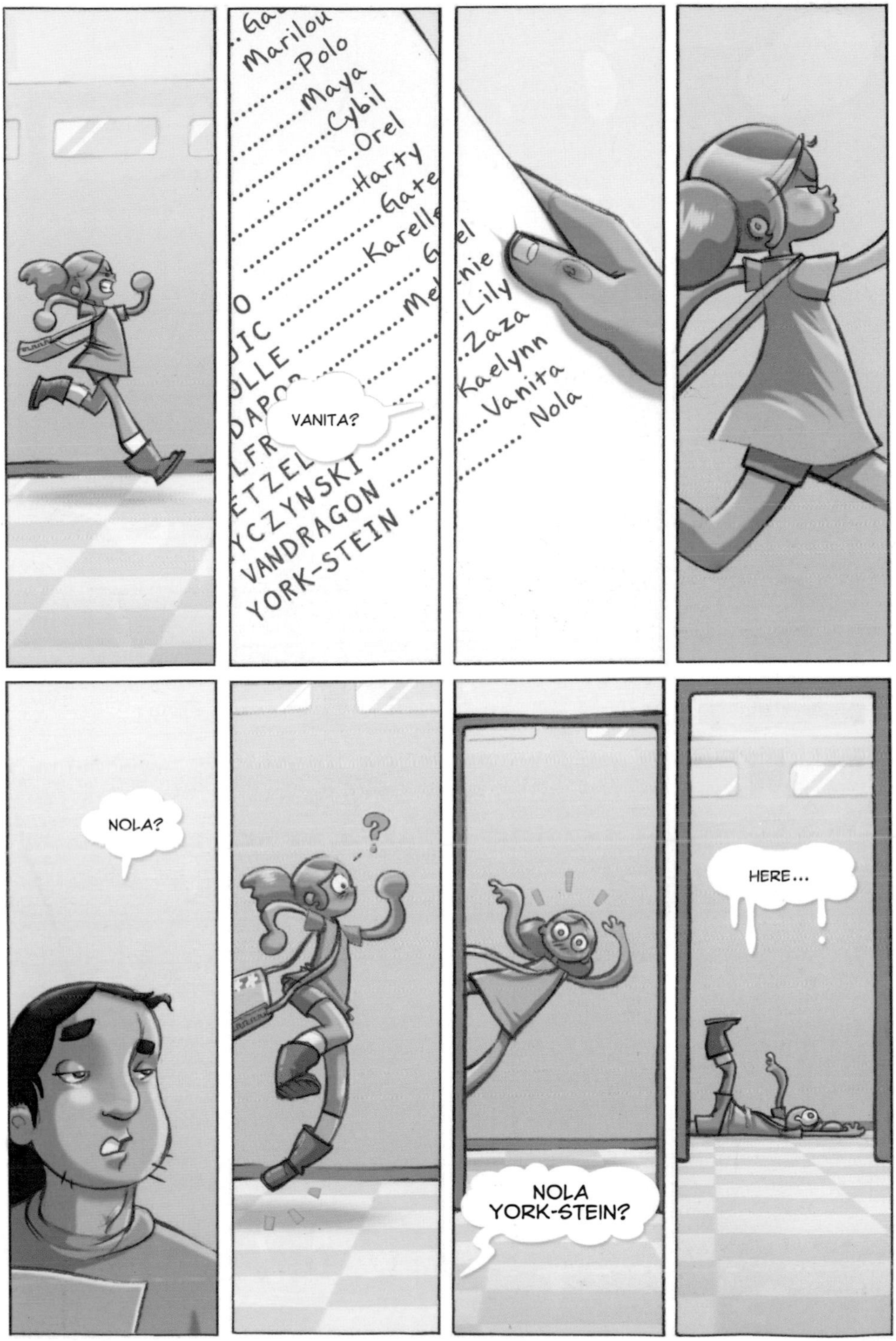
Marilou
Polo
Maya
Cybil
Orel
Harty
Gate
VANDRAGON
YORK-STEIN
VANITA?
Lily
Zaza
Kaelynn
Vanita
Nola
NOLA?
?
NOLA YORK-STEIN?
HERE...

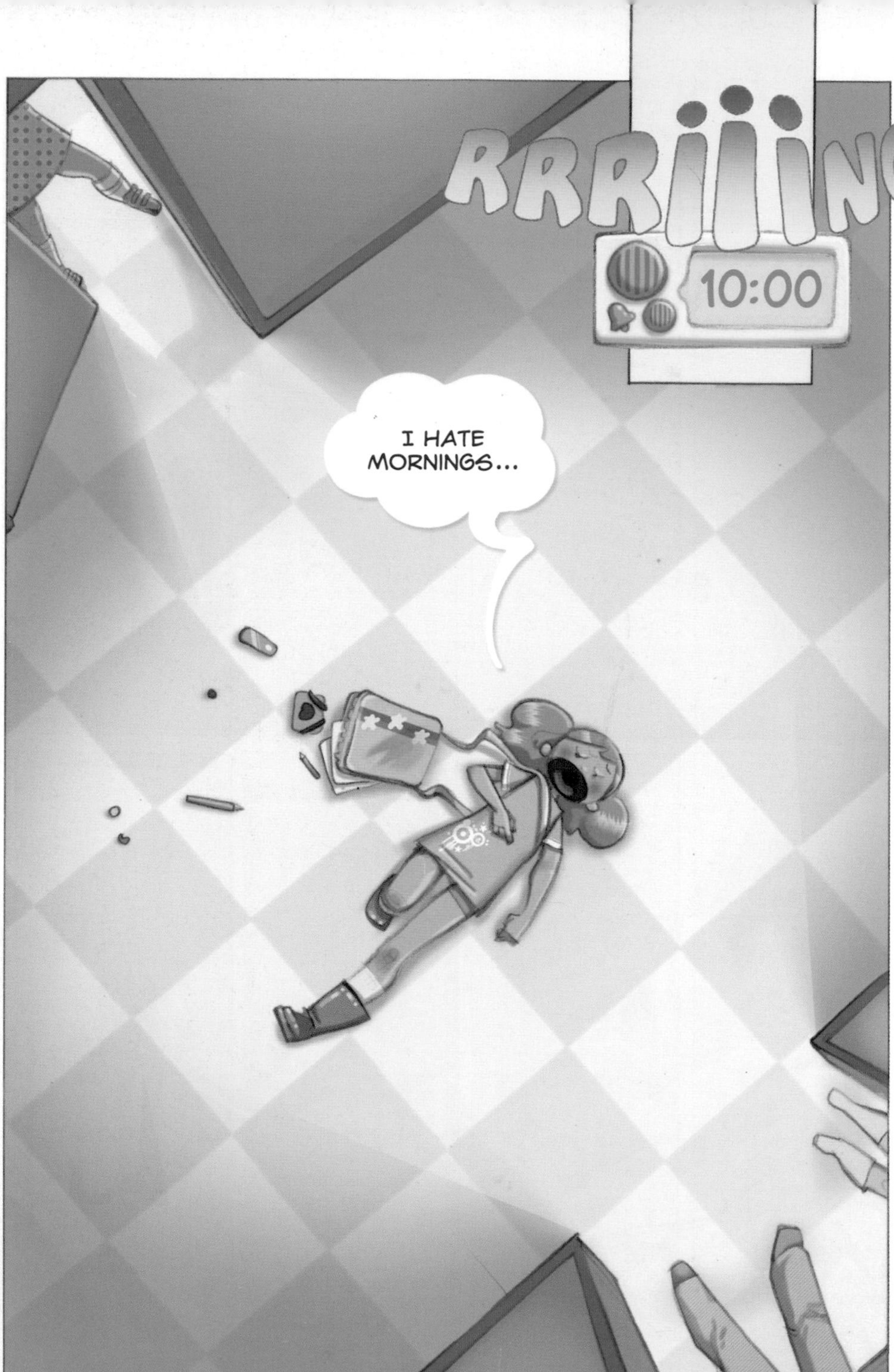
RRRIIIING
10:00
I HATE MORNINGS...

Nola's Worlds #1

changing moon

minikim ★ mariolle ★ pop

GRAPHIC UNIVERSE™ · MINNEAPOLIS · NEW YORK · LONDON

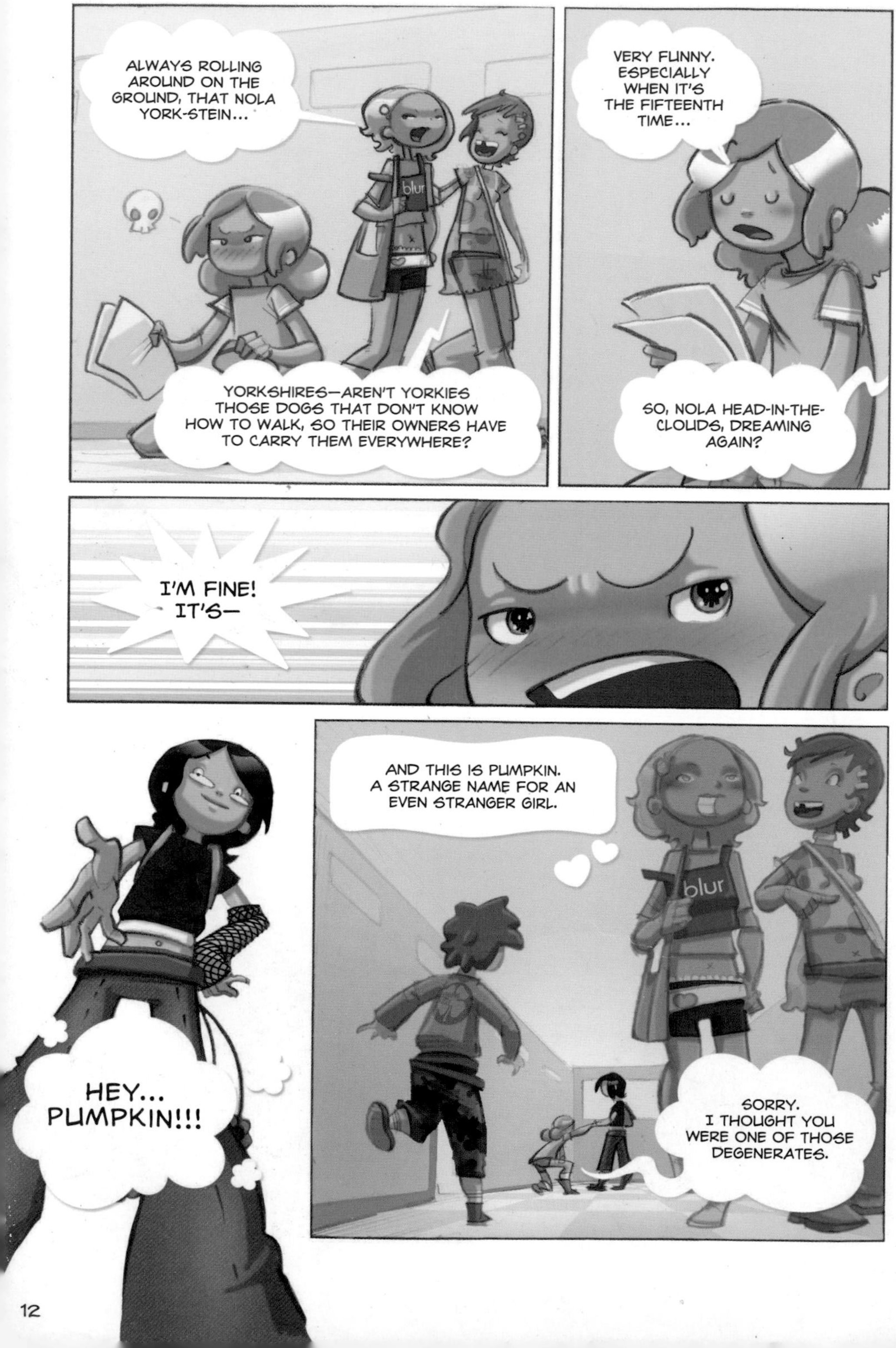
ALWAYS ROLLING AROUND ON THE GROUND, THAT NOLA YORK-STEIN...
YORKSHIRES—AREN'T YORKIES THOSE DOGS THAT DON'T KNOW HOW TO WALK, SO THEIR OWNERS HAVE TO CARRY THEM EVERYWHERE?
VERY FUNNY. ESPECIALLY WHEN IT'S THE FIFTEENTH TIME...
SO, NOLA HEAD-IN-THE-CLOUDS, DREAMING AGAIN?
I'M FINE! IT'S—
HEY... PUMPKIN!!!
AND THIS IS PUMPKIN. A STRANGE NAME FOR AN EVEN STRANGER GIRL.
SORRY. I THOUGHT YOU WERE ONE OF THOSE DEGENERATES.

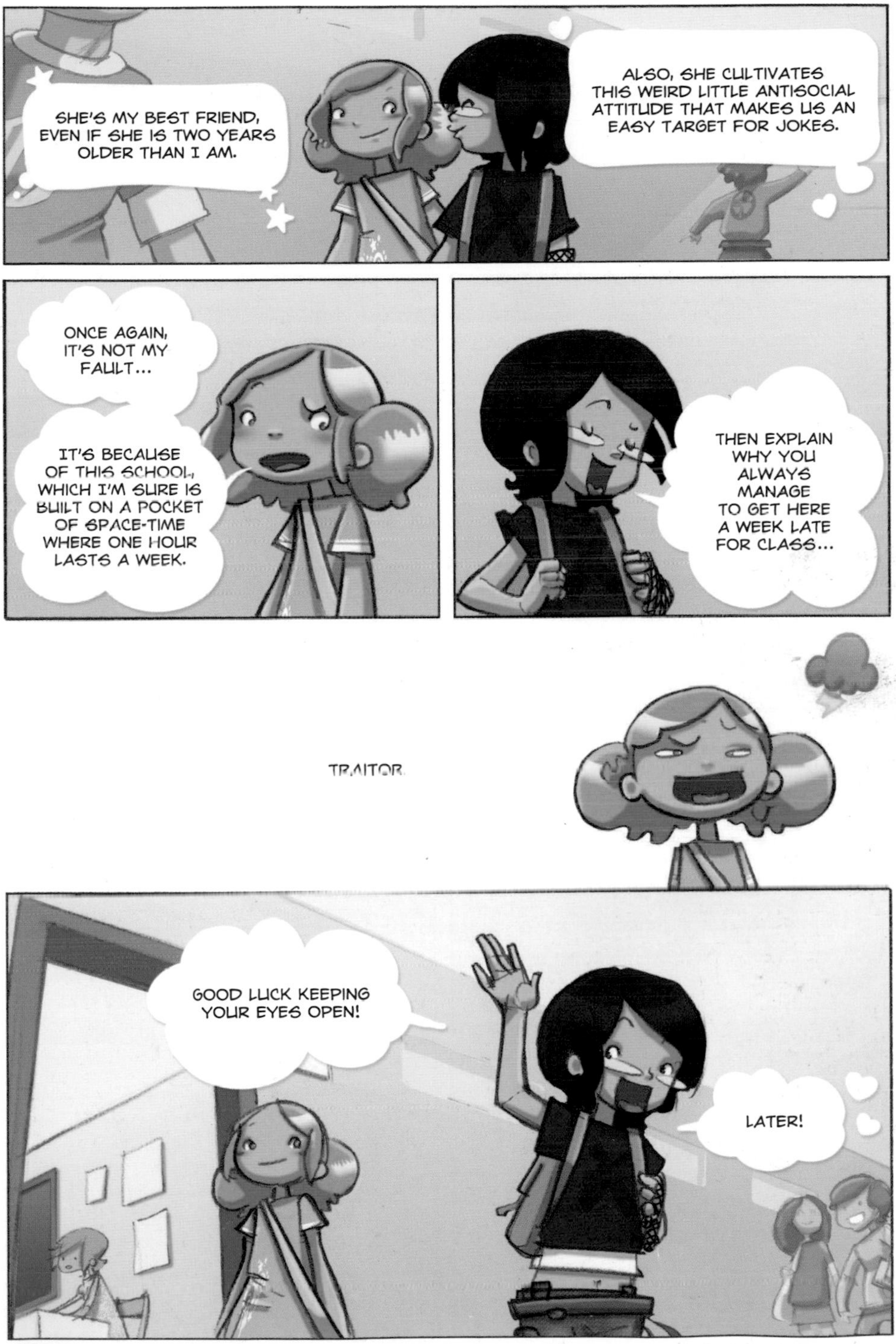
SHE'S MY BEST FRIEND, EVEN IF SHE IS TWO YEARS OLDER THAN I AM.
ALSO, SHE CULTIVATES THIS WEIRD LITTLE ANTISOCIAL ATTITUDE THAT MAKES US AN EASY TARGET FOR JOKES.
ONCE AGAIN, IT'S NOT MY FAULT...
IT'S BECAUSE OF THIS SCHOOL, WHICH I'M SURE IS BUILT ON A POCKET OF SPACE-TIME WHERE ONE HOUR LASTS A WEEK.
THEN EXPLAIN WHY YOU ALWAYS MANAGE TO GET HERE A WEEK LATE FOR CLASS...
TRAITOR.
GOOD LUCK KEEPING YOUR EYES OPEN!
LATER!

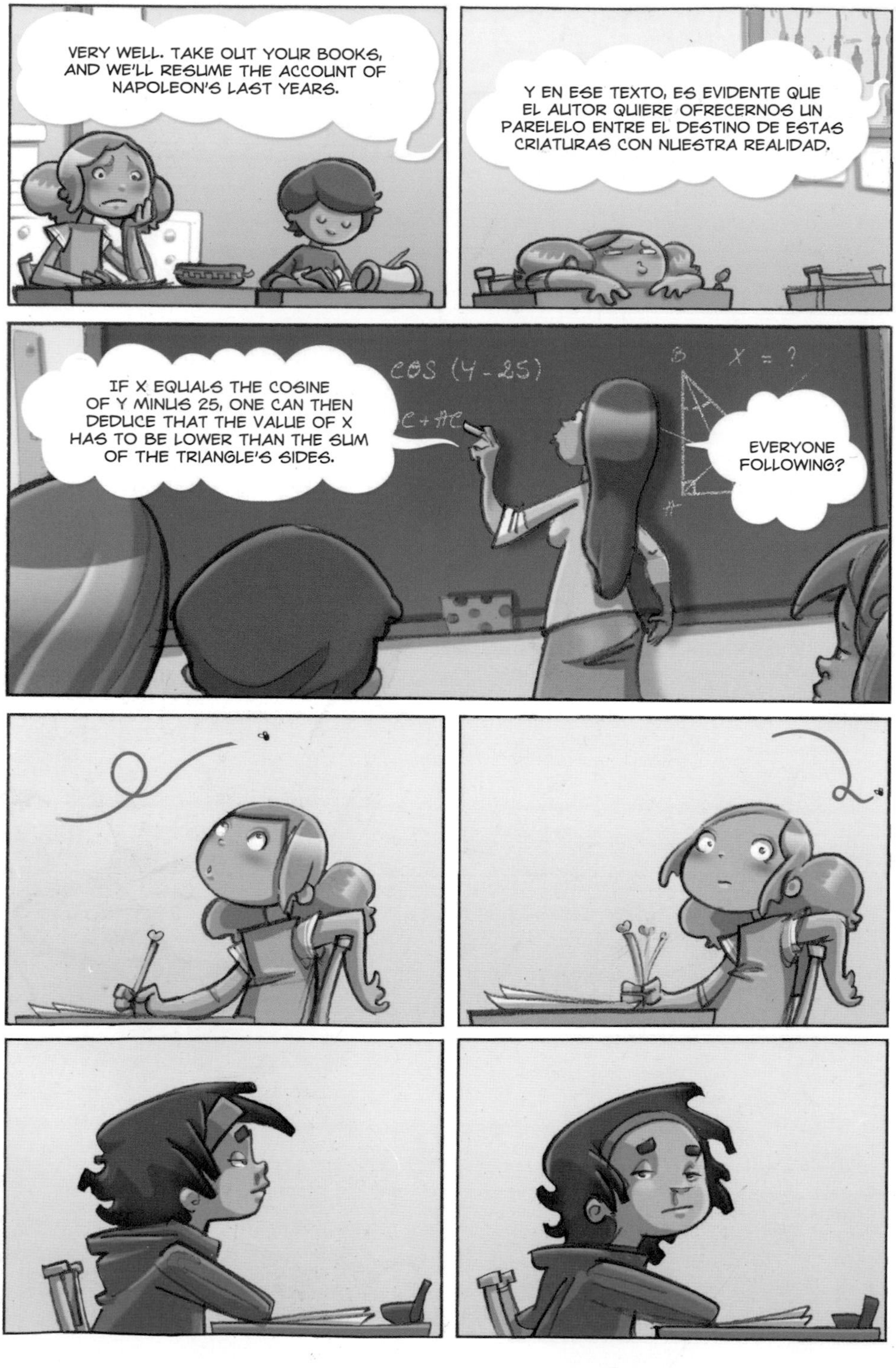
VERY WELL. TAKE OUT YOUR BOOKS, AND WE'LL RESUME THE ACCOUNT OF NAPOLEON'S LAST YEARS.
Y EN ESE TEXTO, ES EVIDENTE QUE EL AUTOR QUIERE OFRECERNOS UN PARELELO ENTRE EL DESTINO DE ESTAS CRIATURAS CON NUESTRA REALIDAD.
COS (Y - 25)
X = ?
IF X EQUALS THE COSINE OF Y MINUS 25, ONE CAN THEN DEDUCE THAT THE VALUE OF X HAS TO BE LOWER THAN THE SUM OF THE TRIANGLE'S SIDES.
EVERYONE FOLLOWING?

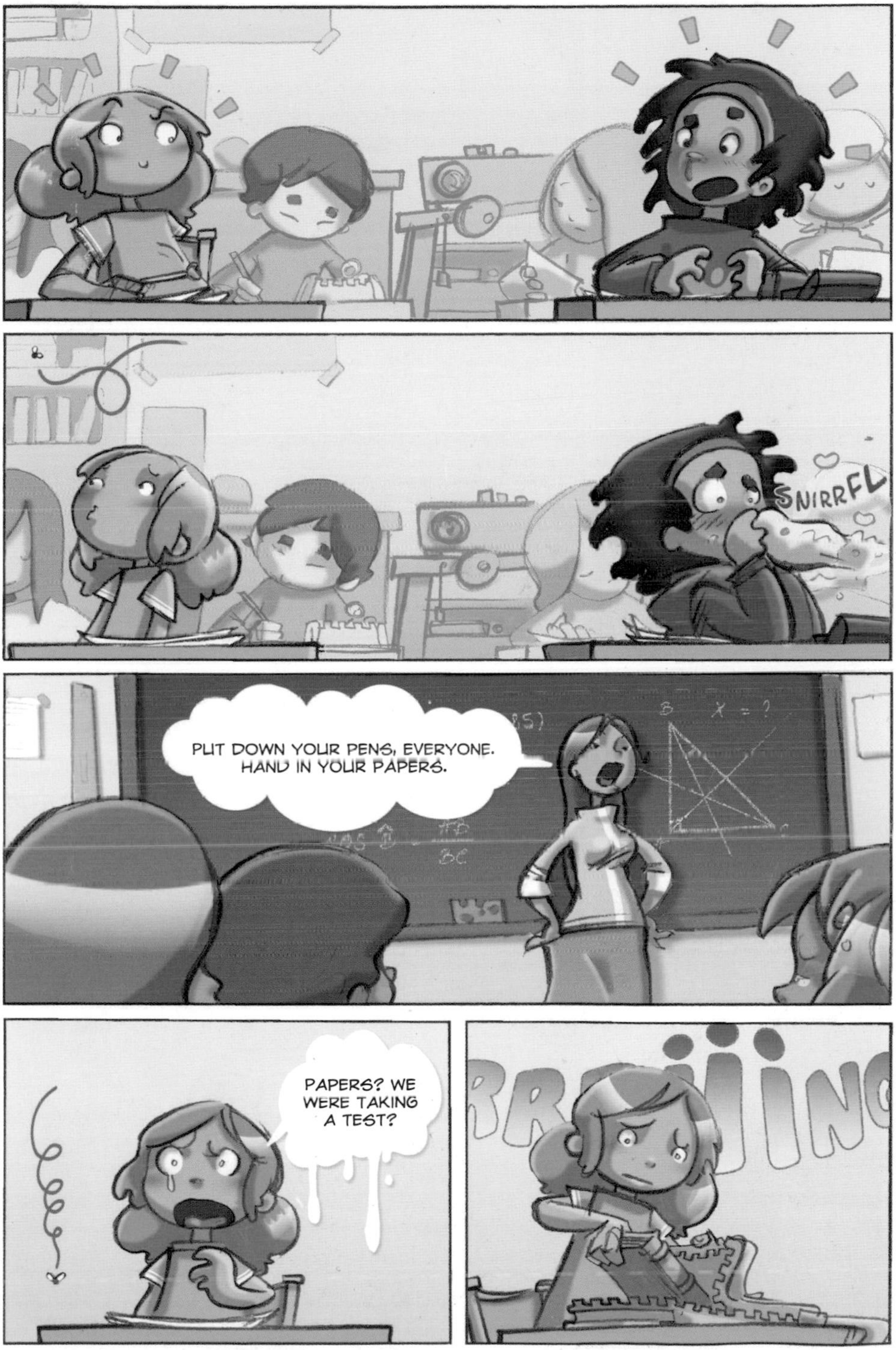
SNIRRFL
PUT DOWN YOUR PENS, EVERYONE. HAND IN YOUR PAPERS.
PAPERS? WE WERE TAKING A TEST?

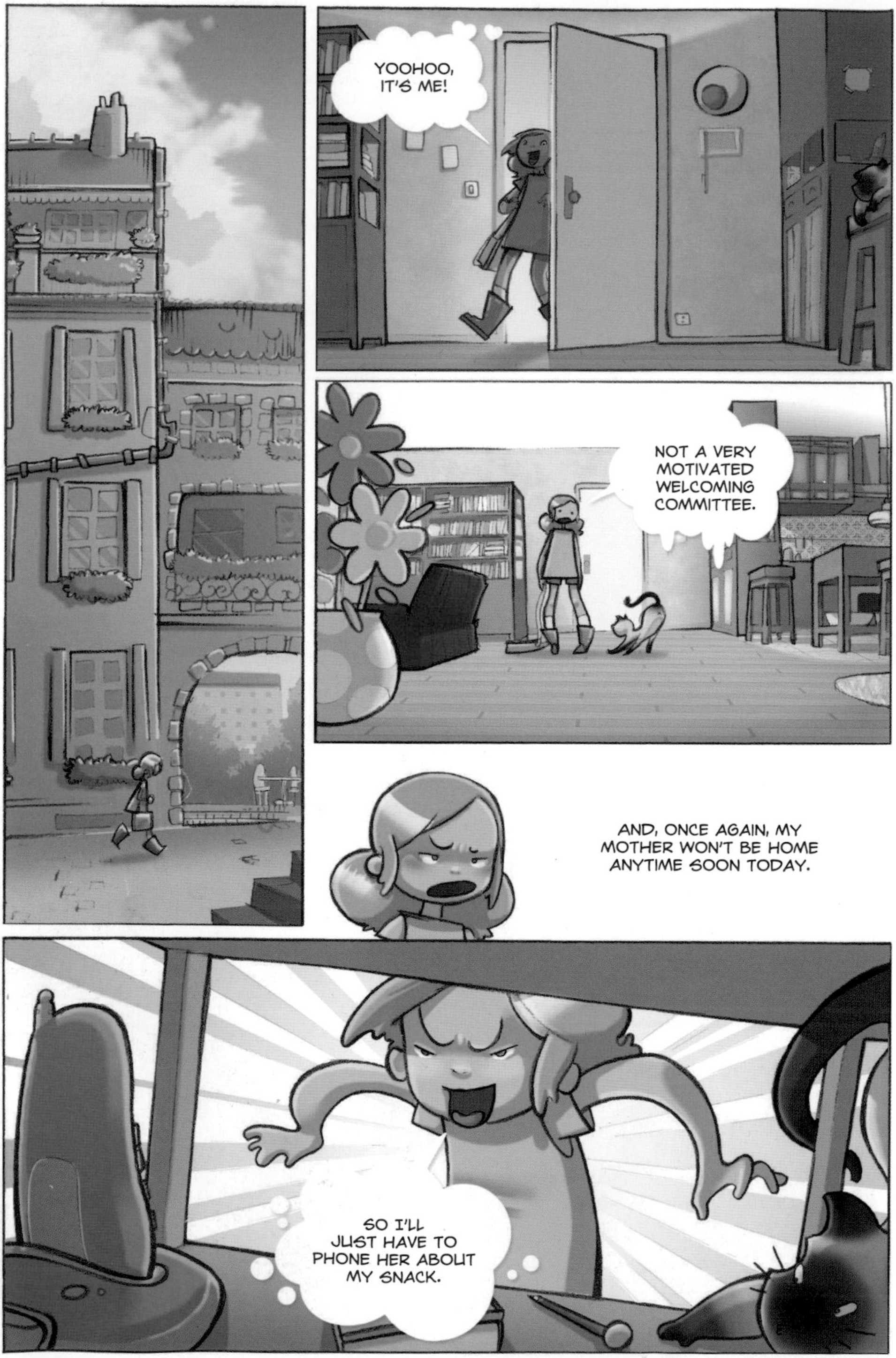
YOOHOO, IT'S ME!
NOT A VERY MOTIVATED WELCOMING COMMITTEE.
AND, ONCE AGAIN, MY MOTHER WON'T BE HOME ANYTIME SOON TODAY.
SO I'LL JUST HAVE TO PHONE HER ABOUT MY SNACK.

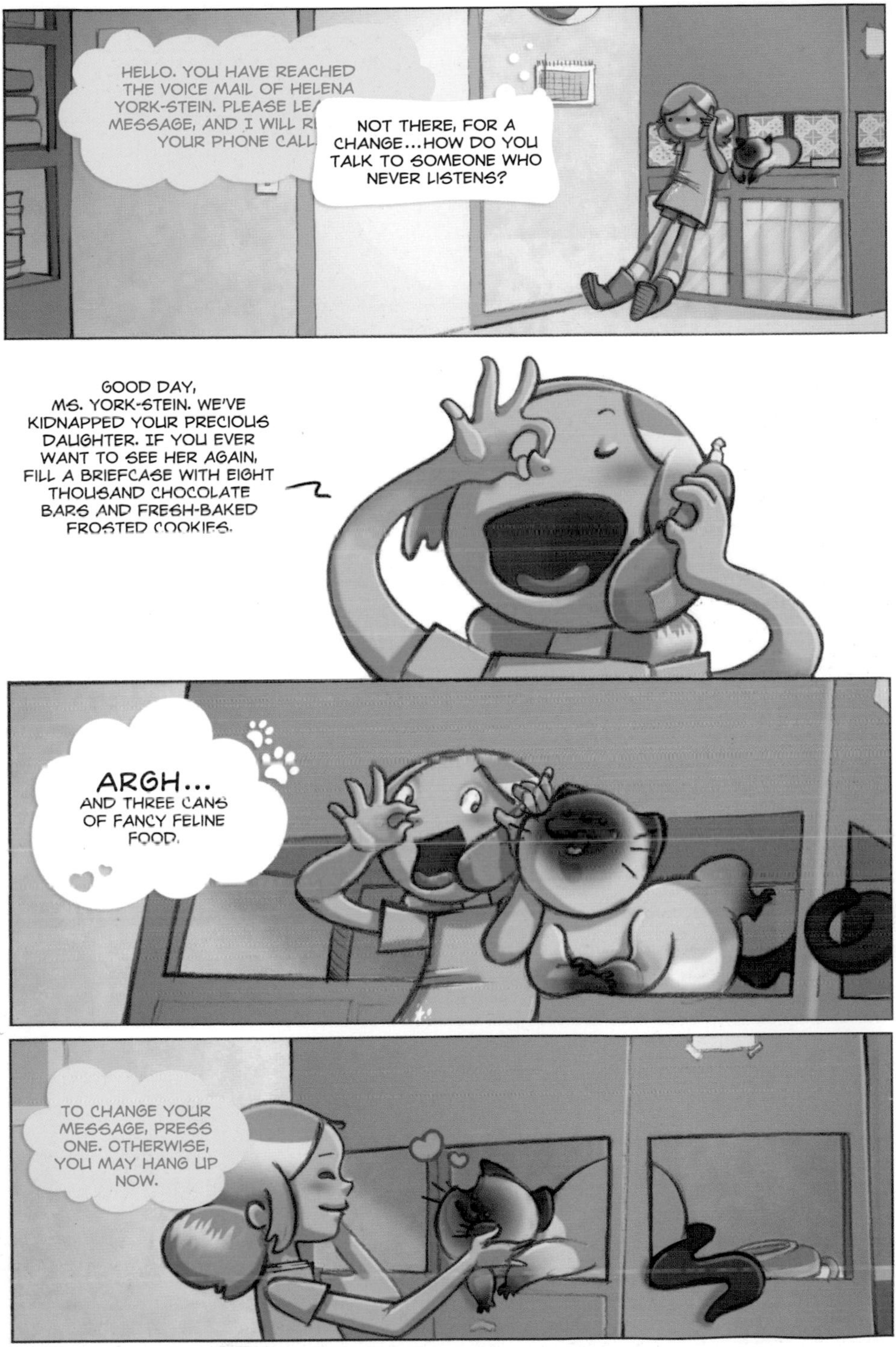
HELLO. YOU HAVE REACHED THE VOICE MAIL OF HELENA YORK-STEIN. PLEASE LEA MESSAGE, AND I WILL R YOUR PHONE CALL
NOT THERE, FOR A CHANGE...HOW DO YOU TALK TO SOMEONE WHO NEVER LISTENS?
GOOD DAY, MS. YORK-STEIN. WE'VE KIDNAPPED YOUR PRECIOUS DAUGHTER. IF YOU EVER WANT TO SEE HER AGAIN, FILL A BRIEFCASE WITH EIGHT THOUSAND CHOCOLATE BARS AND FRESH-BAKED FROSTED COOKIES.
ARGH... AND THREE CANS OF FANCY FELINE FOOD.
TO CHANGE YOUR MESSAGE, PRESS ONE. OTHERWISE, YOU MAY HANG UP NOW.

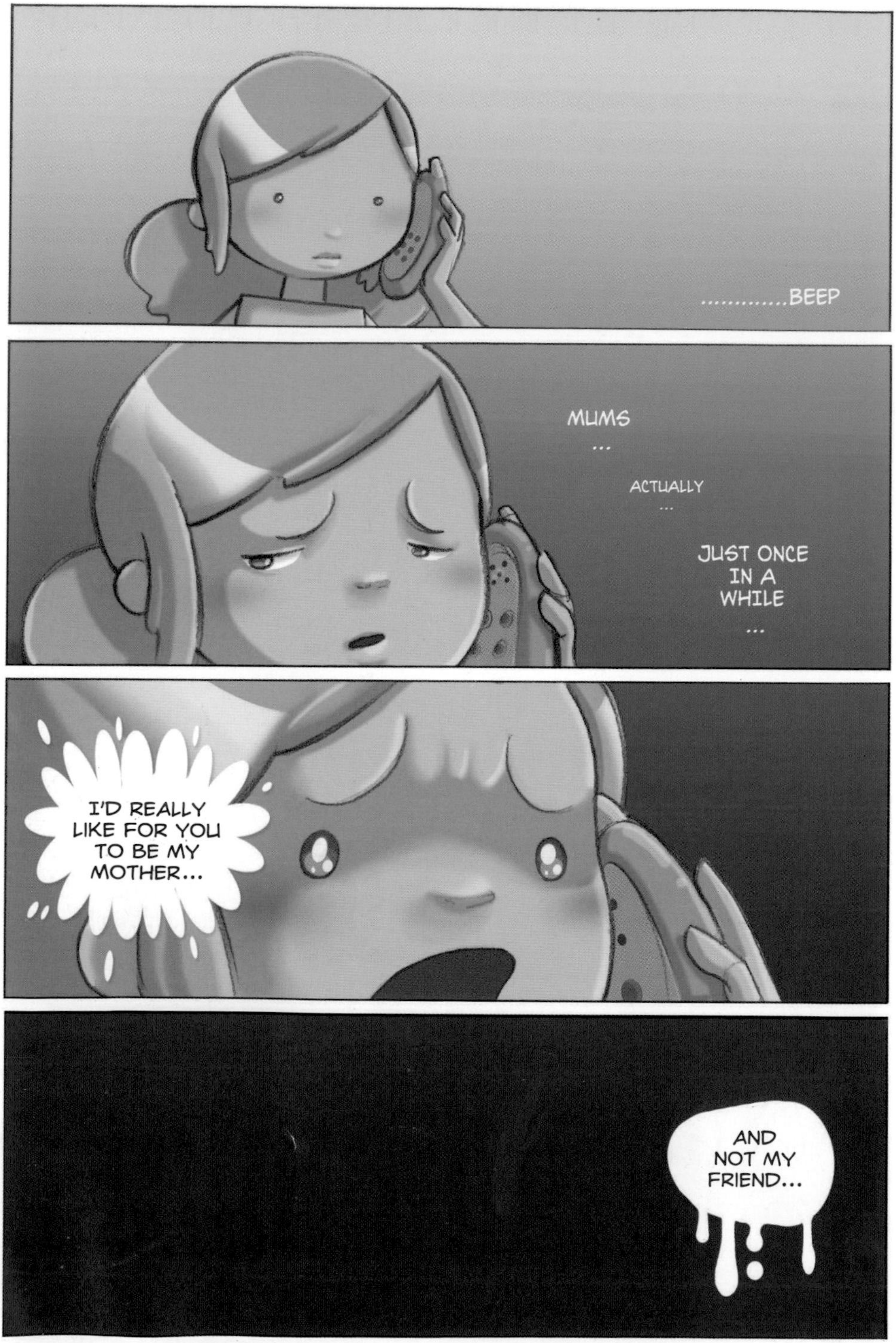
.............BEEP
MUMS
...
ACTUALLY
...
JUST ONCE IN A WHILE
...
I'D REALLY LIKE FOR YOU TO BE MY MOTHER...
AND NOT MY FRIEND...

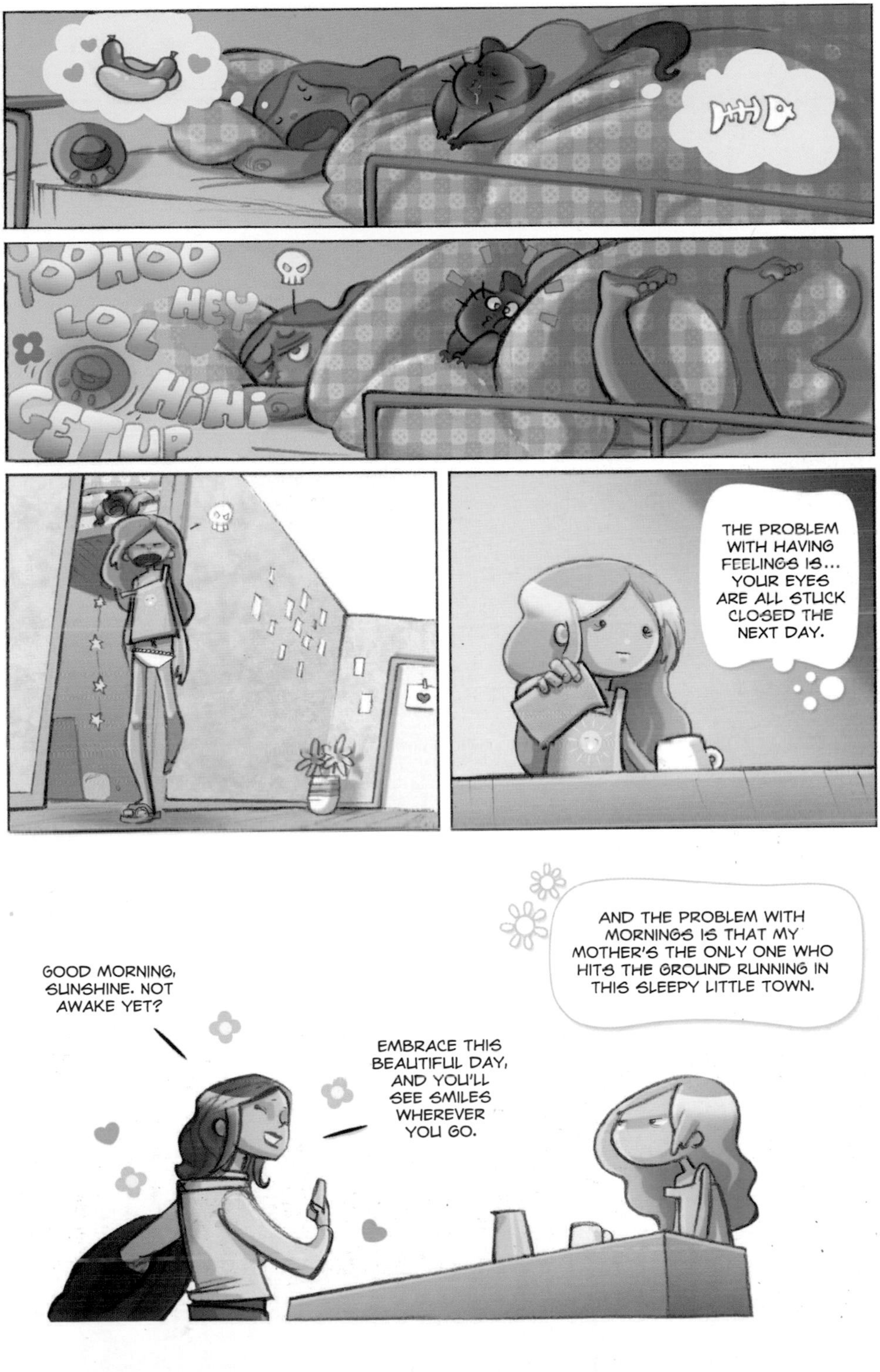
YOOHOO
HEY
LOL
HIHI
GET UP
THE PROBLEM WITH HAVING FEELINGS IS... YOUR EYES ARE ALL STUCK CLOSED THE NEXT DAY.
AND THE PROBLEM WITH MORNINGS IS THAT MY MOTHER'S THE ONLY ONE WHO HITS THE GROUND RUNNING IN THIS SLEEPY LITTLE TOWN.
GOOD MORNING, SUNSHINE. NOT AWAKE YET?
EMBRACE THIS BEAUTIFUL DAY, AND YOU'LL SEE SMILES WHEREVER YOU GO.

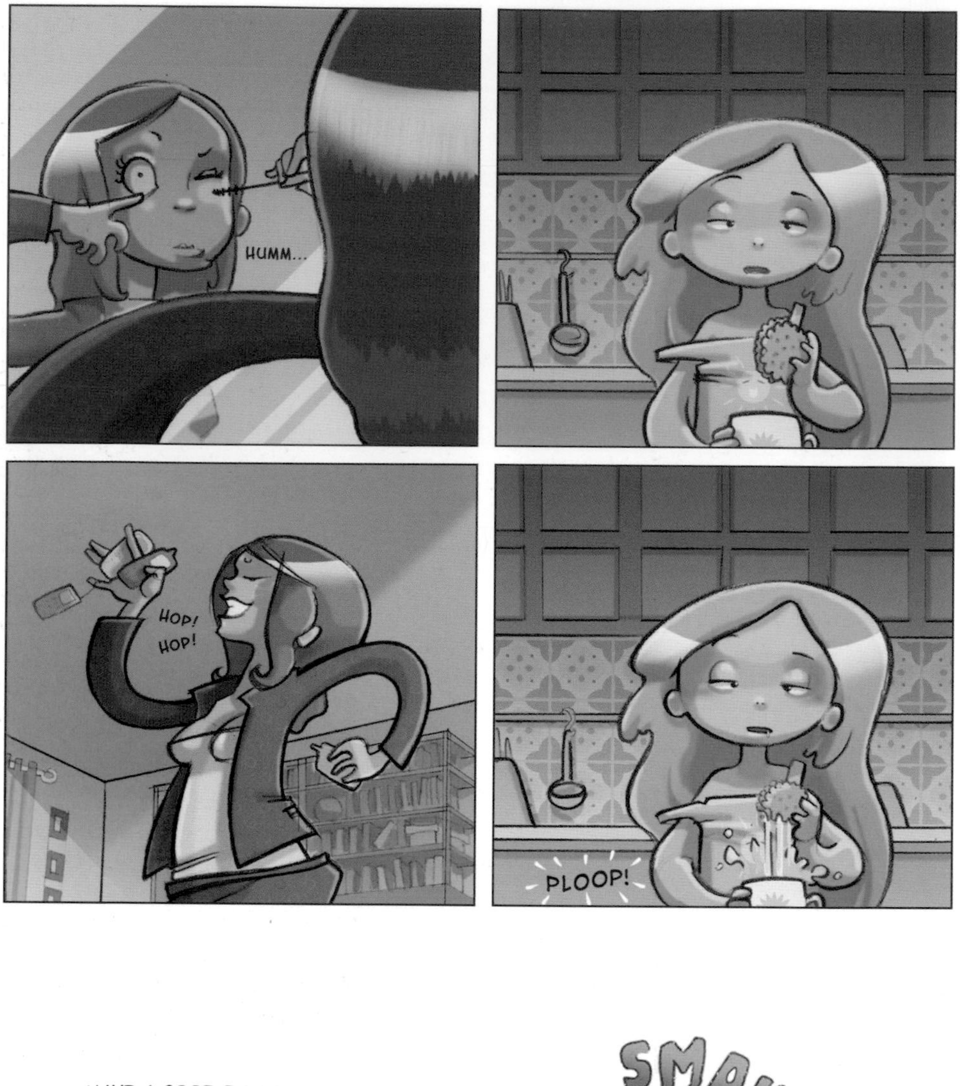
HUMM...
HOP! HOP!
PLOOP!
HAVE A GOOD DAY, DARLING. I LEFT YOU SOMETHING IN THE FRIDGE, ALL READY TO GO. IT'S WEDNESDAY—DON'T FORGET YOU COME HOME FOR LUNCH TODAY.
SMAK

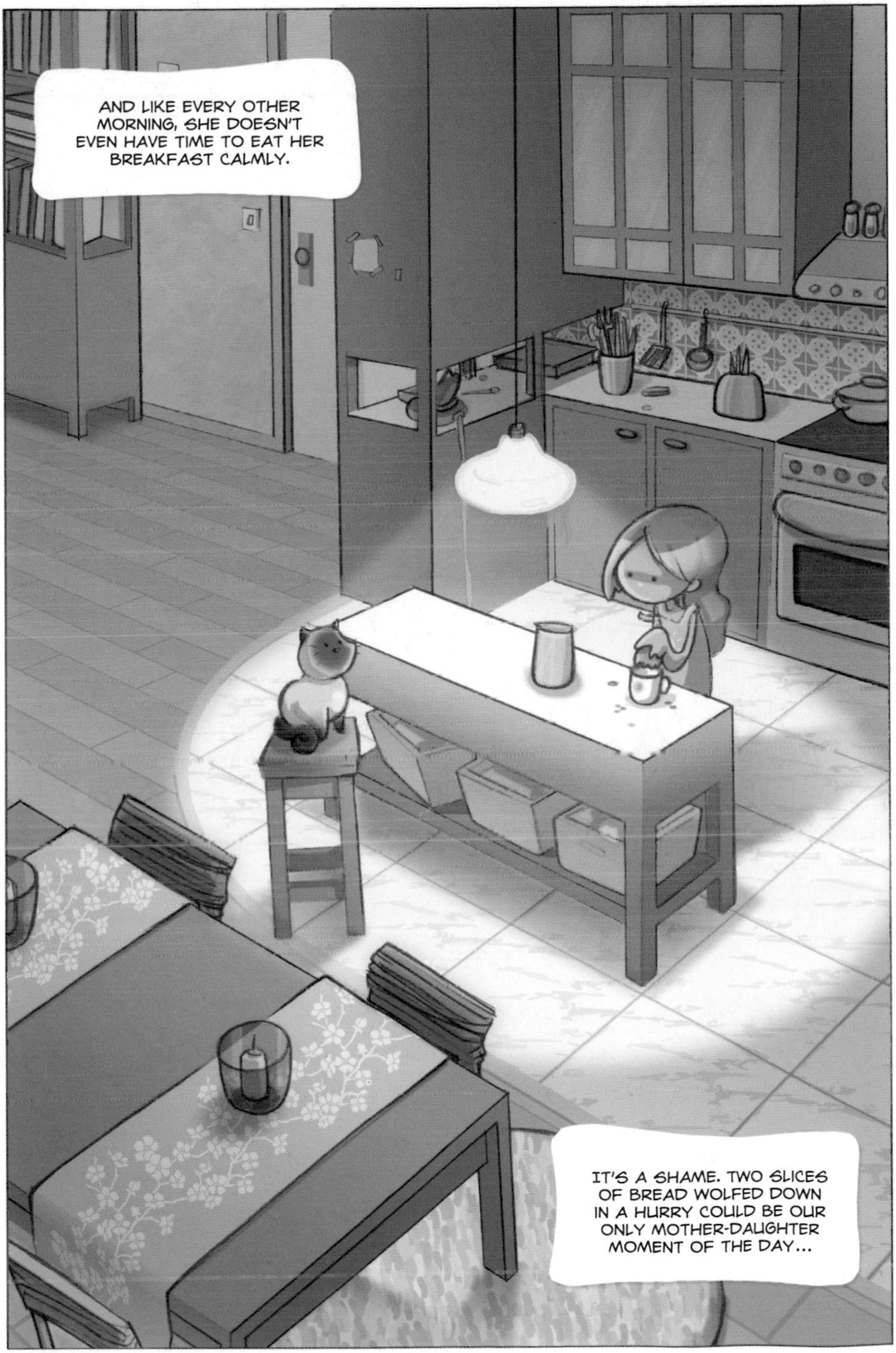
AND LIKE EVERY OTHER MORNING, SHE DOESN'T EVEN HAVE TIME TO EAT HER BREAKFAST CALMLY.
IT'S A SHAME. TWO SLICES OF BREAD WOLFED DOWN IN A HURRY COULD BE OUR ONLY MOTHER-DAUGHTER MOMENT OF THE DAY...

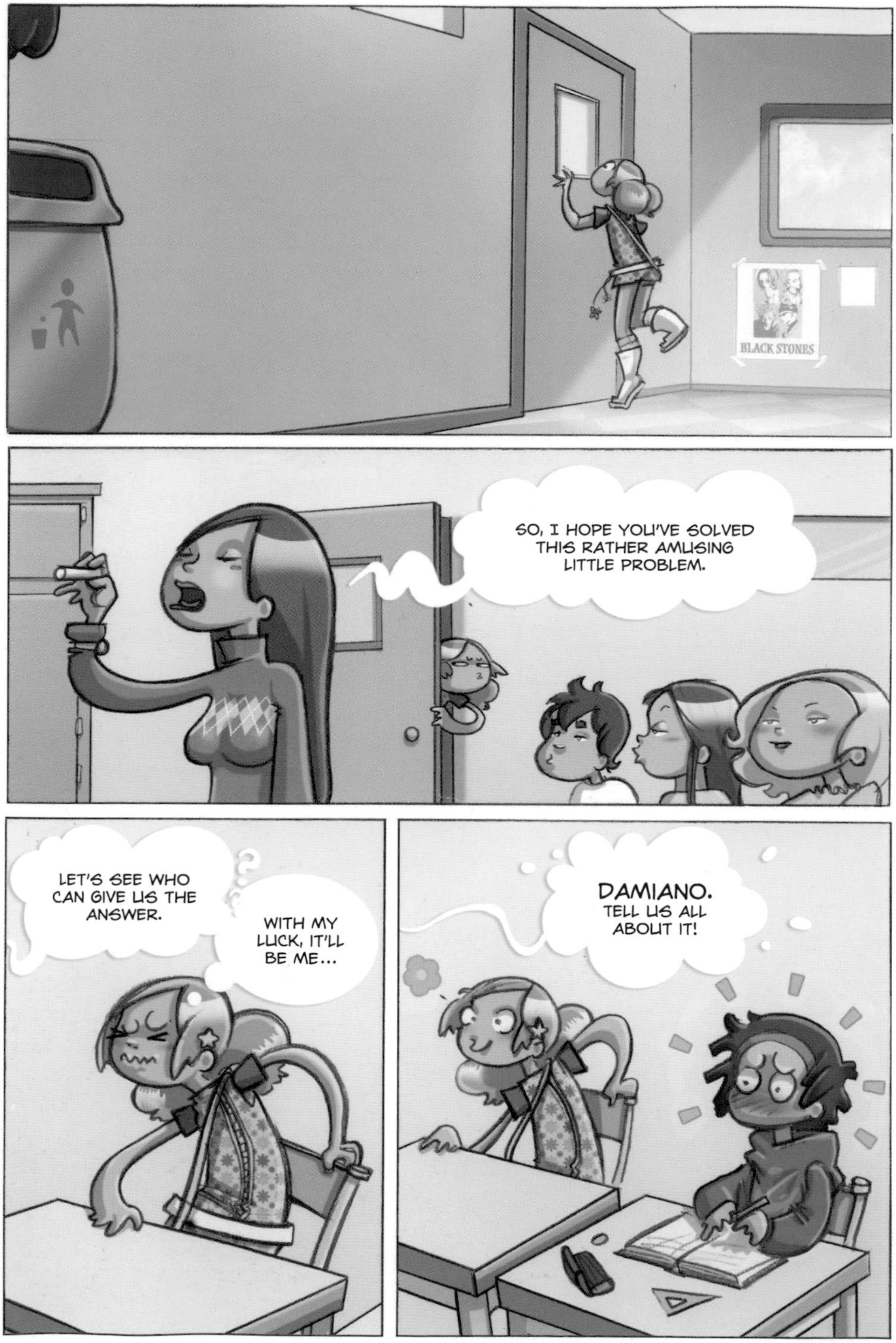
BLACK STONES
SO, I HOPE YOU'VE SOLVED THIS RATHER AMUSING LITTLE PROBLEM.
LET'S SEE WHO CAN GIVE US THE ANSWER.
WITH MY LUCK, IT'LL BE ME...
DAMIANO. TELL US ALL ABOUT IT!

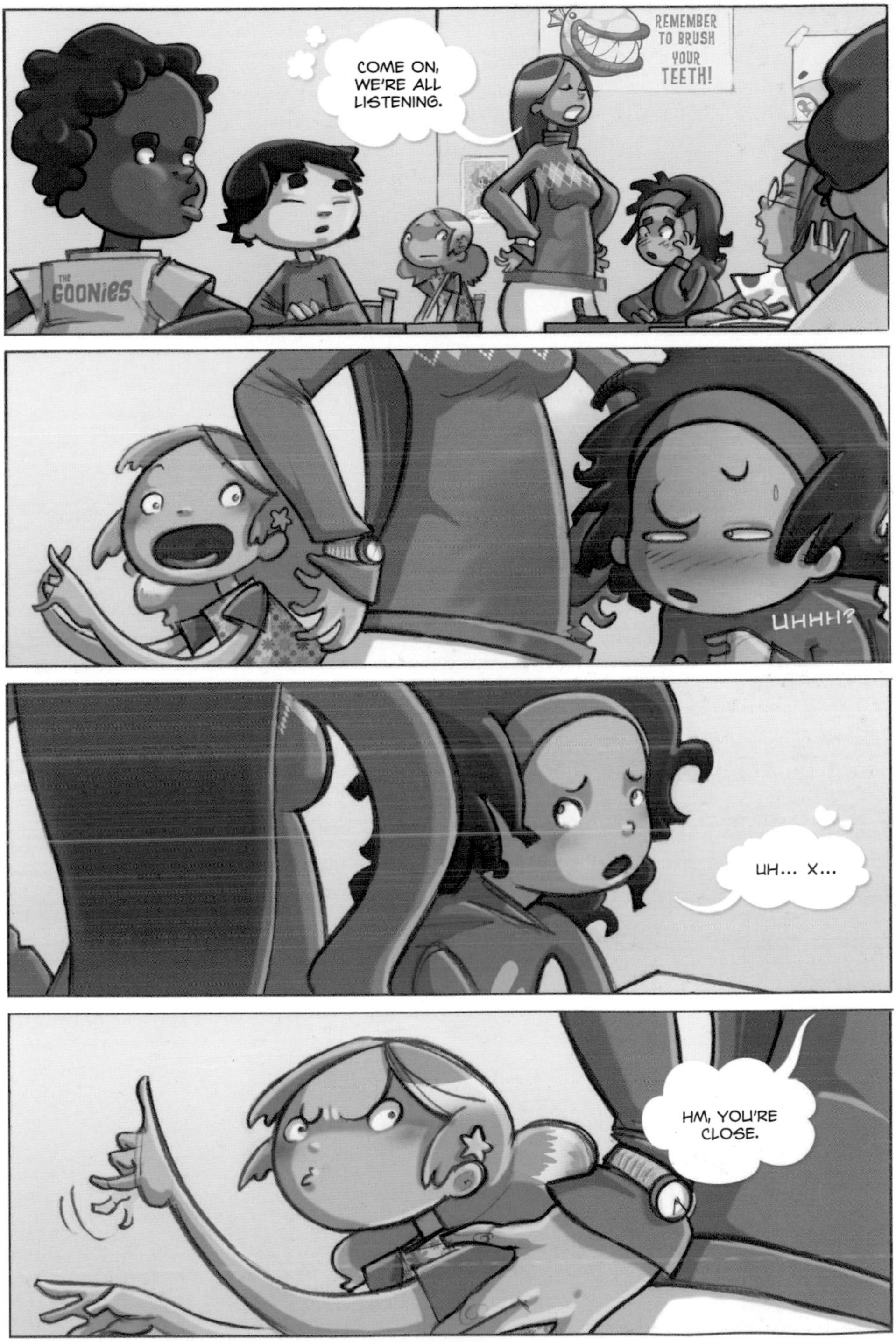
REMEMBER TO BRUSH YOUR TEETH!
COME ON, WE'RE ALL LISTENING.
THE GOONIES
UHHH?
UH... X...
HM, YOU'RE CLOSE.

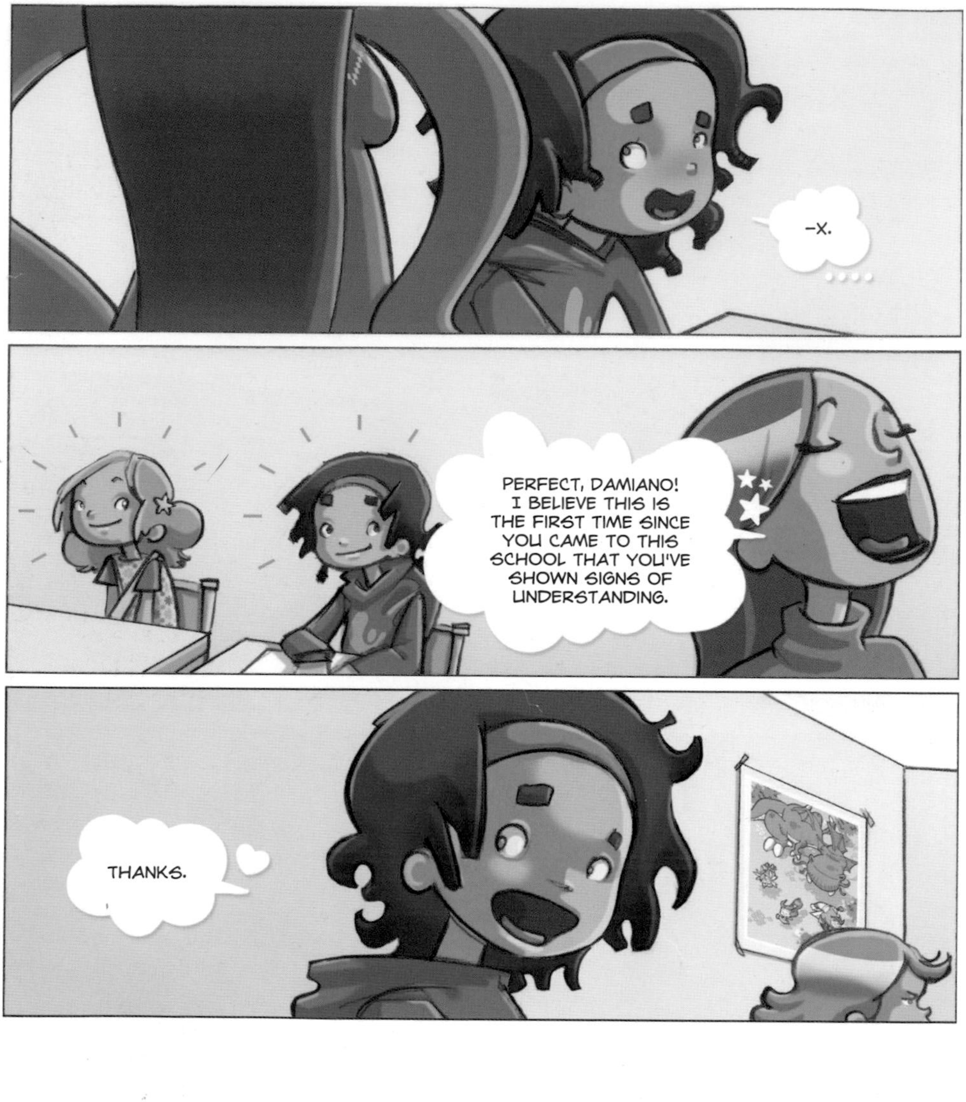

-X.
PERFECT, DAMIANO! I BELIEVE THIS IS THE FIRST TIME SINCE YOU CAME TO THIS SCHOOL THAT YOU'VE SHOWN SIGNS OF UNDERSTANDING.
THANKS.

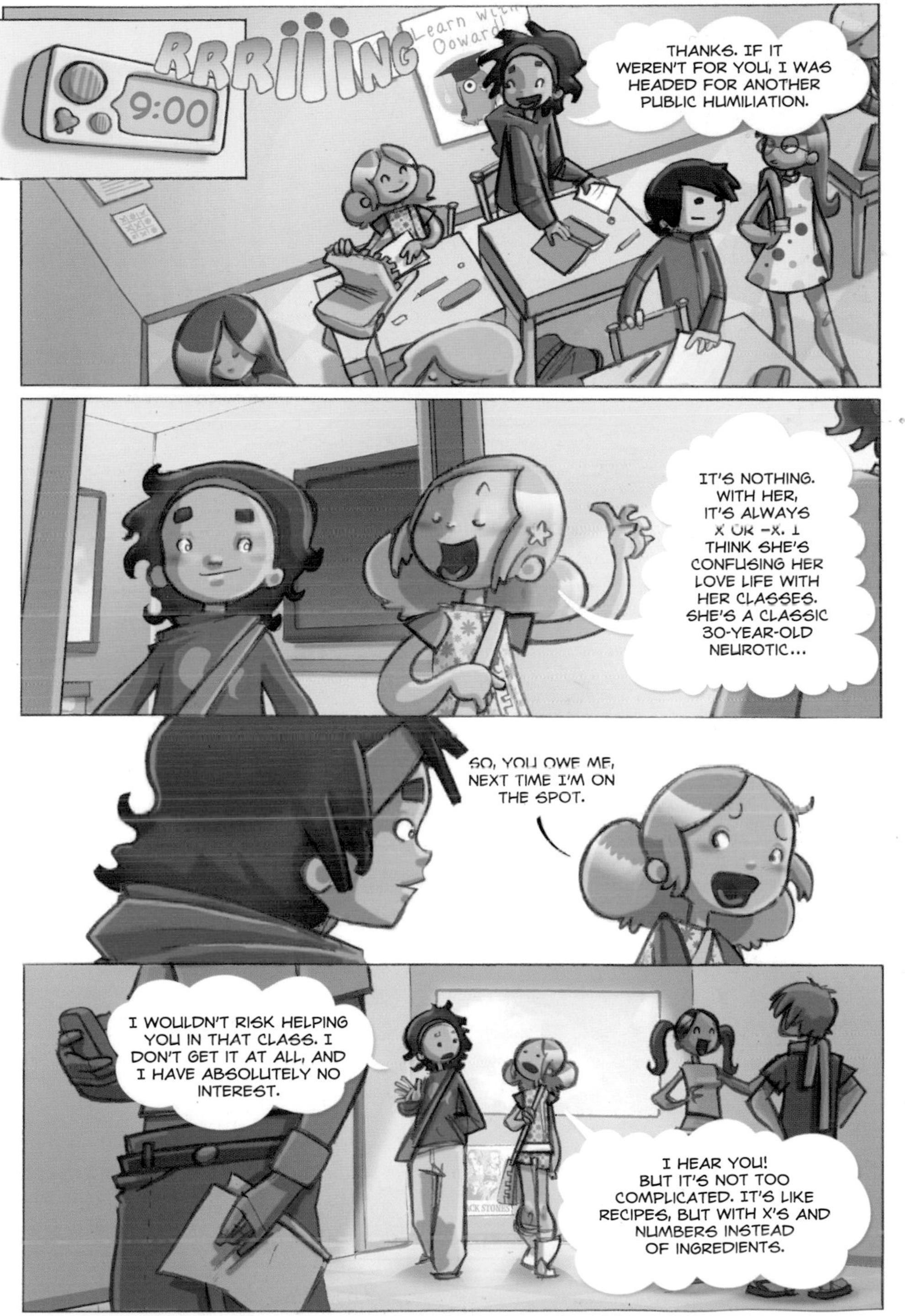
RRRIIING
9:00
Learn with Ooward!
THANKS. IF IT WEREN'T FOR YOU, I WAS HEADED FOR ANOTHER PUBLIC HUMILIATION.
IT'S NOTHING. WITH HER, IT'S ALWAYS X OR –X. I THINK SHE'S CONFUSING HER LOVE LIFE WITH HER CLASSES. SHE'S A CLASSIC 30-YEAR-OLD NEUROTIC...
SO, YOU OWE ME, NEXT TIME I'M ON THE SPOT.
I WOULDN'T RISK HELPING YOU IN THAT CLASS. I DON'T GET IT AT ALL, AND I HAVE ABSOLUTELY NO INTEREST.
I HEAR YOU! BUT IT'S NOT TOO COMPLICATED. IT'S LIKE RECIPES, BUT WITH X'S AND NUMBERS INSTEAD OF INGREDIENTS.

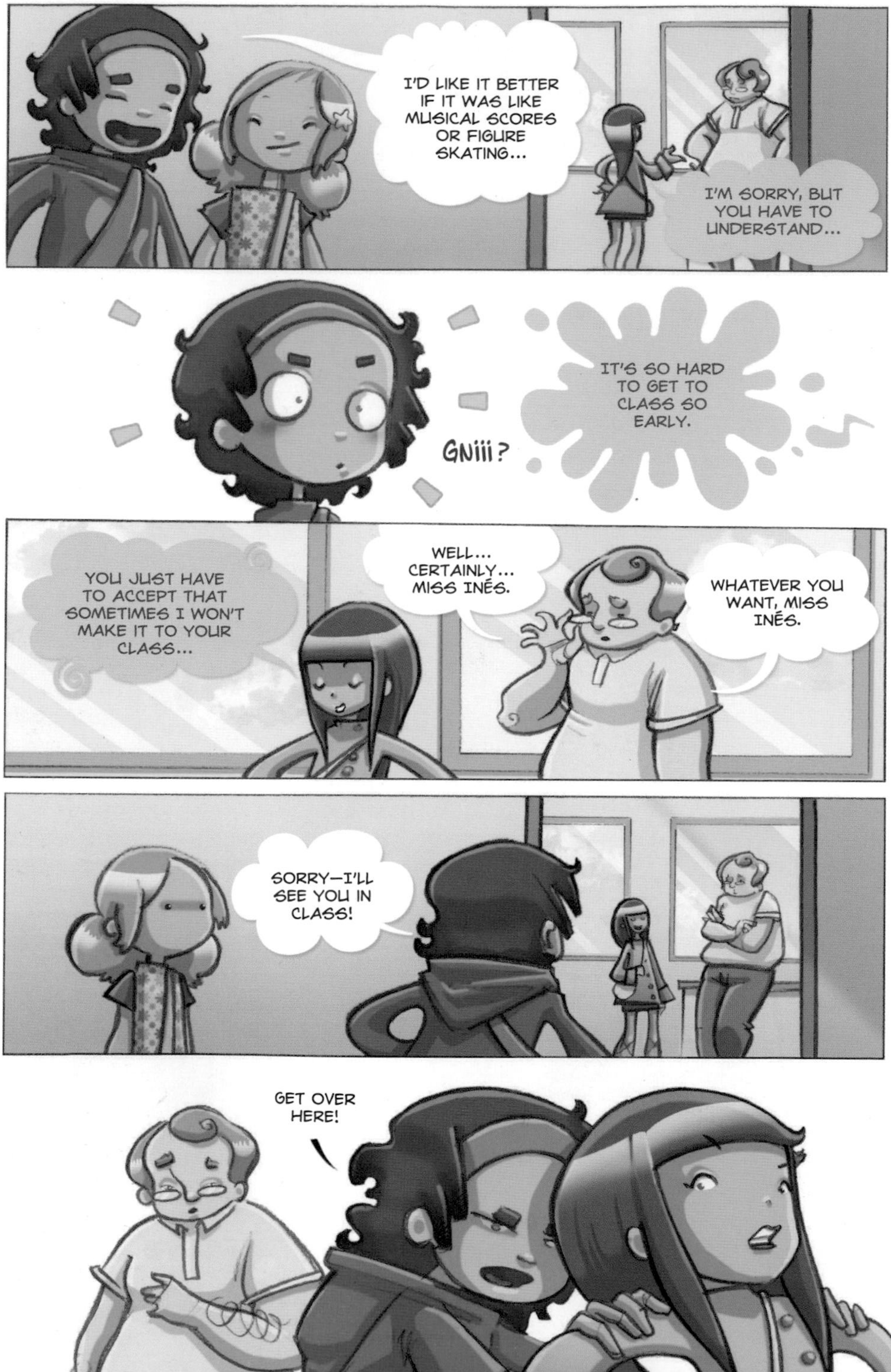
I'D LIKE IT BETTER IF IT WAS LIKE MUSICAL SCORES OR FIGURE SKATING...
I'M SORRY, BUT YOU HAVE TO UNDERSTAND...
GNiii?
IT'S SO HARD TO GET TO CLASS SO EARLY.
YOU JUST HAVE TO ACCEPT THAT SOMETIMES I WON'T MAKE IT TO YOUR CLASS...
WELL... CERTAINLY... MISS INÉS.
WHATEVER YOU WANT, MISS INÉS.
SORRY—I'LL SEE YOU IN CLASS!
GET OVER HERE!

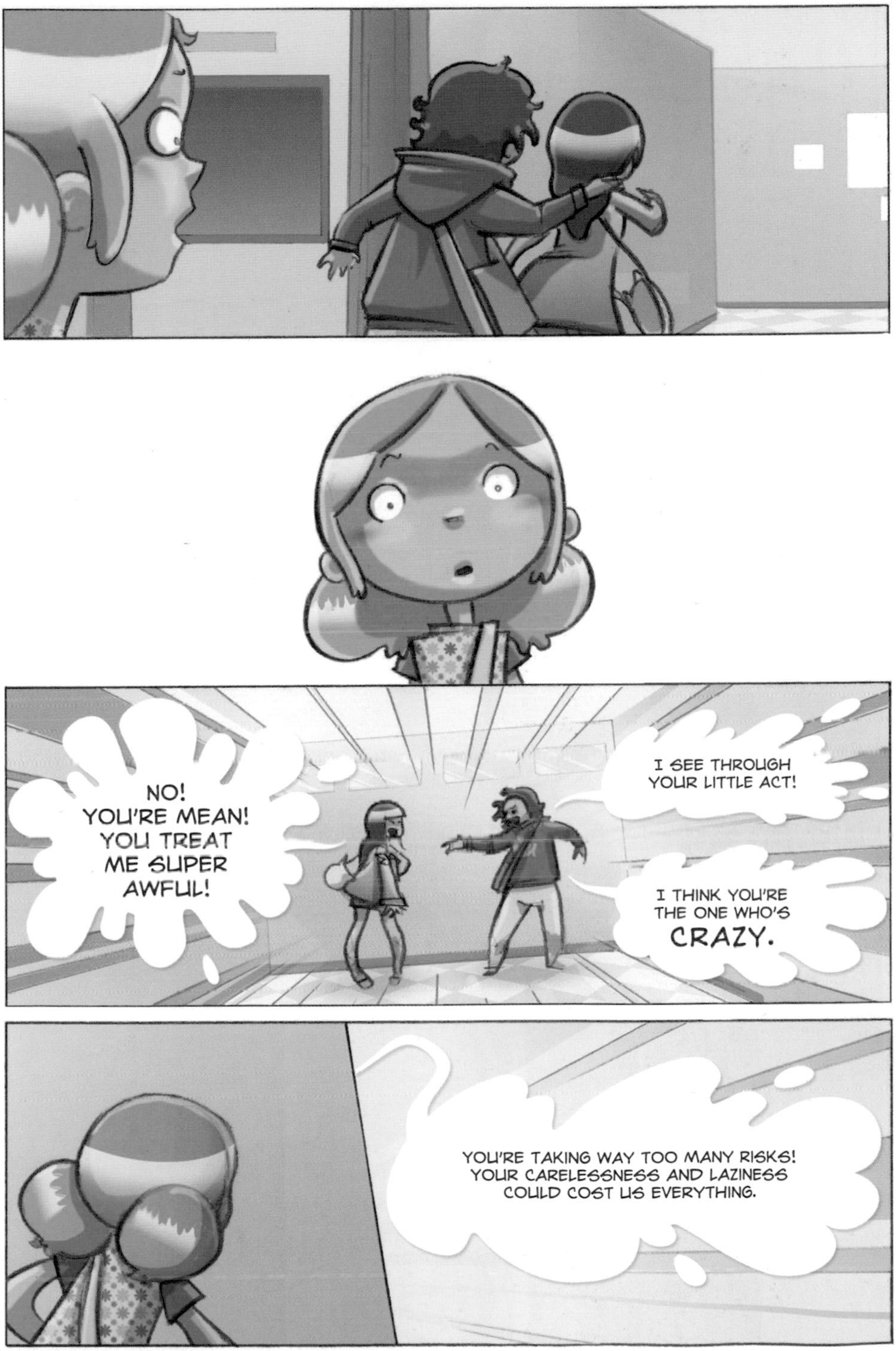
NO! YOU'RE MEAN! YOU TREAT ME SUPER AWFUL!
I SEE THROUGH YOUR LITTLE ACT!
I THINK YOU'RE THE ONE WHO'S CRAZY.
YOU'RE TAKING WAY TOO MANY RISKS! YOUR CARELESSNESS AND LAZINESS COULD COST US EVERYTHING.

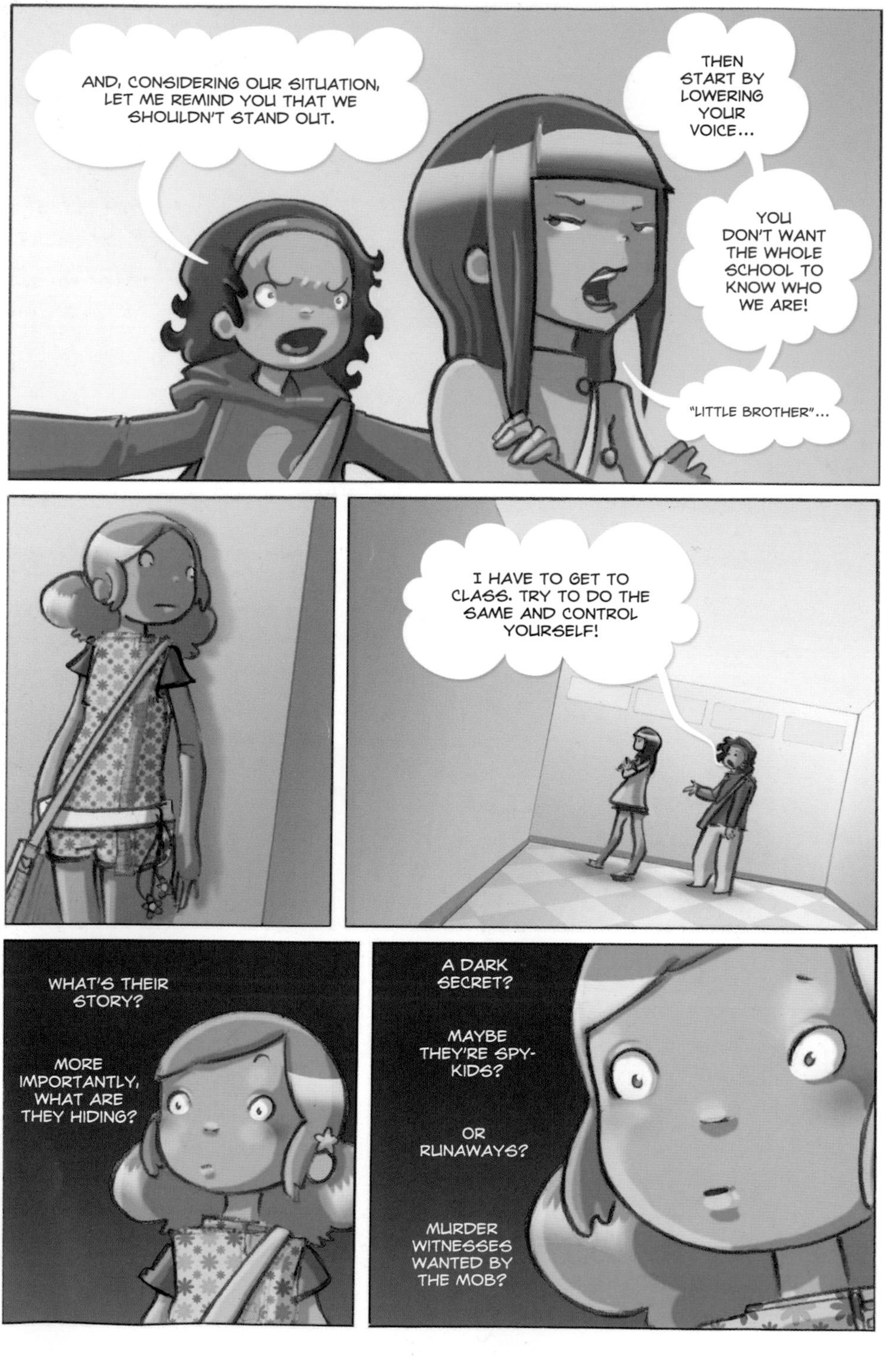
AND, CONSIDERING OUR SITUATION, LET ME REMIND YOU THAT WE SHOULDN'T STAND OUT.
THEN START BY LOWERING YOUR VOICE...
YOU DON'T WANT THE WHOLE SCHOOL TO KNOW WHO WE ARE!
"LITTLE BROTHER"...
I HAVE TO GET TO CLASS. TRY TO DO THE SAME AND CONTROL YOURSELF!
WHAT'S THEIR STORY?
MORE IMPORTANTLY, WHAT ARE THEY HIDING?
A DARK SECRET?
MAYBE THEY'RE SPY-KIDS?
OR RUNAWAYS?
MURDER WITNESSES WANTED BY THE MOB?

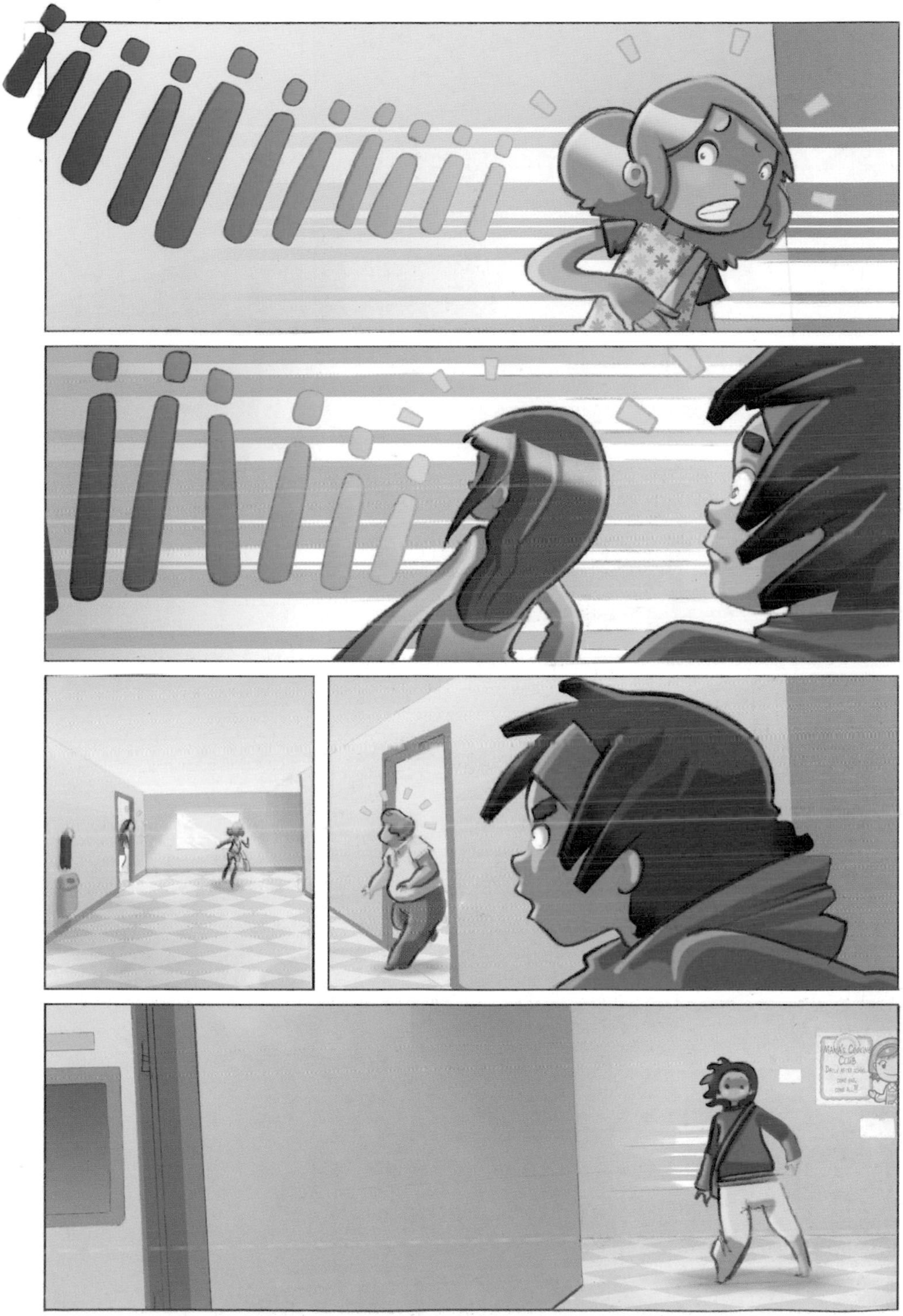
CLUB

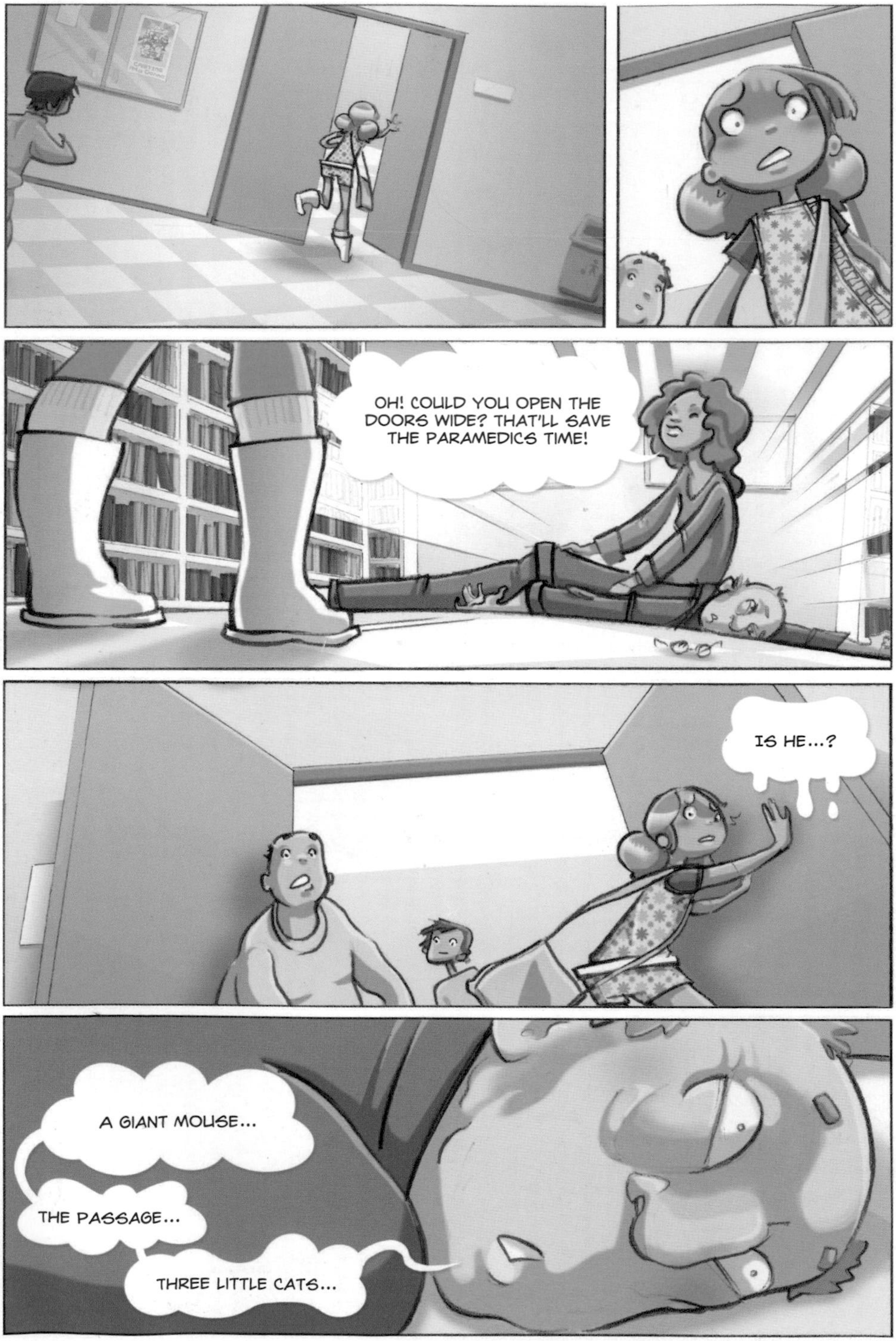
OH! COULD YOU OPEN THE DOORS WIDE? THAT'LL SAVE THE PARAMEDICS TIME!
IS HE...?
A GIANT MOUSE...
THE PASSAGE...
THREE LITTLE CATS...

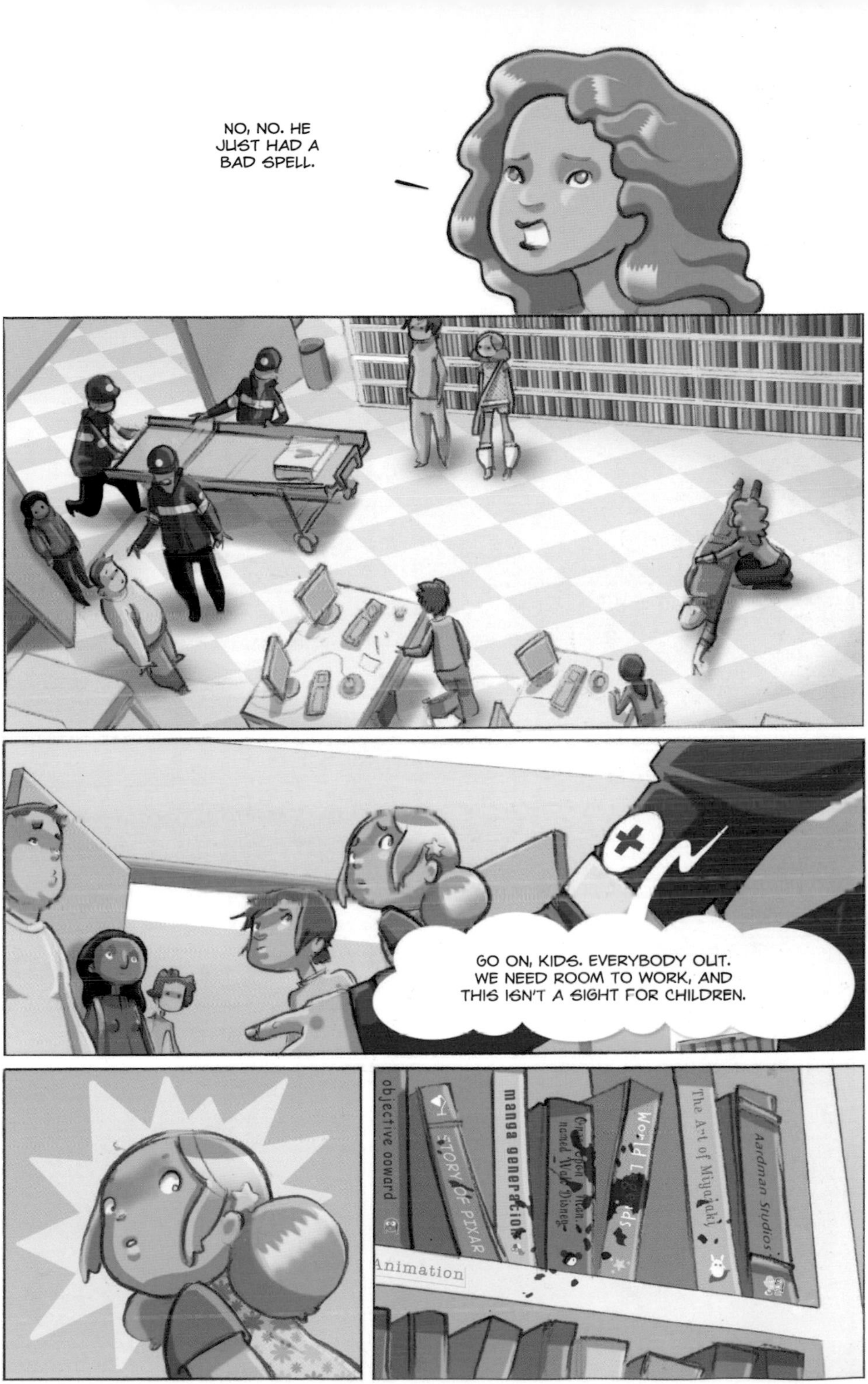
NO, NO. HE JUST HAD A BAD SPELL.
GO ON, KIDS. EVERYBODY OUT. WE NEED ROOM TO WORK, AND THIS ISN'T A SIGHT FOR CHILDREN.
objective oward
STORY OF PIXAR
manga generation
Aardman Studios
Animation

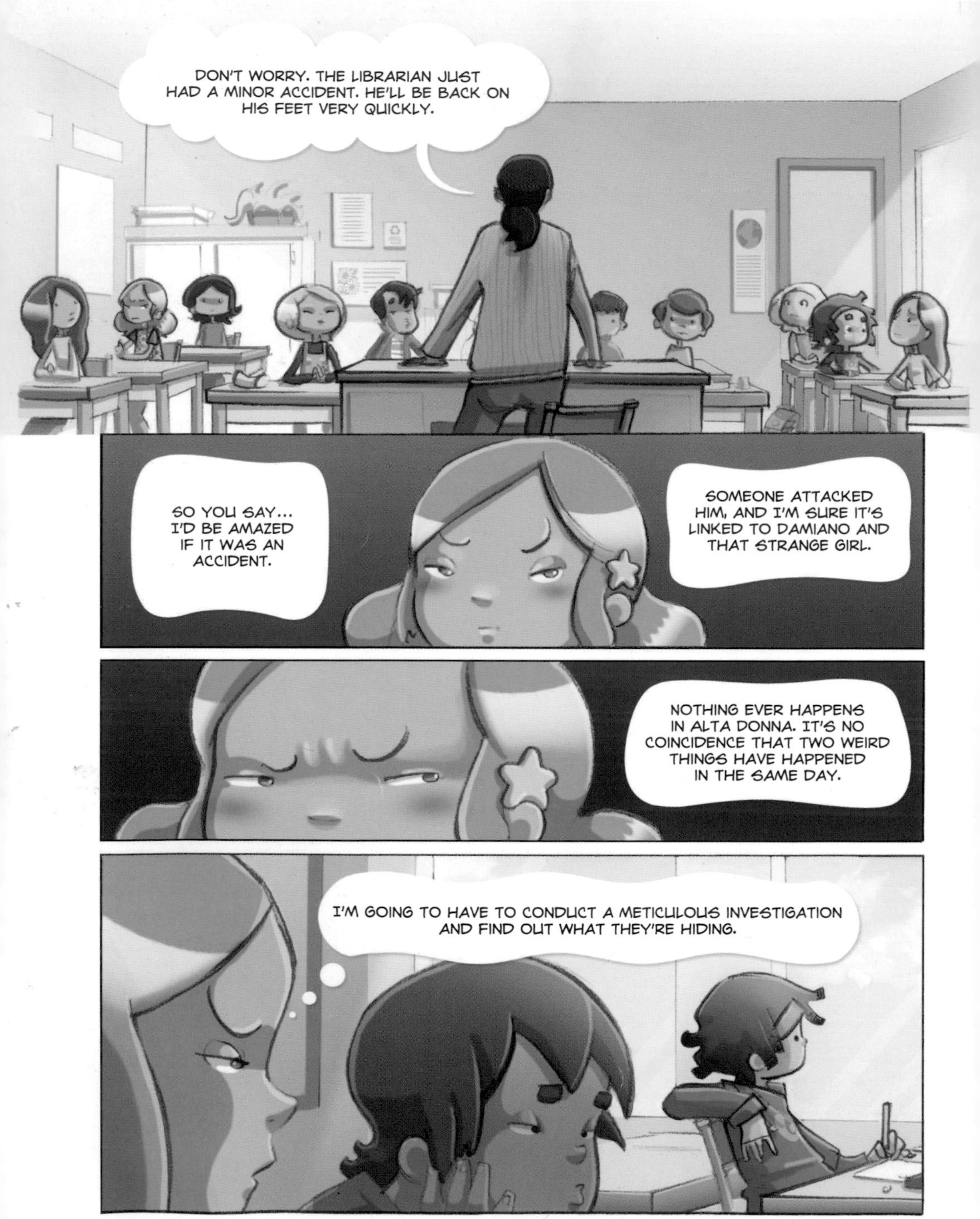
DON'T WORRY. THE LIBRARIAN JUST HAD A MINOR ACCIDENT. HE'LL BE BACK ON HIS FEET VERY QUICKLY.
SO YOU SAY... I'D BE AMAZED IF IT WAS AN ACCIDENT.
SOMEONE ATTACKED HIM, AND I'M SURE IT'S LINKED TO DAMIANO AND THAT STRANGE GIRL.
NOTHING EVER HAPPENS IN ALTA DONNA. IT'S NO COINCIDENCE THAT TWO WEIRD THINGS HAVE HAPPENED IN THE SAME DAY.
I'M GOING TO HAVE TO CONDUCT A METICULOUS INVESTIGATION AND FIND OUT WHAT THEY'RE HIDING.

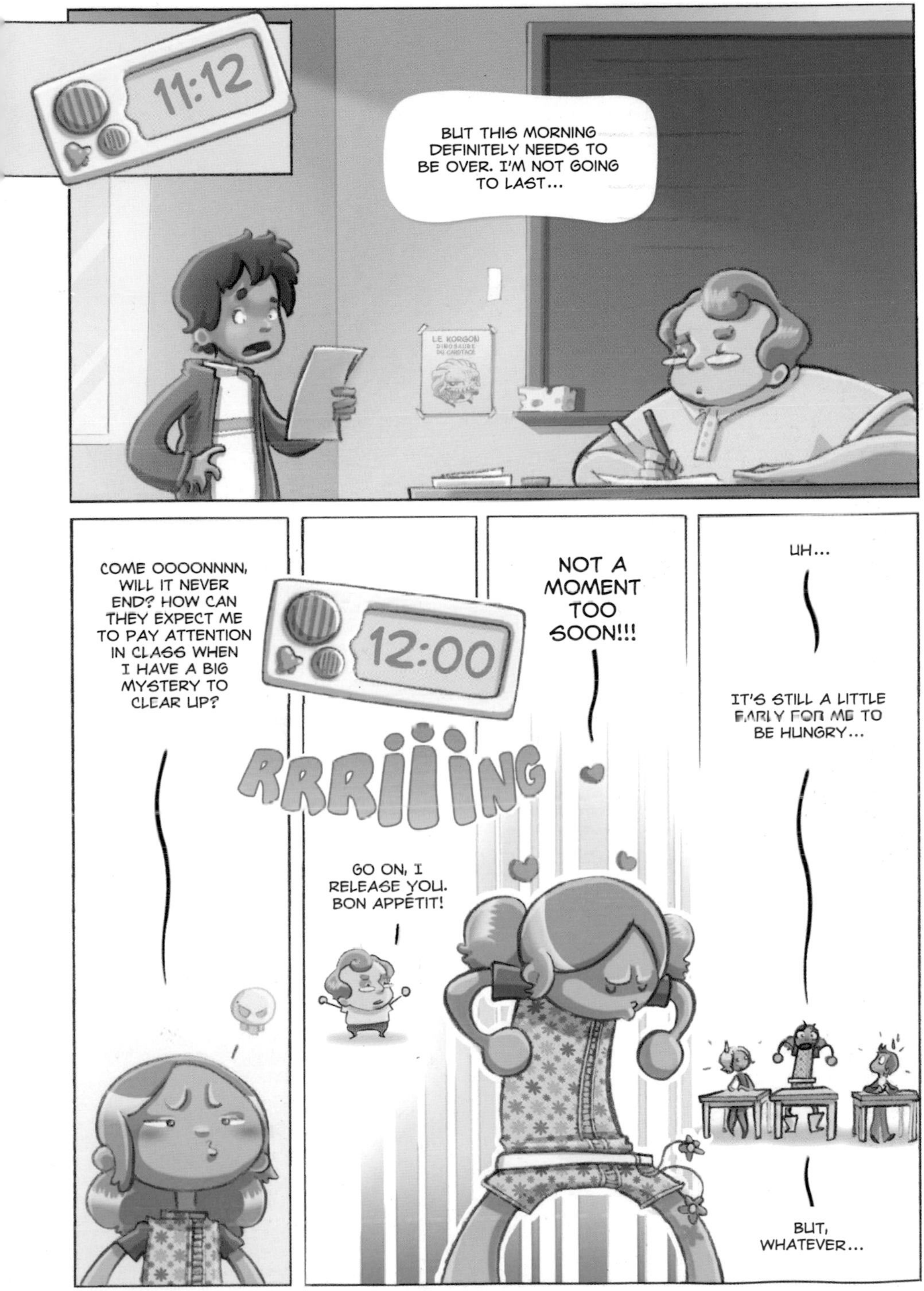
11:12
BUT THIS MORNING DEFINITELY NEEDS TO BE OVER. I'M NOT GOING TO LAST...
LE KORGON
COME OOOONNNN, WILL IT NEVER END? HOW CAN THEY EXPECT ME TO PAY ATTENTION IN CLASS WHEN I HAVE A BIG MYSTERY TO CLEAR UP?
12:00
RRRIIIING
GO ON, I RELEASE YOU. BON APPÉTIT!
NOT A MOMENT TOO SOON!!!
UH...
IT'S STILL A LITTLE EARLY FOR ME TO BE HUNGRY...
BUT, WHATEVER...

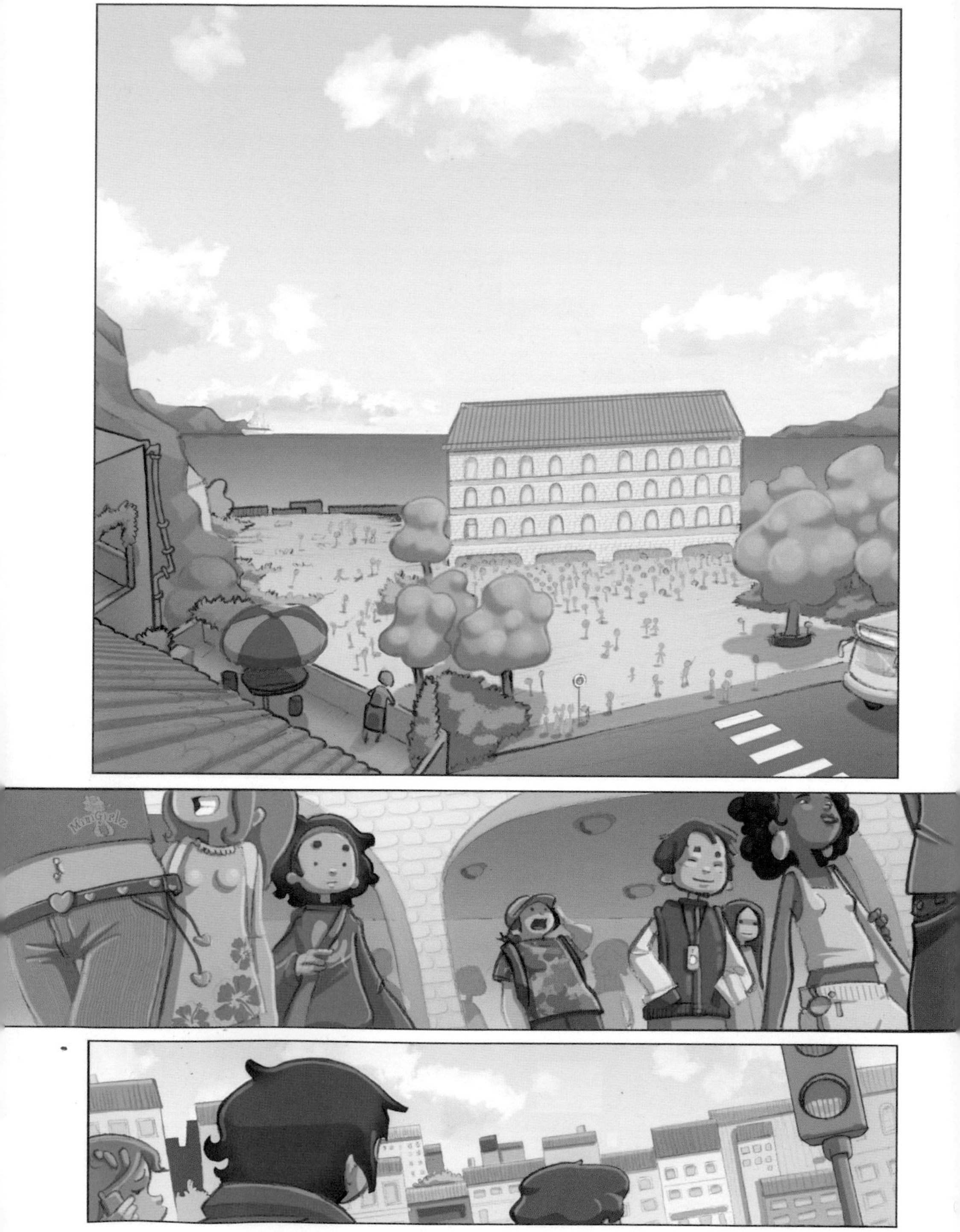

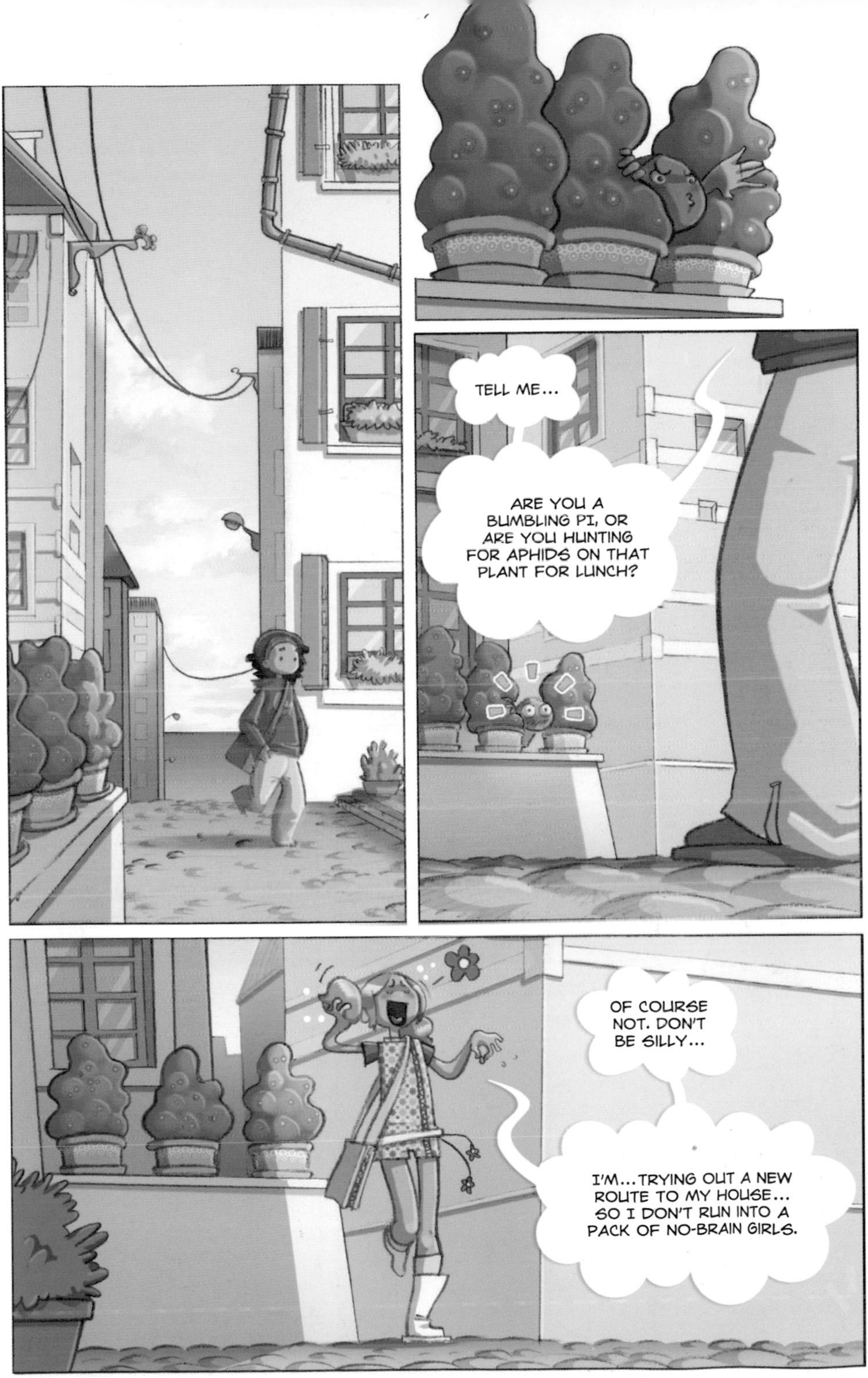
TELL ME...
ARE YOU A BUMBLING PI, OR ARE YOU HUNTING FOR APHIDS ON THAT PLANT FOR LUNCH?
OF COURSE NOT. DON'T BE SILLY...
I'M...TRYING OUT A NEW ROUTE TO MY HOUSE... SO I DON'T RUN INTO A PACK OF NO-BRAIN GIRLS.

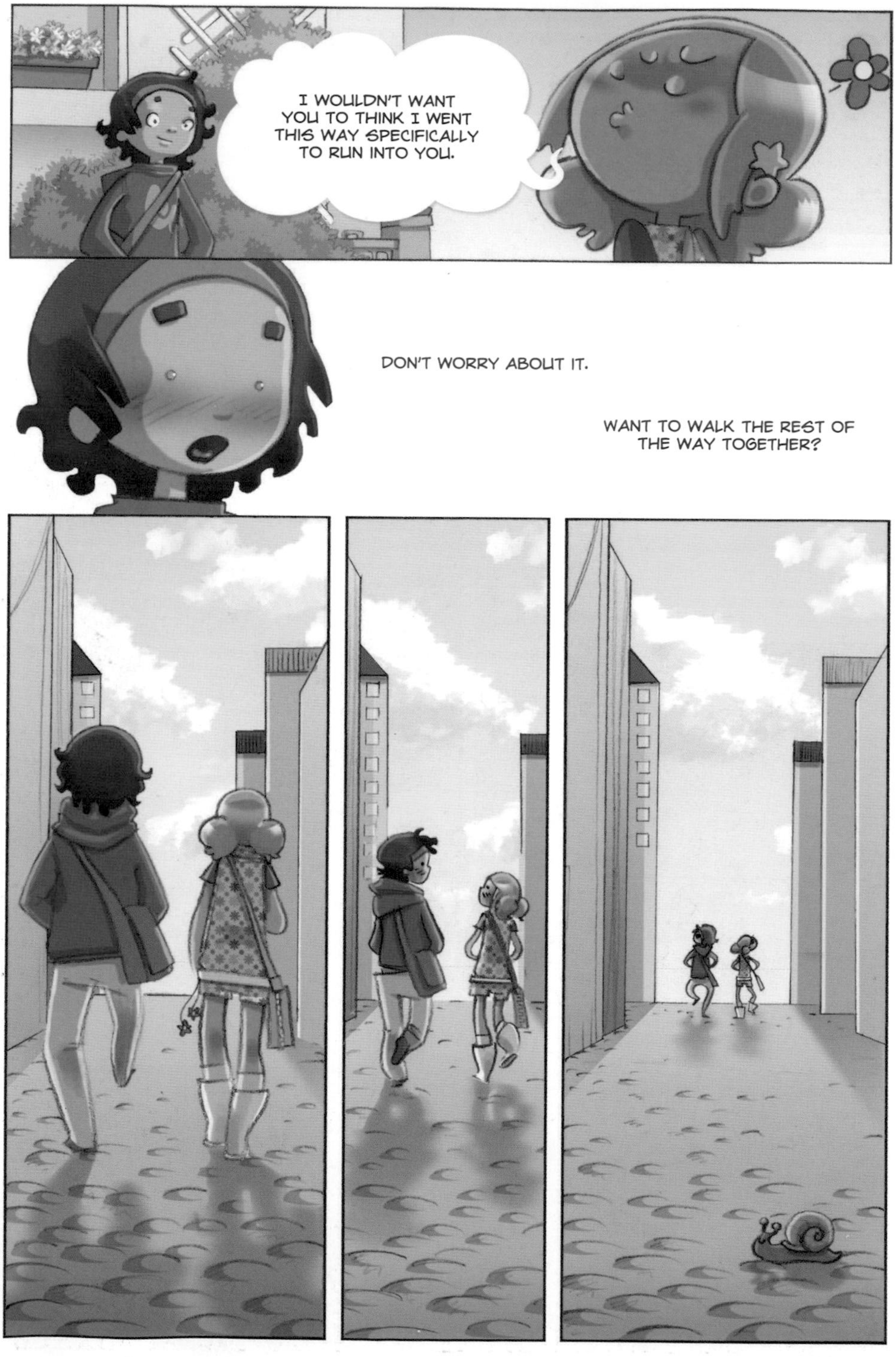
I WOULDN'T WANT YOU TO THINK I WENT THIS WAY SPECIFICALLY TO RUN INTO YOU.
DON'T WORRY ABOUT IT.
WANT TO WALK THE REST OF THE WAY TOGETHER?

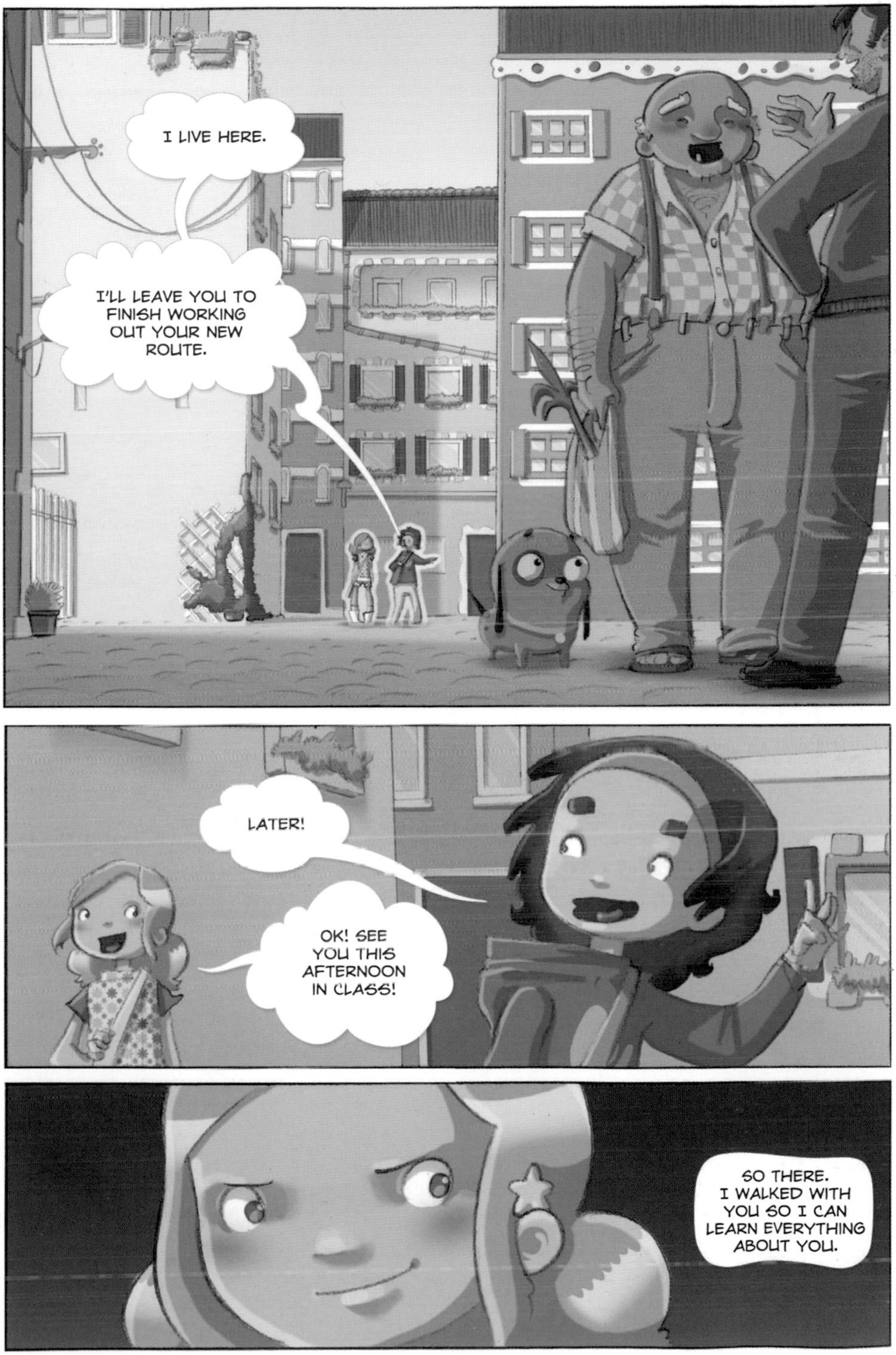
I LIVE HERE.
I'LL LEAVE YOU TO FINISH WORKING OUT YOUR NEW ROUTE.
LATER!
OK! SEE YOU THIS AFTERNOON IN CLASS!
SO THERE. I WALKED WITH YOU SO I CAN LEARN EVERYTHING ABOUT YOU.

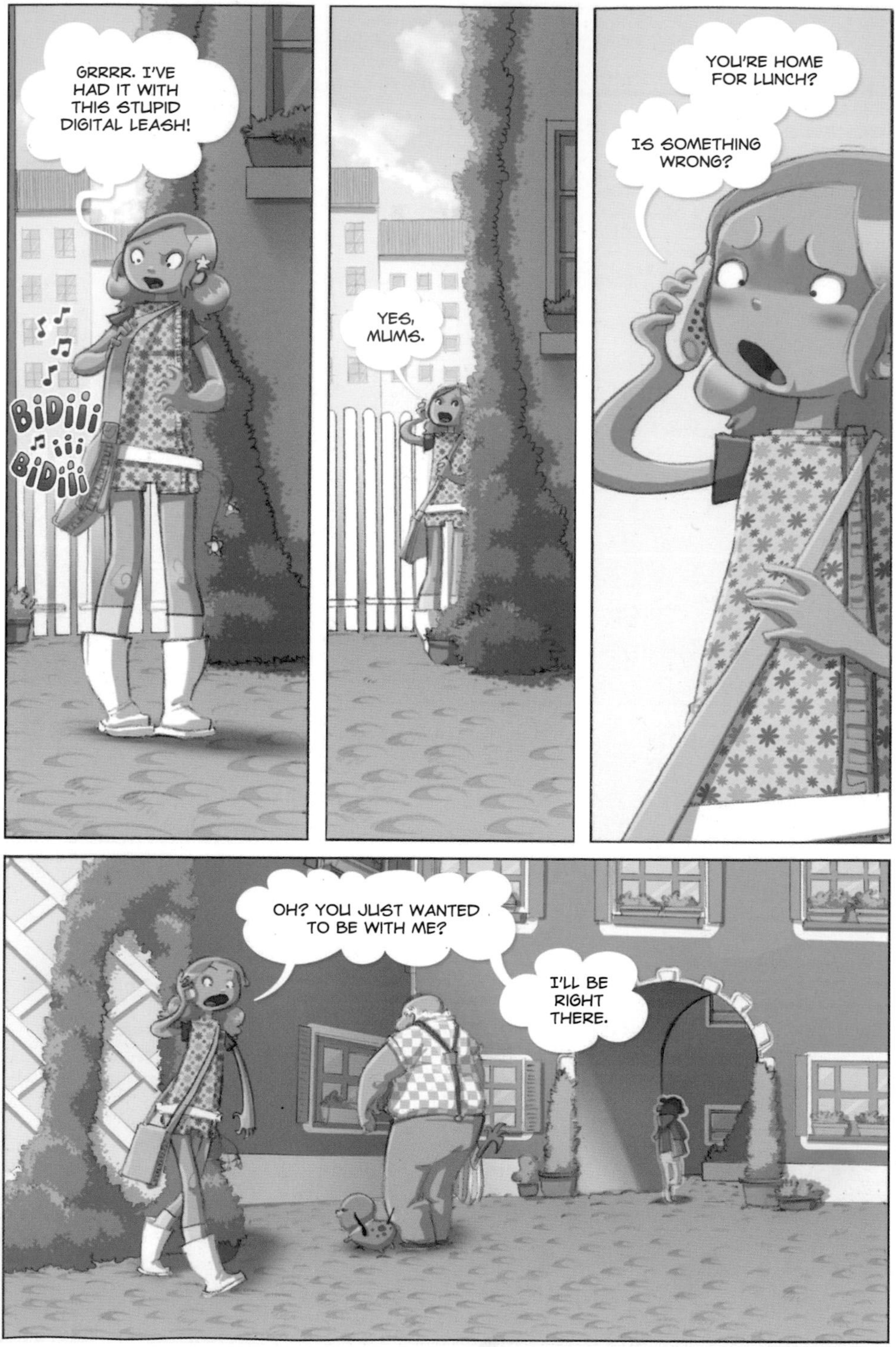
GRRRR. I'VE HAD IT WITH THIS STUPID DIGITAL LEASH!
BIDIIII BIDIIII
YES, MUMS.
YOU'RE HOME FOR LUNCH?
IS SOMETHING WRONG?
OH? YOU JUST WANTED TO BE WITH ME?
I'LL BE RIGHT THERE.

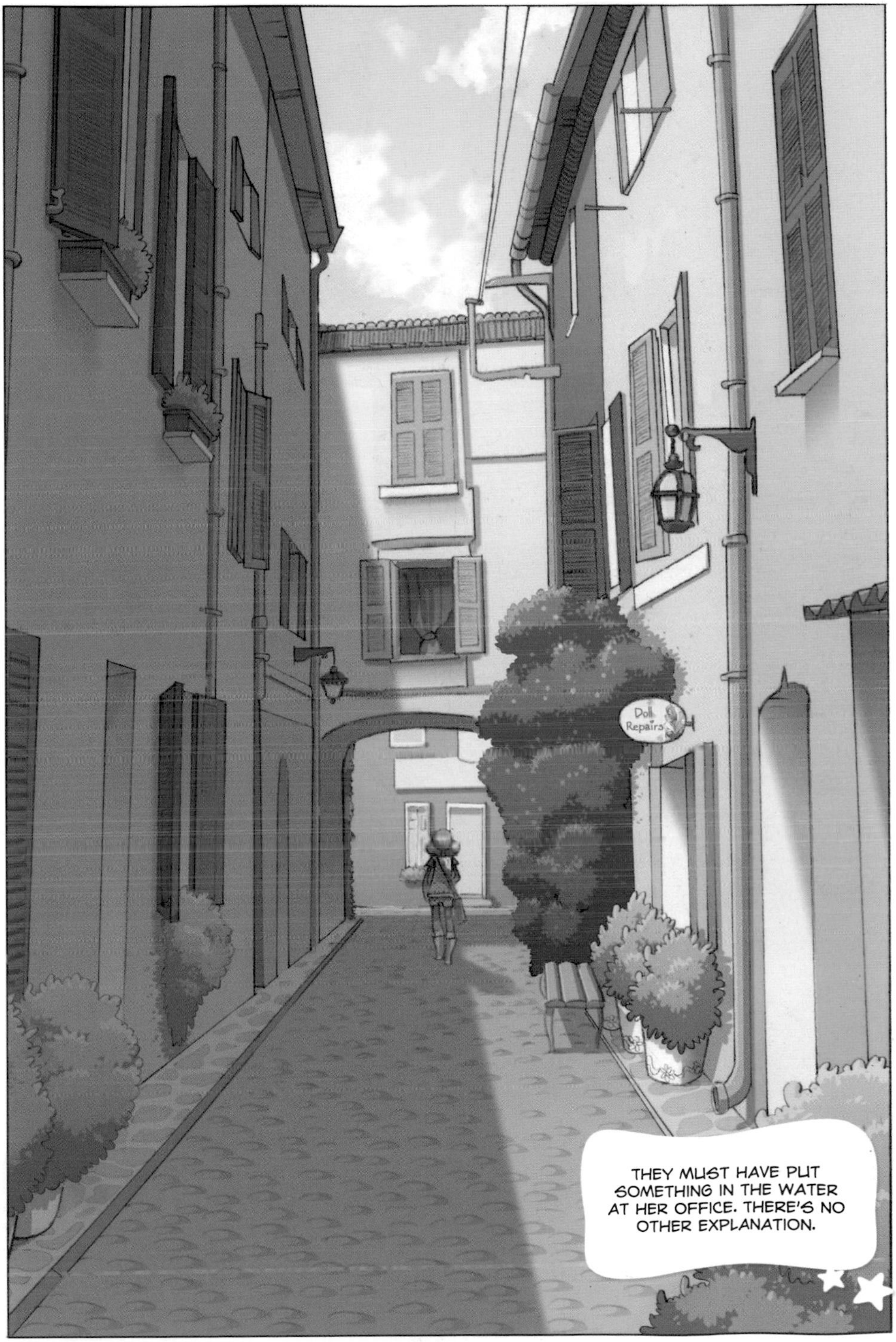
Doll Repairs
THEY MUST HAVE PUT SOMETHING IN THE WATER AT HER OFFICE. THERE'S NO OTHER EXPLANATION.

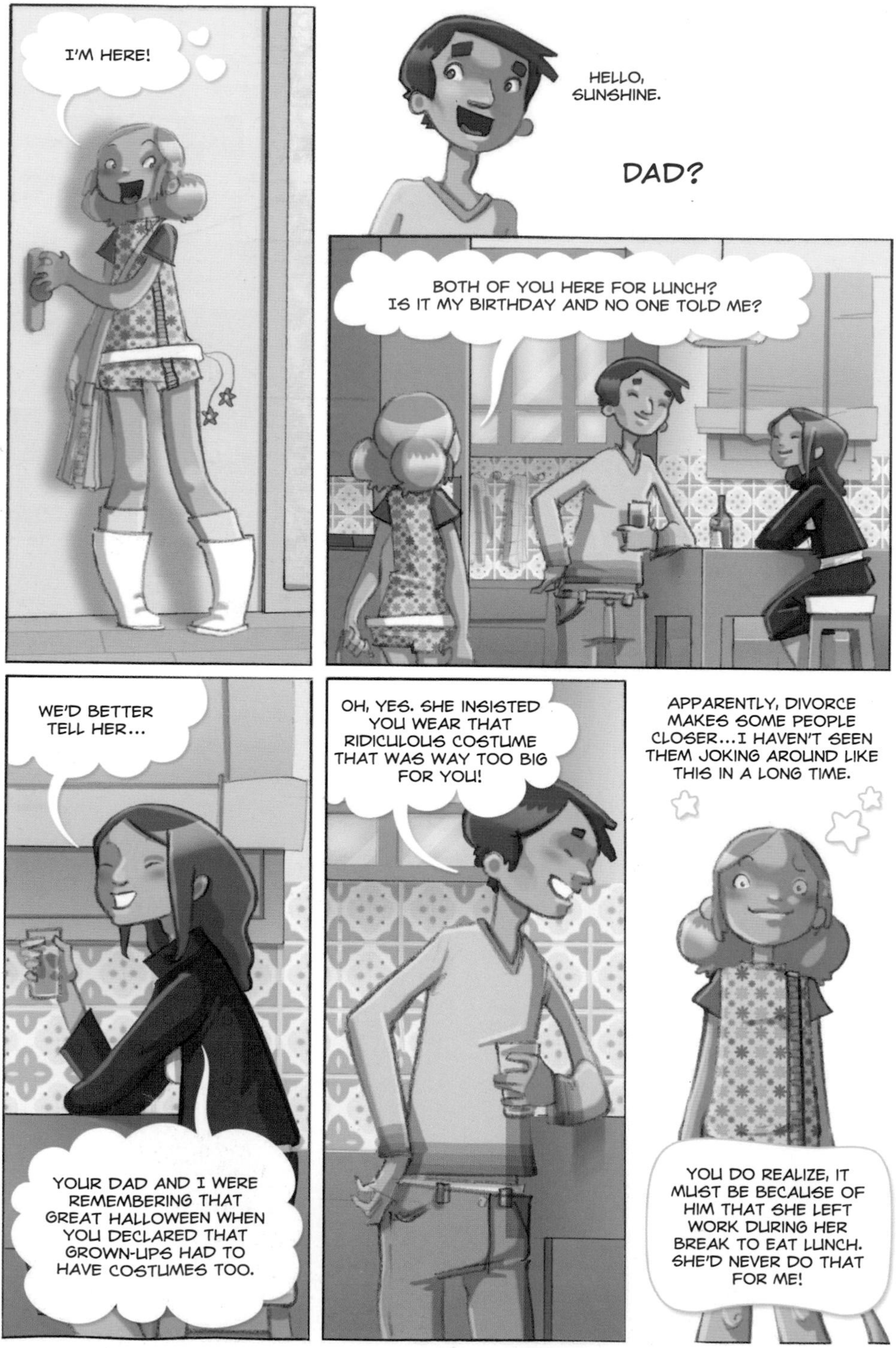
I'M HERE!
HELLO, SUNSHINE.
DAD?
BOTH OF YOU HERE FOR LUNCH? IS IT MY BIRTHDAY AND NO ONE TOLD ME?
WE'D BETTER TELL HER...
YOUR DAD AND I WERE REMEMBERING THAT GREAT HALLOWEEN WHEN YOU DECLARED THAT GROWN-UPS HAD TO HAVE COSTUMES TOO.
OH, YES. SHE INSISTED YOU WEAR THAT RIDICULOUS COSTUME THAT WAS WAY TOO BIG FOR YOU!
APPARENTLY, DIVORCE MAKES SOME PEOPLE CLOSER...I HAVEN'T SEEN THEM JOKING AROUND LIKE THIS IN A LONG TIME.
YOU DO REALIZE, IT MUST BE BECAUSE OF HIM THAT SHE LEFT WORK DURING HER BREAK TO EAT LUNCH. SHE'D NEVER DO THAT FOR ME!

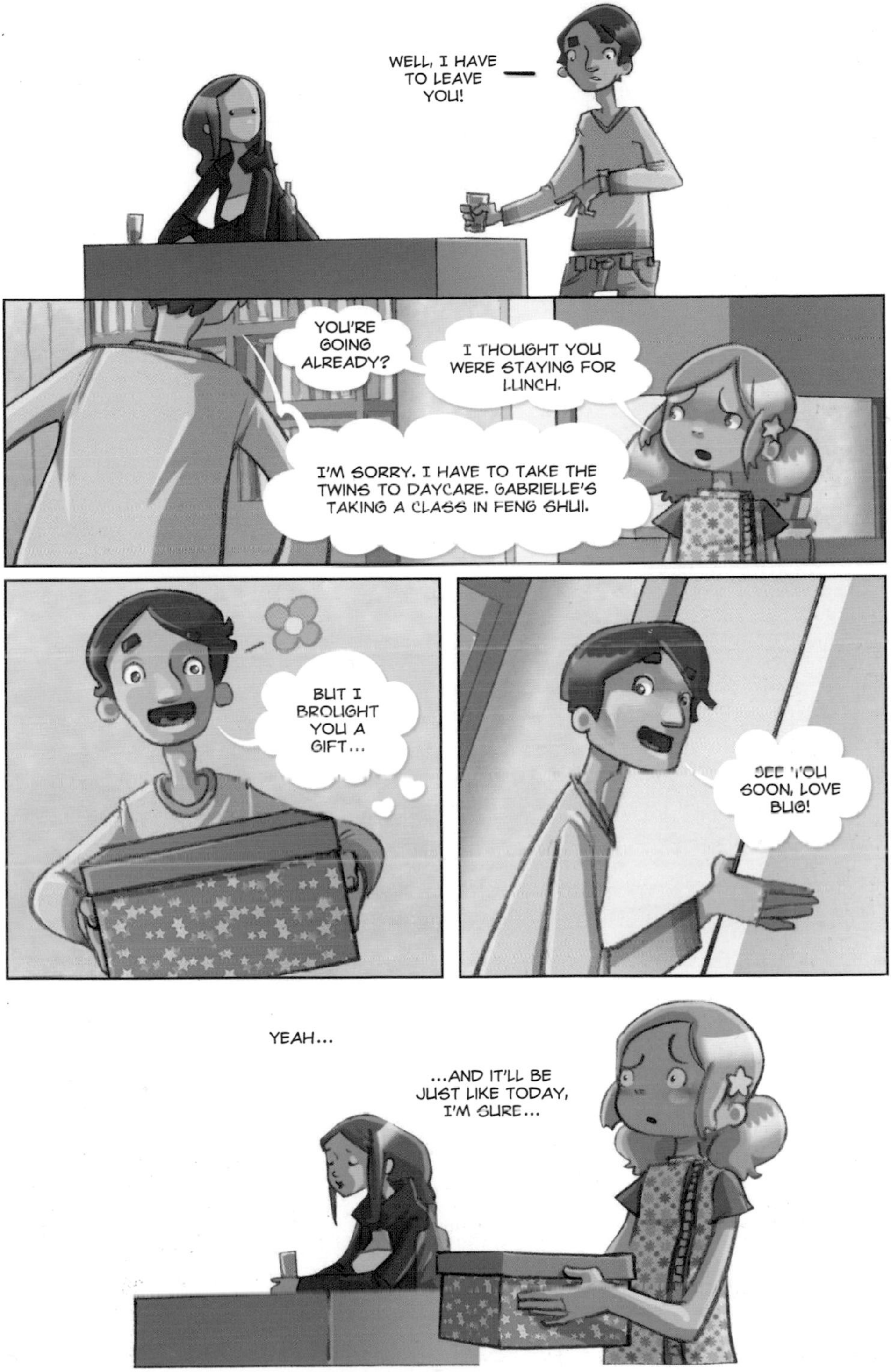
WELL, I HAVE TO LEAVE YOU!
YOU'RE GOING ALREADY?
I THOUGHT YOU WERE STAYING FOR LUNCH.
I'M SORRY. I HAVE TO TAKE THE TWINS TO DAYCARE. GABRIELLE'S TAKING A CLASS IN FENG SHUI.
BUT I BROUGHT YOU A GIFT...
SEE YOU SOON, LOVE BUG!
YEAH...
...AND IT'LL BE JUST LIKE TODAY, I'M SURE...

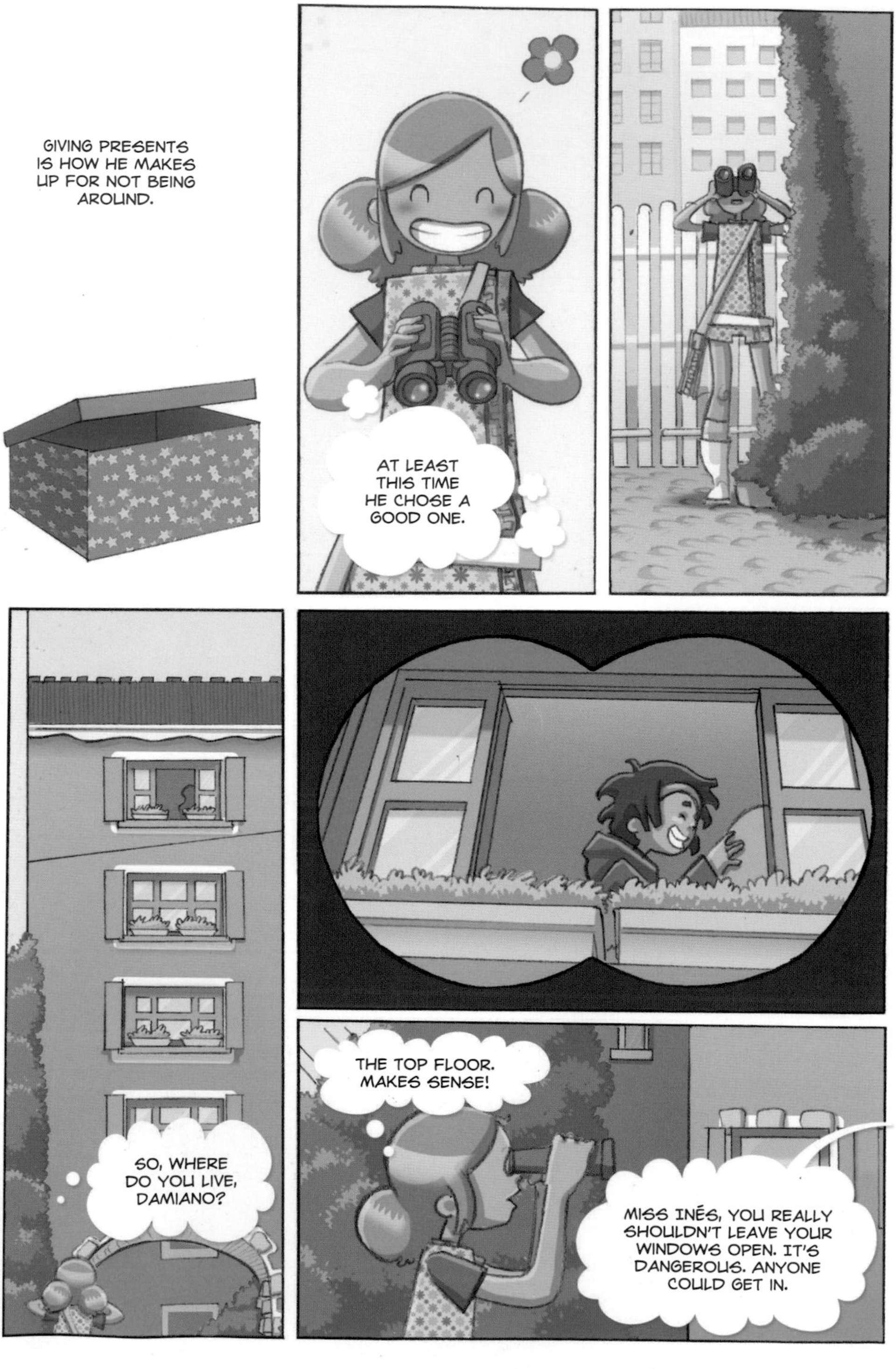
GIVING PRESENTS IS HOW HE MAKES UP FOR NOT BEING AROUND.
AT LEAST THIS TIME HE CHOSE A GOOD ONE.
SO, WHERE DO YOU LIVE, DAMIANO?
THE TOP FLOOR. MAKES SENSE!
MISS INÉS, YOU REALLY SHOULDN'T LEAVE YOUR WINDOWS OPEN. IT'S DANGEROUS. ANYONE COULD GET IN.

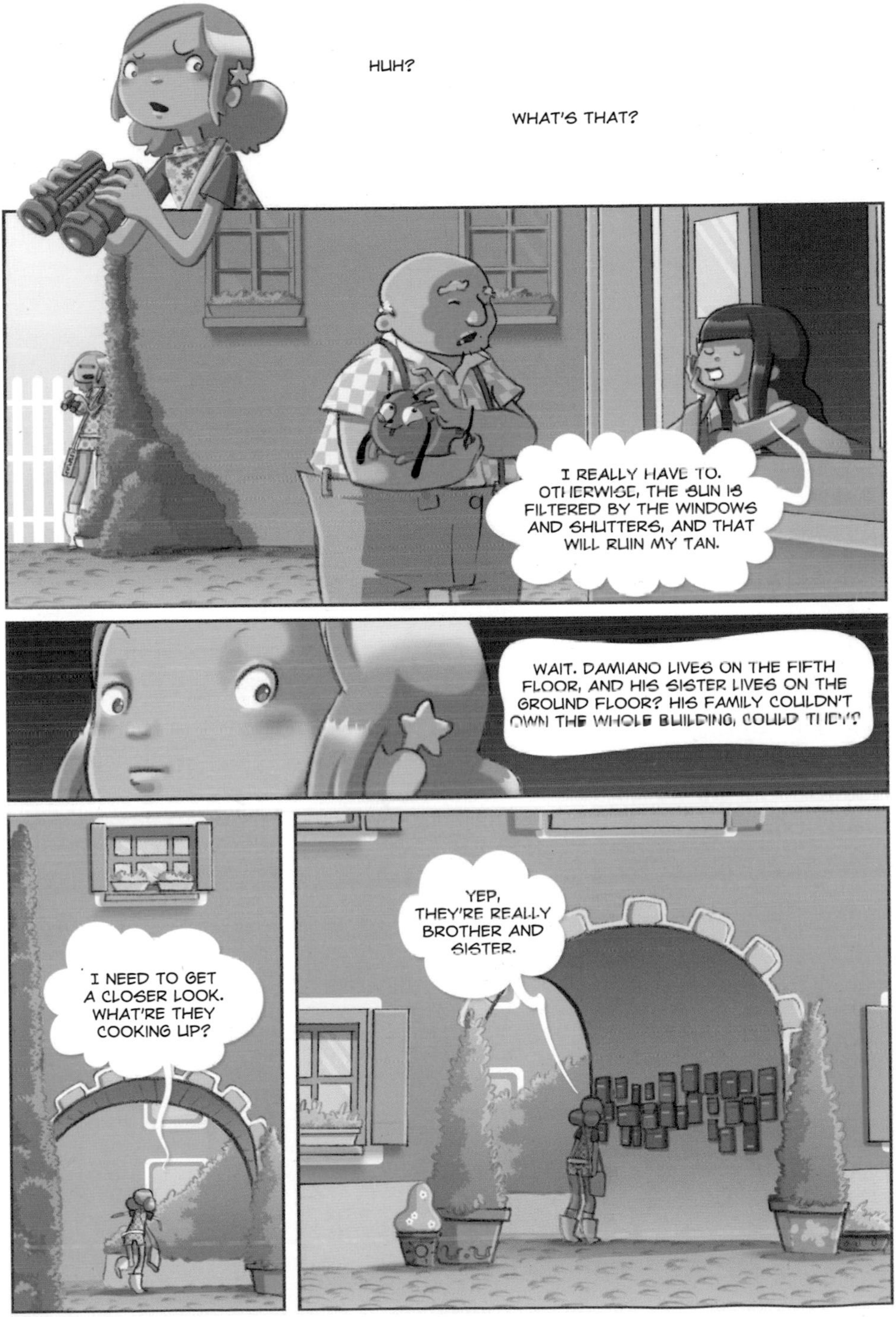
HUH?
WHAT'S THAT?
I REALLY HAVE TO. OTHERWISE, THE SUN IS FILTERED BY THE WINDOWS AND SHUTTERS, AND THAT WILL RUIN MY TAN.
WAIT. DAMIANO LIVES ON THE FIFTH FLOOR, AND HIS SISTER LIVES ON THE GROUND FLOOR? HIS FAMILY COULDN'T OWN THE WHOLE BUILDING, COULD THEY?
I NEED TO GET A CLOSER LOOK. WHAT'RE THEY COOKING UP?
YEP, THEY'RE REALLY BROTHER AND SISTER.

BUT THEY EACH HAVE THEIR OWN APARTMENT. THEY'RE DEFINITELY DIFFERENT...
Inés
Damiano
Apt.D3
CLAAAC!!!
A1
AGENT NOLA STEIN, I BELIEVE OUR TARGET HAS JUST GONE OUT. SHE WON'T KNOW SHE'S BEING FOLLOWED.

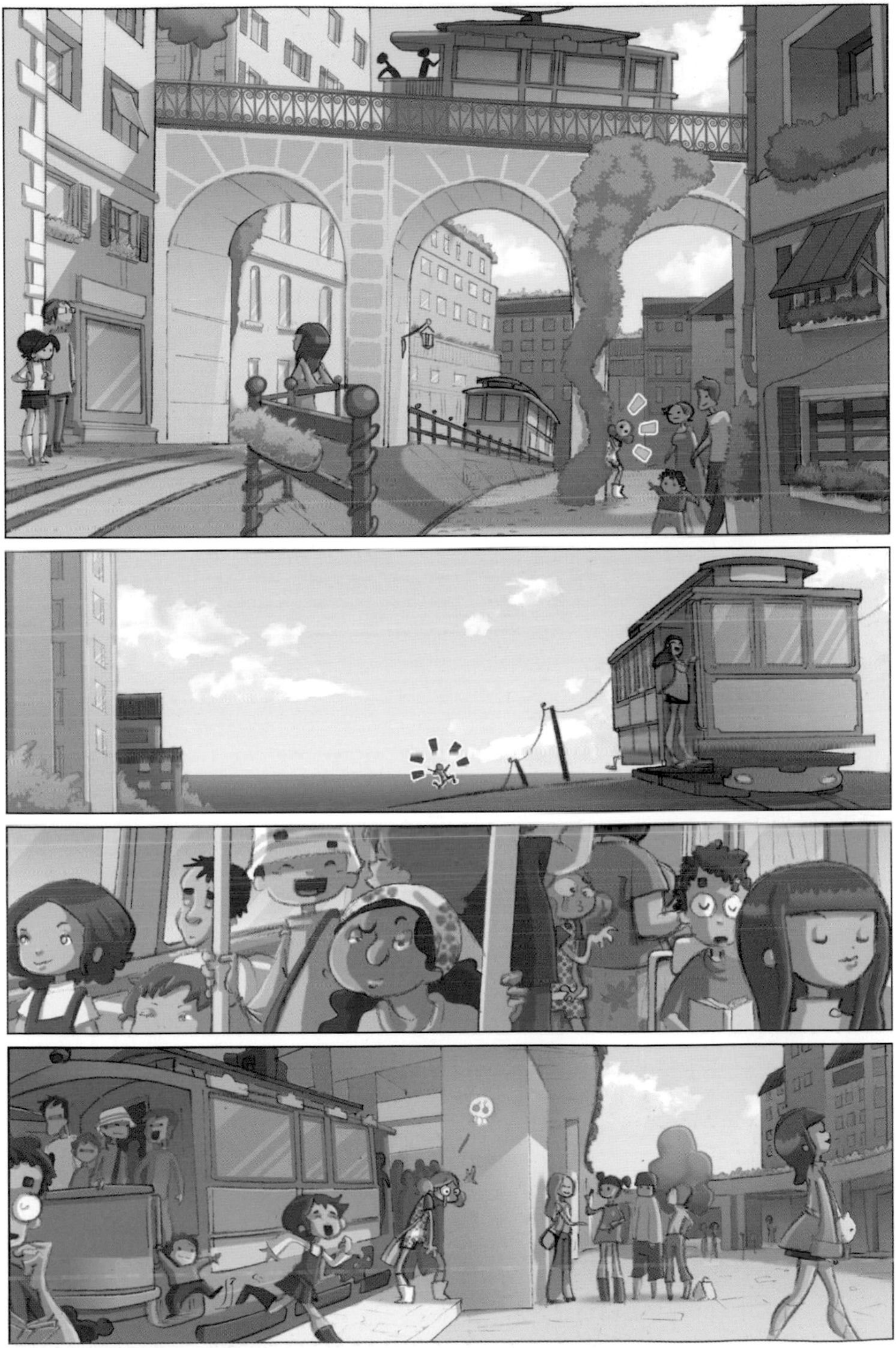

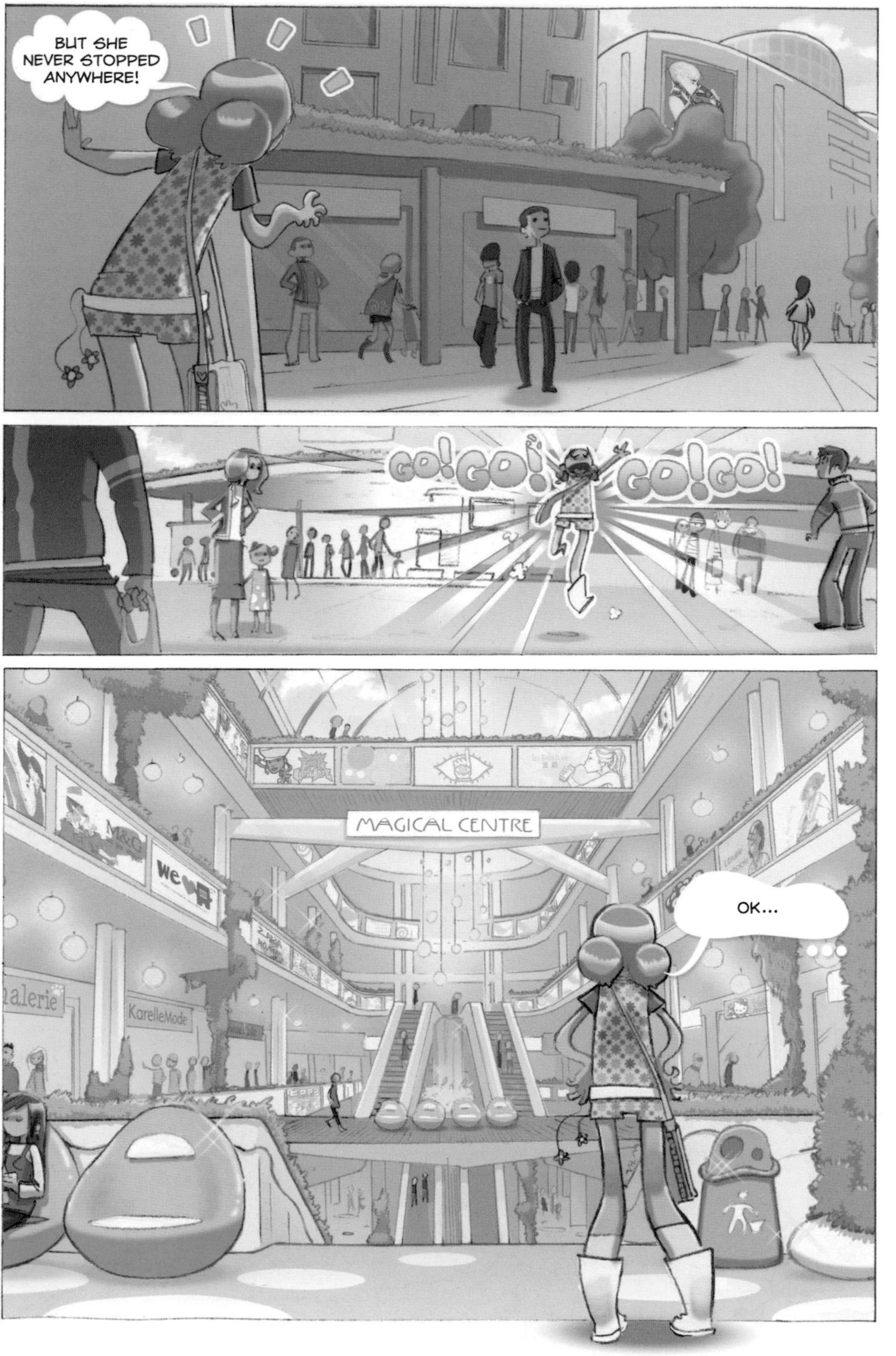
BUT SHE NEVER STOPPED ANYWHERE!
GO! GO! GO! GO!
MAGICAL CENTRE
OK...

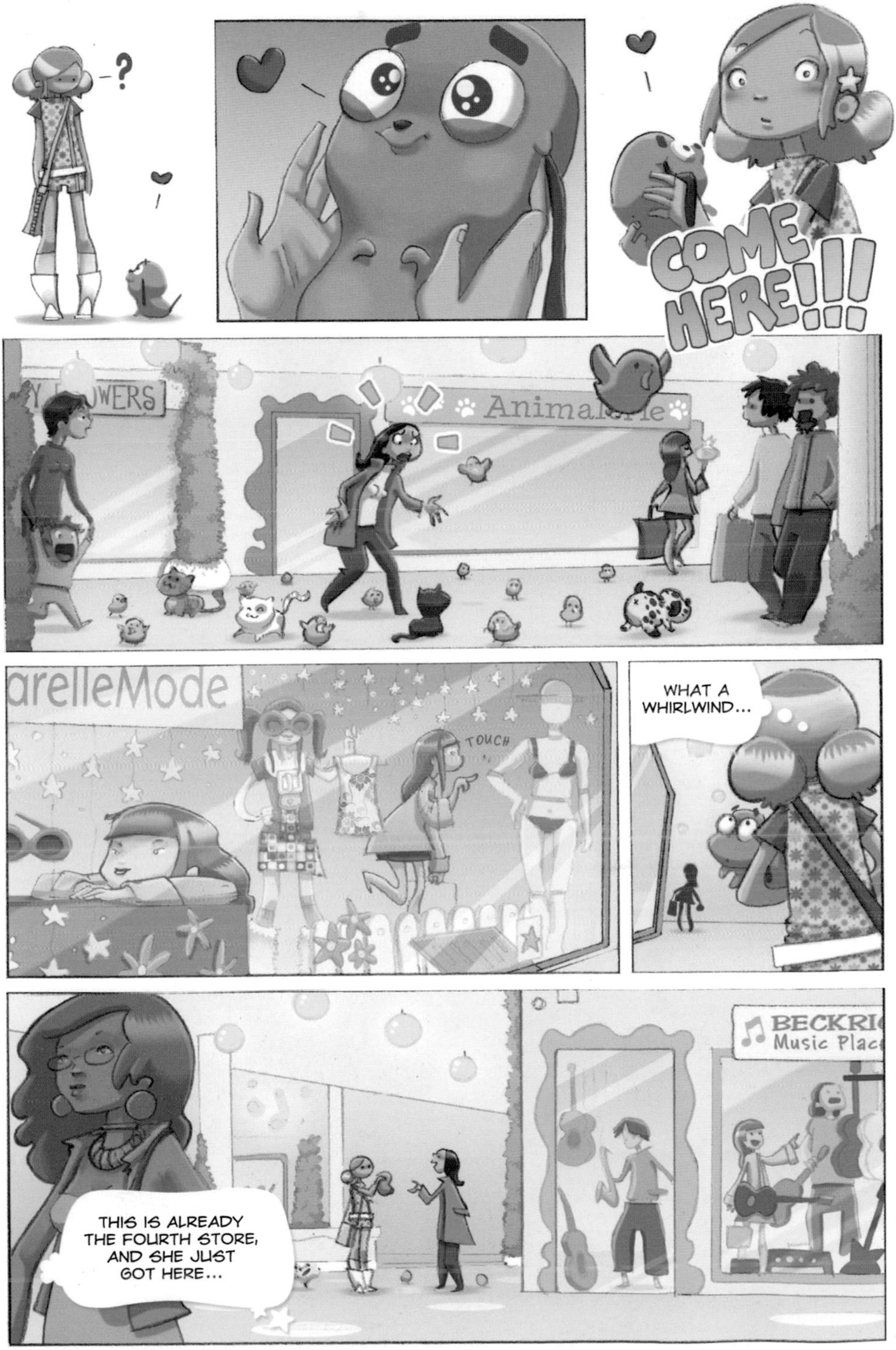
?
COME HERE!!!
Y FLOWERS
Animalerie
arelleMode
TOUCH
WHAT A WHIRLWIND...
BECKRI
Music Plac
THIS IS ALREADY THE FOURTH STORE, AND SHE JUST GOT HERE...

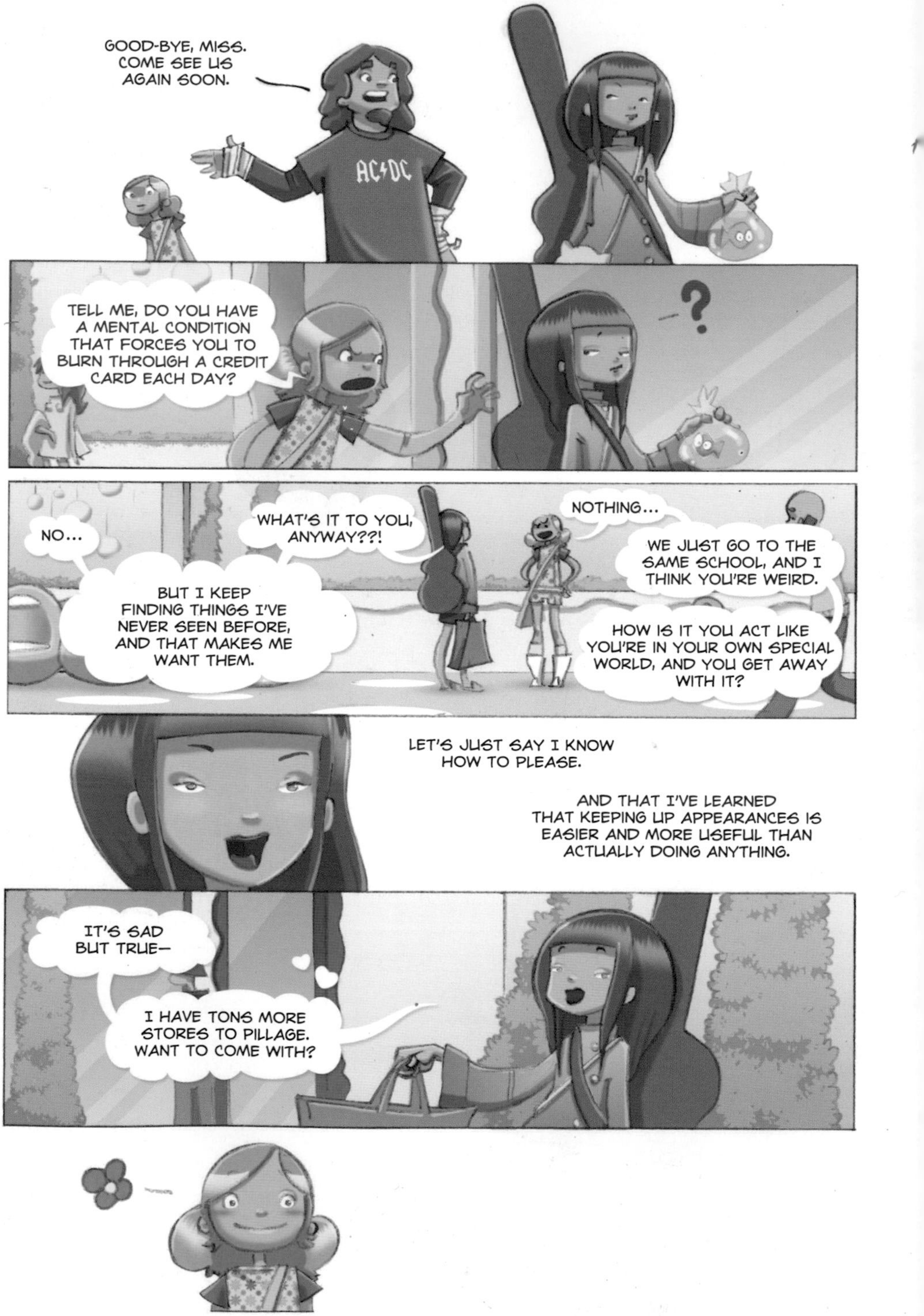
GOOD-BYE, MISS. COME SEE US AGAIN SOON.
AC/DC
TELL ME, DO YOU HAVE A MENTAL CONDITION THAT FORCES YOU TO BURN THROUGH A CREDIT CARD EACH DAY?
?
NO...
BUT I KEEP FINDING THINGS I'VE NEVER SEEN BEFORE, AND THAT MAKES ME WANT THEM.
WHAT'S IT TO YOU, ANYWAY??!
NOTHING...
WE JUST GO TO THE SAME SCHOOL, AND I THINK YOU'RE WEIRD.
HOW IS IT YOU ACT LIKE YOU'RE IN YOUR OWN SPECIAL WORLD, AND YOU GET AWAY WITH IT?
LET'S JUST SAY I KNOW HOW TO PLEASE.
AND THAT I'VE LEARNED THAT KEEPING UP APPEARANCES IS EASIER AND MORE USEFUL THAN ACTUALLY DOING ANYTHING.
IT'S SAD BUT TRUE—
I HAVE TONS MORE STORES TO PILLAGE. WANT TO COME WITH?

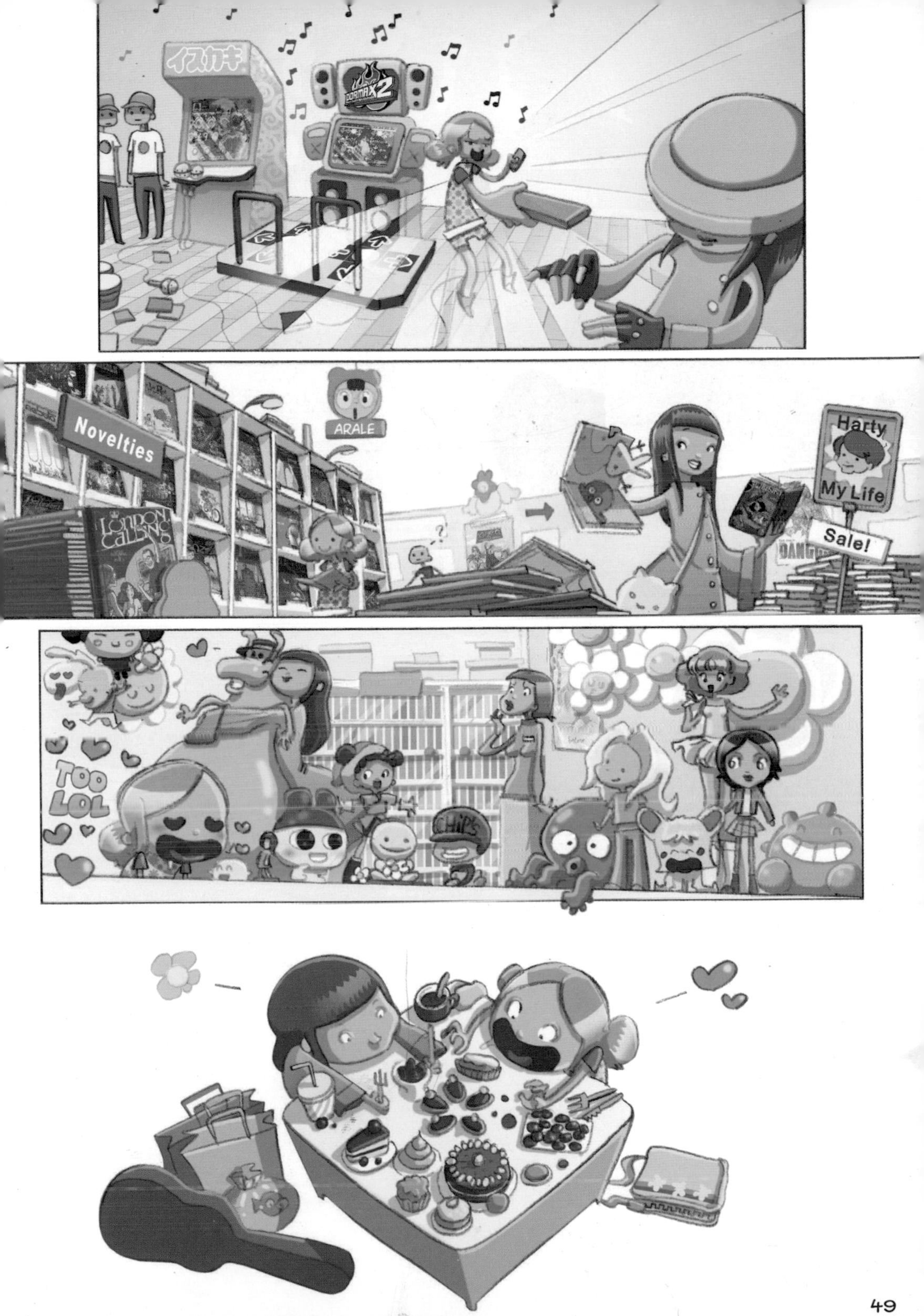
イスカキ
DDRMAX 2
Novelties
ARALE
LONDON CALLING
Harty
My Life
Sale!
TOO LOL
CHIP's

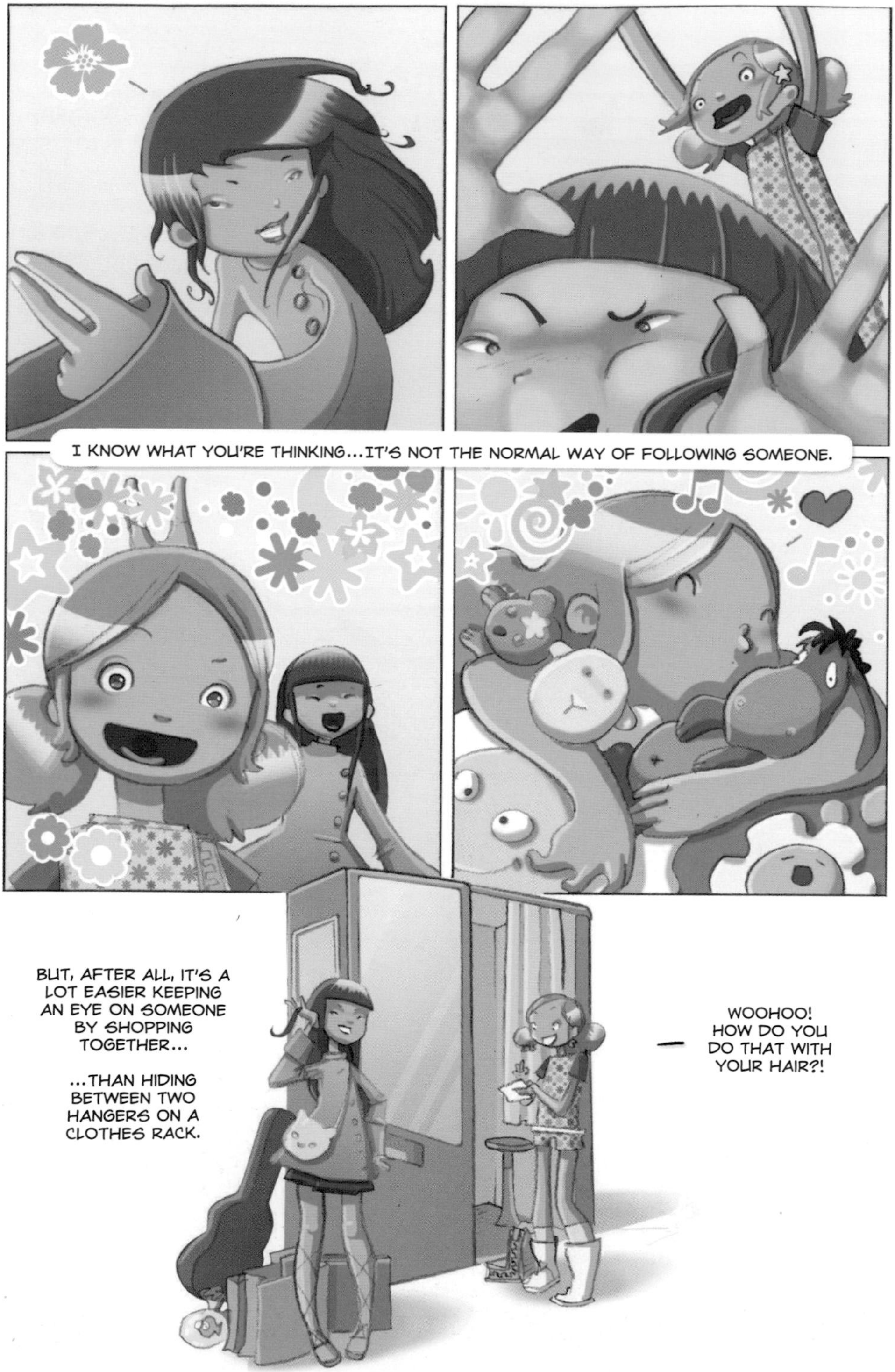

I KNOW WHAT YOU'RE THINKING...IT'S NOT THE NORMAL WAY OF FOLLOWING SOMEONE.
BUT, AFTER ALL, IT'S A LOT EASIER KEEPING AN EYE ON SOMEONE BY SHOPPING TOGETHER...
...THAN HIDING BETWEEN TWO HANGERS ON A CLOTHES RACK.
WOOHOO! HOW DO YOU DO THAT WITH YOUR HAIR?!

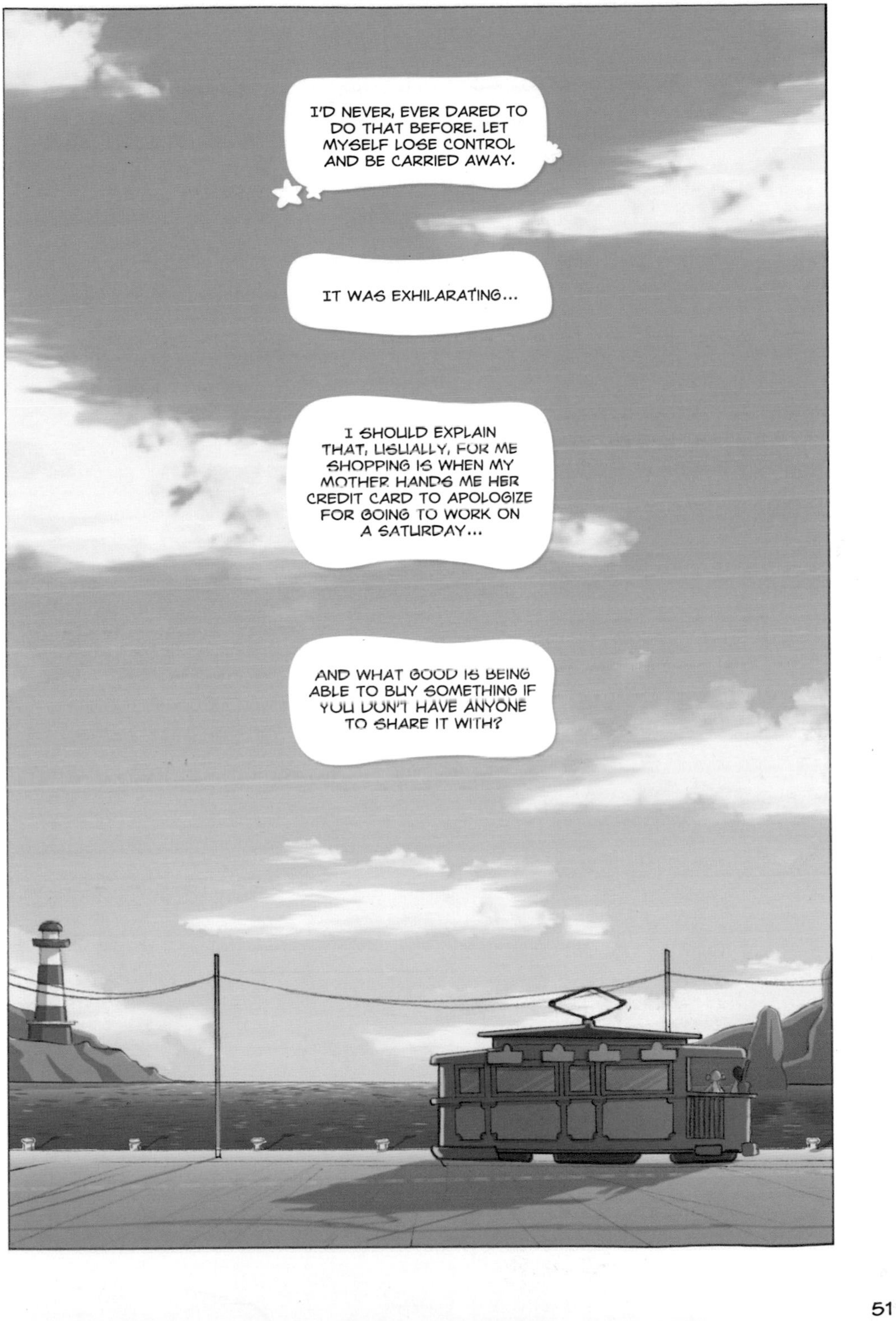
I'D NEVER, EVER DARED TO DO THAT BEFORE. LET MYSELF LOSE CONTROL AND BE CARRIED AWAY.
IT WAS EXHILARATING...
I SHOULD EXPLAIN THAT, USUALLY, FOR ME SHOPPING IS WHEN MY MOTHER HANDS ME HER CREDIT CARD TO APOLOGIZE FOR GOING TO WORK ON A SATURDAY...
AND WHAT GOOD IS BEING ABLE TO BUY SOMETHING IF YOU DON'T HAVE ANYONE TO SHARE IT WITH?

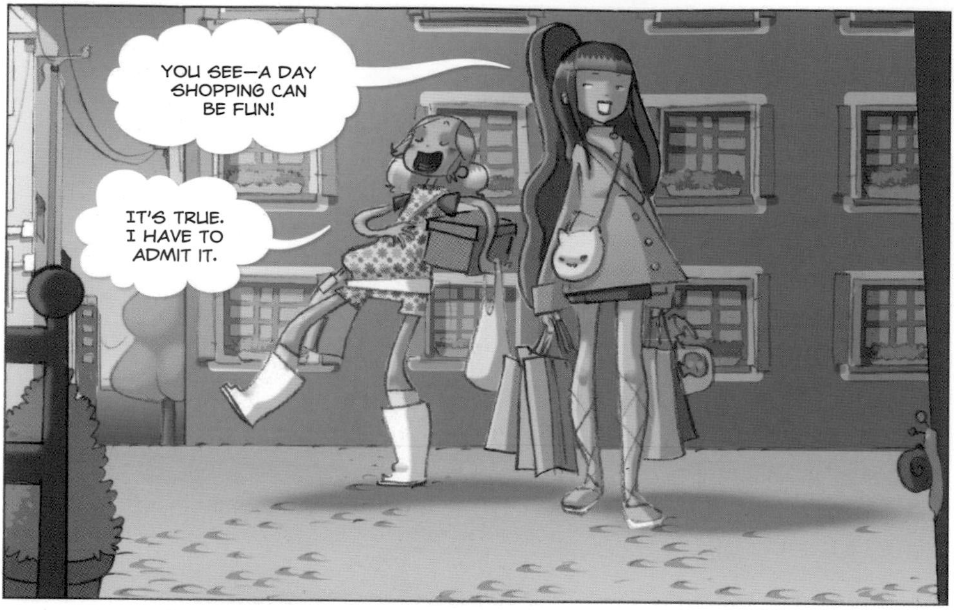
YOU SEE—A DAY SHOPPING CAN BE FUN!
IT'S TRUE. I HAVE TO ADMIT IT.

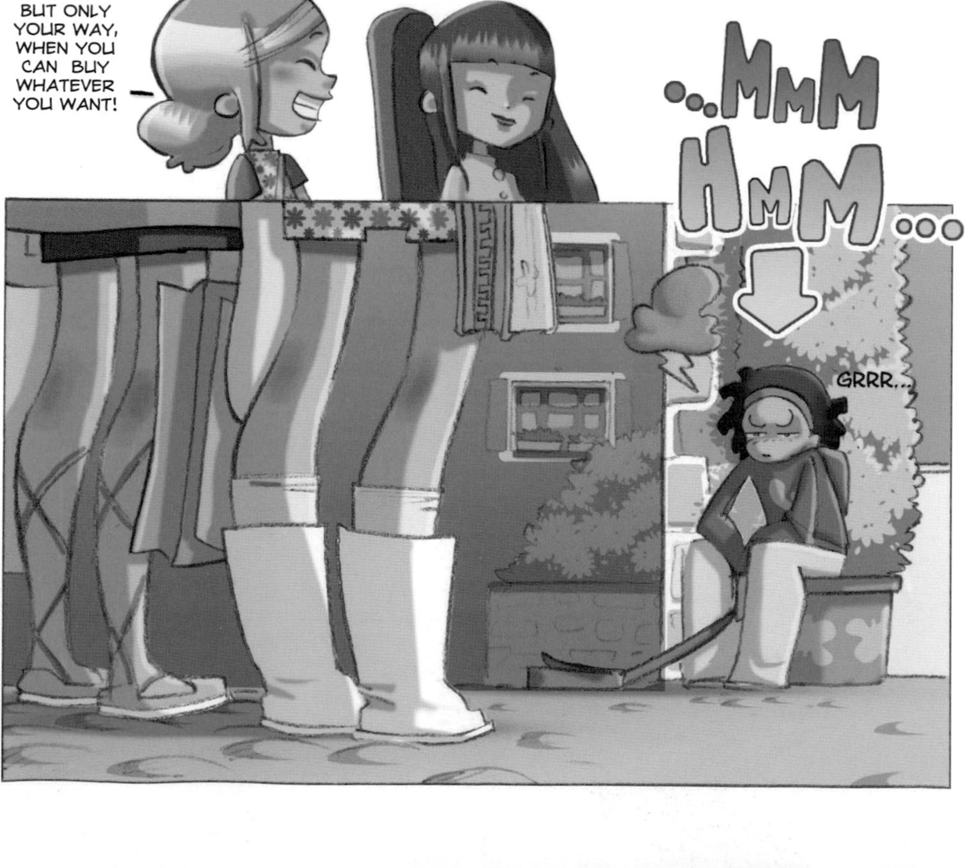
BUT ONLY YOUR WAY, WHEN YOU CAN BUY WHATEVER YOU WANT!
...MMM HMM...
GRRR...

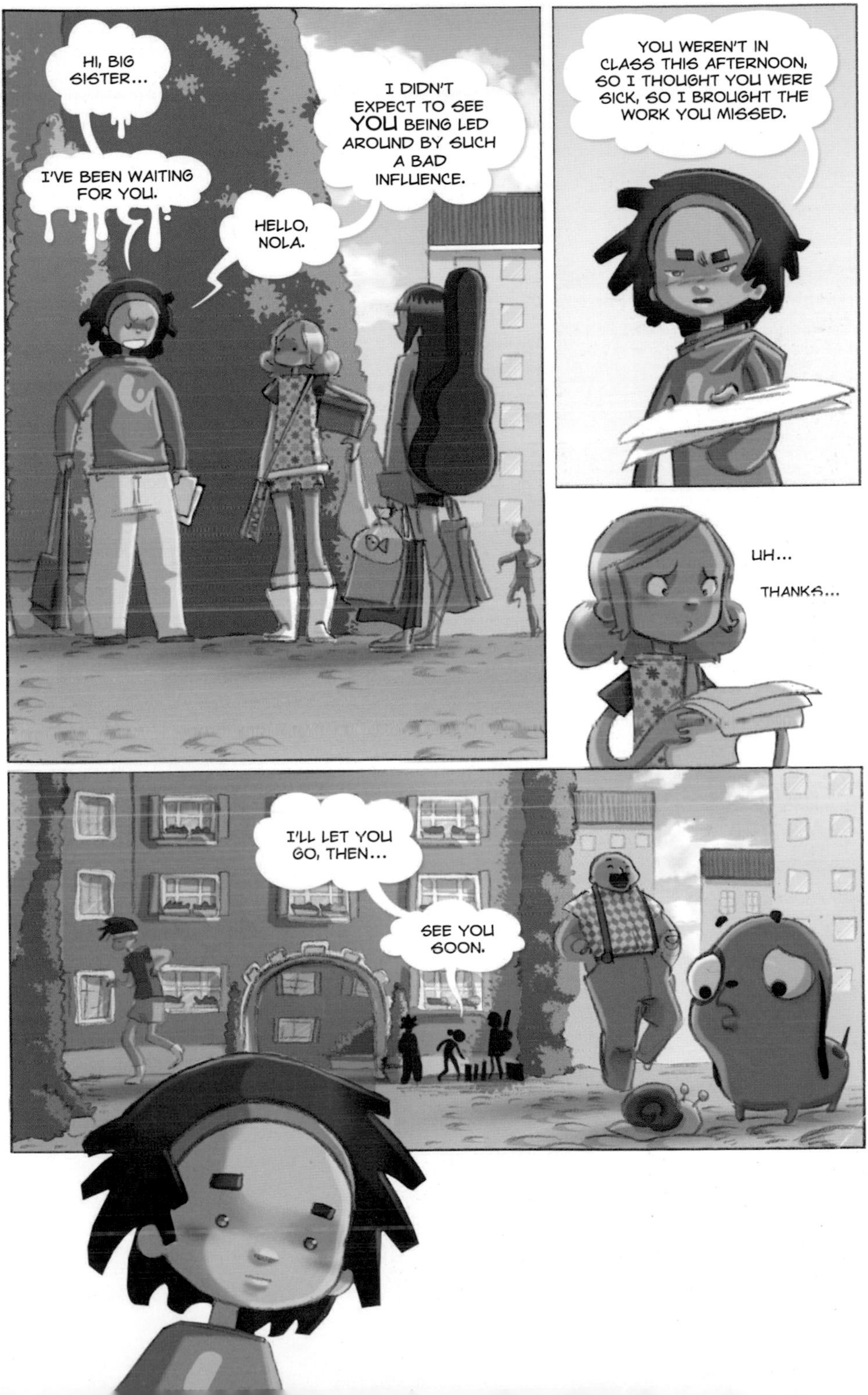
HI, BIG SISTER...
I'VE BEEN WAITING FOR YOU.
HELLO, NOLA.
I DIDN'T EXPECT TO SEE YOU BEING LED AROUND BY SUCH A BAD INFLUENCE.
YOU WEREN'T IN CLASS THIS AFTERNOON, SO I THOUGHT YOU WERE SICK, SO I BROUGHT THE WORK YOU MISSED.
UH...
THANKS...
I'LL LET YOU GO, THEN...
SEE YOU SOON.

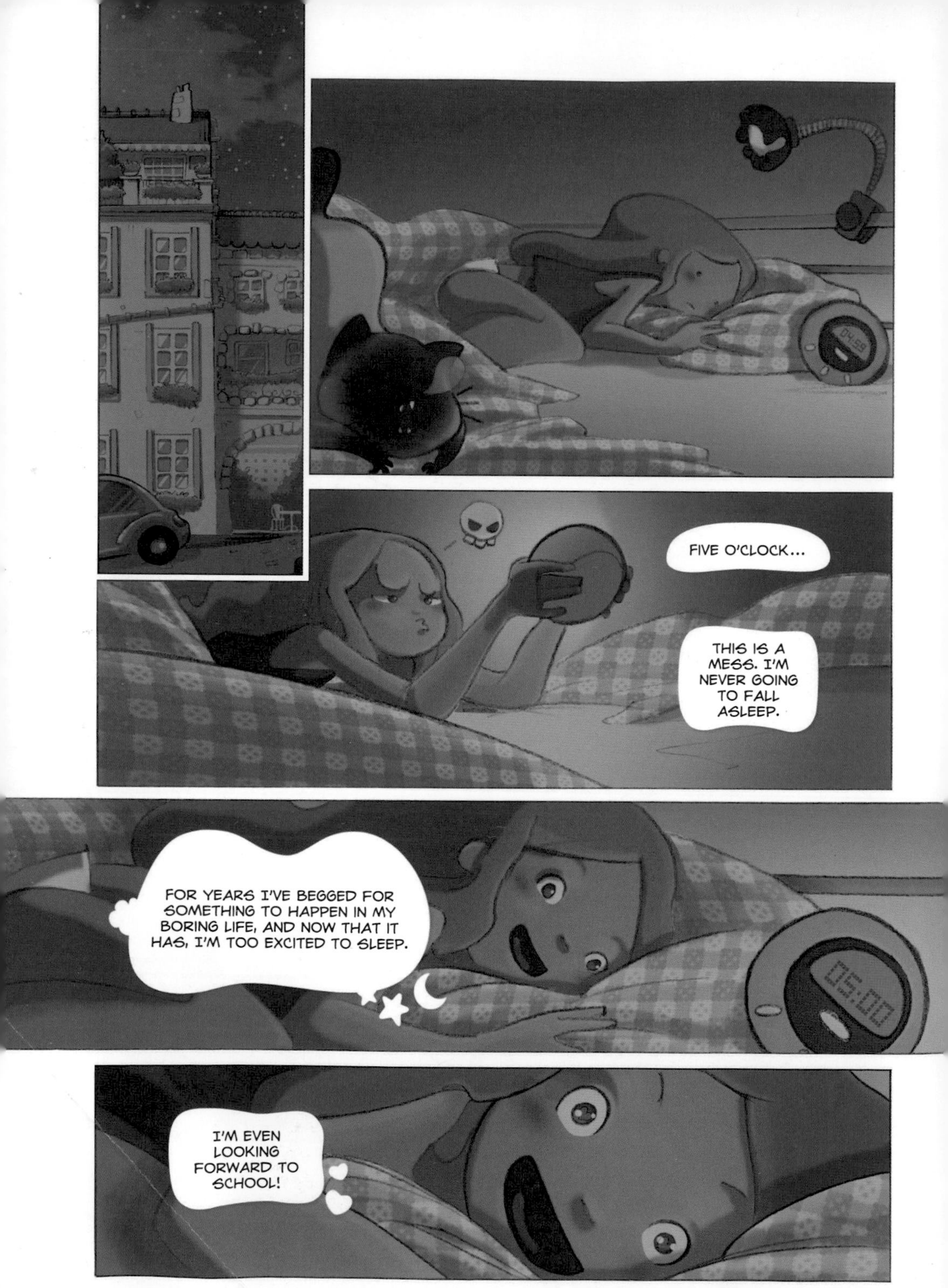
FIVE O'CLOCK...
THIS IS A MESS. I'M NEVER GOING TO FALL ASLEEP.
FOR YEARS I'VE BEGGED FOR SOMETHING TO HAPPEN IN MY BORING LIFE, AND NOW THAT IT HAS, I'M TOO EXCITED TO SLEEP.
I'M EVEN LOOKING FORWARD TO SCHOOL!

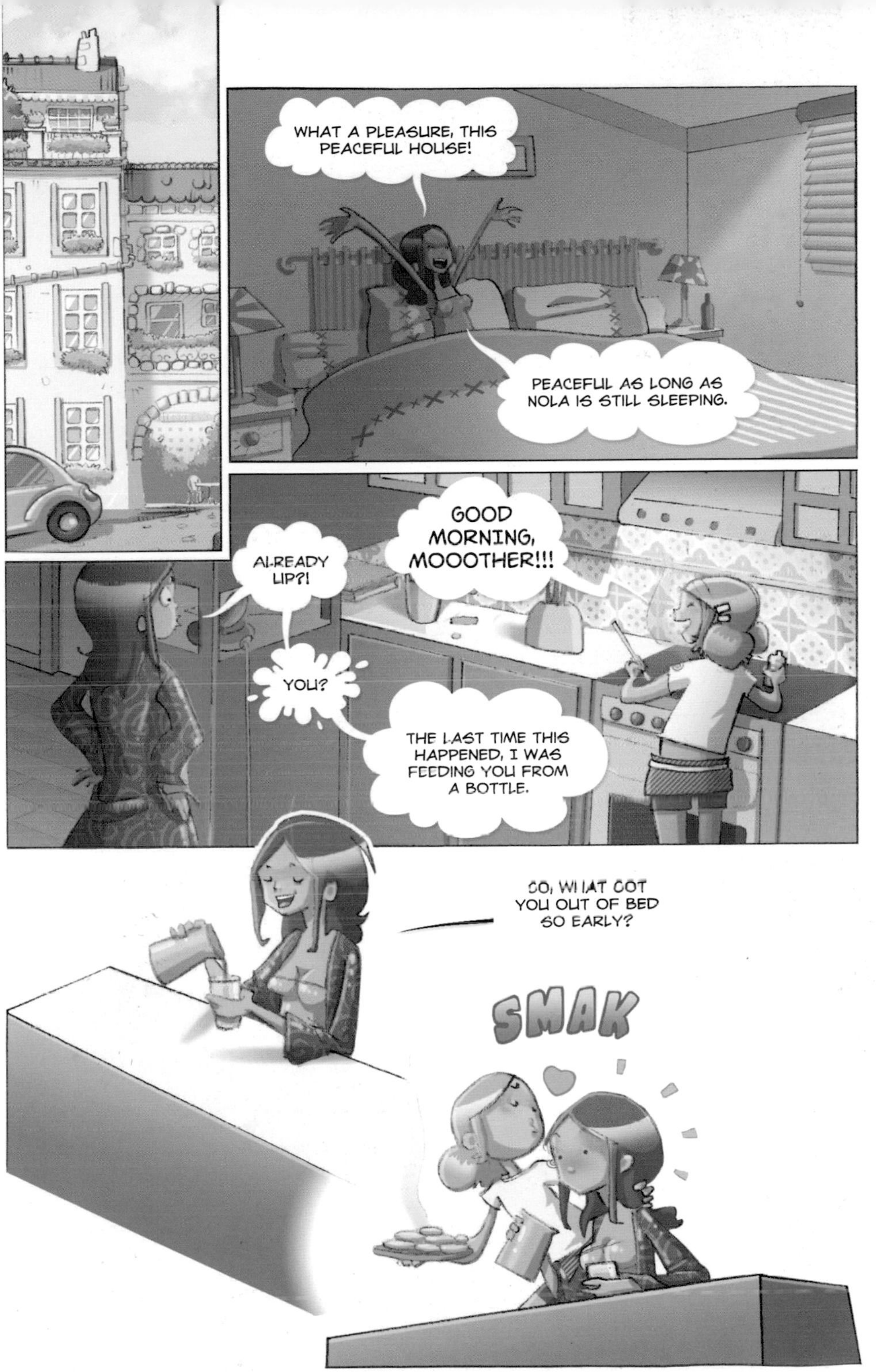
WHAT A PLEASURE, THIS PEACEFUL HOUSE!
PEACEFUL AS LONG AS NOLA IS STILL SLEEPING.
GOOD MORNING, MOOOTHER!!!
ALREADY UP?!
YOU?
THE LAST TIME THIS HAPPENED, I WAS FEEDING YOU FROM A BOTTLE.
SO, WHAT GOT YOU OUT OF BED SO EARLY?
SMAK

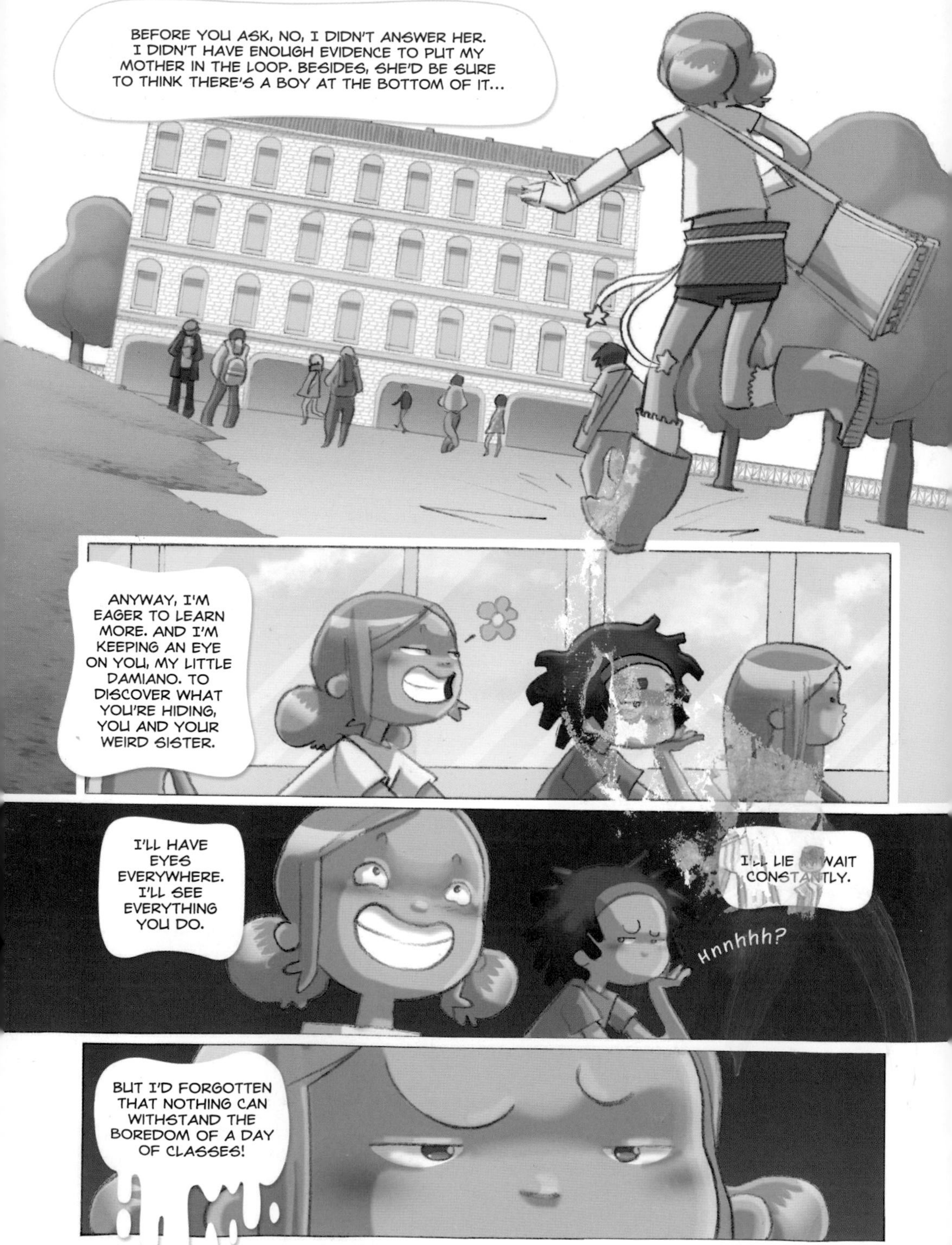
BEFORE YOU ASK, NO, I DIDN'T ANSWER HER. I DIDN'T HAVE ENOUGH EVIDENCE TO PUT MY MOTHER IN THE LOOP. BESIDES, SHE'D BE SURE TO THINK THERE'S A BOY AT THE BOTTOM OF IT...
ANYWAY, I'M EAGER TO LEARN MORE. AND I'M KEEPING AN EYE ON YOU, MY LITTLE DAMIANO. TO DISCOVER WHAT YOU'RE HIDING, YOU AND YOUR WEIRD SISTER.
I'LL HAVE EYES EVERYWHERE. I'LL SEE EVERYTHING YOU DO.
I'LL LIE WAIT CONSTANTLY.
Hnnhhh?
BUT I'D FORGOTTEN THAT NOTHING CAN WITHSTAND THE BOREDOM OF A DAY OF CLASSES!

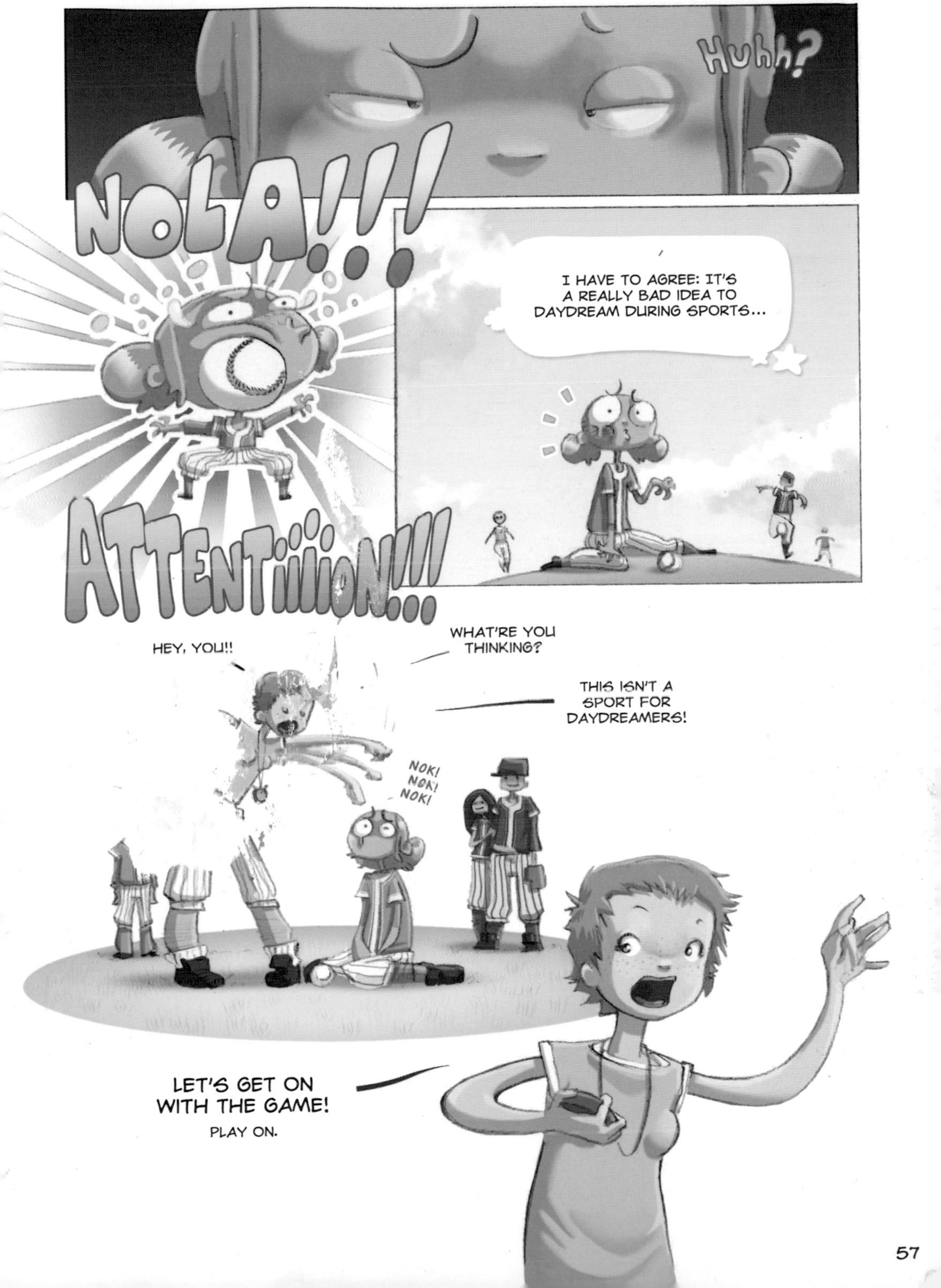

Huhh?
NOLA!!!...
ATTENTiiiiiON!!!...
I HAVE TO AGREE: IT'S A REALLY BAD IDEA TO DAYDREAM DURING SPORTS...
HEY, YOU!!
WHAT'RE YOU THINKING?
THIS ISN'T A SPORT FOR DAYDREAMERS!
NOK! NOK! NOK!
LET'S GET ON WITH THE GAME!
PLAY ON.

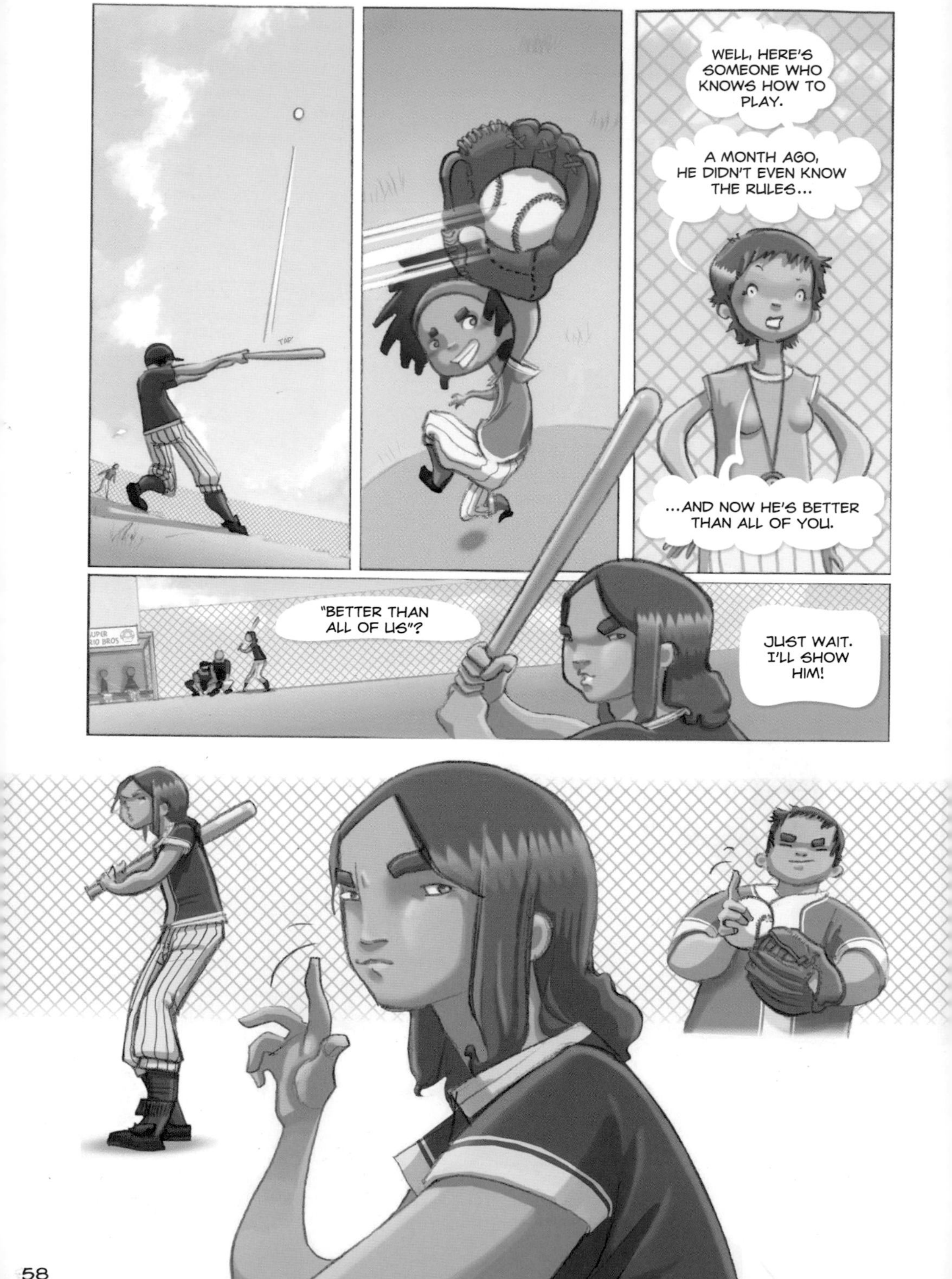
TAP
WELL, HERE'S SOMEONE WHO KNOWS HOW TO PLAY.
A MONTH AGO, HE DIDN'T EVEN KNOW THE RULES...
...AND NOW HE'S BETTER THAN ALL OF YOU.
"BETTER THAN ALL OF US"?
JUST WAIT. I'LL SHOW HIM!

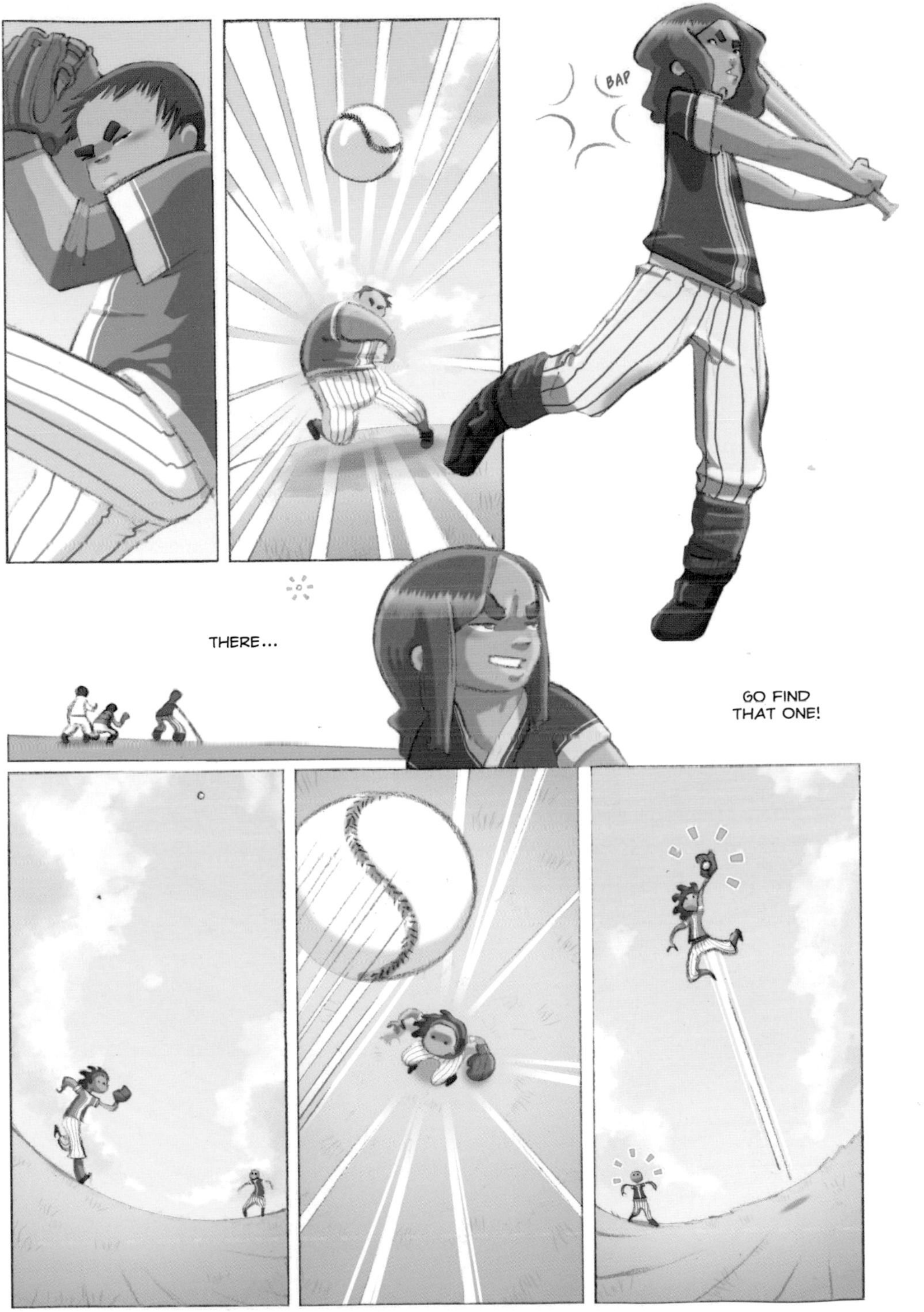
BAP
THERE...
GO FIND THAT ONE!

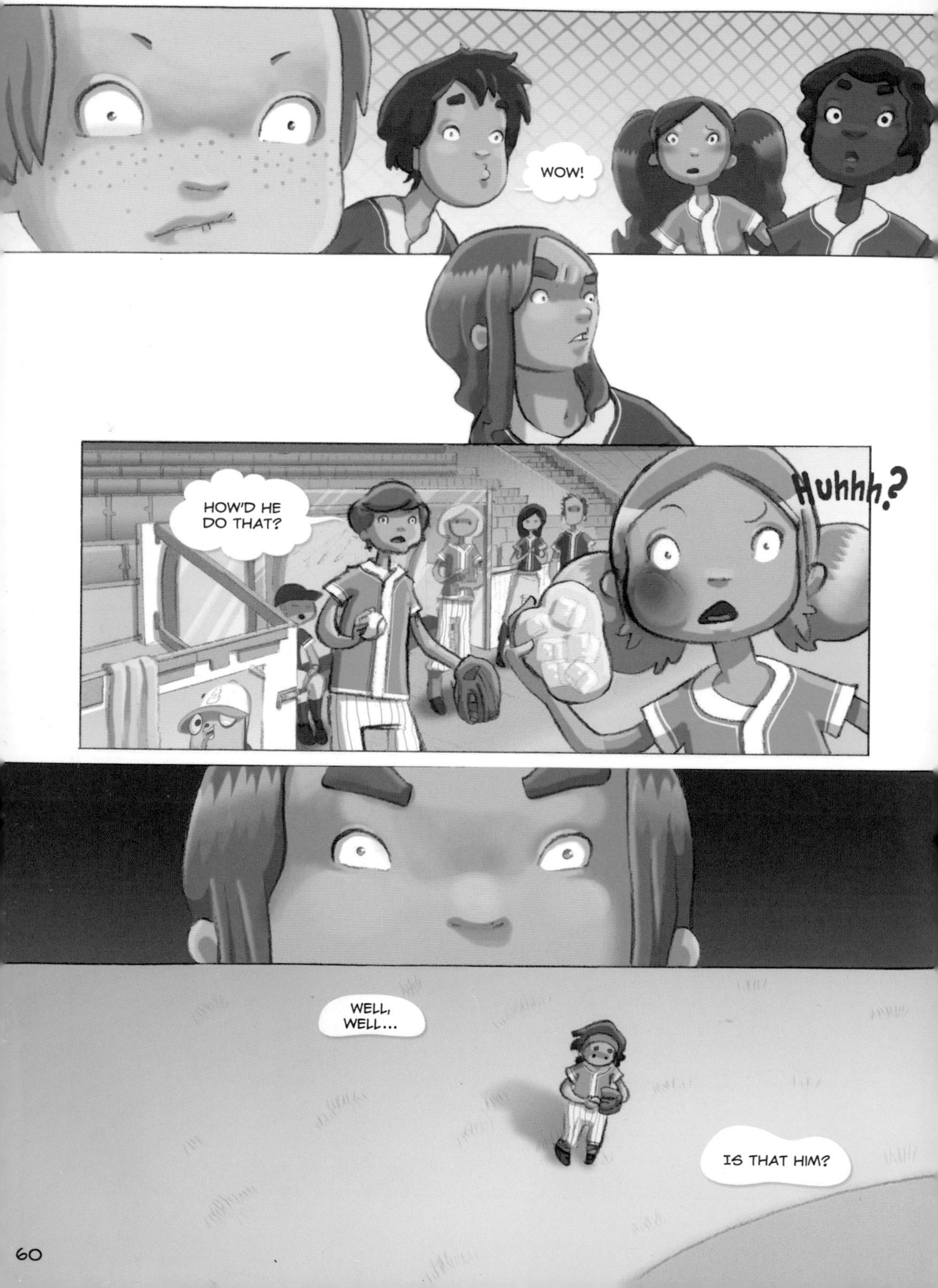
WOW!
HOW'D HE DO THAT?
Huhhh?
WELL, WELL...
IS THAT HIM?

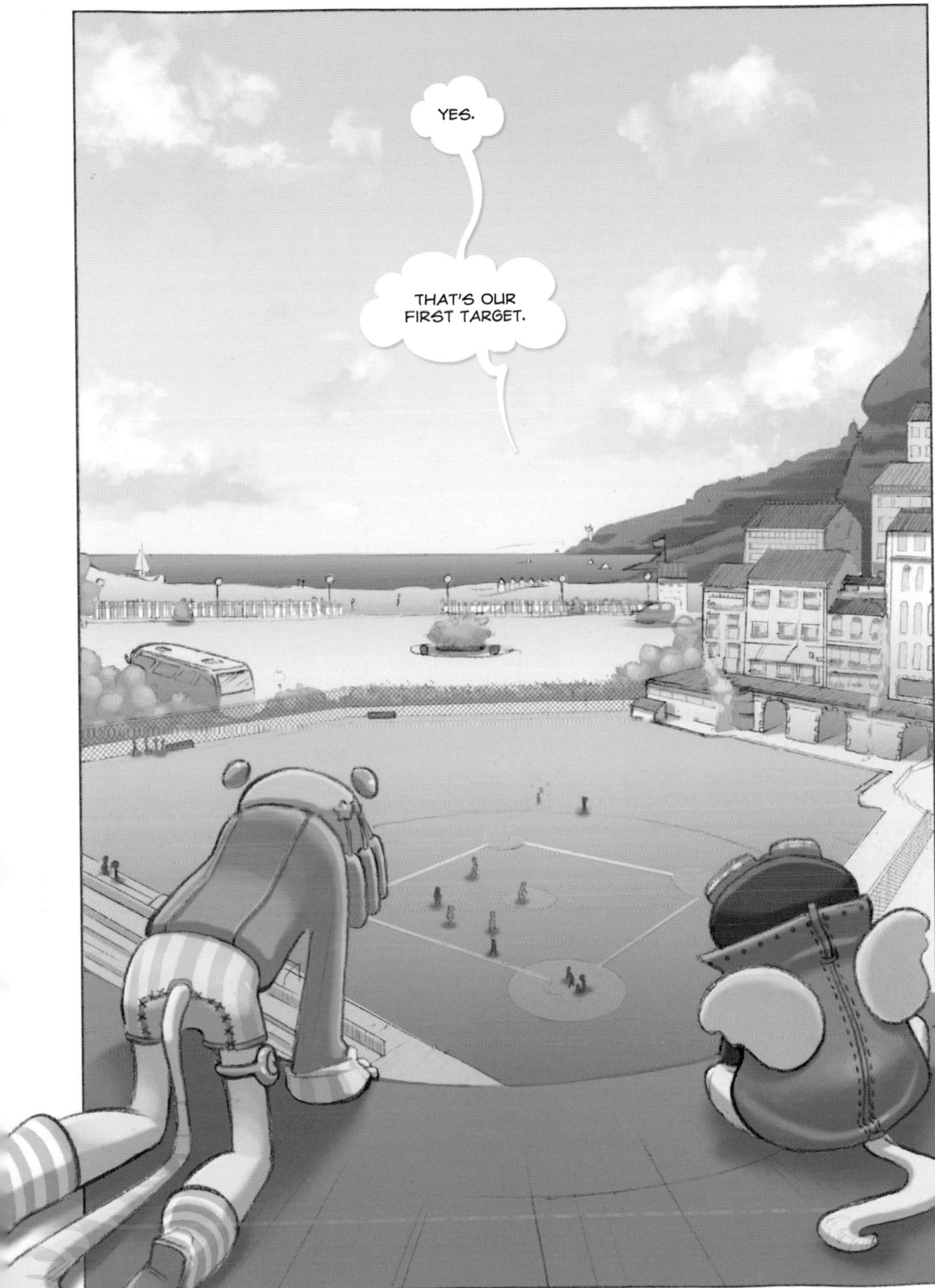
YES.
THAT'S OUR FIRST TARGET.

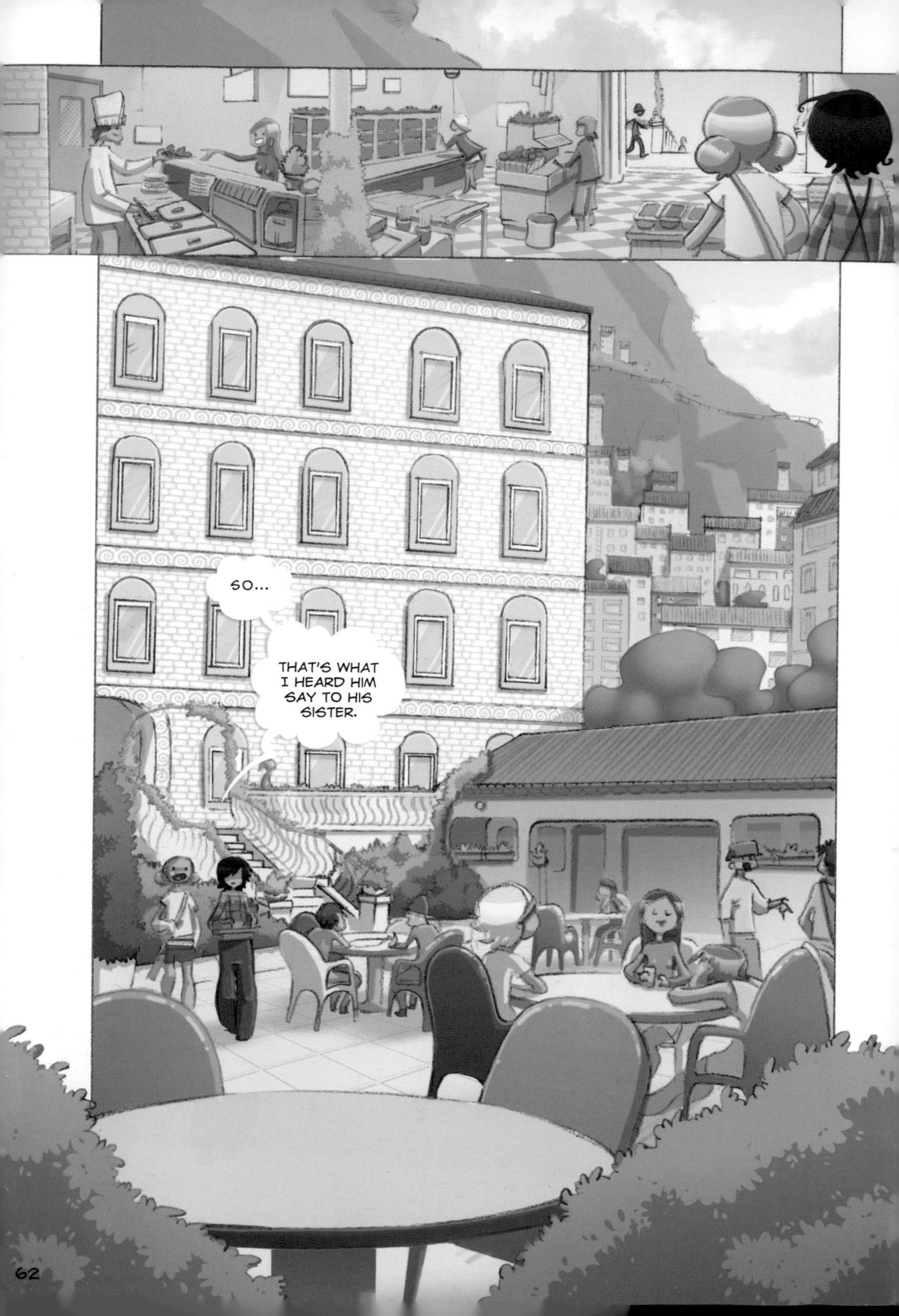
SO...
THAT'S WHAT I HEARD HIM SAY TO HIS SISTER.

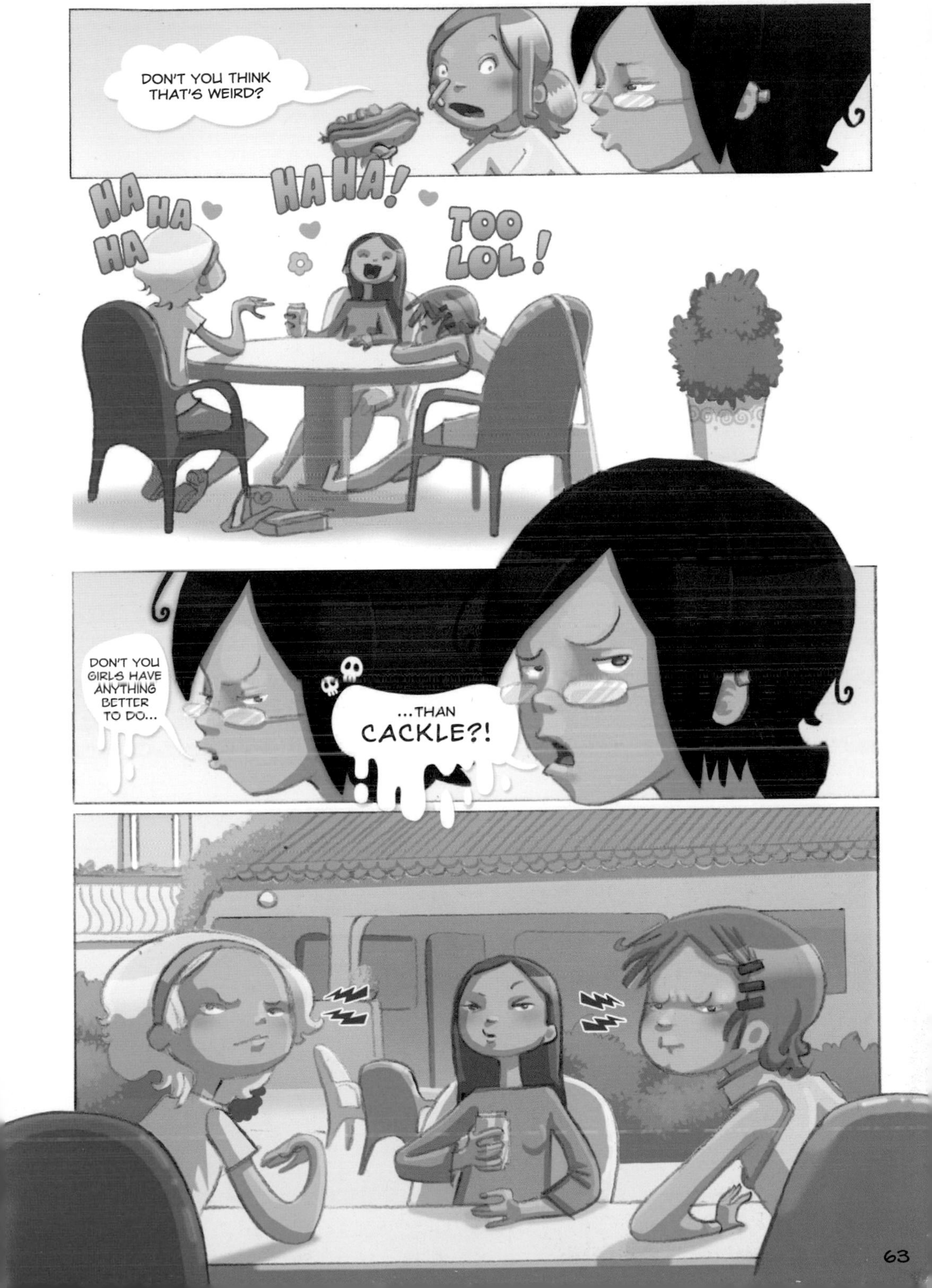

DON'T YOU THINK THAT'S WEIRD?
HA HA HA HA
HA HA!
TOO LOL!
DON'T YOU GIRLS HAVE ANYTHING BETTER TO DO...
...THAN CACKLE?!

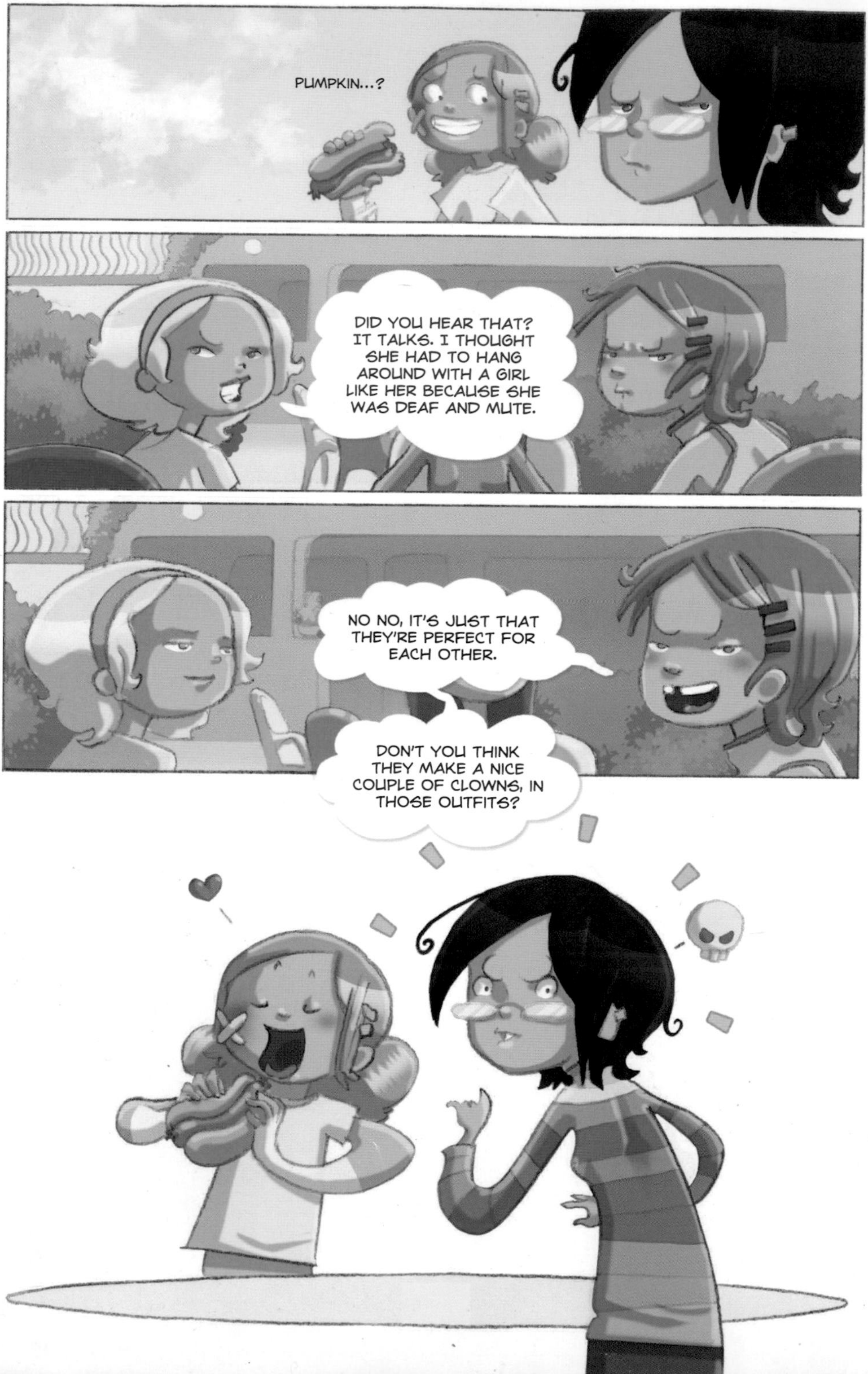
PUMPKIN...?
DID YOU HEAR THAT? IT TALKS. I THOUGHT SHE HAD TO HANG AROUND WITH A GIRL LIKE HER BECAUSE SHE WAS DEAF AND MUTE.
NO NO, IT'S JUST THAT THEY'RE PERFECT FOR EACH OTHER.
DON'T YOU THINK THEY MAKE A NICE COUPLE OF CLOWNS, IN THOSE OUTFITS?

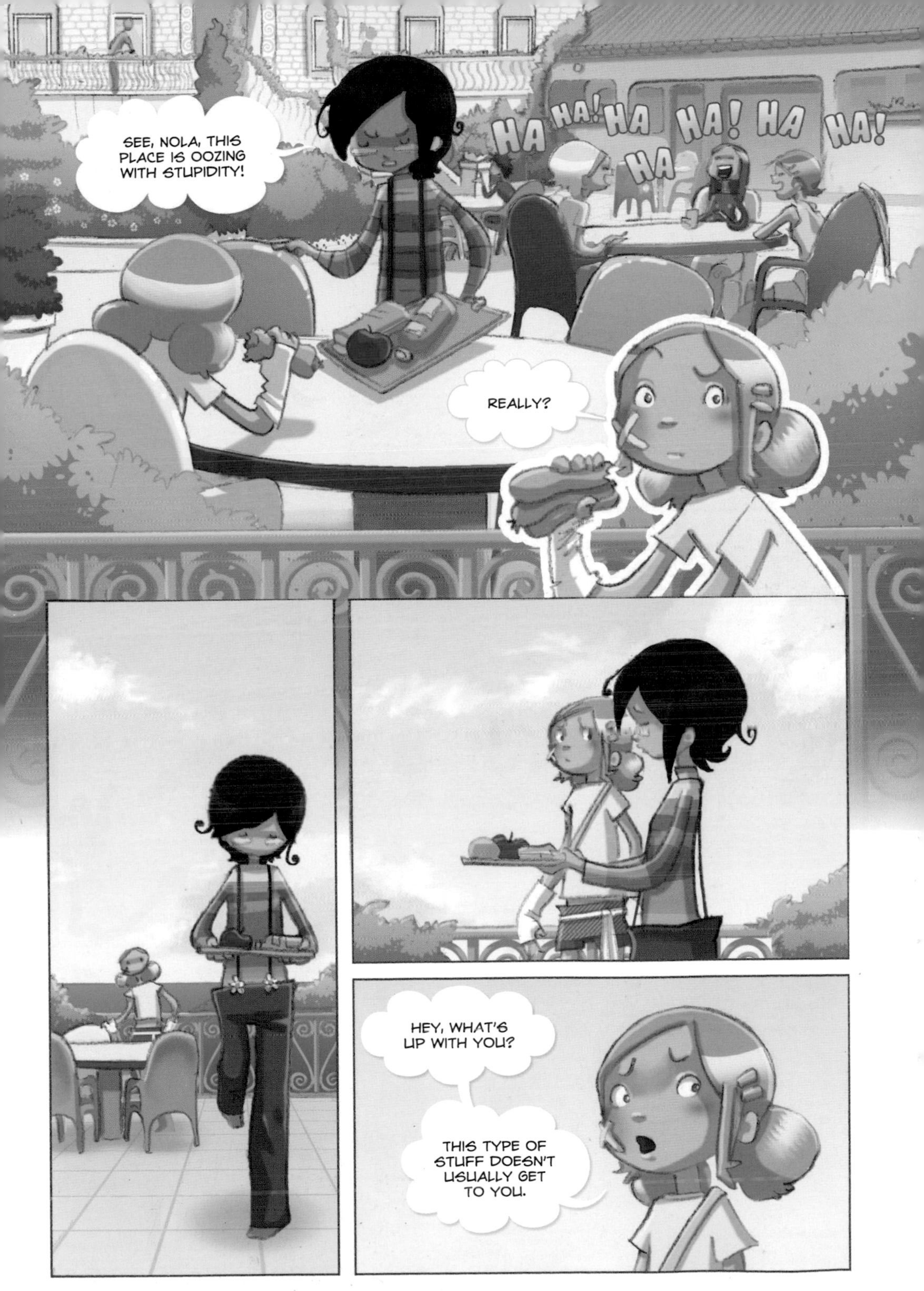
SEE, NOLA, THIS PLACE IS OOZING WITH STUPIDITY!
HA HA! HA HA! HA HA HA!
REALLY?
HEY, WHAT'S UP WITH YOU?
THIS TYPE OF STUFF DOESN'T USUALLY GET TO YOU.

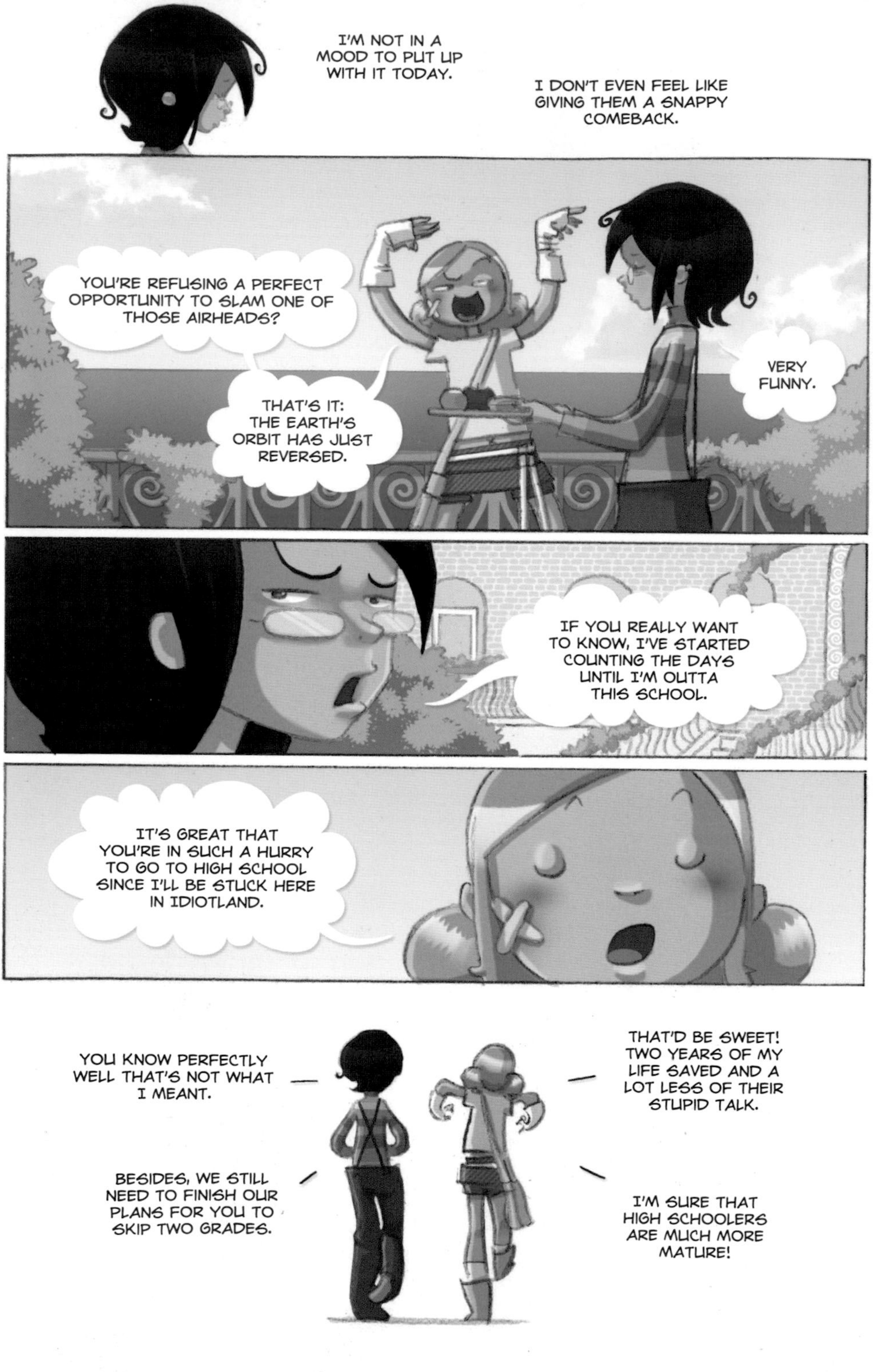
I'M NOT IN A MOOD TO PUT UP WITH IT TODAY.
I DON'T EVEN FEEL LIKE GIVING THEM A SNAPPY COMEBACK.
YOU'RE REFUSING A PERFECT OPPORTUNITY TO SLAM ONE OF THOSE AIRHEADS?
THAT'S IT: THE EARTH'S ORBIT HAS JUST REVERSED.
VERY FUNNY.
IF YOU REALLY WANT TO KNOW, I'VE STARTED COUNTING THE DAYS UNTIL I'M OUTTA THIS SCHOOL.
IT'S GREAT THAT YOU'RE IN SUCH A HURRY TO GO TO HIGH SCHOOL SINCE I'LL BE STUCK HERE IN IDIOTLAND.
YOU KNOW PERFECTLY WELL THAT'S NOT WHAT I MEANT.
THAT'D BE SWEET! TWO YEARS OF MY LIFE SAVED AND A LOT LESS OF THEIR STUPID TALK.
BESIDES, WE STILL NEED TO FINISH OUR PLANS FOR YOU TO SKIP TWO GRADES.
I'M SURE THAT HIGH SCHOOLERS ARE MUCH MORE MATURE!

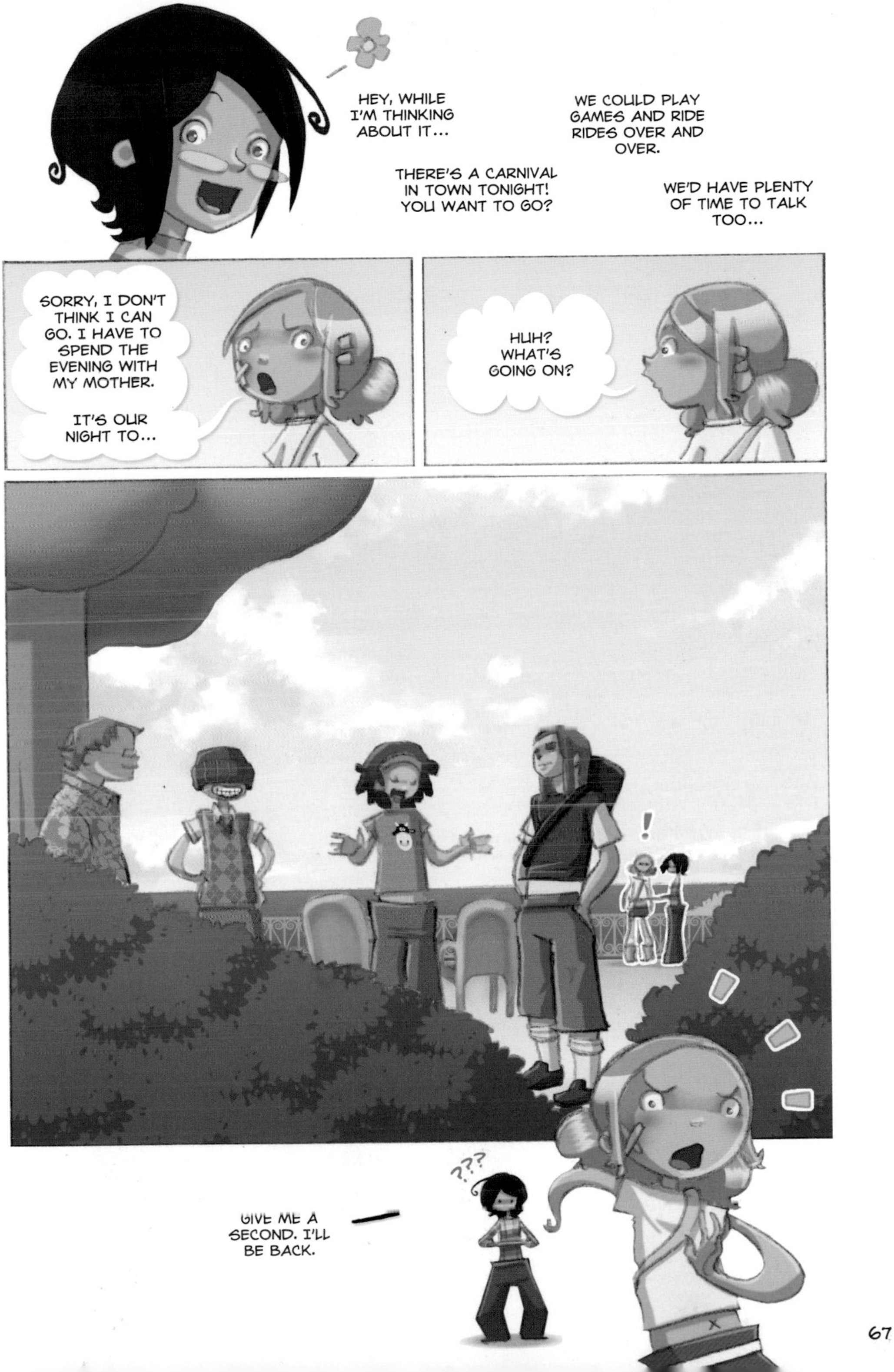
HEY, WHILE I'M THINKING ABOUT IT...
THERE'S A CARNIVAL IN TOWN TONIGHT! YOU WANT TO GO?
WE COULD PLAY GAMES AND RIDE RIDES OVER AND OVER.
WE'D HAVE PLENTY OF TIME TO TALK TOO...
SORRY, I DON'T THINK I CAN GO. I HAVE TO SPEND THE EVENING WITH MY MOTHER.
IT'S OUR NIGHT TO...
HUH? WHAT'S GOING ON?
!
???
GIVE ME A SECOND. I'LL BE BACK.

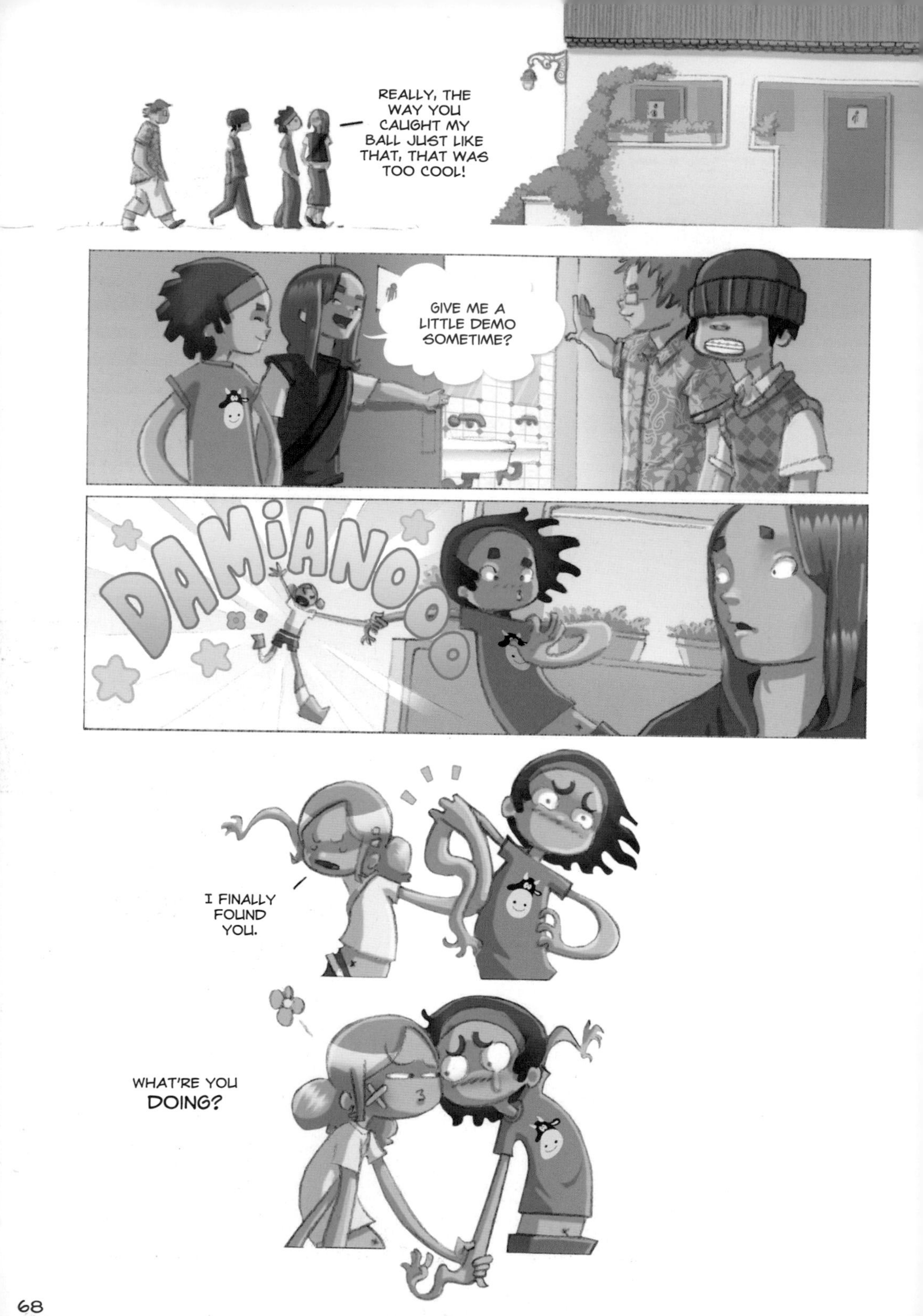
REALLY, THE WAY YOU CAUGHT MY BALL JUST LIKE THAT, THAT WAS TOO COOL!
GIVE ME A LITTLE DEMO SOMETIME?
DAMIANOOOO
I FINALLY FOUND YOU.
WHAT'RE YOU DOING?

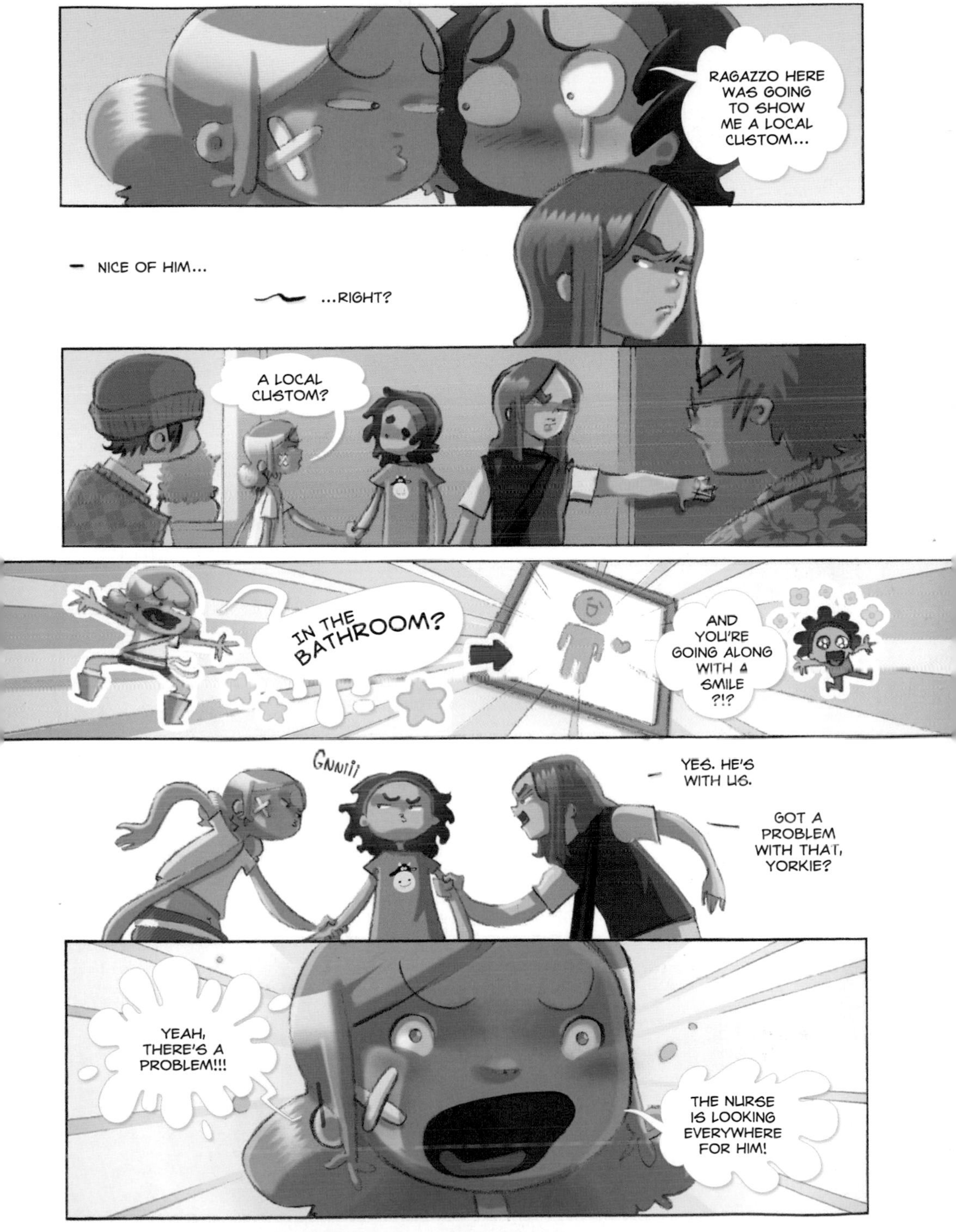
RAGAZZO HERE WAS GOING TO SHOW ME A LOCAL CUSTOM...
NICE OF HIM...
...RIGHT?
A LOCAL CUSTOM?
IN THE BATHROOM?
AND YOU'RE GOING ALONG WITH A SMILE ?!?
GNNIII
YES. HE'S WITH US.
GOT A PROBLEM WITH THAT, YORKIE?
YEAH, THERE'S A PROBLEM!!!
THE NURSE IS LOOKING EVERYWHERE FOR HIM!

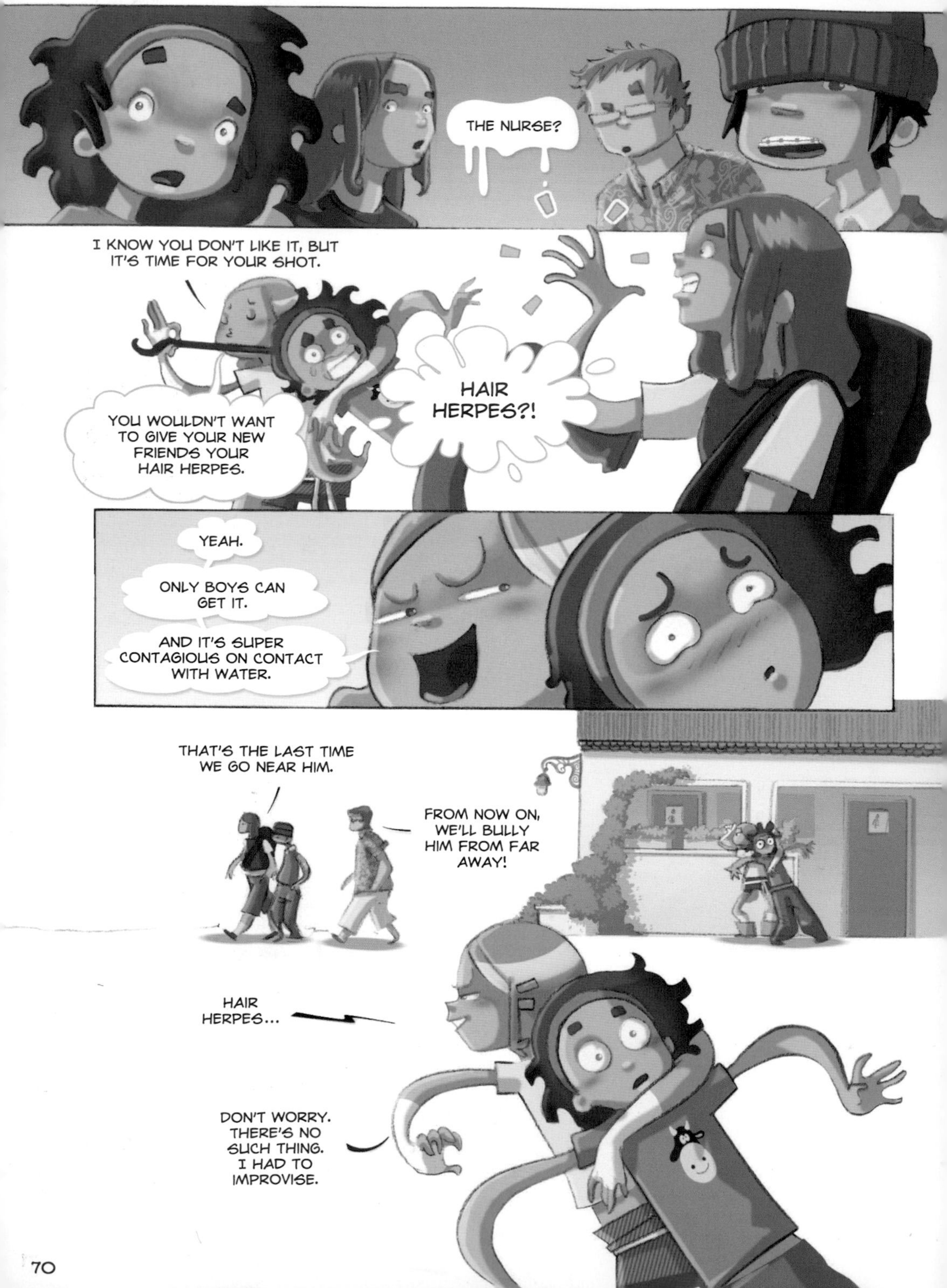
THE NURSE?
I KNOW YOU DON'T LIKE IT, BUT IT'S TIME FOR YOUR SHOT.
YOU WOULDN'T WANT TO GIVE YOUR NEW FRIENDS YOUR HAIR HERPES.
HAIR HERPES?!
YEAH.
ONLY BOYS CAN GET IT.
AND IT'S SUPER CONTAGIOUS ON CONTACT WITH WATER.
THAT'S THE LAST TIME WE GO NEAR HIM.
FROM NOW ON, WE'LL BULLY HIM FROM FAR AWAY!
HAIR HERPES...
DON'T WORRY. THERE'S NO SUCH THING. I HAD TO IMPROVISE.

WHY DID YOU DO THAT?

YOU KNOW WHAT KIND OF REPUTATION I'M GONNA HAVE NOW?

YOU'D RATHER HAVE THEM SHOW YOU THEIR LOCAL CUSTOM?

A HEAD FIRST BATH IN THE **TOILET?!**

OH...

WELL, THAT WAS A CLEVER RESCUE PLAN...

YOU KNOW...

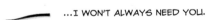 ...I WON'T ALWAYS NEED YOU.

BUT...

THANKS ALL THE SAME!

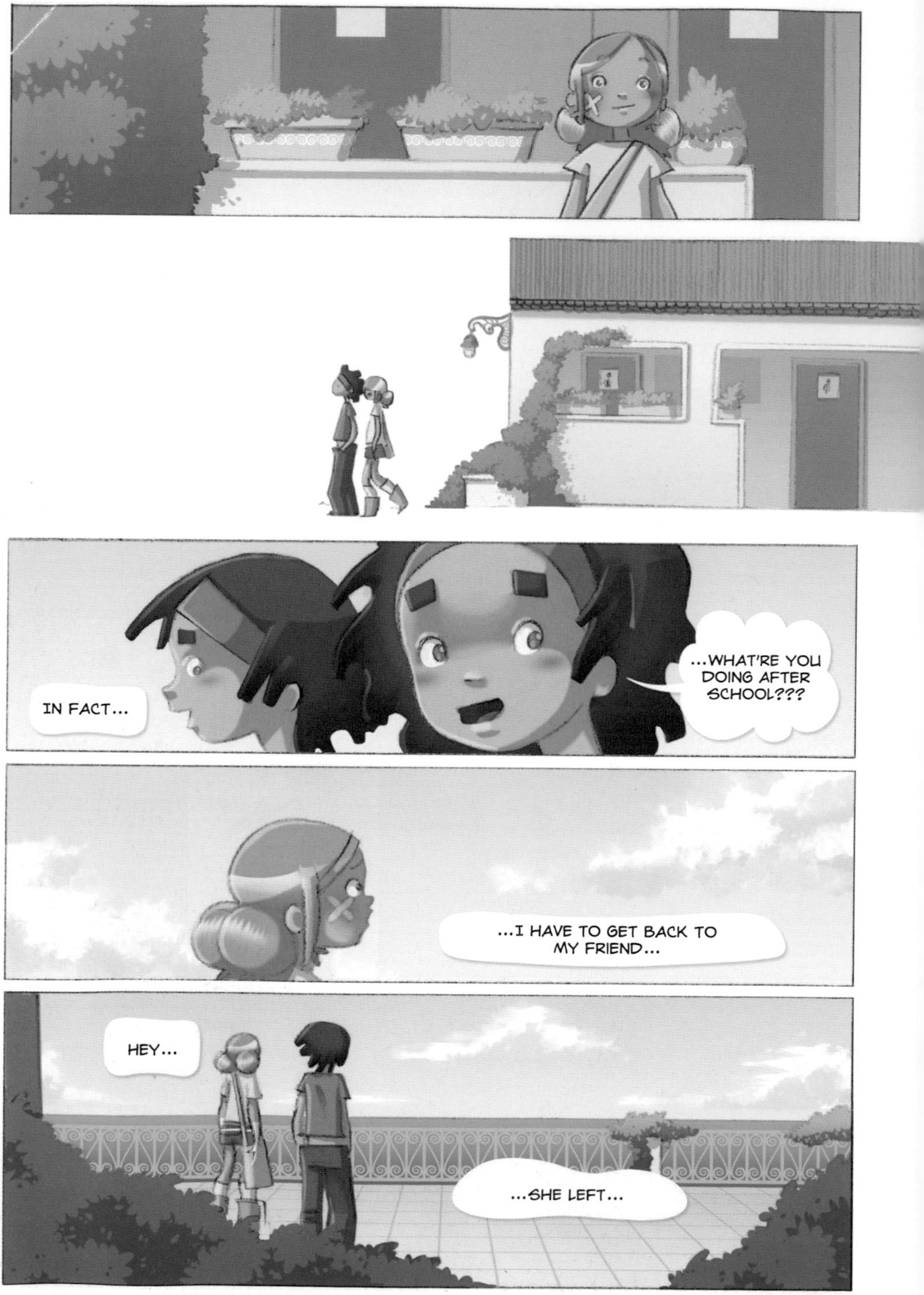
IN FACT...
...WHAT'RE YOU DOING AFTER SCHOOL???
...I HAVE TO GET BACK TO MY FRIEND...
HEY...
...SHE LEFT...

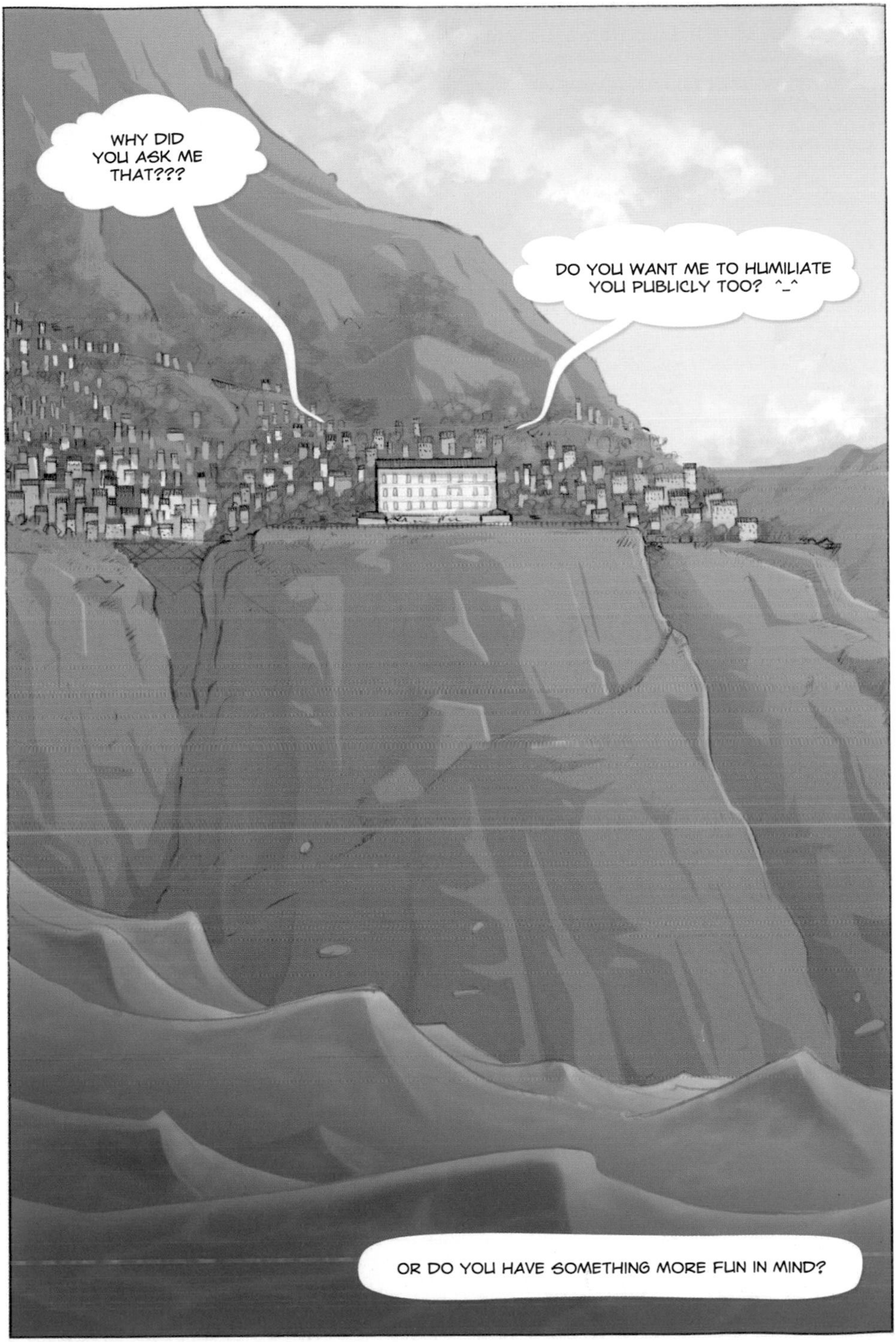
WHY DID YOU ASK ME THAT???
DO YOU WANT ME TO HUMILIATE YOU PUBLICLY TOO? ^_^
OR DO YOU HAVE SOMETHING MORE FUN IN MIND?

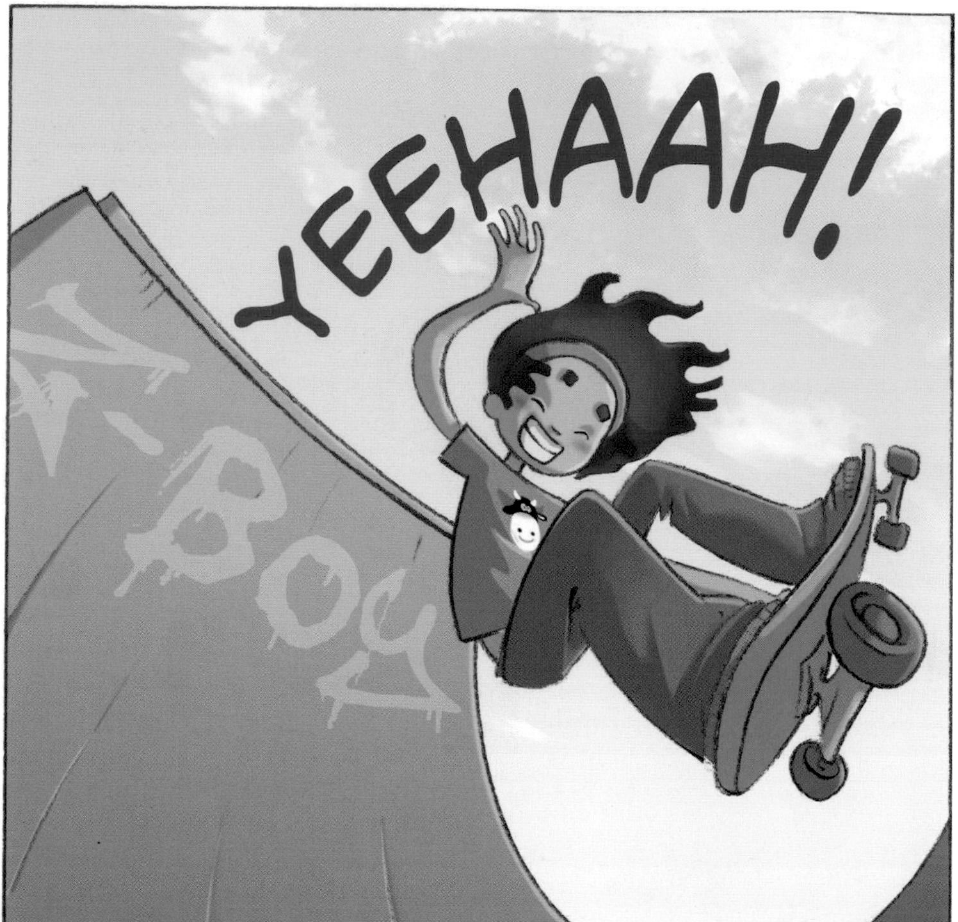
YEEHAAH!

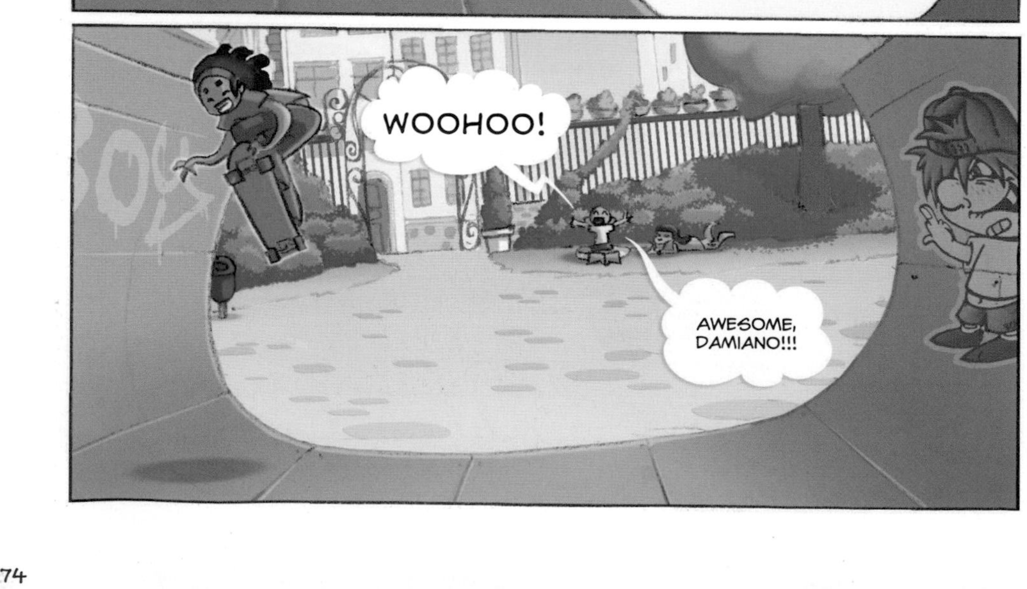
WOOHOO!
AWESOME, DAMIANO!!!

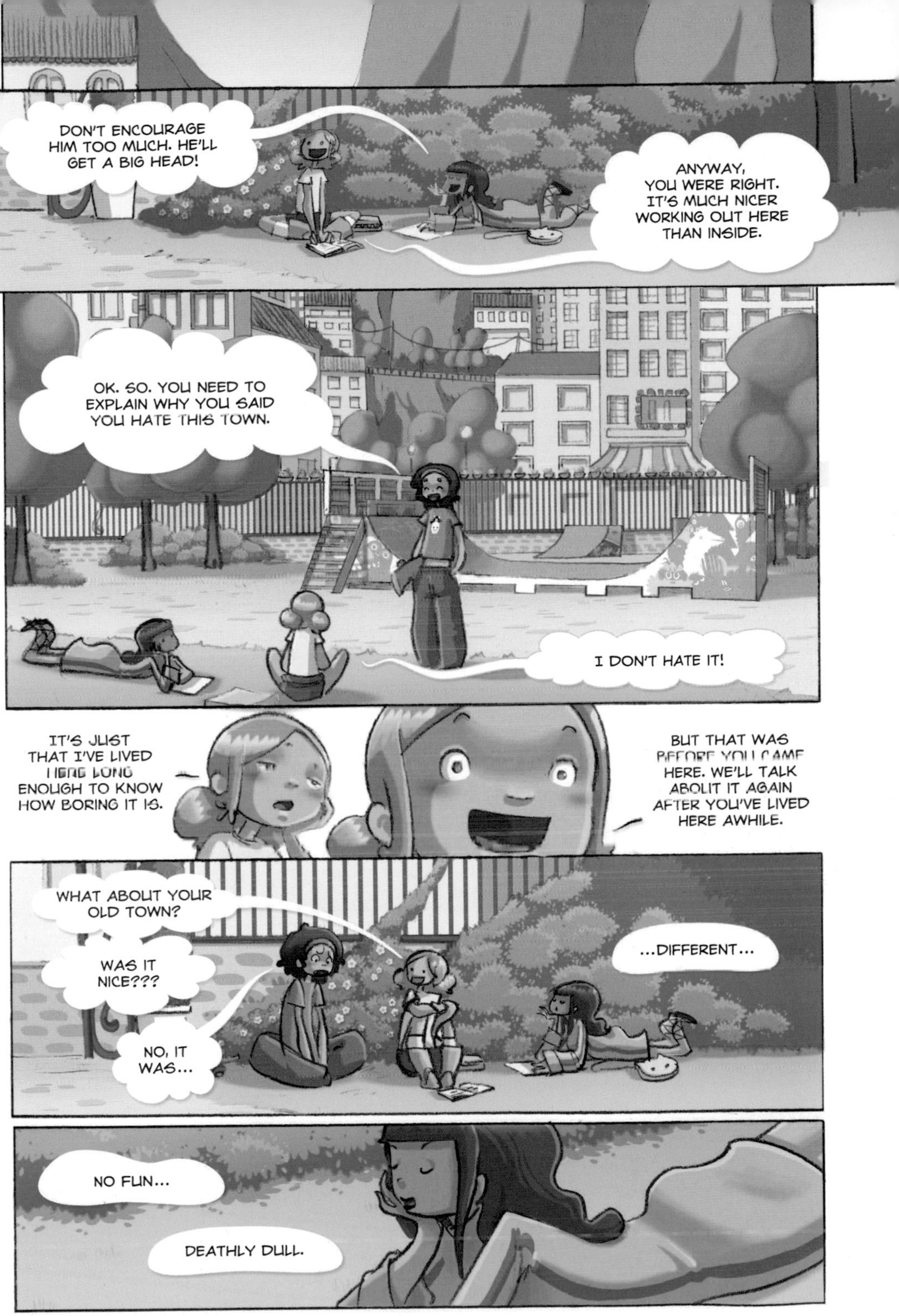
DON'T ENCOURAGE HIM TOO MUCH. HE'LL GET A BIG HEAD!
ANYWAY, YOU WERE RIGHT. IT'S MUCH NICER WORKING OUT HERE THAN INSIDE.
OK. SO. YOU NEED TO EXPLAIN WHY YOU SAID YOU HATE THIS TOWN.
I DON'T HATE IT!
IT'S JUST THAT I'VE LIVED HERE LONG ENOUGH TO KNOW HOW BORING IT IS.
BUT THAT WAS BEFORE YOU CAME HERE. WE'LL TALK ABOUT IT AGAIN AFTER YOU'VE LIVED HERE AWHILE.
WHAT ABOUT YOUR OLD TOWN?
WAS IT NICE???
NO, IT WAS...
...DIFFERENT...
NO FUN...
DEATHLY DULL.

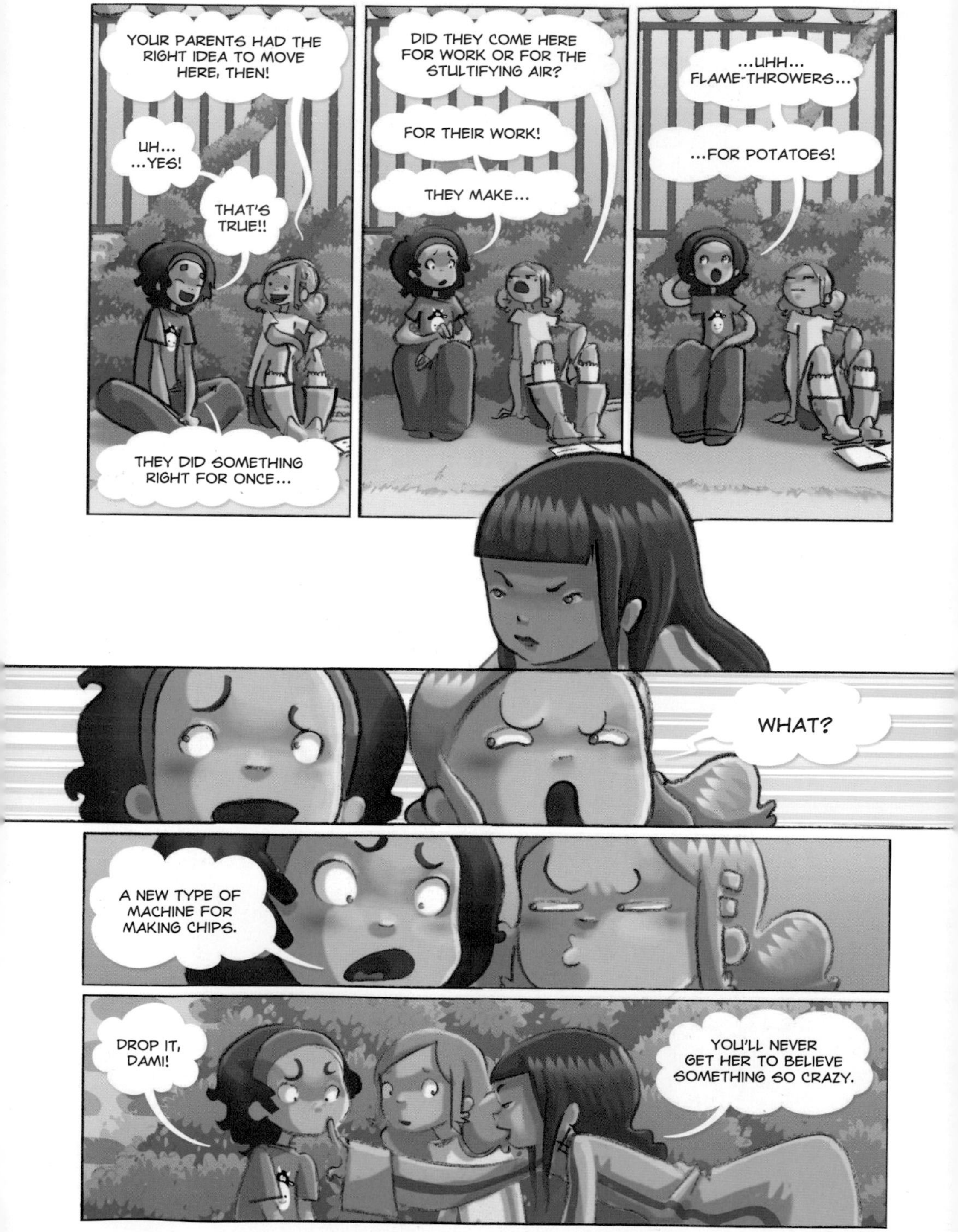
YOUR PARENTS HAD THE RIGHT IDEA TO MOVE HERE, THEN!
UH... ...YES!
THAT'S TRUE!!
THEY DID SOMETHING RIGHT FOR ONCE...
DID THEY COME HERE FOR WORK OR FOR THE STULTIFYING AIR?
FOR THEIR WORK!
THEY MAKE...
...UHH... FLAME-THROWERS...
...FOR POTATOES!
WHAT?
A NEW TYPE OF MACHINE FOR MAKING CHIPS.
DROP IT, DAMI!
YOU'LL NEVER GET HER TO BELIEVE SOMETHING SO CRAZY.

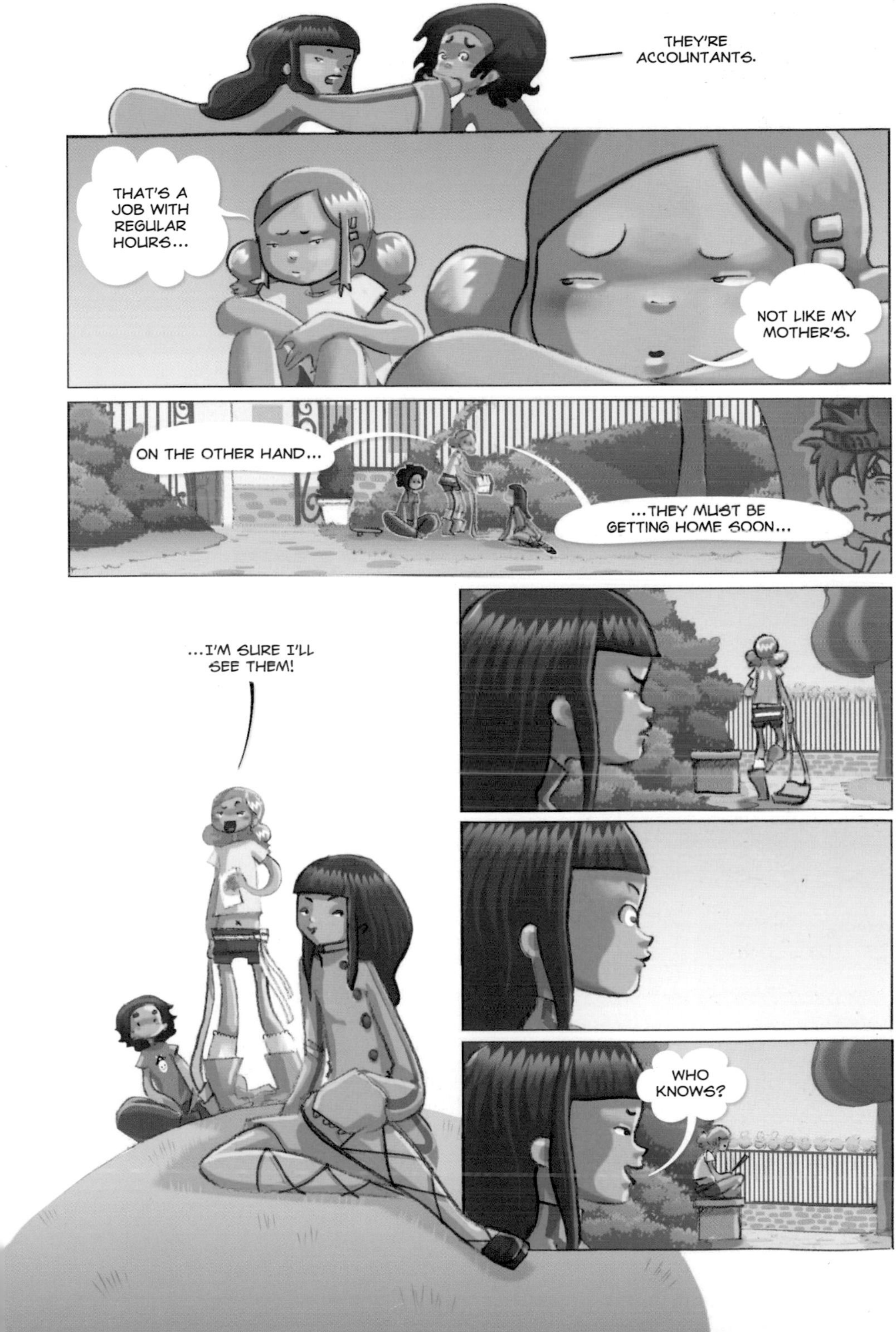
THEY'RE ACCOUNTANTS.
THAT'S A JOB WITH REGULAR HOURS...
NOT LIKE MY MOTHER'S.
ON THE OTHER HAND...
...THEY MUST BE GETTING HOME SOON...
...I'M SURE I'LL SEE THEM!
WHO KNOWS?

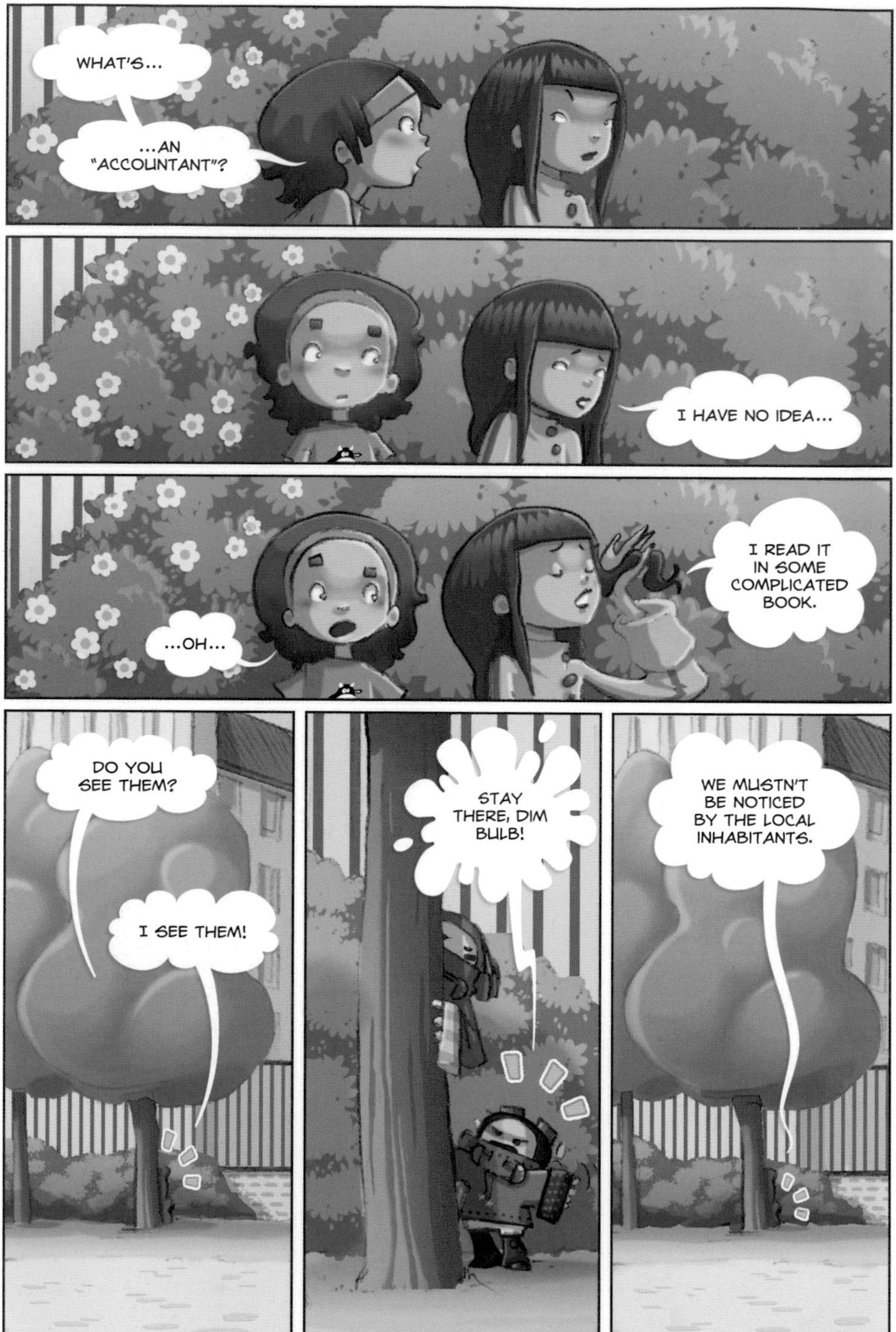
WHAT'S...
...AN "ACCOUNTANT"?
I HAVE NO IDEA...
I READ IT IN SOME COMPLICATED BOOK.
...OH...
DO YOU SEE THEM?
I SEE THEM!
STAY THERE, DIM BULB!
WE MUSTN'T BE NOTICED BY THE LOCAL INHABITANTS.

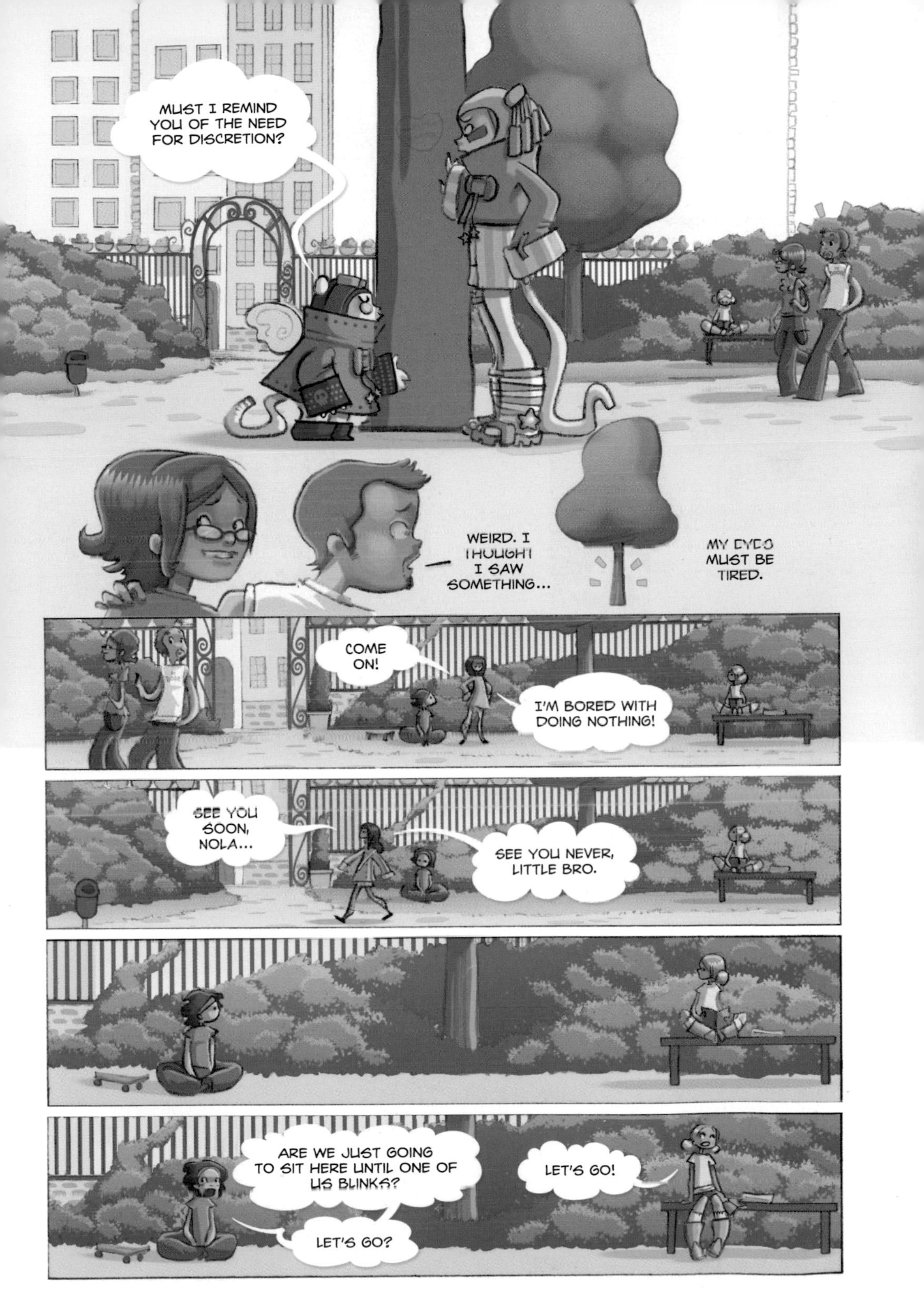

MUST I REMIND YOU OF THE NEED FOR DISCRETION?
WEIRD. I THOUGHT I SAW SOMETHING...
MY EYES MUST BE TIRED.
COME ON!
I'M BORED WITH DOING NOTHING!
SEE YOU SOON, NOLA...
SEE YOU NEVER, LITTLE BRO.
ARE WE JUST GOING TO SIT HERE UNTIL ONE OF US BLINKS?
LET'S GO!
LET'S GO?

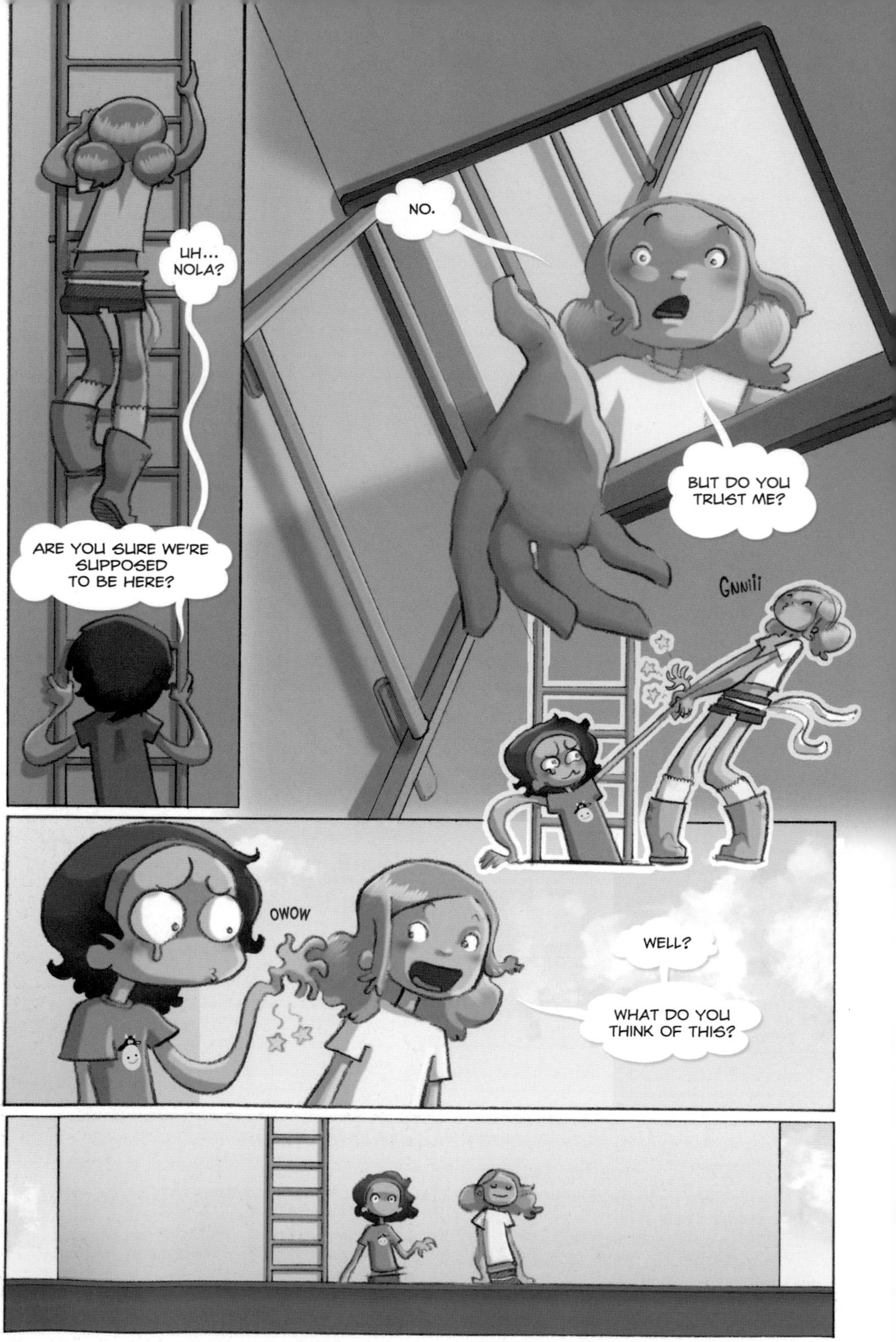
UH... NOLA?
ARE YOU SURE WE'RE SUPPOSED TO BE HERE?
NO.
BUT DO YOU TRUST ME?
GNNIII
OWOW
WELL?
WHAT DO YOU THINK OF THIS?

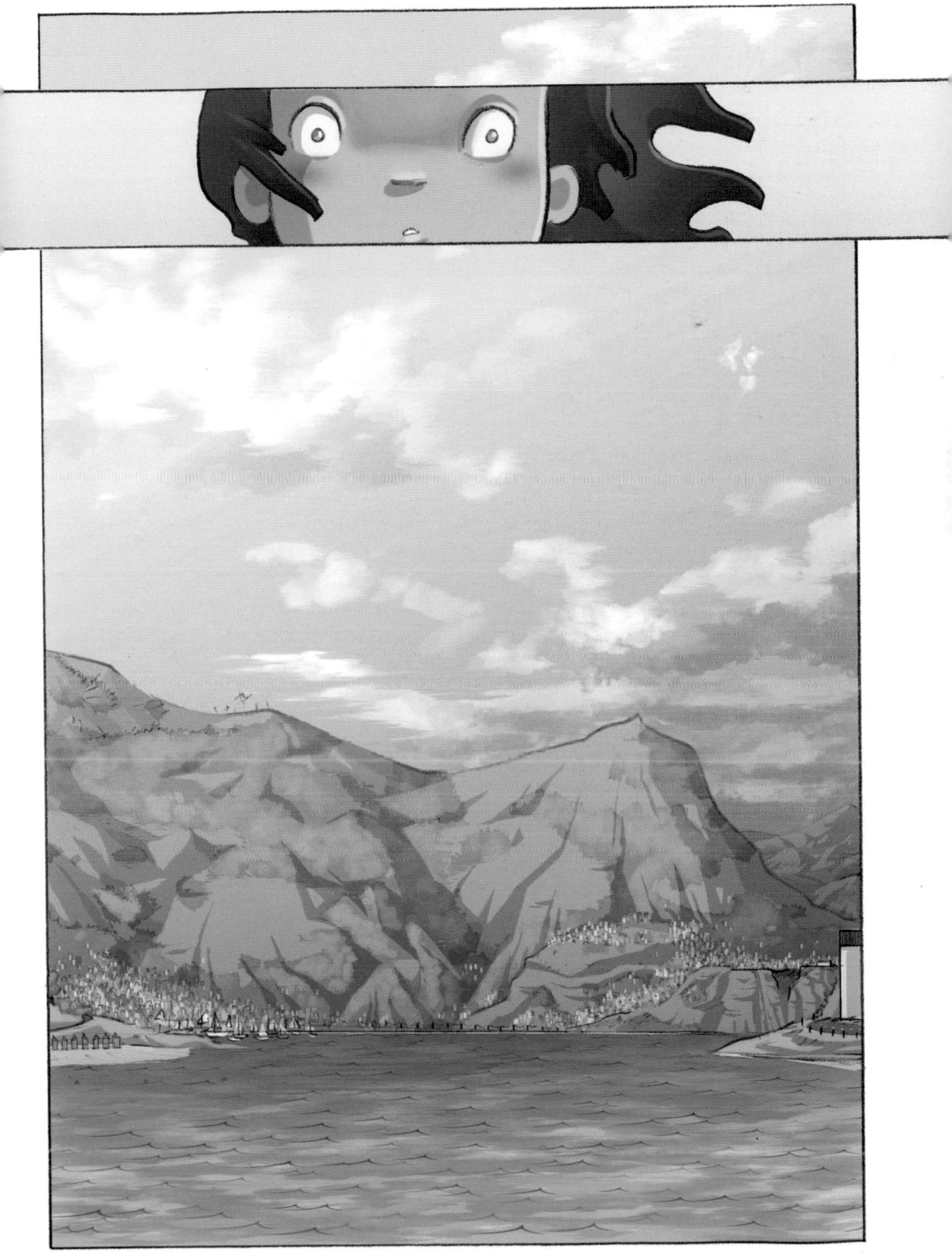

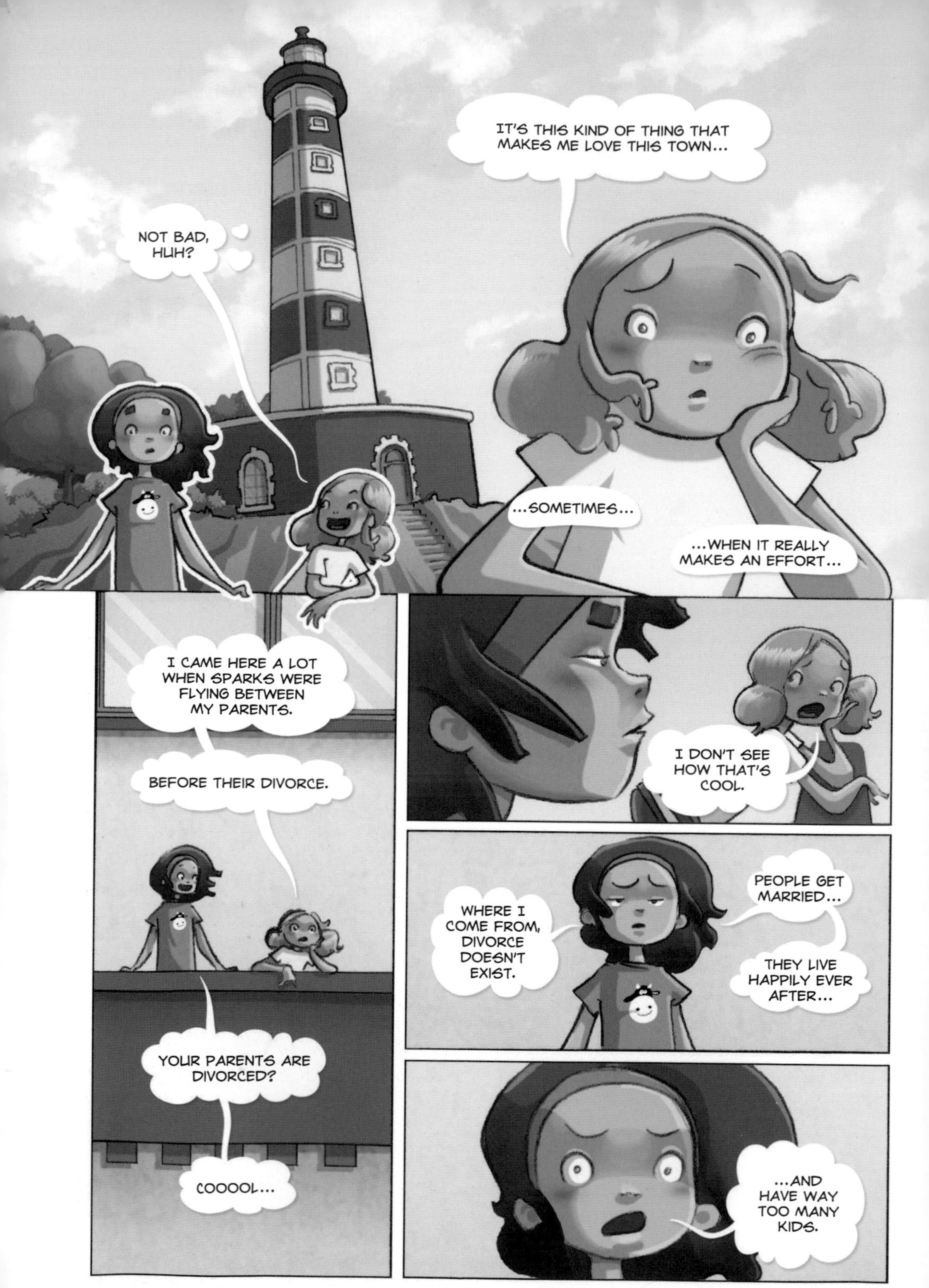
NOT BAD, HUH?
IT'S THIS KIND OF THING THAT MAKES ME LOVE THIS TOWN...
...SOMETIMES...
...WHEN IT REALLY MAKES AN EFFORT...
I CAME HERE A LOT WHEN SPARKS WERE FLYING BETWEEN MY PARENTS.
BEFORE THEIR DIVORCE.
YOUR PARENTS ARE DIVORCED?
COOOOL...
I DON'T SEE HOW THAT'S COOL.
WHERE I COME FROM, DIVORCE DOESN'T EXIST.
PEOPLE GET MARRIED...
THEY LIVE HAPPILY EVER AFTER...
...AND HAVE WAY TOO MANY KIDS.

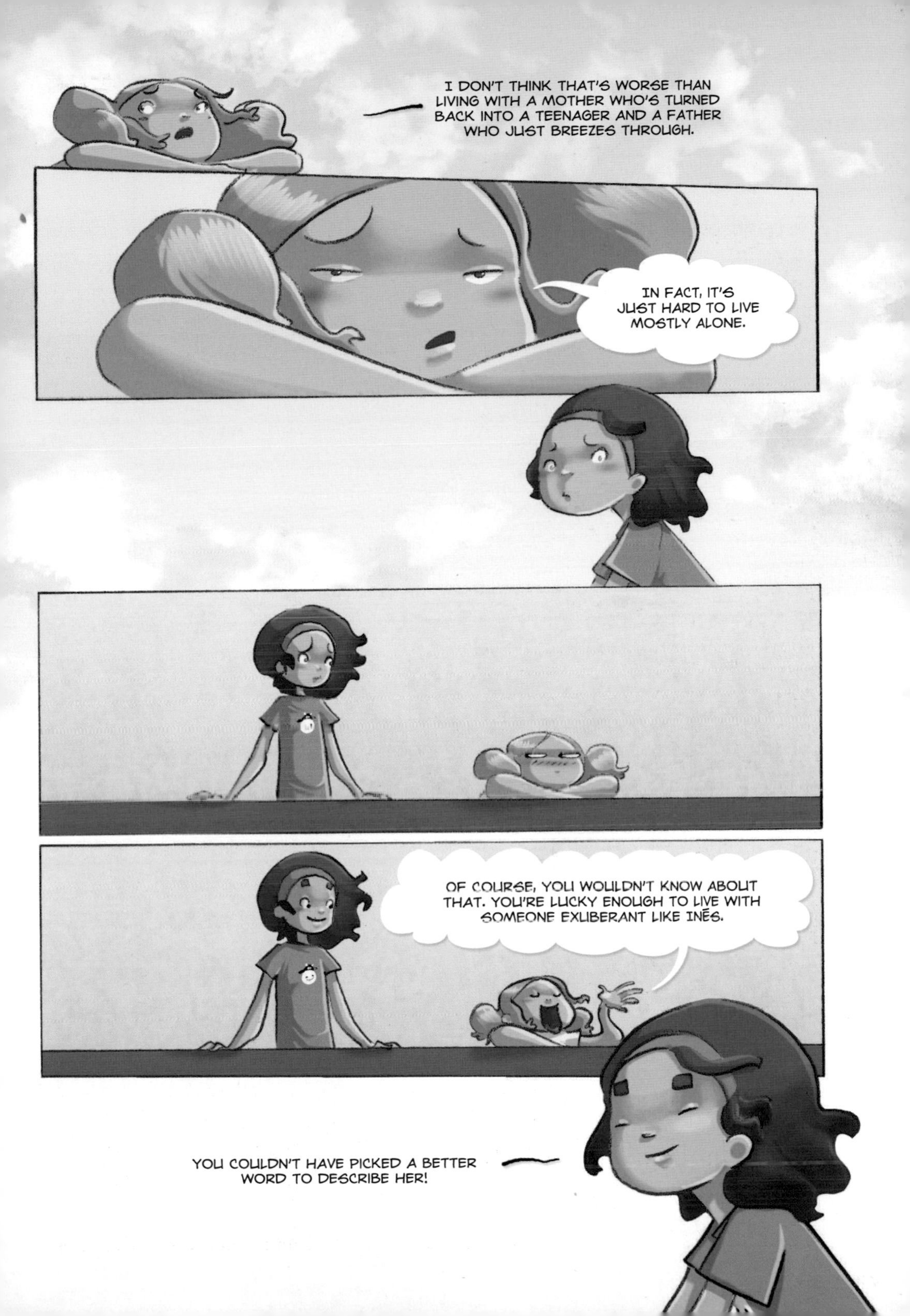
I DON'T THINK THAT'S WORSE THAN LIVING WITH A MOTHER WHO'S TURNED BACK INTO A TEENAGER AND A FATHER WHO JUST BREEZES THROUGH.
IN FACT, IT'S JUST HARD TO LIVE MOSTLY ALONE.
OF COURSE, YOU WOULDN'T KNOW ABOUT THAT. YOU'RE LUCKY ENOUGH TO LIVE WITH SOMEONE EXUBERANT LIKE INÉS.
YOU COULDN'T HAVE PICKED A BETTER WORD TO DESCRIBE HER!

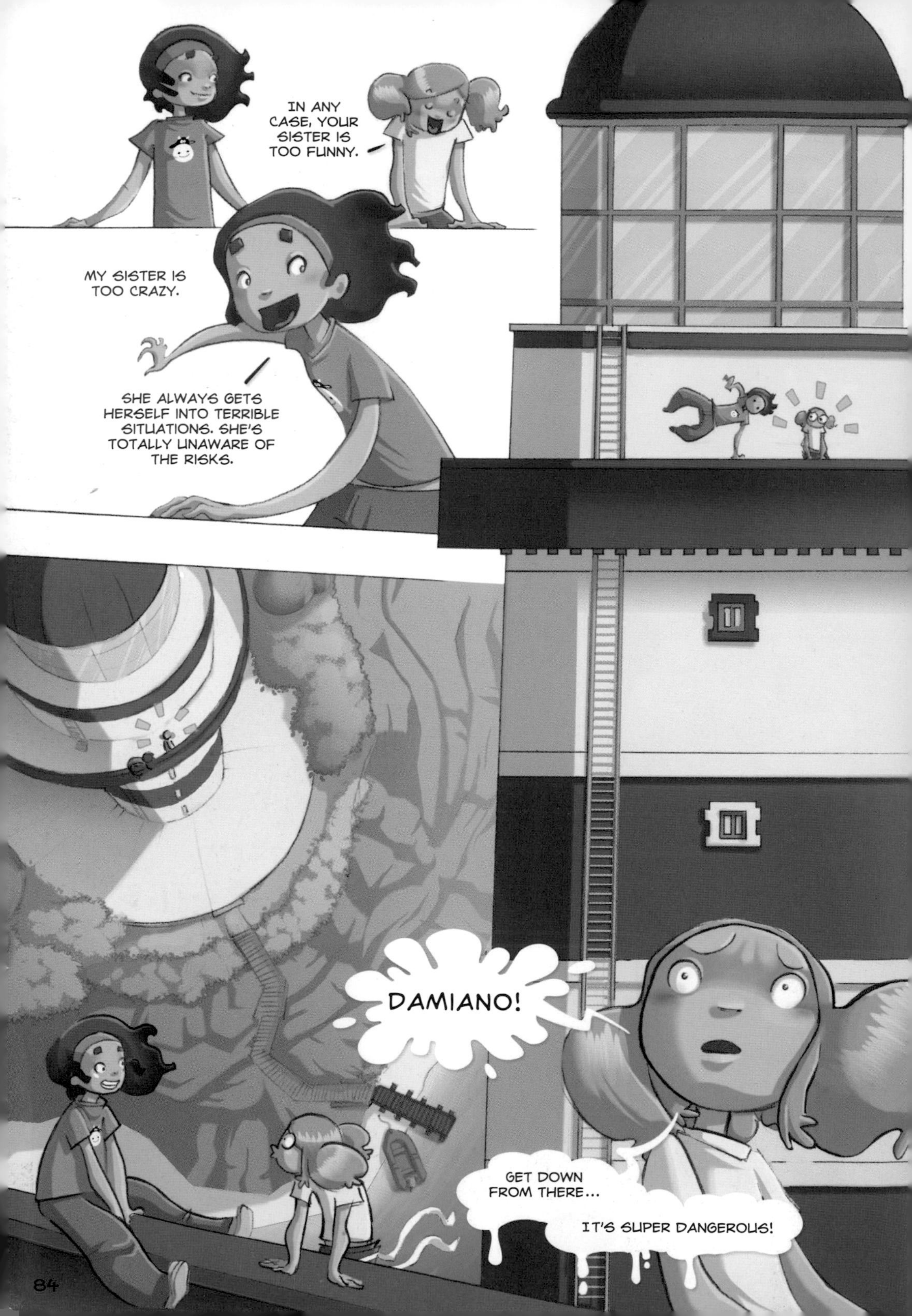
IN ANY CASE, YOUR SISTER IS TOO FUNNY.
MY SISTER IS TOO CRAZY.
SHE ALWAYS GETS HERSELF INTO TERRIBLE SITUATIONS. SHE'S TOTALLY UNAWARE OF THE RISKS.
DAMIANO!
GET DOWN FROM THERE...
IT'S SUPER DANGEROUS!

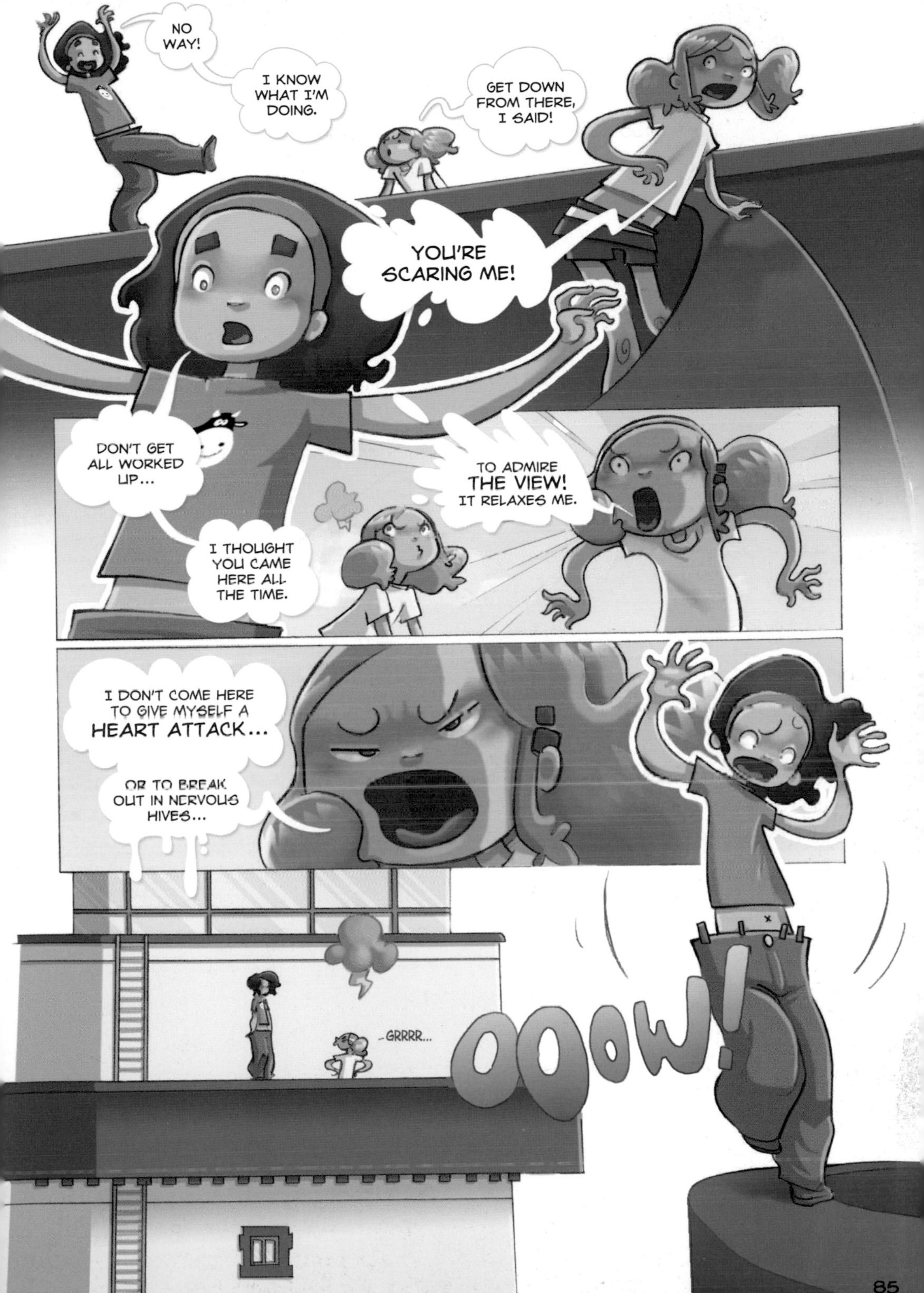
NO WAY!
I KNOW WHAT I'M DOING.
GET DOWN FROM THERE, I SAID!
YOU'RE SCARING ME!
DON'T GET ALL WORKED UP...
I THOUGHT YOU CAME HERE ALL THE TIME.
TO ADMIRE THE VIEW! IT RELAXES ME.
I DON'T COME HERE TO GIVE MYSELF A HEART ATTACK...
OR TO BREAK OUT IN NERVOUS HIVES...
-GRRRR...
OOOW!

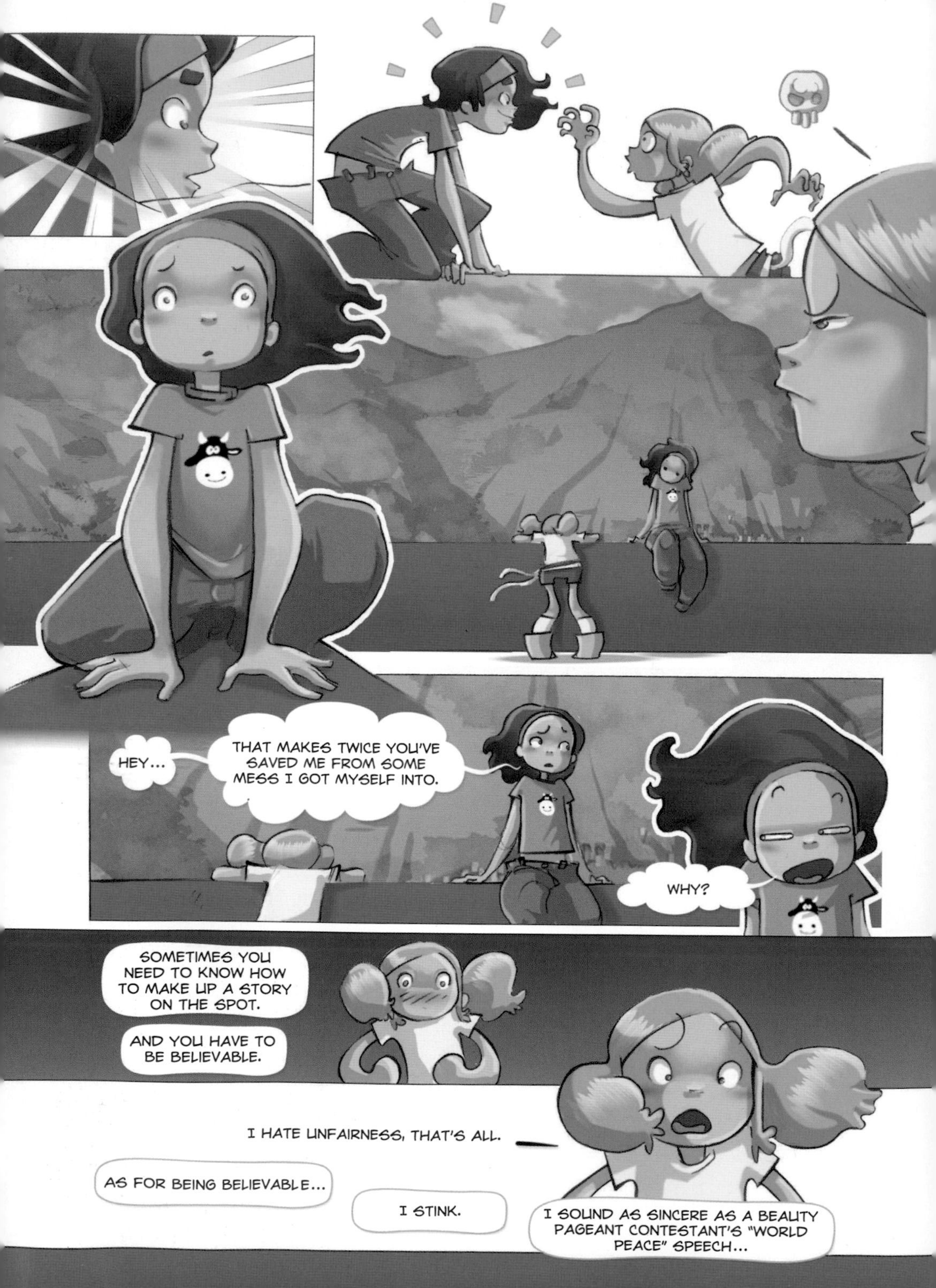
HEY...
THAT MAKES TWICE YOU'VE SAVED ME FROM SOME MESS I GOT MYSELF INTO.
WHY?
SOMETIMES YOU NEED TO KNOW HOW TO MAKE UP A STORY ON THE SPOT.
AND YOU HAVE TO BE BELIEVABLE.
I HATE UNFAIRNESS, THAT'S ALL.
AS FOR BEING BELIEVABLE...
I STINK.
I SOUND AS SINCERE AS A BEAUTY PAGEANT CONTESTANT'S "WORLD PEACE" SPEECH...

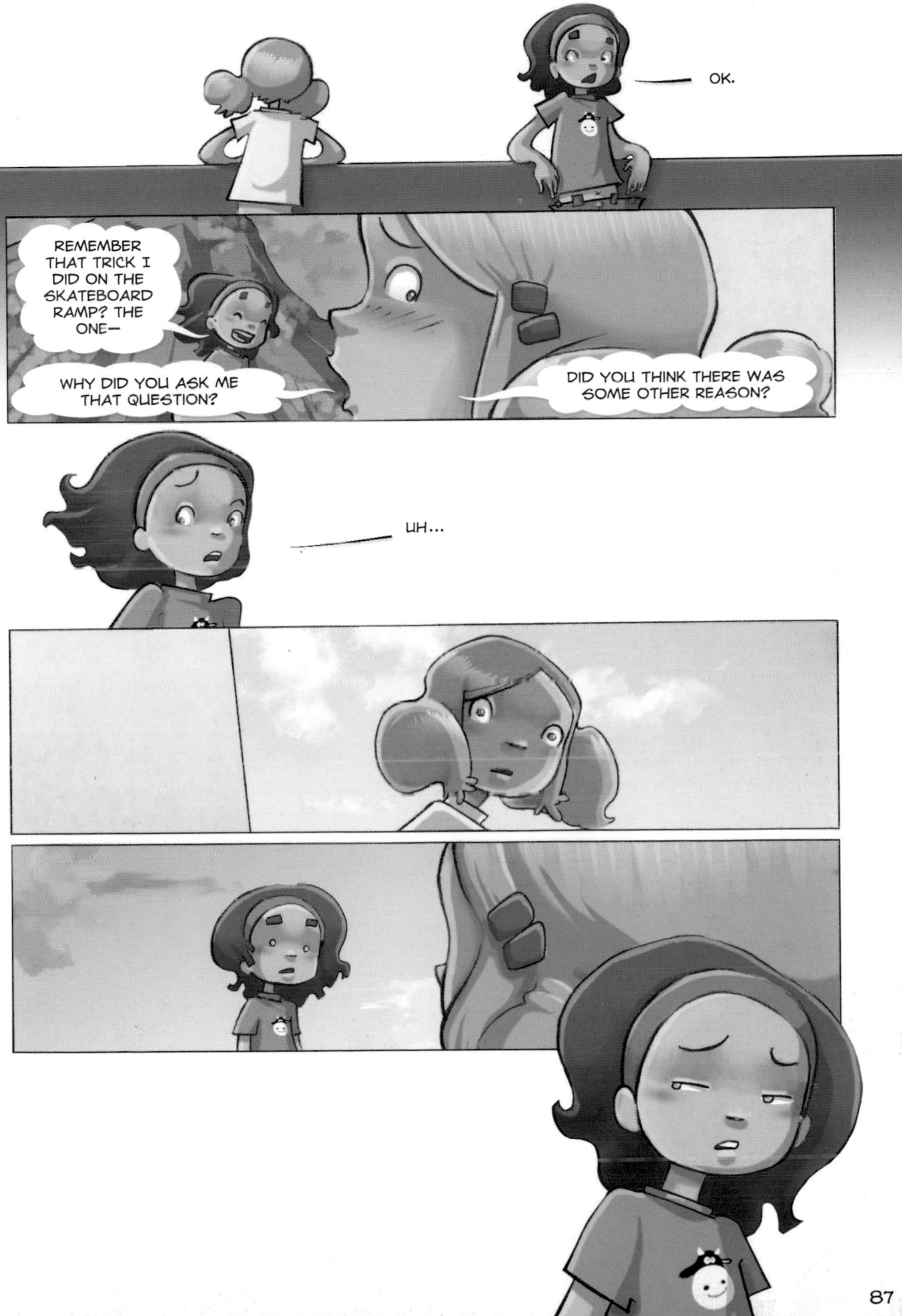
OK.
REMEMBER THAT TRICK I DID ON THE SKATEBOARD RAMP? THE ONE—
WHY DID YOU ASK ME THAT QUESTION?
DID YOU THINK THERE WAS SOME OTHER REASON?
UH...

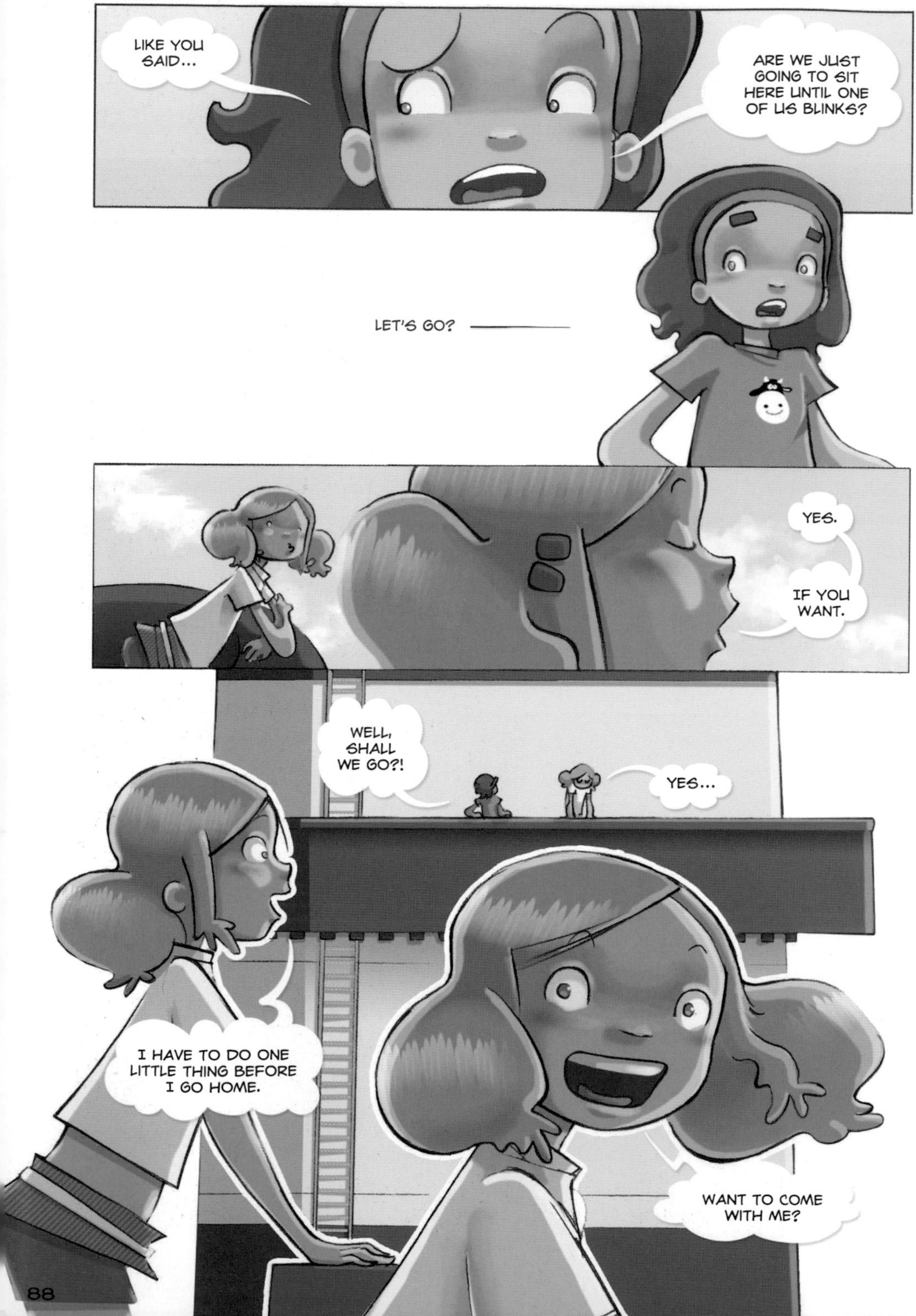
LIKE YOU SAID...
ARE WE JUST GOING TO SIT HERE UNTIL ONE OF US BLINKS?
LET'S GO?
YES.
IF YOU WANT.
WELL, SHALL WE GO?!
YES...
I HAVE TO DO ONE LITTLE THING BEFORE I GO HOME.
WANT TO COME WITH ME?

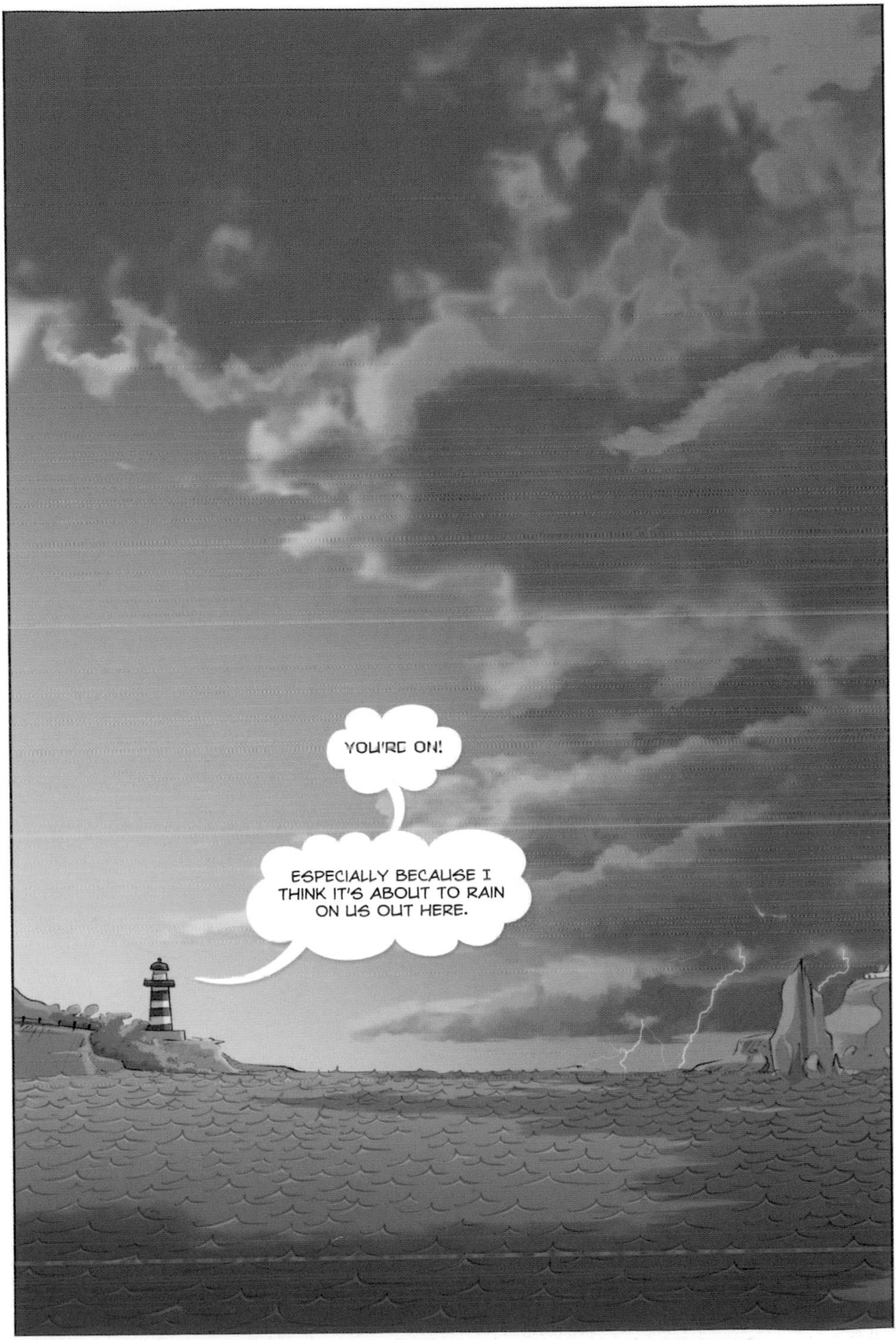
YOU'RE ON!
ESPECIALLY BECAUSE I THINK IT'S ABOUT TO RAIN ON US OUT HERE.

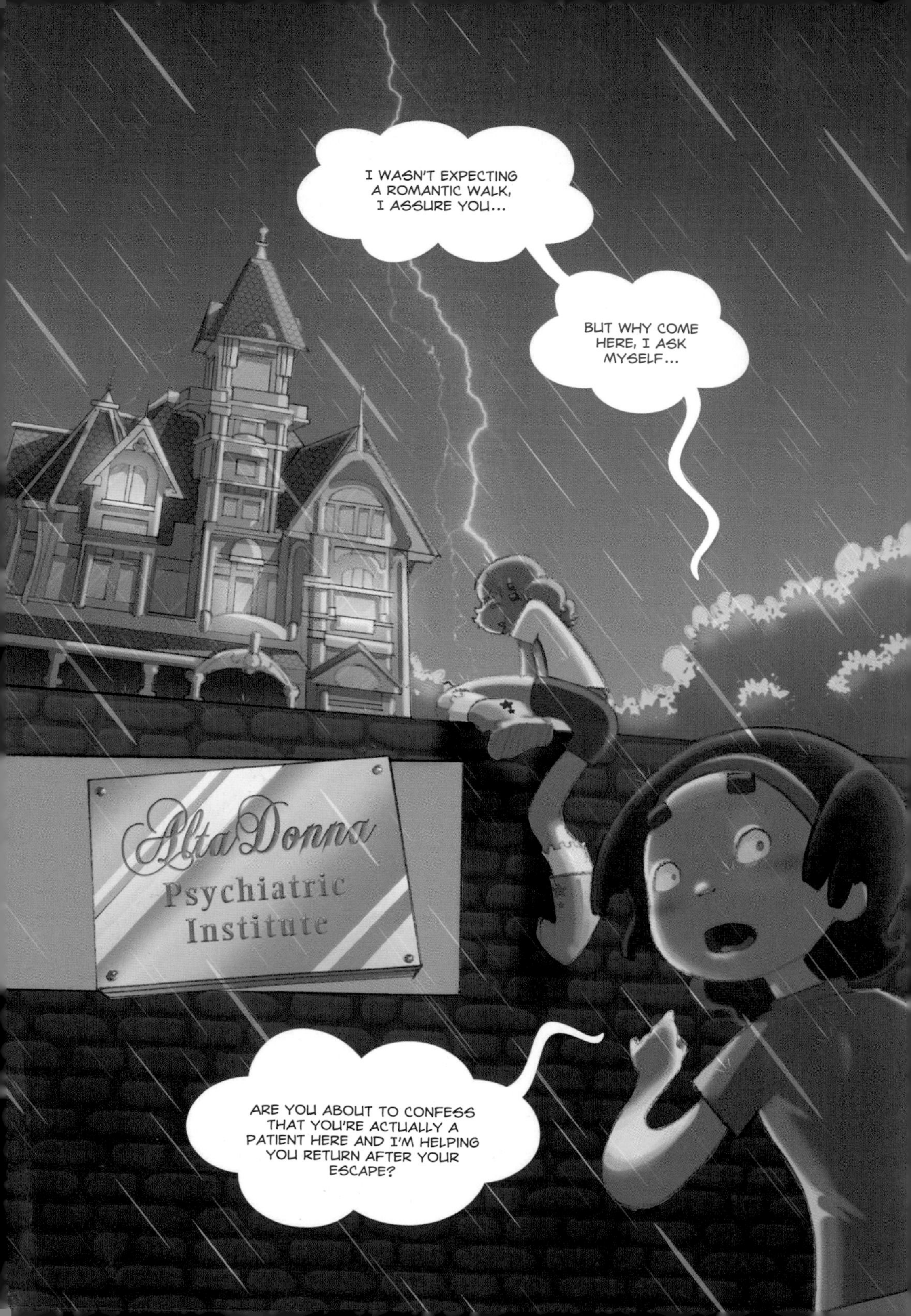
I WASN'T EXPECTING A ROMANTIC WALK, I ASSURE YOU...
BUT WHY COME HERE, I ASK MYSELF...
AltaDonna
Psychiatric
Institute
ARE YOU ABOUT TO CONFESS THAT YOU'RE ACTUALLY A PATIENT HERE AND I'M HELPING YOU RETURN AFTER YOUR ESCAPE?

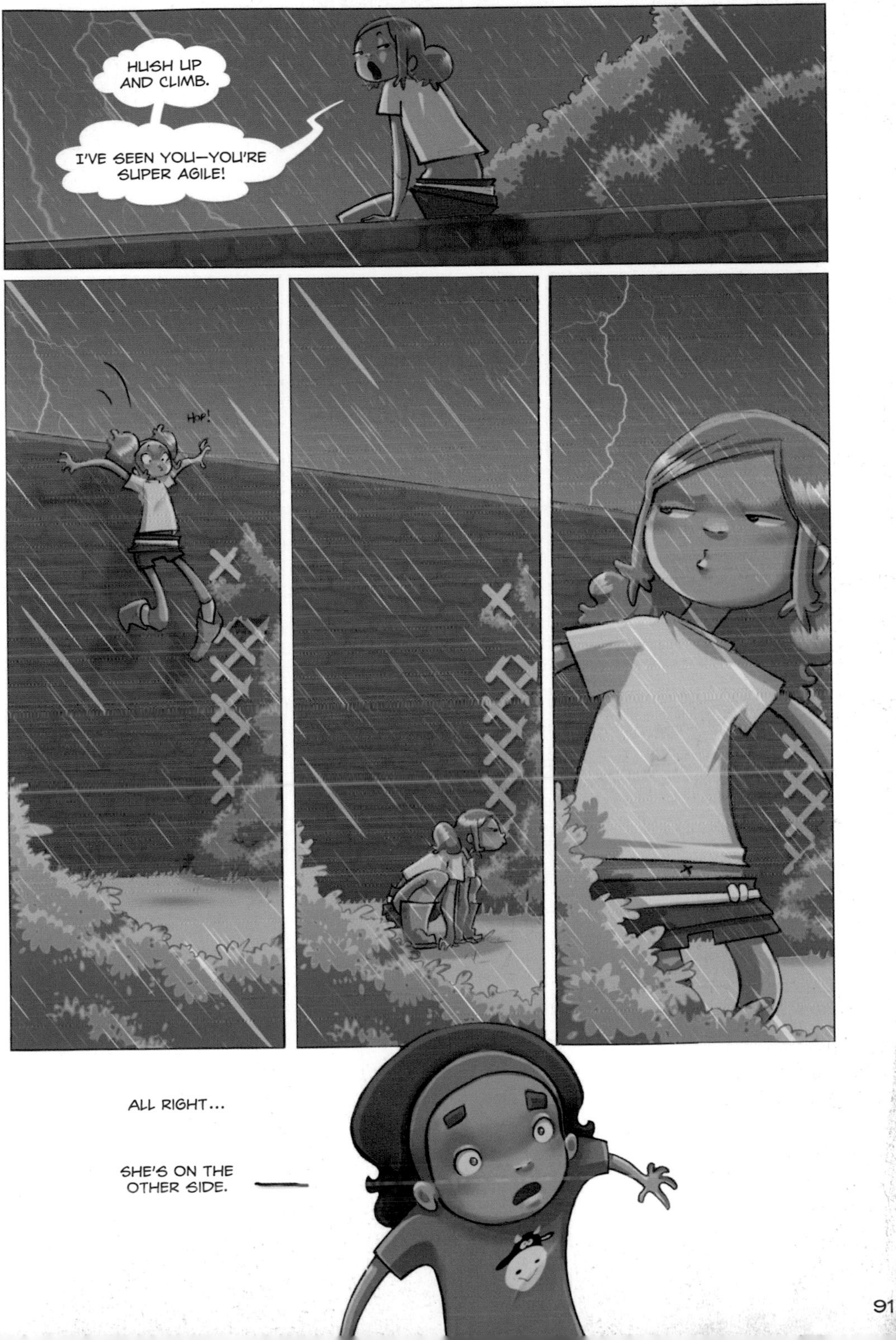
HUSH UP AND CLIMB.
I'VE SEEN YOU—YOU'RE SUPER AGILE!
HOP!
ALL RIGHT...
SHE'S ON THE OTHER SIDE.

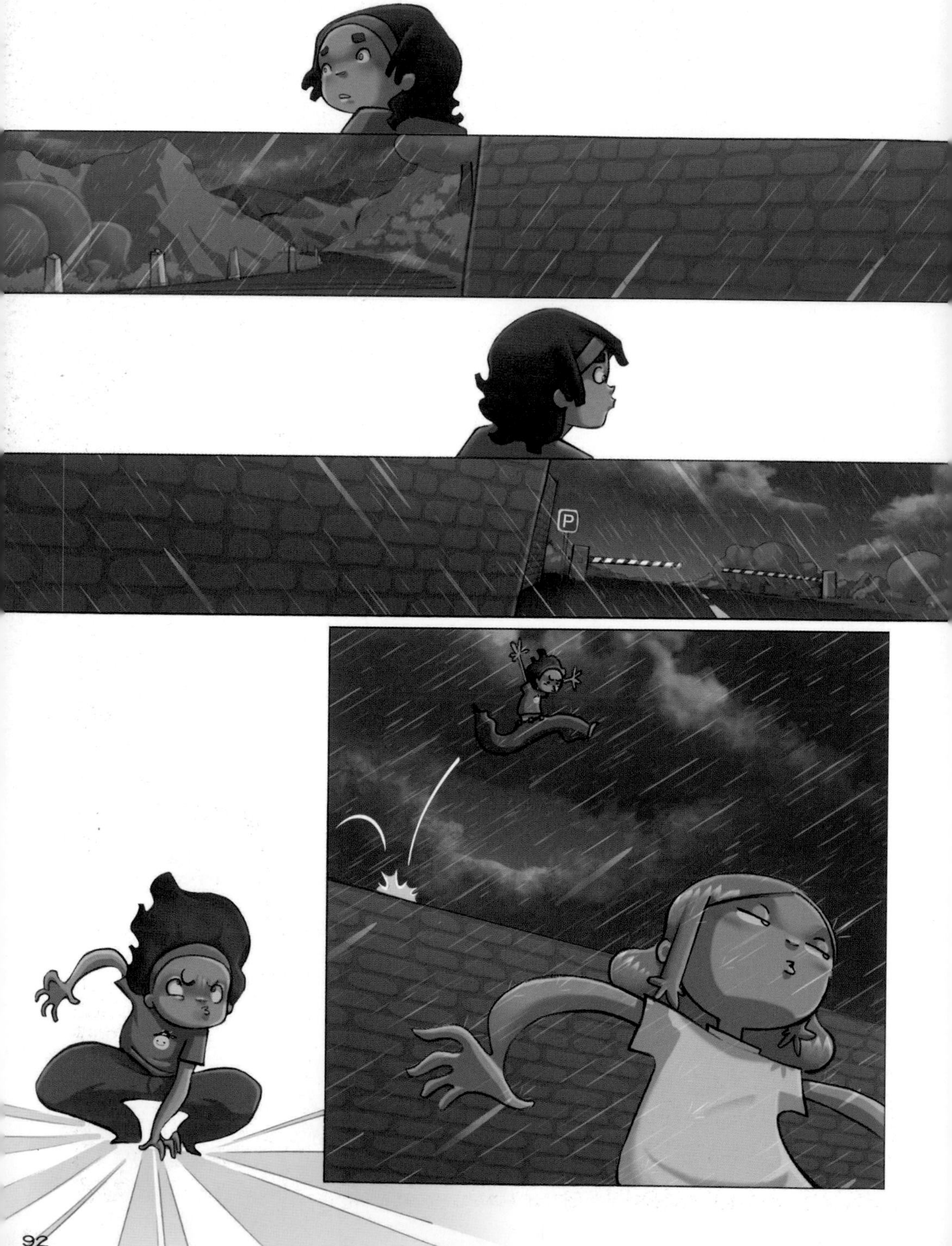
P

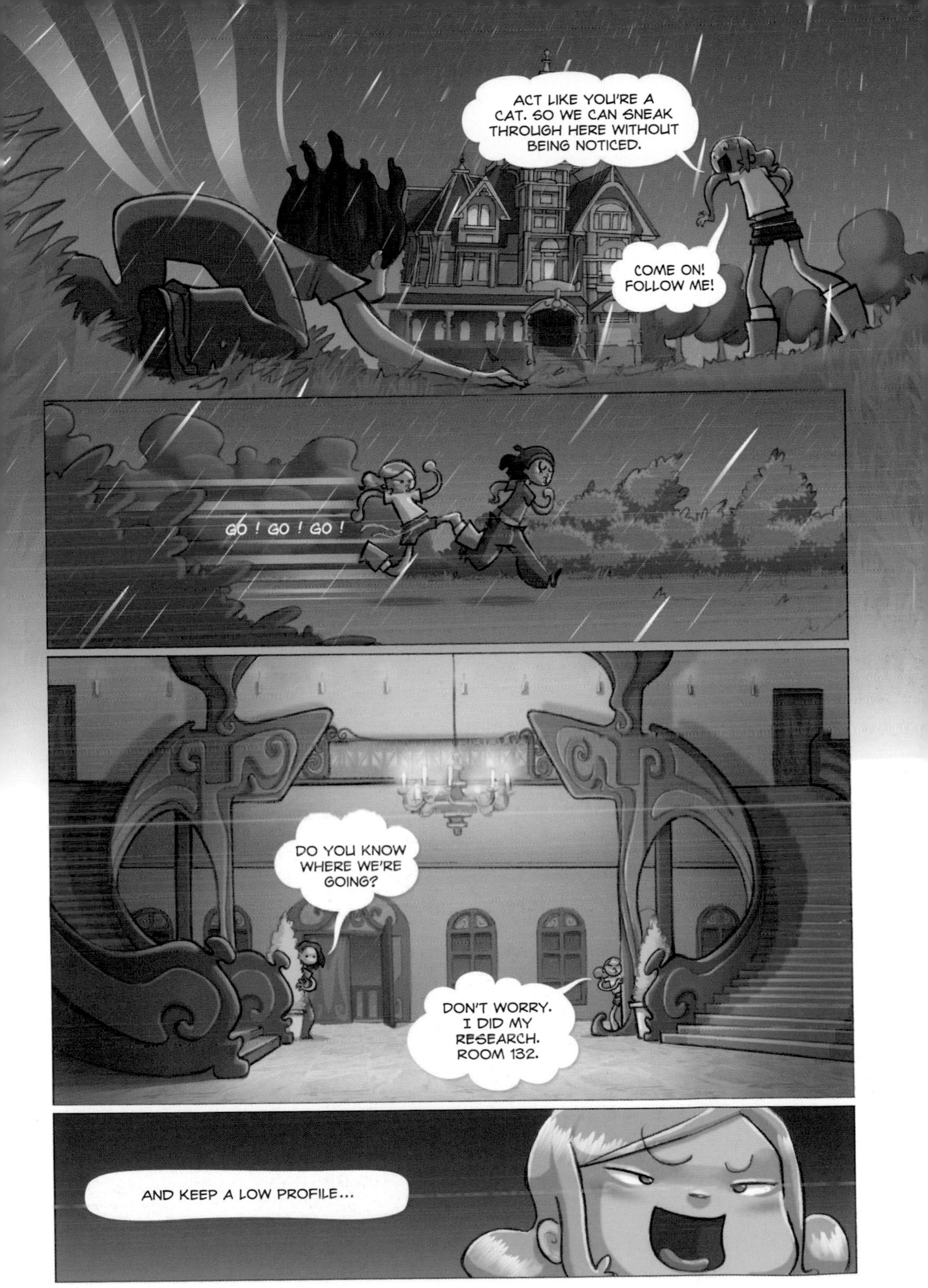
ACT LIKE YOU'RE A CAT. SO WE CAN SNEAK THROUGH HERE WITHOUT BEING NOTICED.
COME ON! FOLLOW ME!
GO ! GO ! GO !
DO YOU KNOW WHERE WE'RE GOING?
DON'T WORRY. I DID MY RESEARCH. ROOM 132.
AND KEEP A LOW PROFILE...

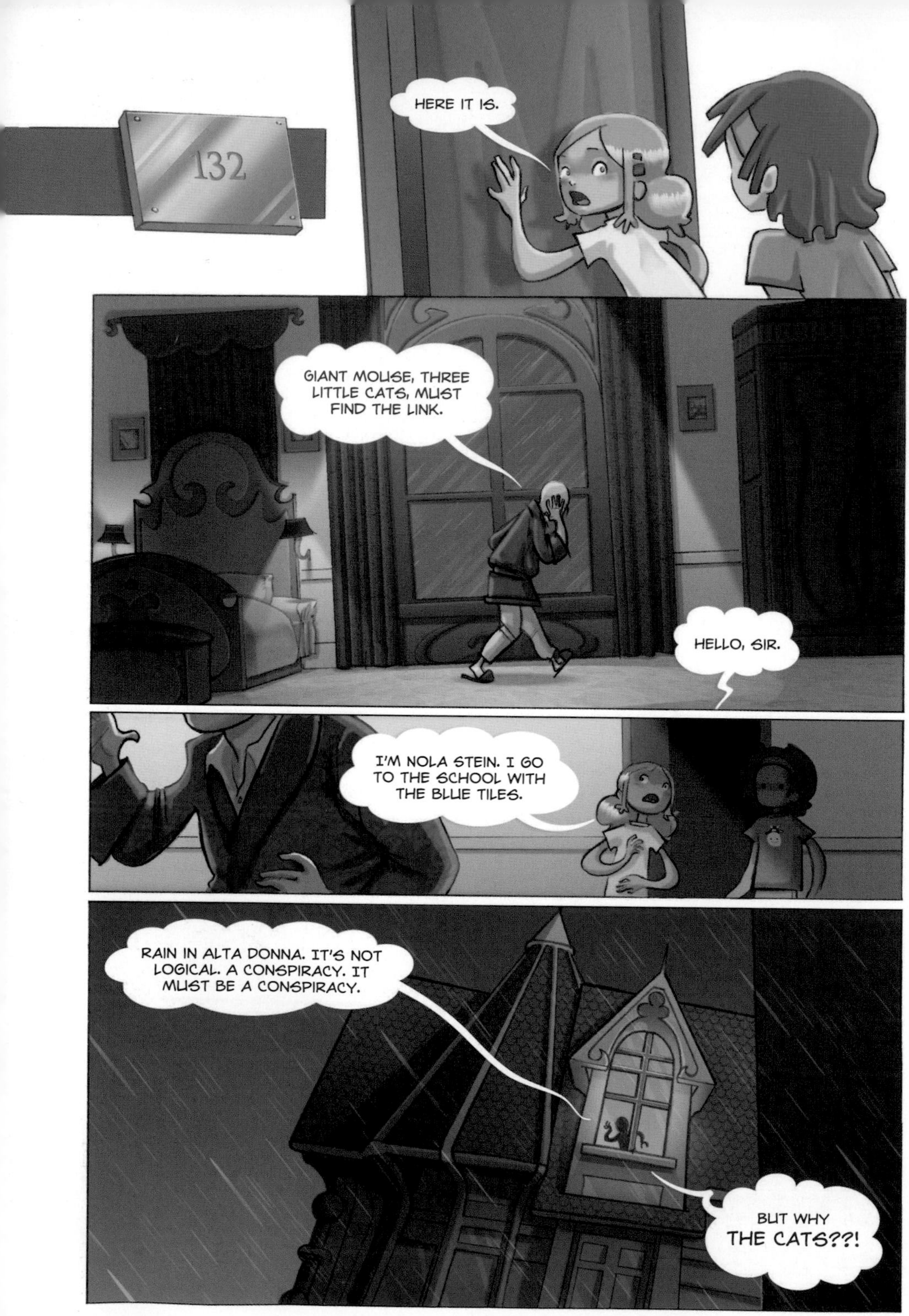
132
HERE IT IS.
GIANT MOUSE, THREE LITTLE CATS, MUST FIND THE LINK.
HELLO, SIR.
I'M NOLA STEIN. I GO TO THE SCHOOL WITH THE BLUE TILES.
RAIN IN ALTA DONNA. IT'S NOT LOGICAL. A CONSPIRACY. IT MUST BE A CONSPIRACY.
BUT WHY THE CATS??!

CATS DON'T LIKE WATER. EVERYONE KNOWS THAT. NOW, AS FOR THE PASSAGE...

SIR...

YOU'RE OUR LIBRARIAN.

YOU REMEMBER—

YOU TOO? YOU'RE LOOKING FOR THE PASSAGE, ALSO? YOU WANT ME FOR WHAT I DID?

AAAH!

HEY!!! LET GO OF HER!

YOU?

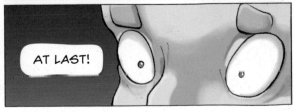

AT LAST!

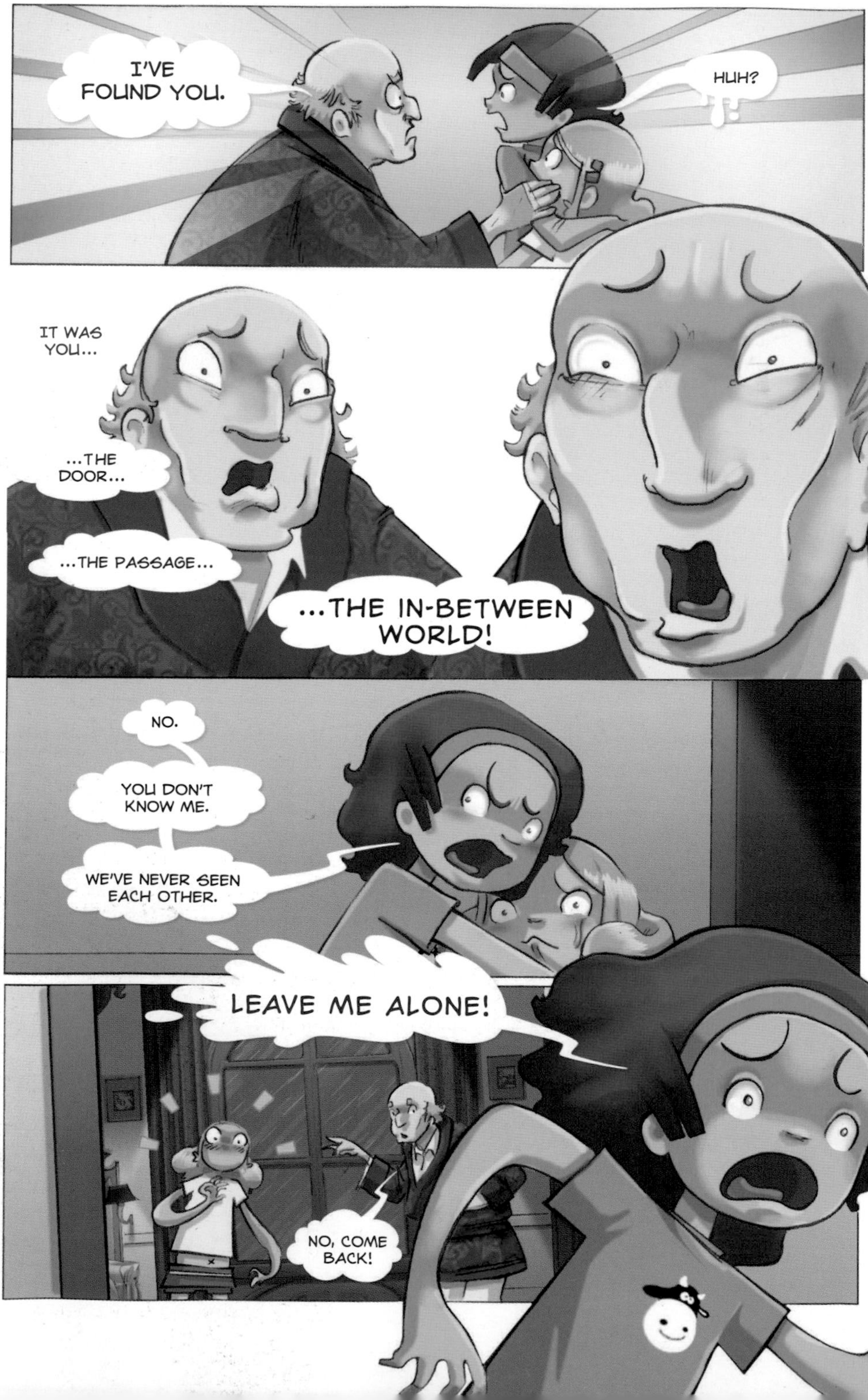
I'VE FOUND YOU.
HUH?
IT WAS YOU...
...THE DOOR...
...THE PASSAGE...
...THE IN-BETWEEN WORLD!
NO.
YOU DON'T KNOW ME.
WE'VE NEVER SEEN EACH OTHER.
LEAVE ME ALONE!
NO, COME BACK!

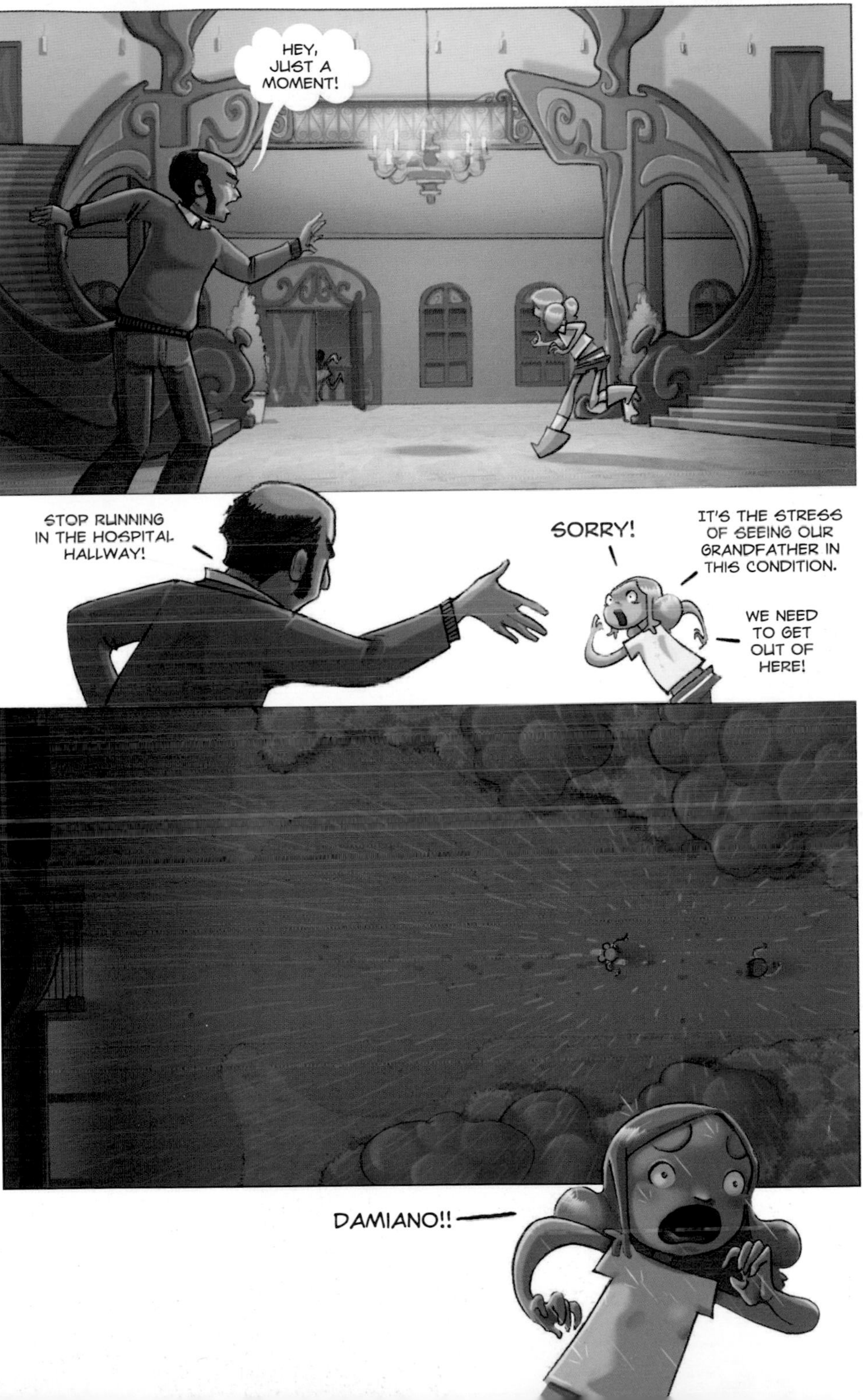
HEY, JUST A MOMENT!
STOP RUNNING IN THE HOSPITAL HALLWAY!
SORRY!
IT'S THE STRESS OF SEEING OUR GRANDFATHER IN THIS CONDITION.
WE NEED TO GET OUT OF HERE!
DAMIANO!!

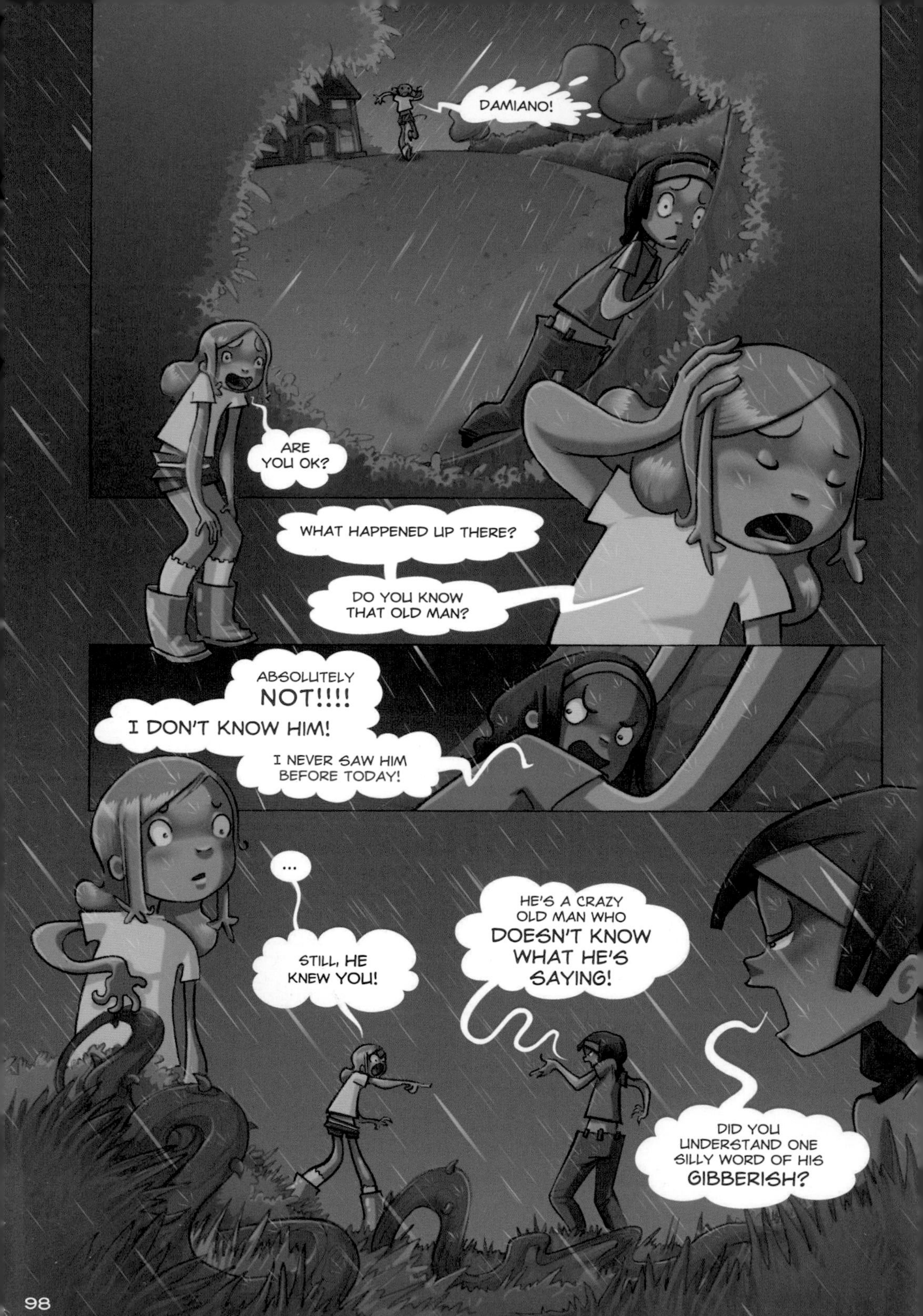
DAMIANO!
ARE YOU OK?
WHAT HAPPENED UP THERE?
DO YOU KNOW THAT OLD MAN?
ABSOLUTELY NOT!!!!
I DON'T KNOW HIM!
I NEVER SAW HIM BEFORE TODAY!
...
STILL, HE KNEW YOU!
HE'S A CRAZY OLD MAN WHO DOESN'T KNOW WHAT HE'S SAYING!
DID YOU UNDERSTAND ONE SILLY WORD OF HIS GIBBERISH?

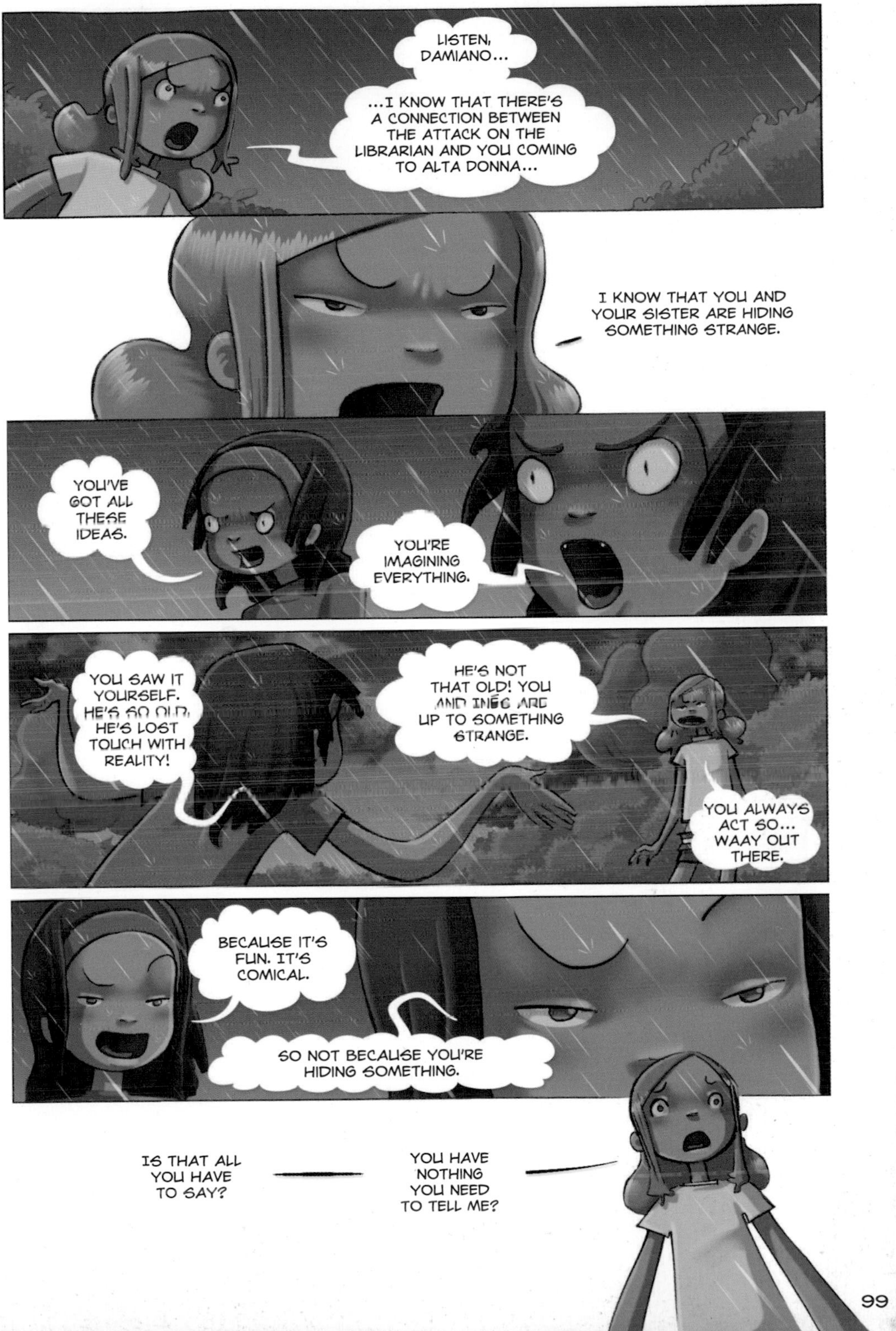
LISTEN, DAMIANO...
...I KNOW THAT THERE'S A CONNECTION BETWEEN THE ATTACK ON THE LIBRARIAN AND YOU COMING TO ALTA DONNA...
I KNOW THAT YOU AND YOUR SISTER ARE HIDING SOMETHING STRANGE.
YOU'VE GOT ALL THESE IDEAS.
YOU'RE IMAGINING EVERYTHING.
YOU SAW IT YOURSELF. HE'S SO OLD, HE'S LOST TOUCH WITH REALITY!
HE'S NOT THAT OLD! YOU AND INÈS ARE UP TO SOMETHING STRANGE.
YOU ALWAYS ACT SO... WAAY OUT THERE.
BECAUSE IT'S FUN. IT'S COMICAL.
SO NOT BECAUSE YOU'RE HIDING SOMETHING.
IS THAT ALL YOU HAVE TO SAY?
YOU HAVE NOTHING YOU NEED TO TELL ME?

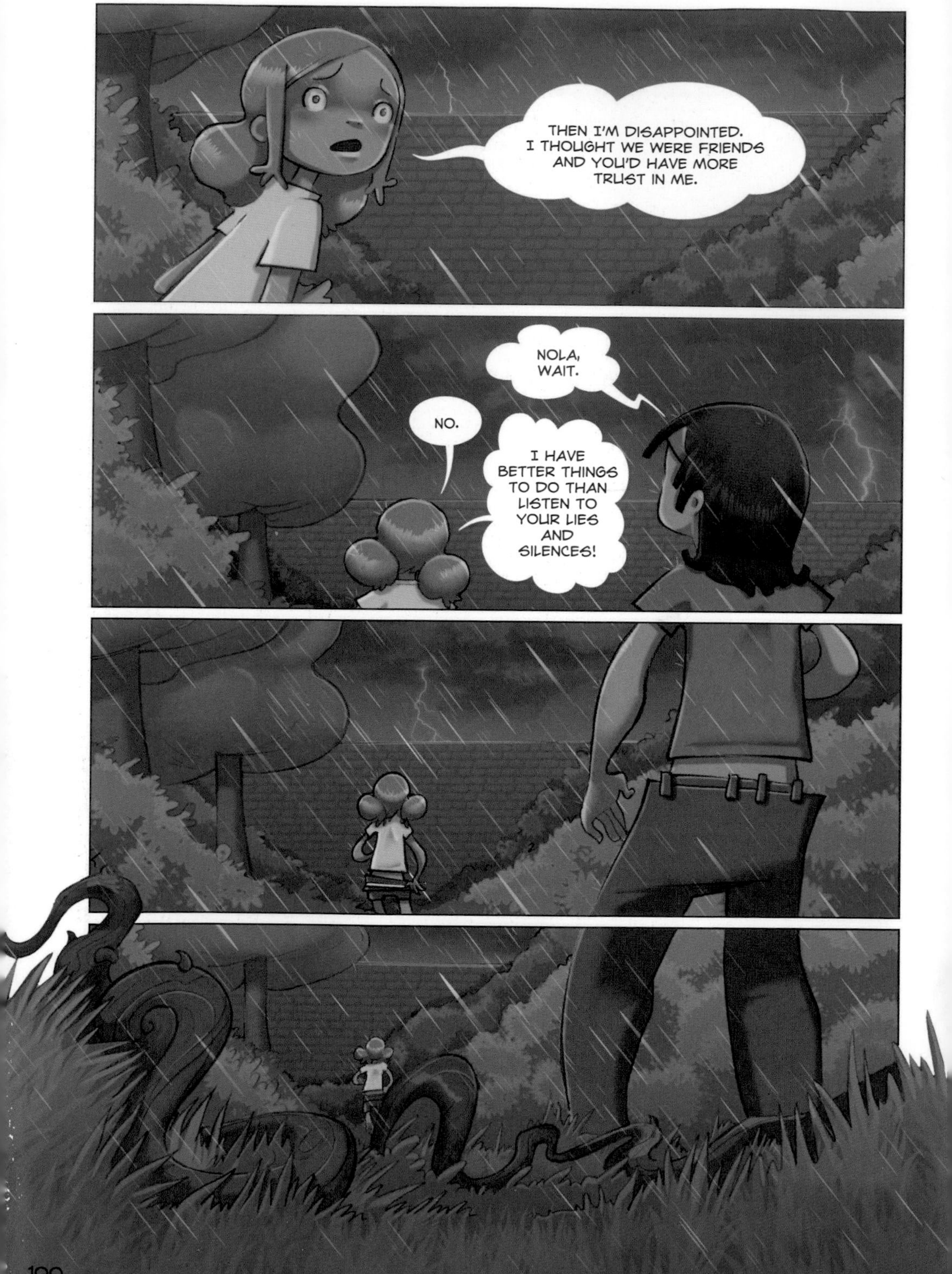
THEN I'M DISAPPOINTED. I THOUGHT WE WERE FRIENDS AND YOU'D HAVE MORE TRUST IN ME.
NOLA, WAIT.
NO.
I HAVE BETTER THINGS TO DO THAN LISTEN TO YOUR LIES AND SILENCES!

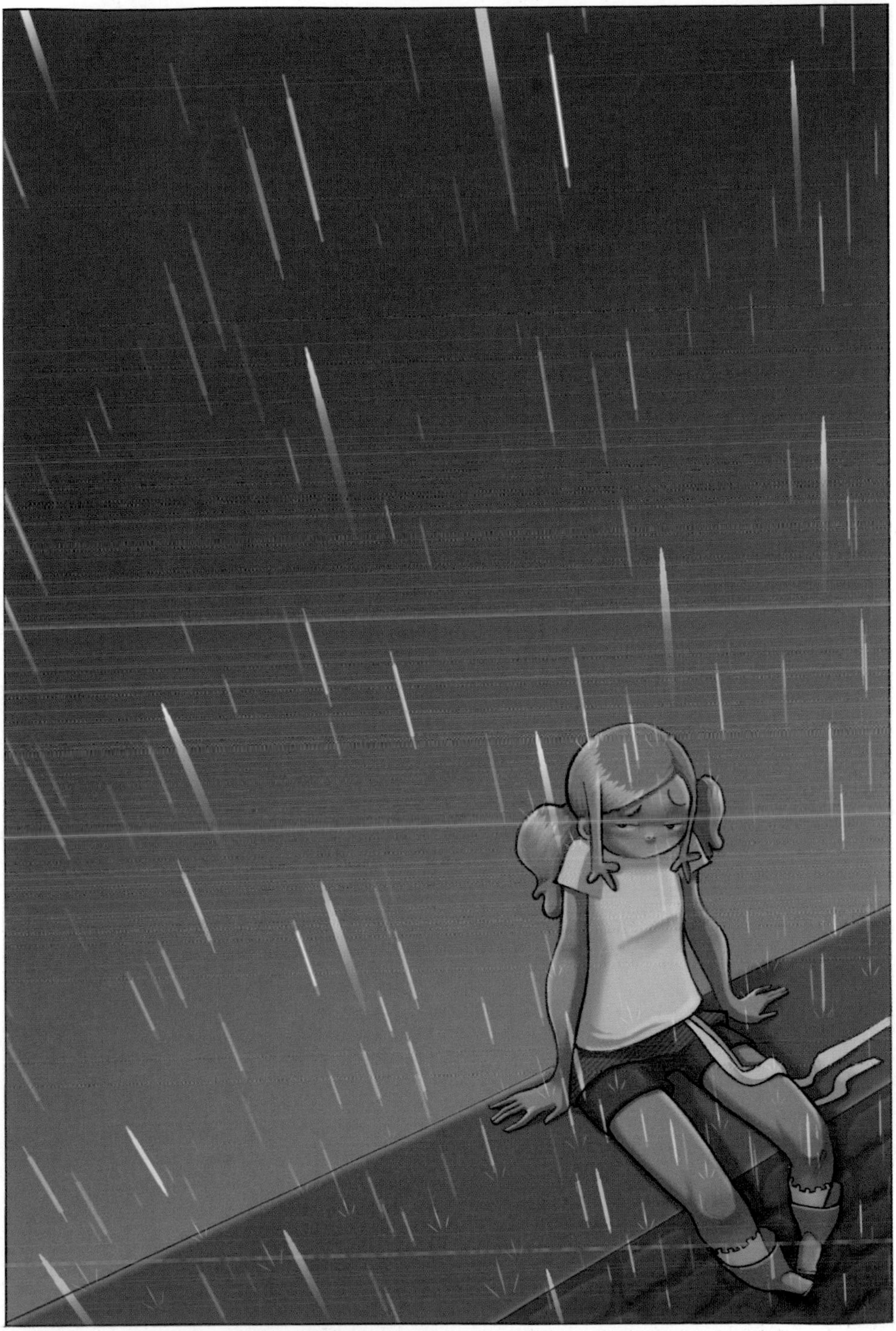

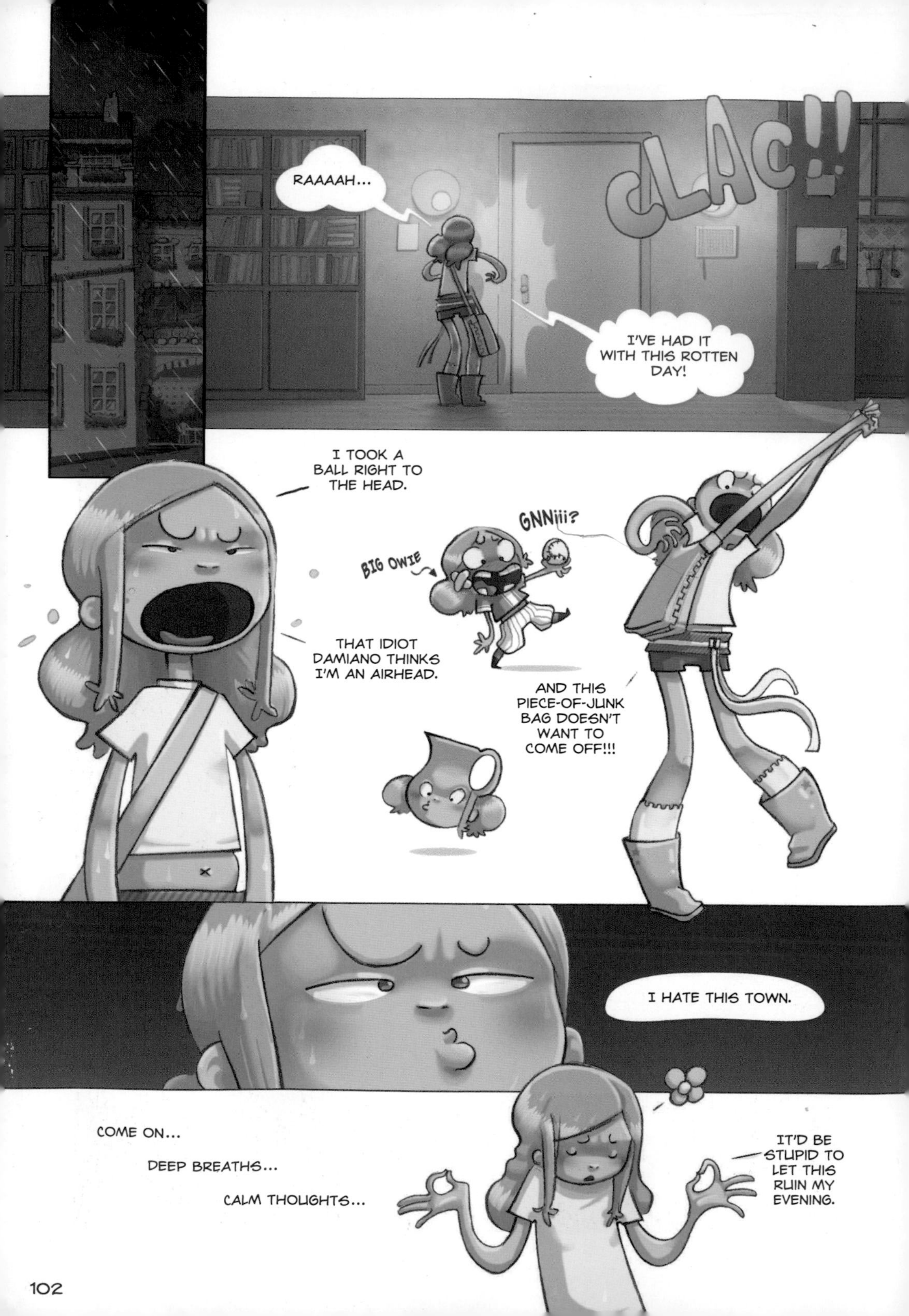
RAAAAH...
CLAC!!
I'VE HAD IT WITH THIS ROTTEN DAY!
I TOOK A BALL RIGHT TO THE HEAD.
BIG OWIE
GNNiii?
THAT IDIOT DAMIANO THINKS I'M AN AIRHEAD.
AND THIS PIECE-OF-JUNK BAG DOESN'T WANT TO COME OFF!!!
I HATE THIS TOWN.
COME ON...
DEEP BREATHS...
CALM THOUGHTS...
IT'D BE STUPID TO LET THIS RUIN MY EVENING.

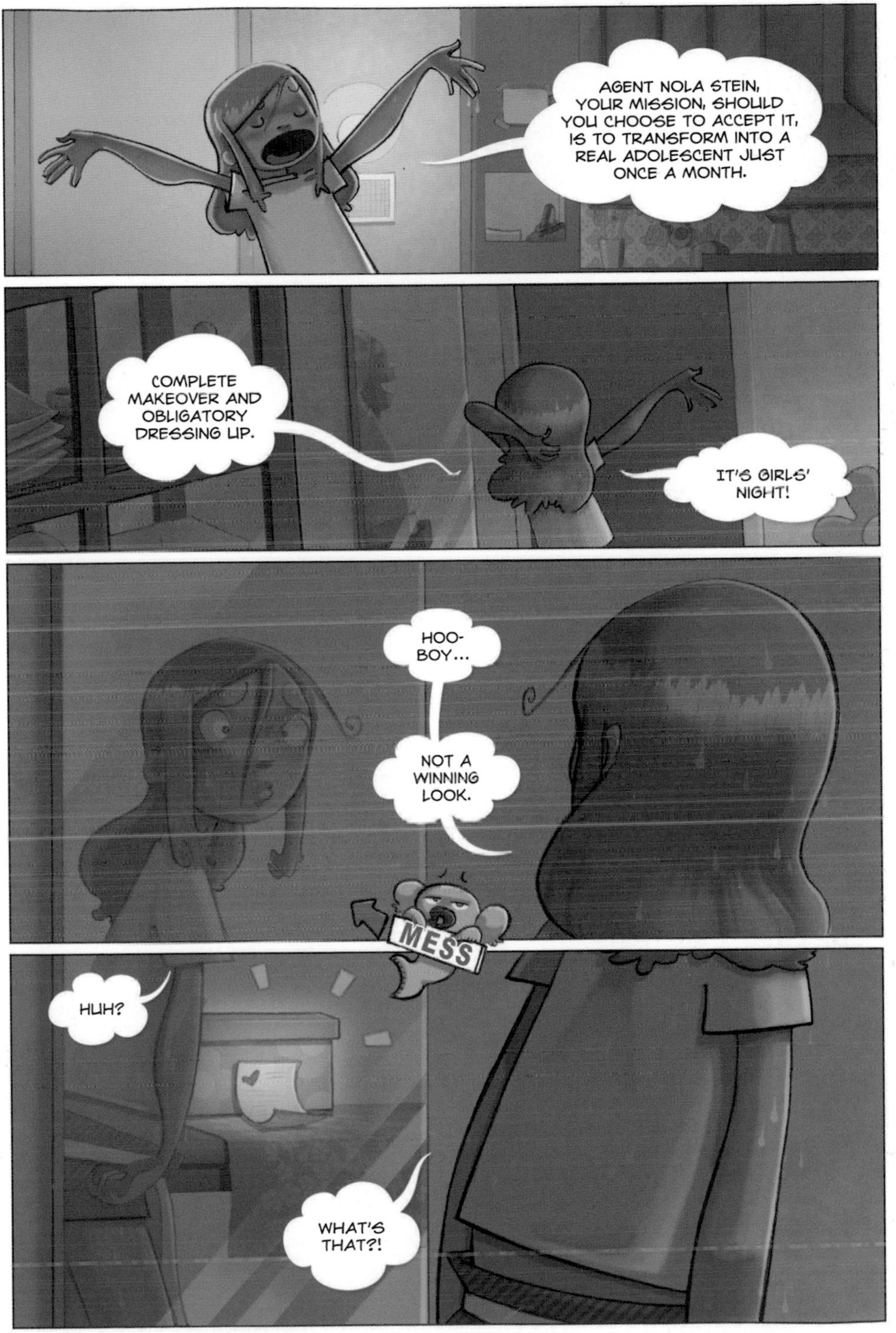
AGENT NOLA STEIN, YOUR MISSION, SHOULD YOU CHOOSE TO ACCEPT IT, IS TO TRANSFORM INTO A REAL ADOLESCENT JUST ONCE A MONTH.
COMPLETE MAKEOVER AND OBLIGATORY DRESSING UP.
IT'S GIRLS' NIGHT!
HOO-BOY...
NOT A WINNING LOOK.
MESS
HUH?
WHAT'S THAT?!

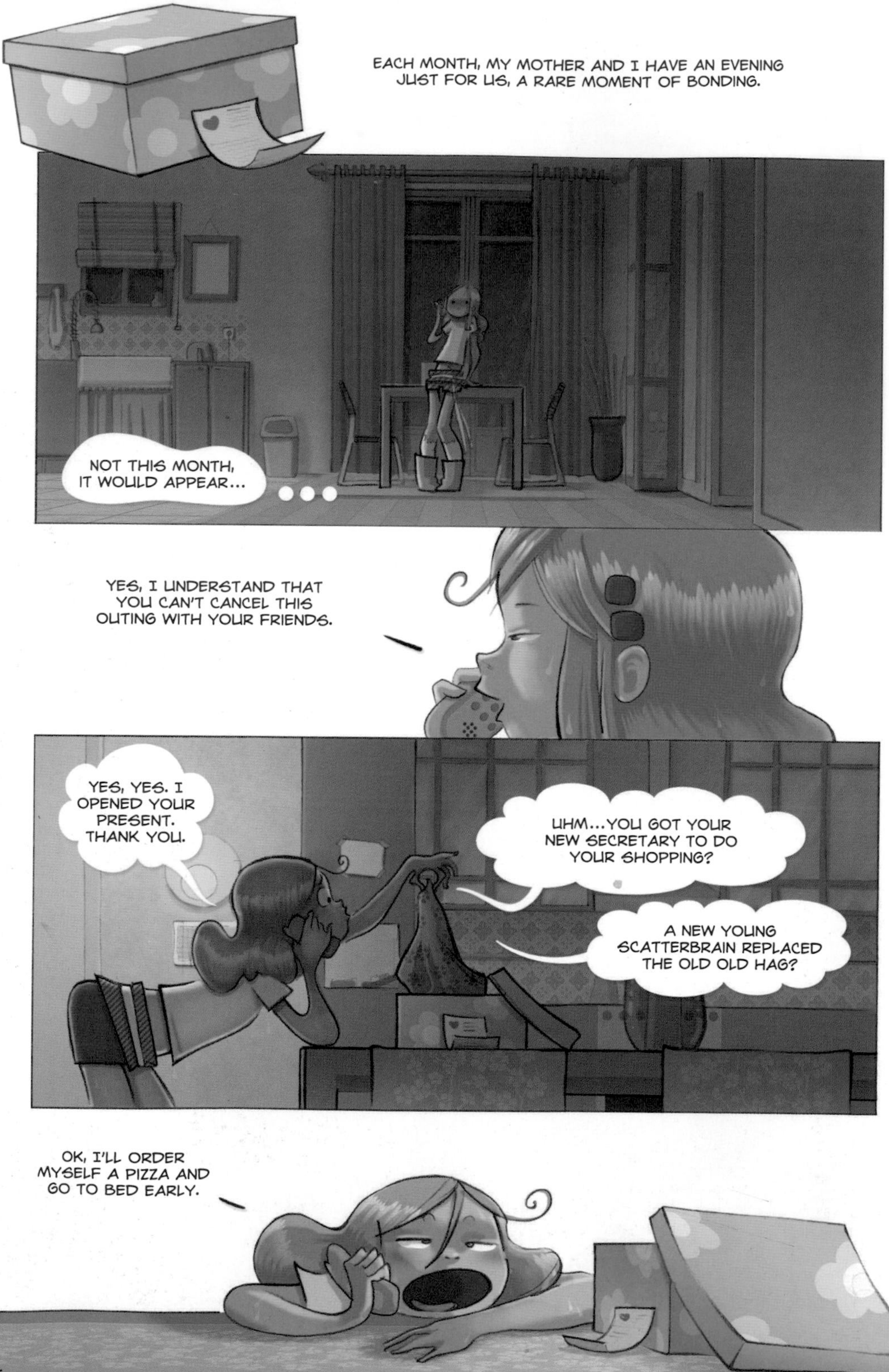
EACH MONTH, MY MOTHER AND I HAVE AN EVENING JUST FOR US, A RARE MOMENT OF BONDING.
NOT THIS MONTH, IT WOULD APPEAR...
YES, I UNDERSTAND THAT YOU CAN'T CANCEL THIS OUTING WITH YOUR FRIENDS.
YES, YES. I OPENED YOUR PRESENT. THANK YOU.
UHM...YOU GOT YOUR NEW SECRETARY TO DO YOUR SHOPPING?
A NEW YOUNG SCATTERBRAIN REPLACED THE OLD OLD HAG?
OK, I'LL ORDER MYSELF A PIZZA AND GO TO BED EARLY.

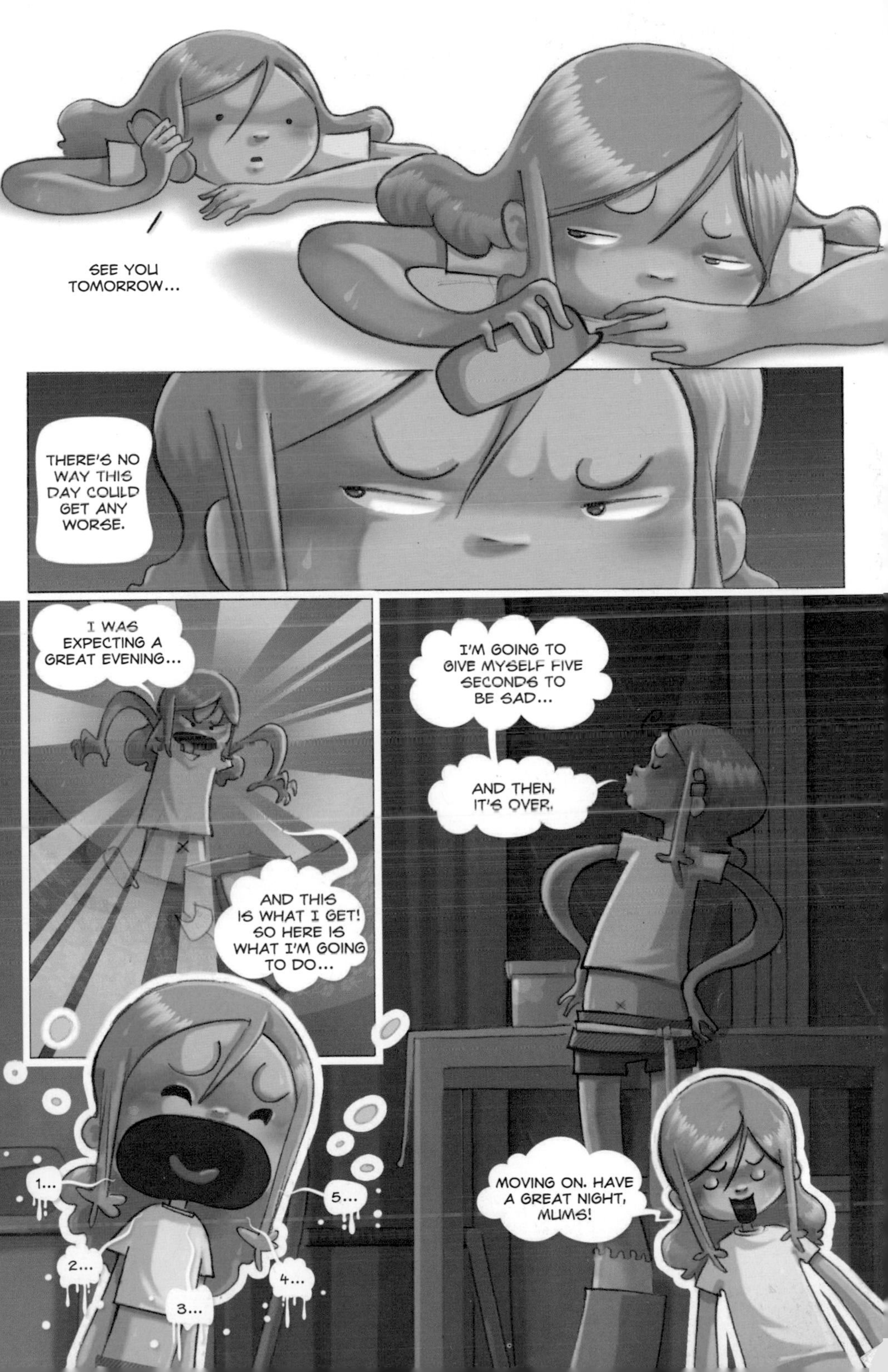
SEE YOU TOMORROW...
THERE'S NO WAY THIS DAY COULD GET ANY WORSE.
I WAS EXPECTING A GREAT EVENING...
AND THIS IS WHAT I GET! SO HERE IS WHAT I'M GOING TO DO...
I'M GOING TO GIVE MYSELF FIVE SECONDS TO BE SAD...
AND THEN, IT'S OVER.
1...
2...
3...
4...
5...
MOVING ON. HAVE A GREAT NIGHT, MUMS!

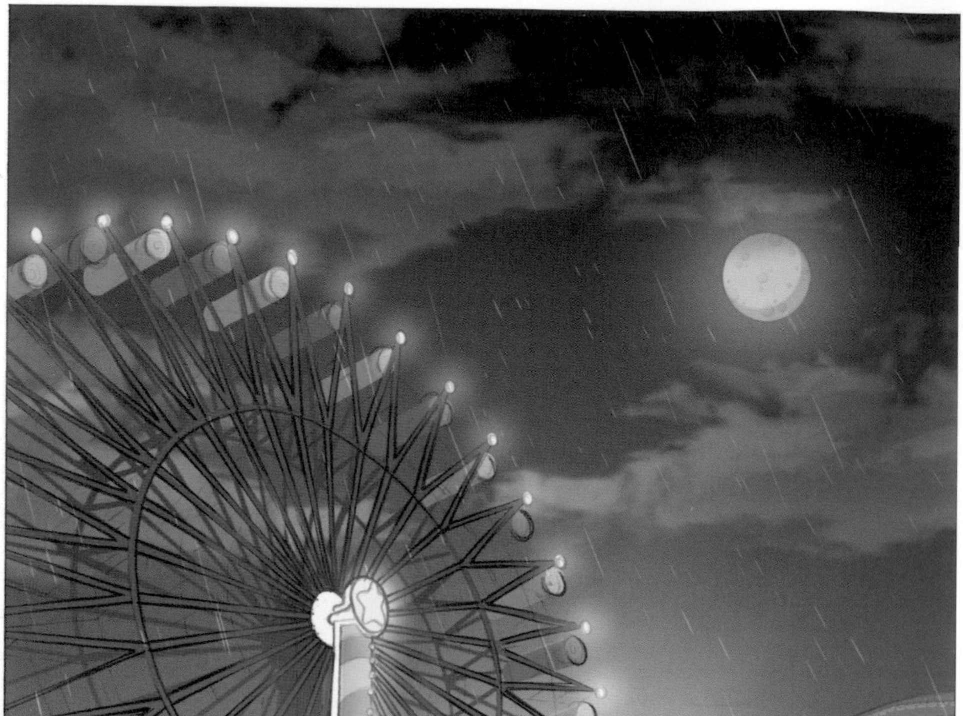

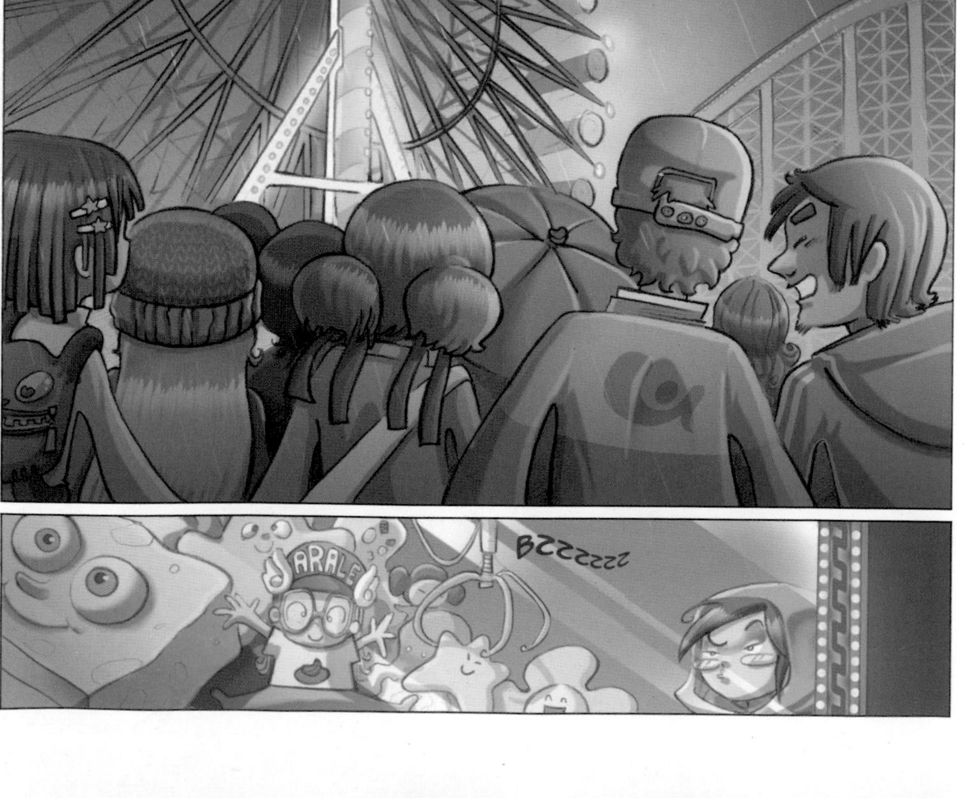
BZZZZZZ
ARALE

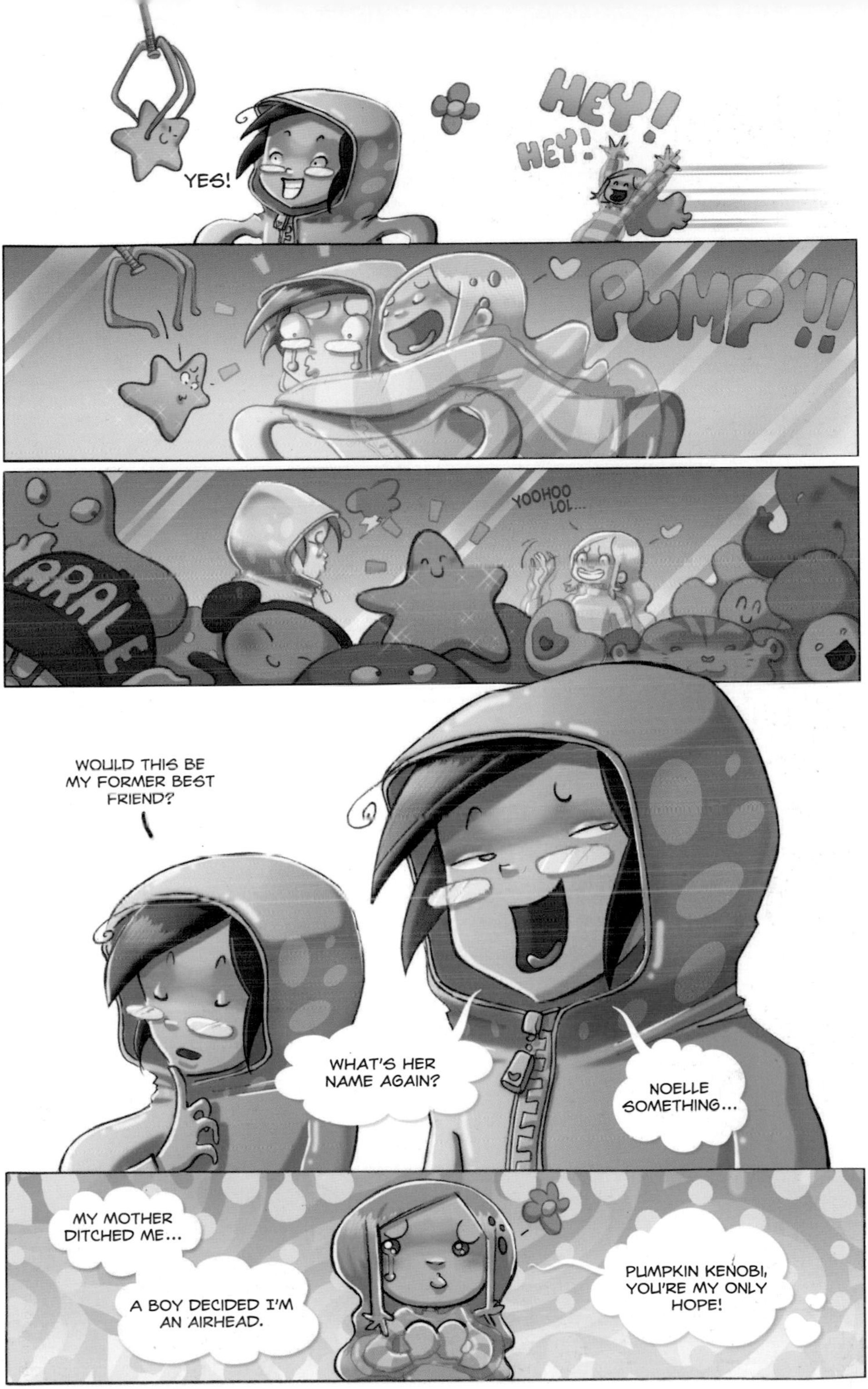
YES!
HEY!
HEY!
PUMP'!!
YOOHOO LOL...
ARALE
WOULD THIS BE MY FORMER BEST FRIEND?
WHAT'S HER NAME AGAIN?
NOELLE SOMETHING...
MY MOTHER DITCHED ME...
A BOY DECIDED I'M AN AIRHEAD.
PUMPKIN KENOBI, YOU'RE MY ONLY HOPE!

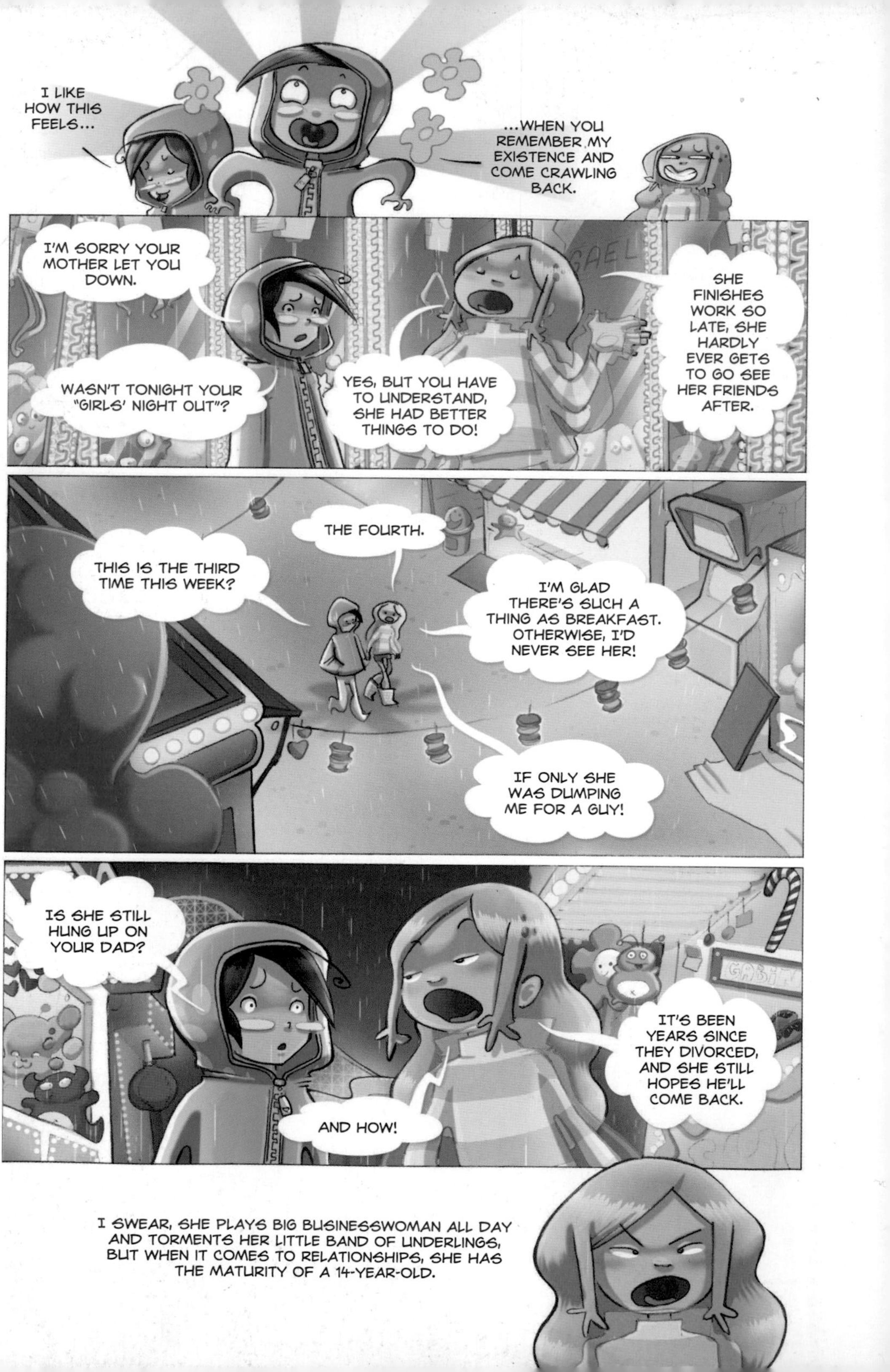
I LIKE HOW THIS FEELS...
...WHEN YOU REMEMBER MY EXISTENCE AND COME CRAWLING BACK.
I'M SORRY YOUR MOTHER LET YOU DOWN.
WASN'T TONIGHT YOUR "GIRLS' NIGHT OUT"?
YES, BUT YOU HAVE TO UNDERSTAND, SHE HAD BETTER THINGS TO DO!
SHE FINISHES WORK SO LATE, SHE HARDLY EVER GETS TO GO SEE HER FRIENDS AFTER.
THIS IS THE THIRD TIME THIS WEEK?
THE FOURTH.
I'M GLAD THERE'S SUCH A THING AS BREAKFAST. OTHERWISE, I'D NEVER SEE HER!
IF ONLY SHE WAS DUMPING ME FOR A GUY!
IS SHE STILL HUNG UP ON YOUR DAD?
IT'S BEEN YEARS SINCE THEY DIVORCED, AND SHE STILL HOPES HE'LL COME BACK.
AND HOW!
I SWEAR, SHE PLAYS BIG BUSINESSWOMAN ALL DAY AND TORMENTS HER LITTLE BAND OF UNDERLINGS, BUT WHEN IT COMES TO RELATIONSHIPS, SHE HAS THE MATURITY OF A 14-YEAR-OLD.

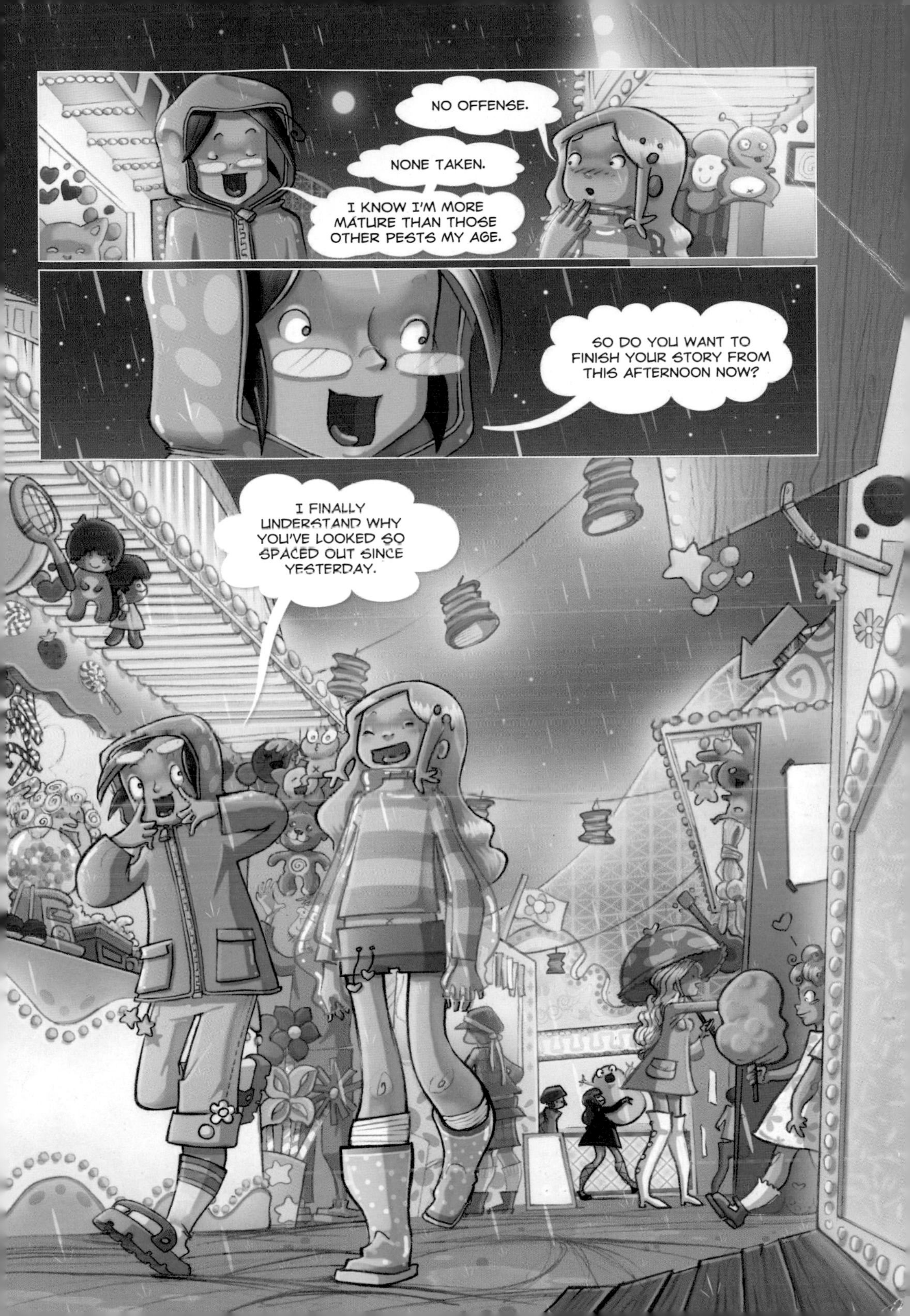
NO OFFENSE.
NONE TAKEN.
I KNOW I'M MORE MATURE THAN THOSE OTHER PESTS MY AGE.
SO DO YOU WANT TO FINISH YOUR STORY FROM THIS AFTERNOON NOW?
I FINALLY UNDERSTAND WHY YOU'VE LOOKED SO SPACED OUT SINCE YESTERDAY.

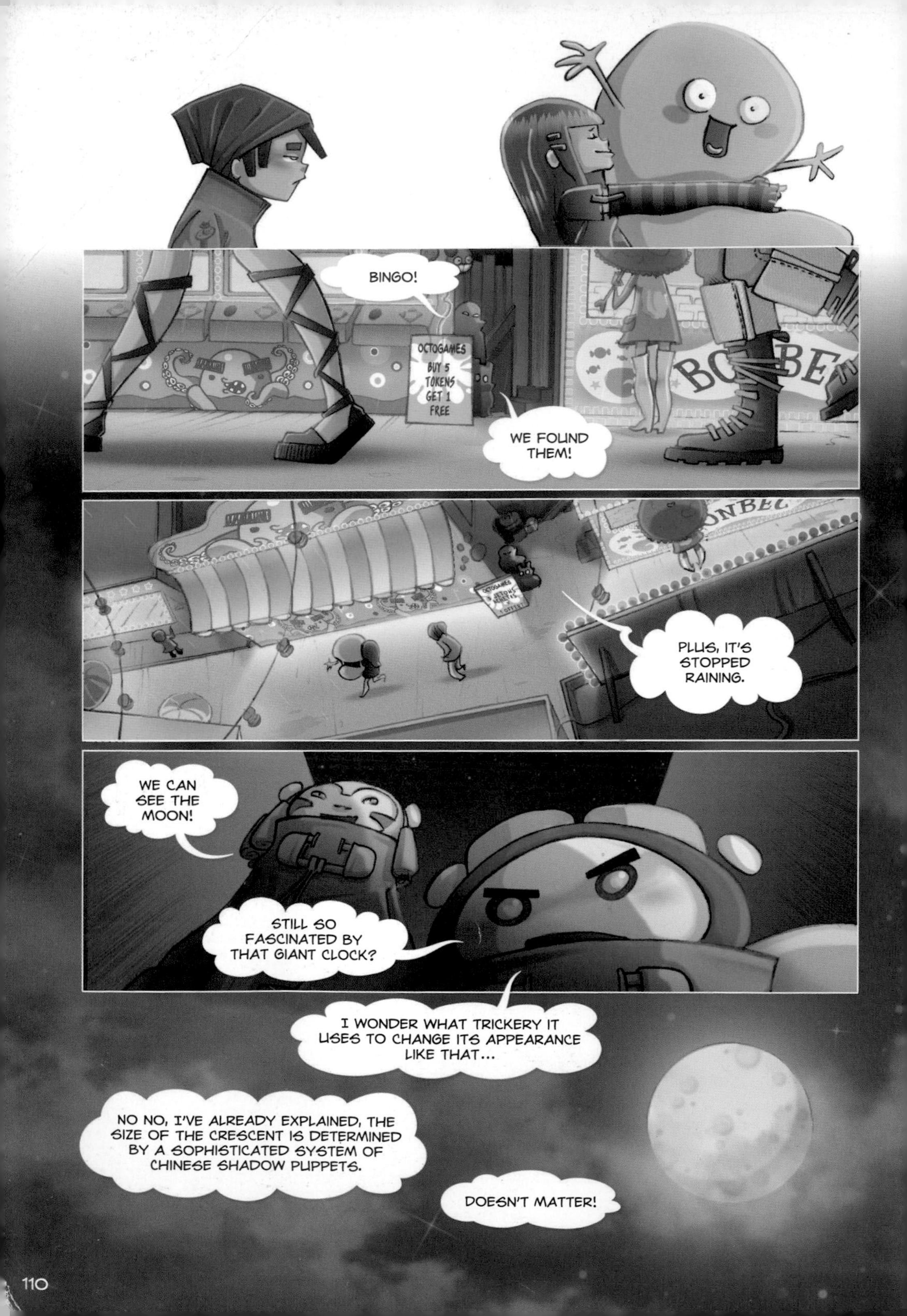
BINGO!
OCTOGAMES BUY 5 TOKENS GET 1 FREE
WE FOUND THEM!
PLUS, IT'S STOPPED RAINING.
WE CAN SEE THE MOON!
STILL SO FASCINATED BY THAT GIANT CLOCK?
I WONDER WHAT TRICKERY IT USES TO CHANGE ITS APPEARANCE LIKE THAT...
NO NO, I'VE ALREADY EXPLAINED, THE SIZE OF THE CRESCENT IS DETERMINED BY A SOPHISTICATED SYSTEM OF CHINESE SHADOW PUPPETS.
DOESN'T MATTER!

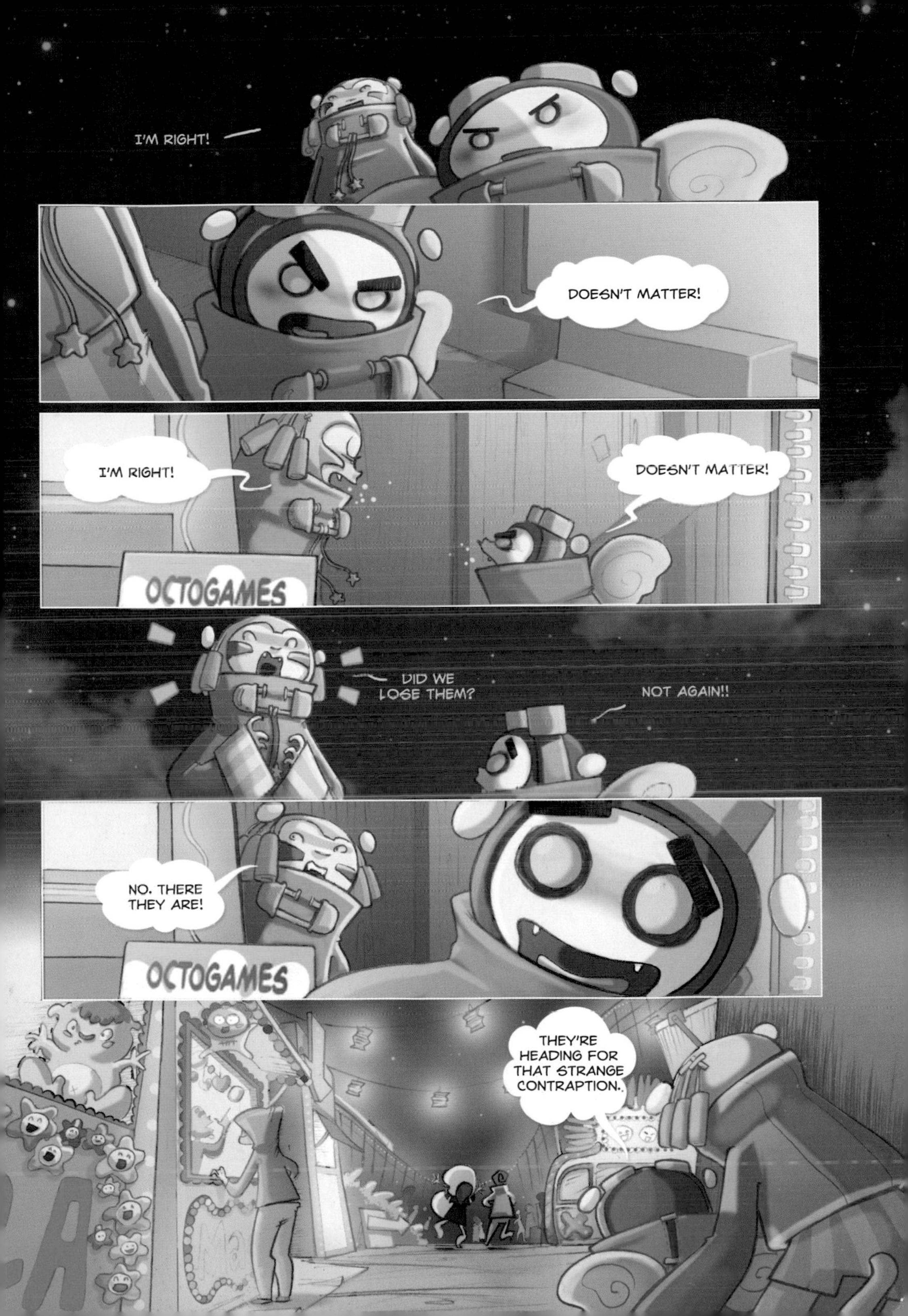
I'M RIGHT!
DOESN'T MATTER!
I'M RIGHT!
DOESN'T MATTER!
OCTOGAMES
DID WE LOSE THEM?
NOT AGAIN!!
NO. THERE THEY ARE!
OCTOGAMES
THEY'RE HEADING FOR THAT STRANGE CONTRAPTION.

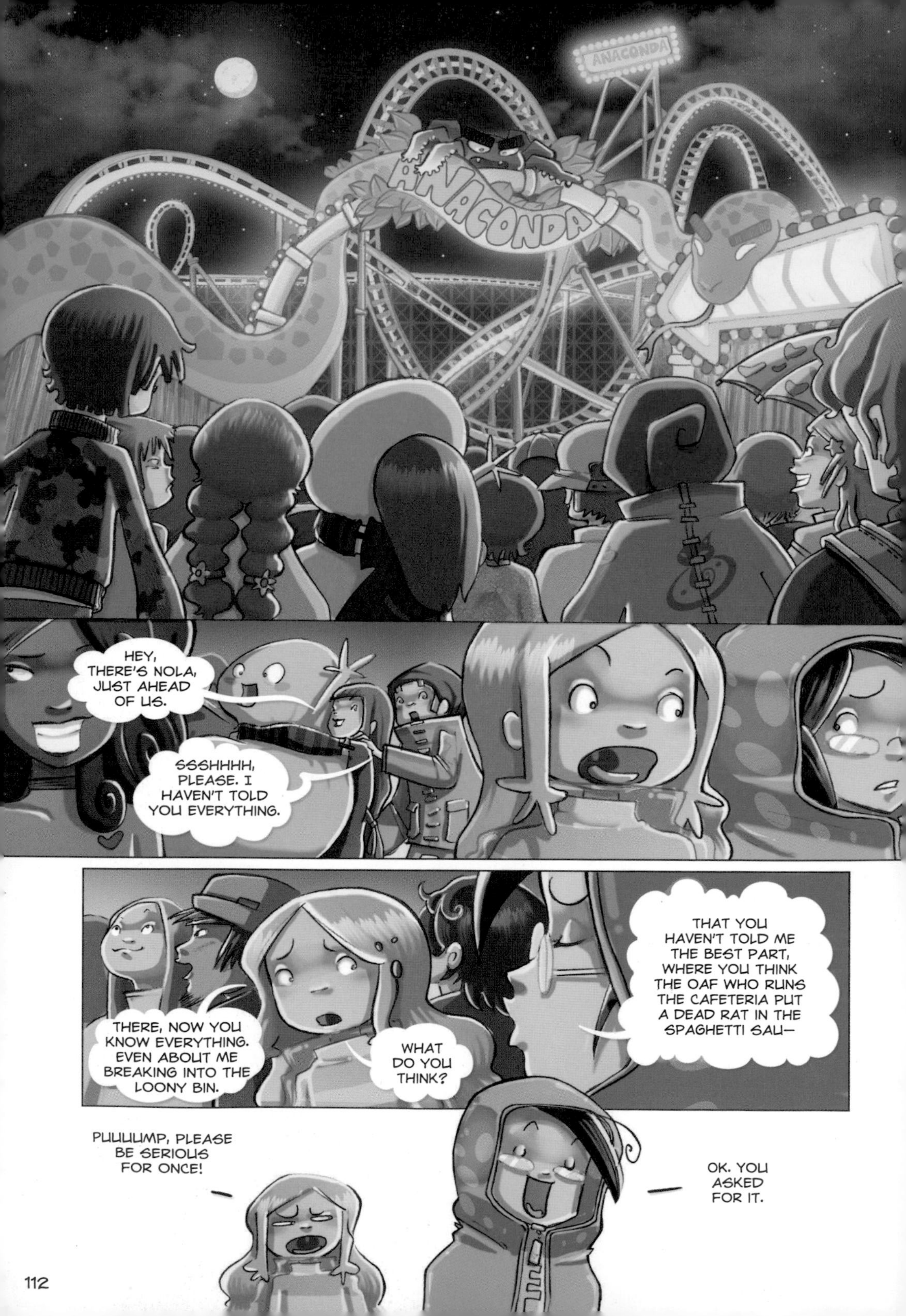
ANACONDA
ANACONDA
HEY, THERE'S NOLA, JUST AHEAD OF US.
SSSHHHH, PLEASE. I HAVEN'T TOLD YOU EVERYTHING.
THERE, NOW YOU KNOW EVERYTHING. EVEN ABOUT ME BREAKING INTO THE LOONY BIN.
WHAT DO YOU THINK?
THAT YOU HAVEN'T TOLD ME THE BEST PART, WHERE YOU THINK THE OAF WHO RUNS THE CAFETERIA PUT A DEAD RAT IN THE SPAGHETTI SAU–
PUUUUMP, PLEASE BE SERIOUS FOR ONCE!
OK. YOU ASKED FOR IT.

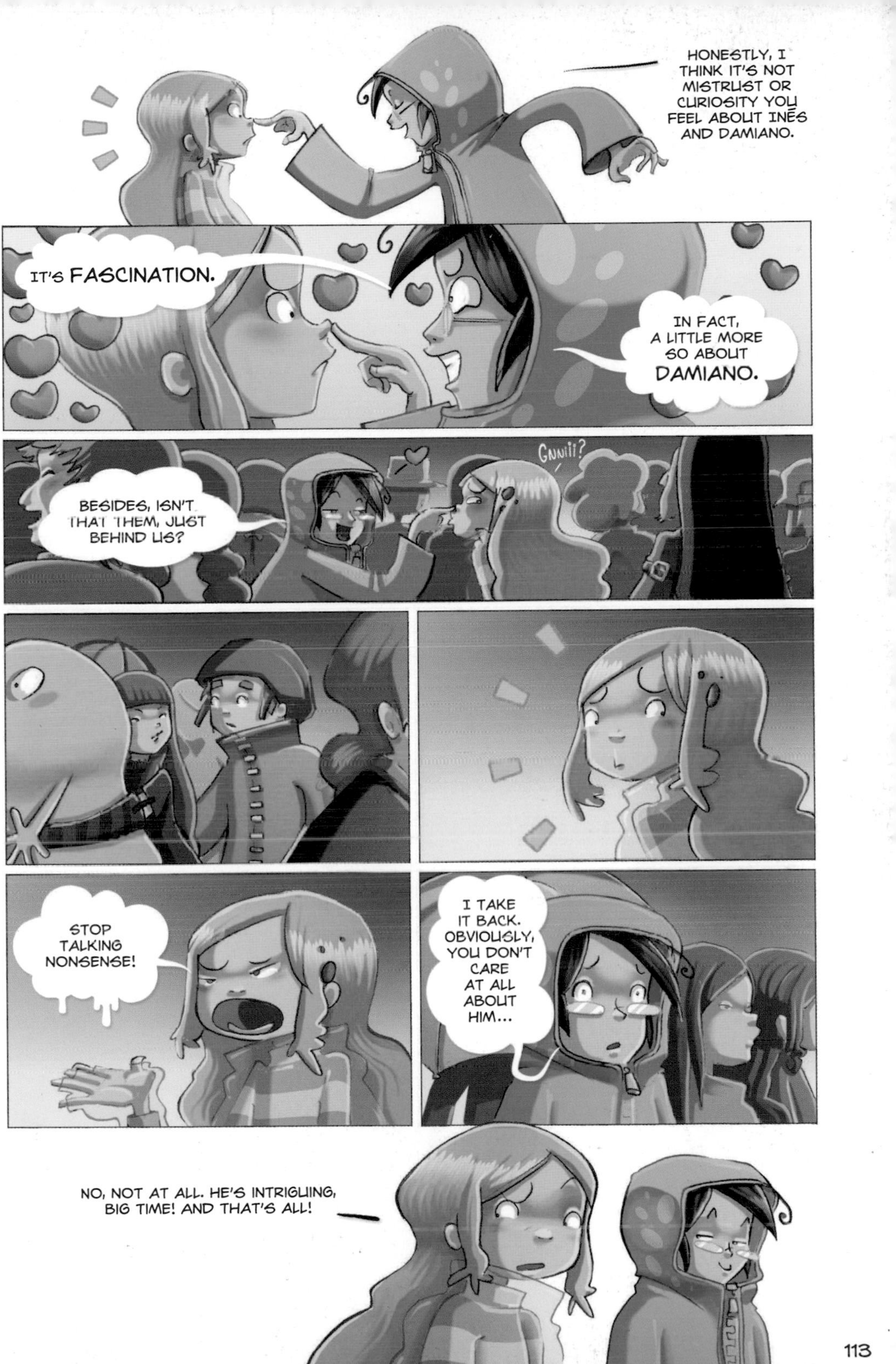

HONESTLY, I THINK IT'S NOT MISTRUST OR CURIOSITY YOU FEEL ABOUT INÉS AND DAMIANO.
IT'S FASCINATION.
IN FACT, A LITTLE MORE SO ABOUT DAMIANO.
BESIDES, ISN'T THAT THEM, JUST BEHIND US?
GNIII?
STOP TALKING NONSENSE!
I TAKE IT BACK. OBVIOUSLY, YOU DON'T CARE AT ALL ABOUT HIM...
NO, NOT AT ALL. HE'S INTRIGUING, BIG TIME! AND THAT'S ALL!

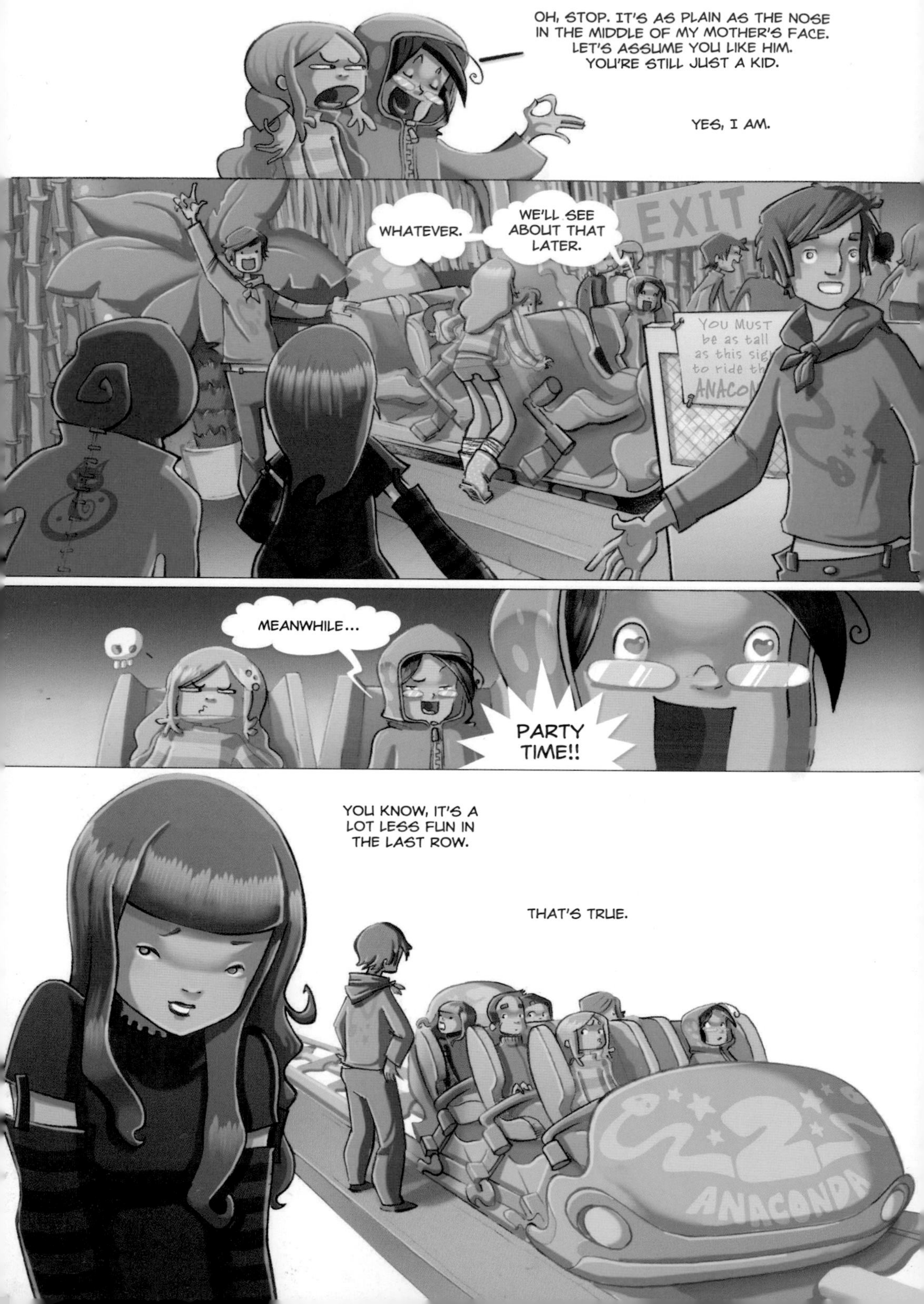

OH, STOP. IT'S AS PLAIN AS THE NOSE IN THE MIDDLE OF MY MOTHER'S FACE. LET'S ASSUME YOU LIKE HIM. YOU'RE STILL JUST A KID.
YES, I AM.
EXIT
WHATEVER.
WE'LL SEE ABOUT THAT LATER.
You Must be as tall
MEANWHILE...
PARTY TIME!!
YOU KNOW, IT'S A LOT LESS FUN IN THE LAST ROW.
THAT'S TRUE.
ANACONDA

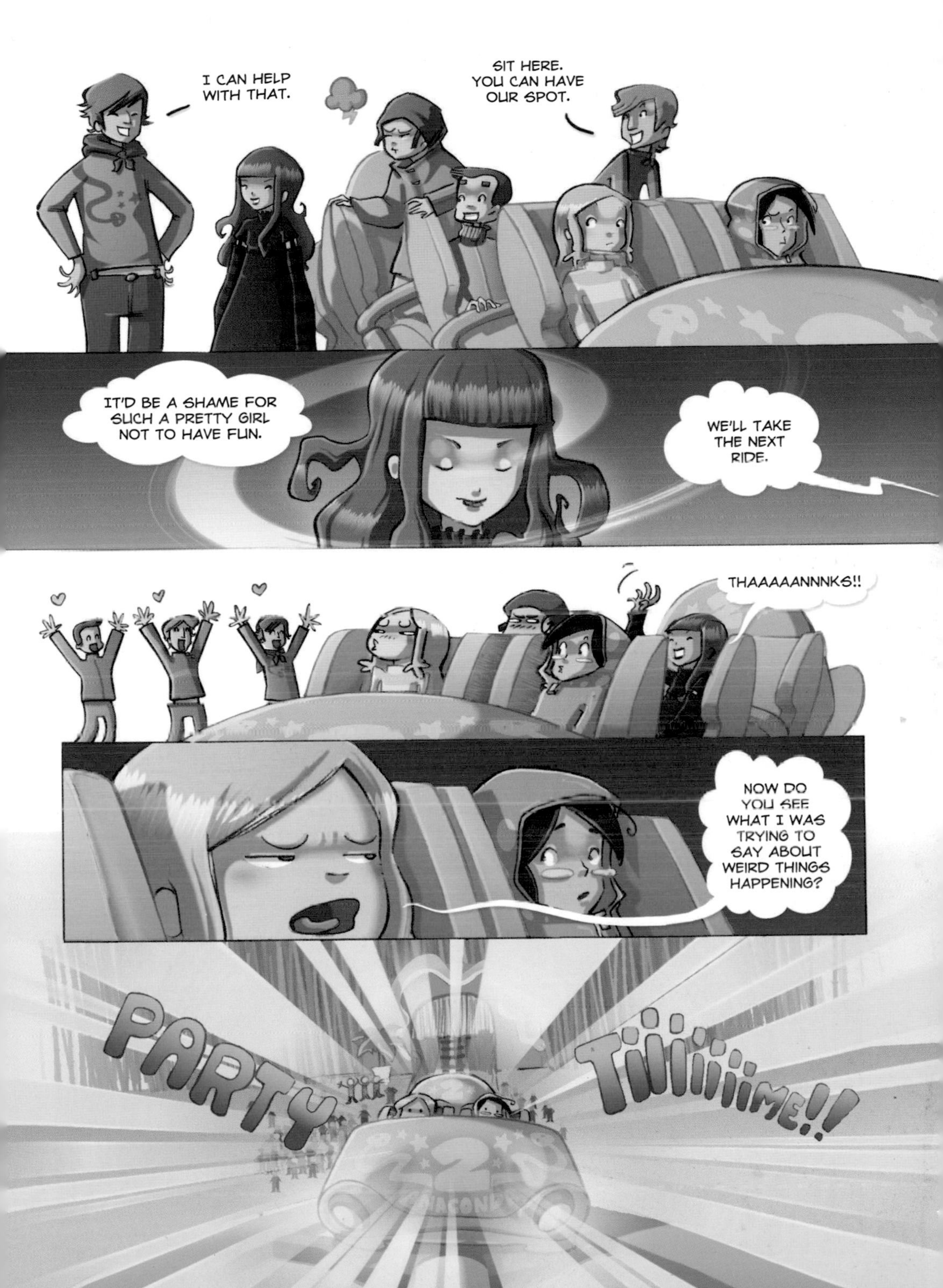

I CAN HELP WITH THAT.
SIT HERE. YOU CAN HAVE OUR SPOT.
IT'D BE A SHAME FOR SUCH A PRETTY GIRL NOT TO HAVE FUN.
WE'LL TAKE THE NEXT RIDE.
THAAAAANNNKS!!
NOW DO YOU SEE WHAT I WAS TRYING TO SAY ABOUT WEIRD THINGS HAPPENING?
PARTY TIIIIIIIME!!

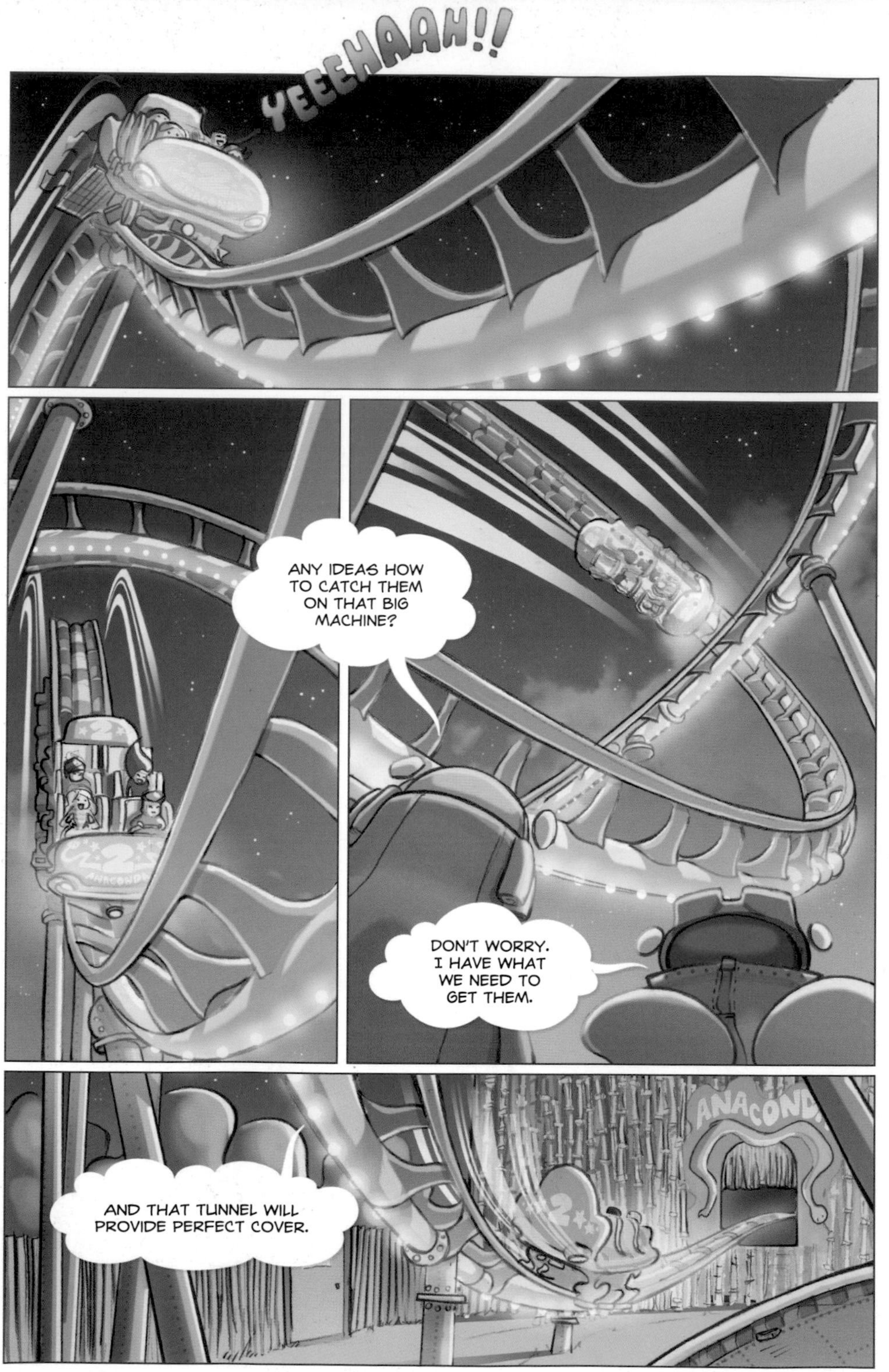
YEEEHAAAH!!
ANY IDEAS HOW TO CATCH THEM ON THAT BIG MACHINE?
DON'T WORRY. I HAVE WHAT WE NEED TO GET THEM.
AND THAT TUNNEL WILL PROVIDE PERFECT COVER.
ANACONDA

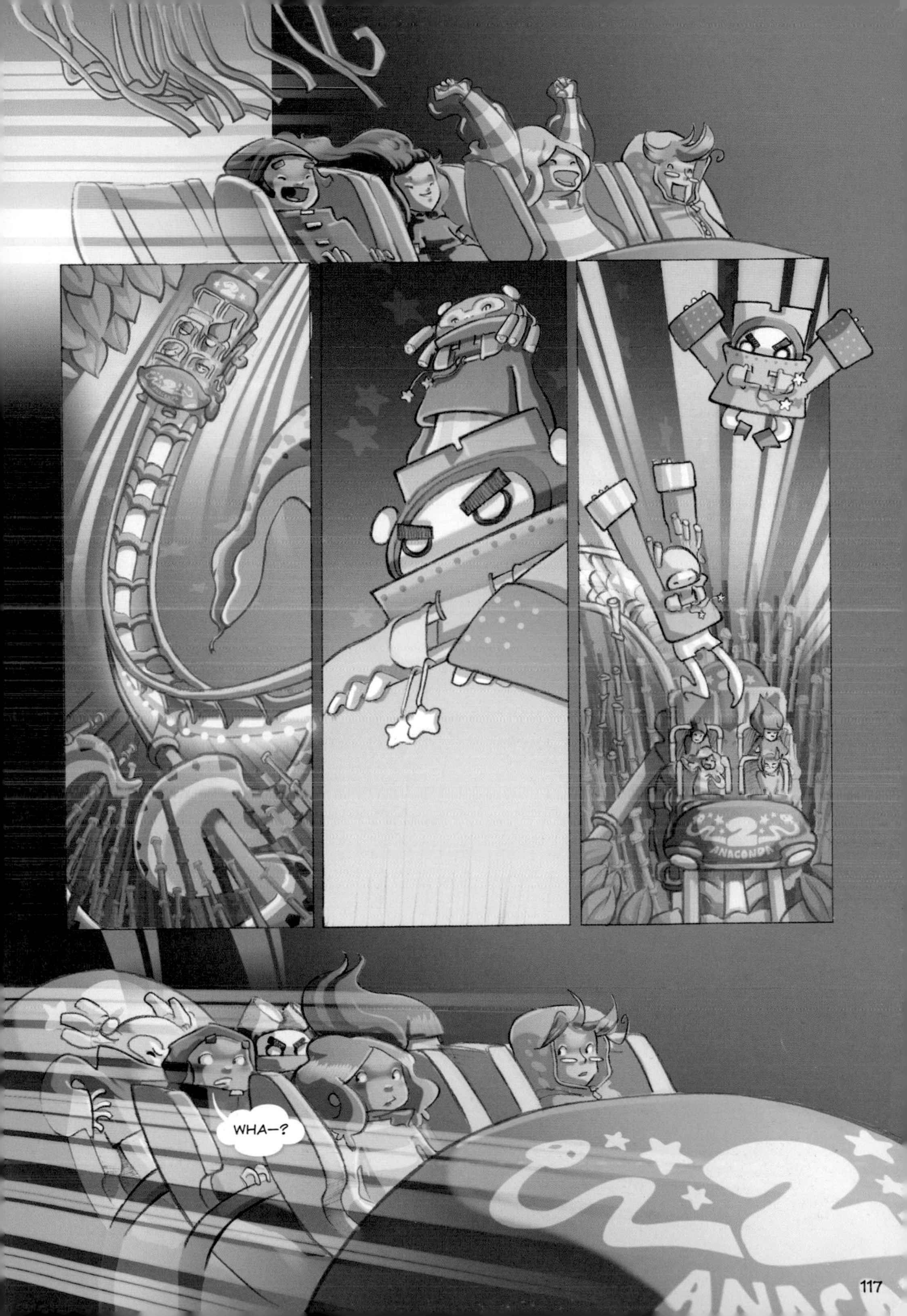

ANACONDA
WHA–?
ANACONDA

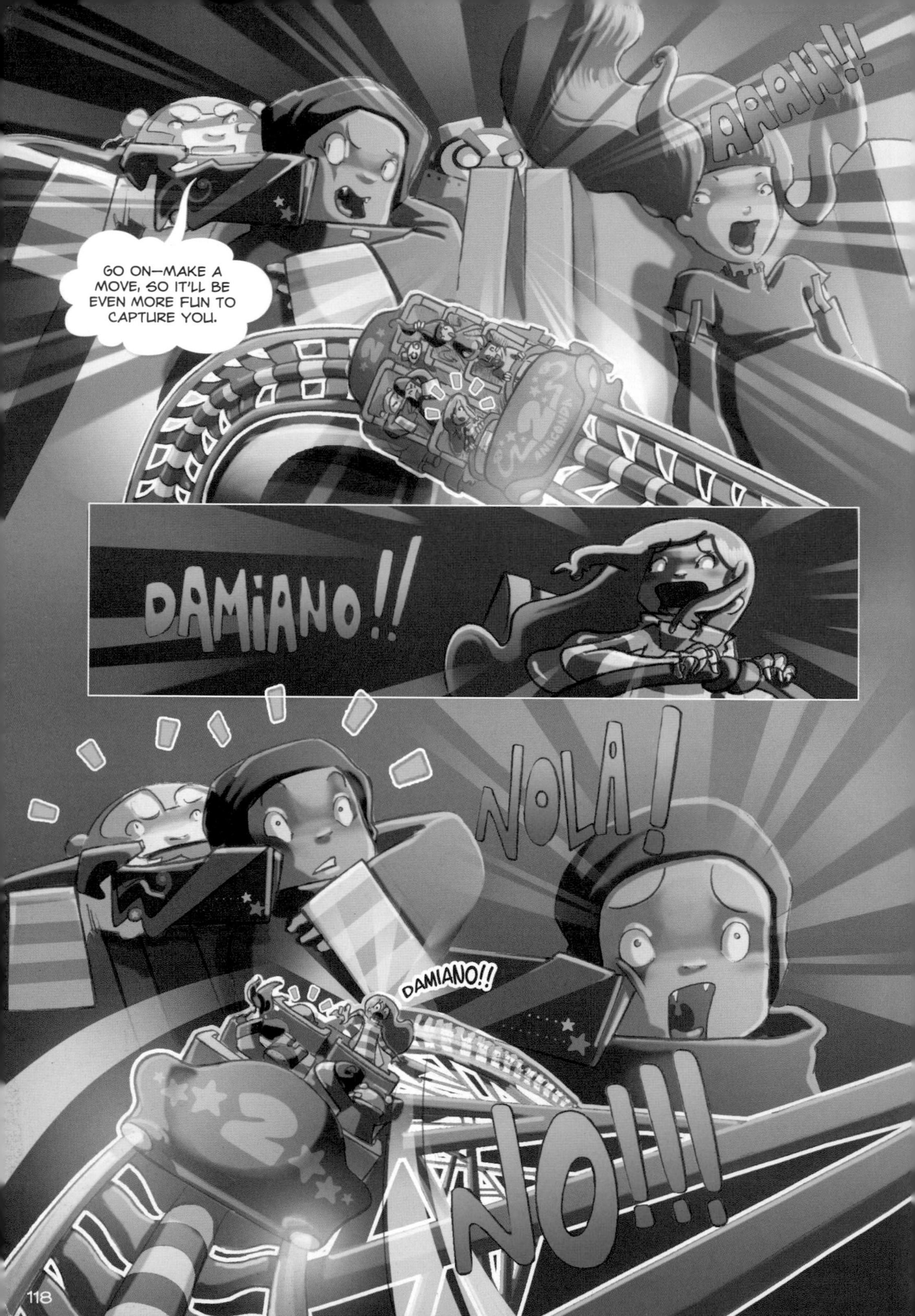
ARRRH!!
GO ON—MAKE A MOVE, SO IT'LL BE EVEN MORE FUN TO CAPTURE YOU.
DAMIANO!!
NOLA!
DAMIANO!!
NO!!!

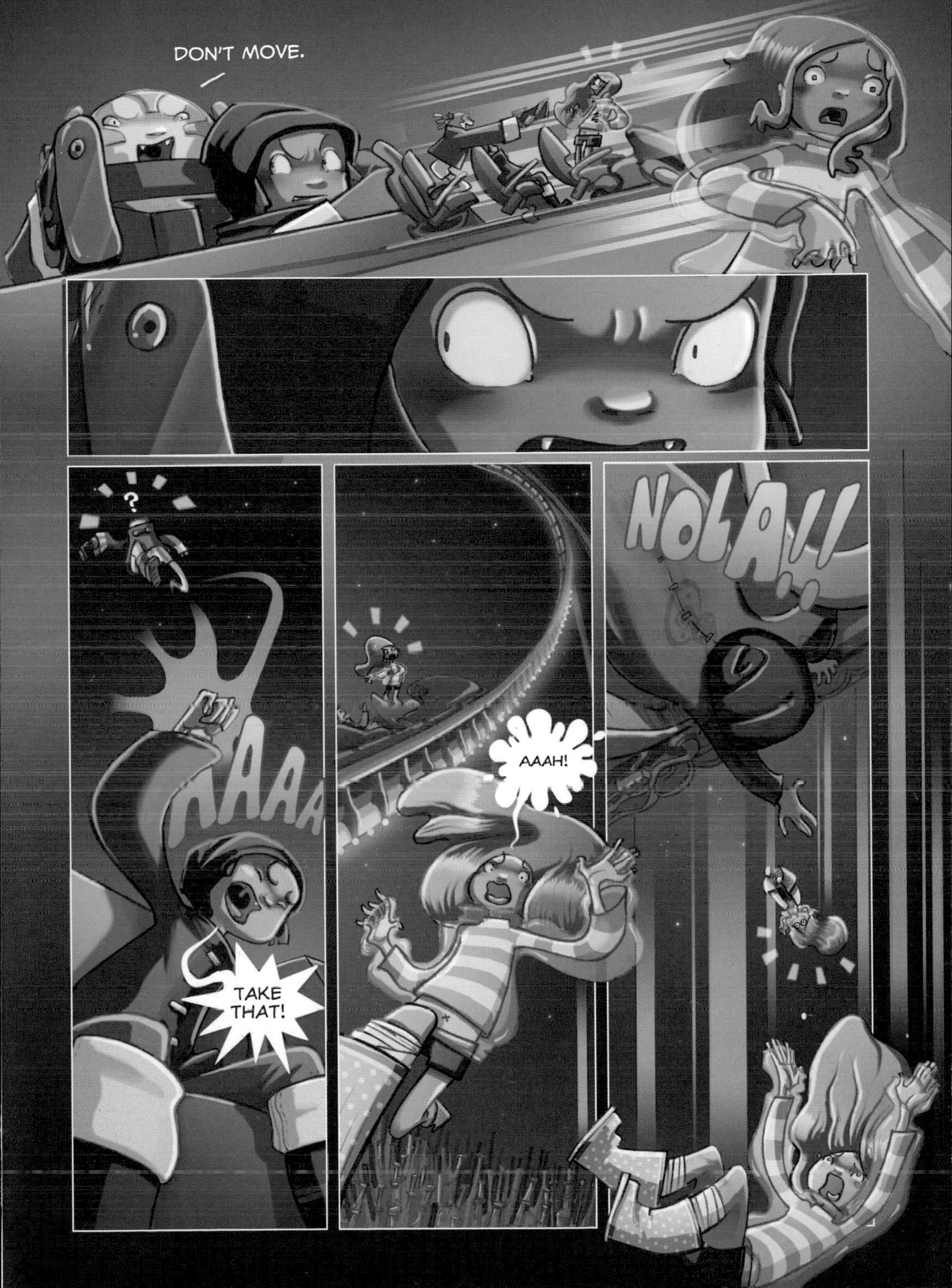
DON'T MOVE.
AAAA
TAKE THAT!
AAAH!
NOLA!!

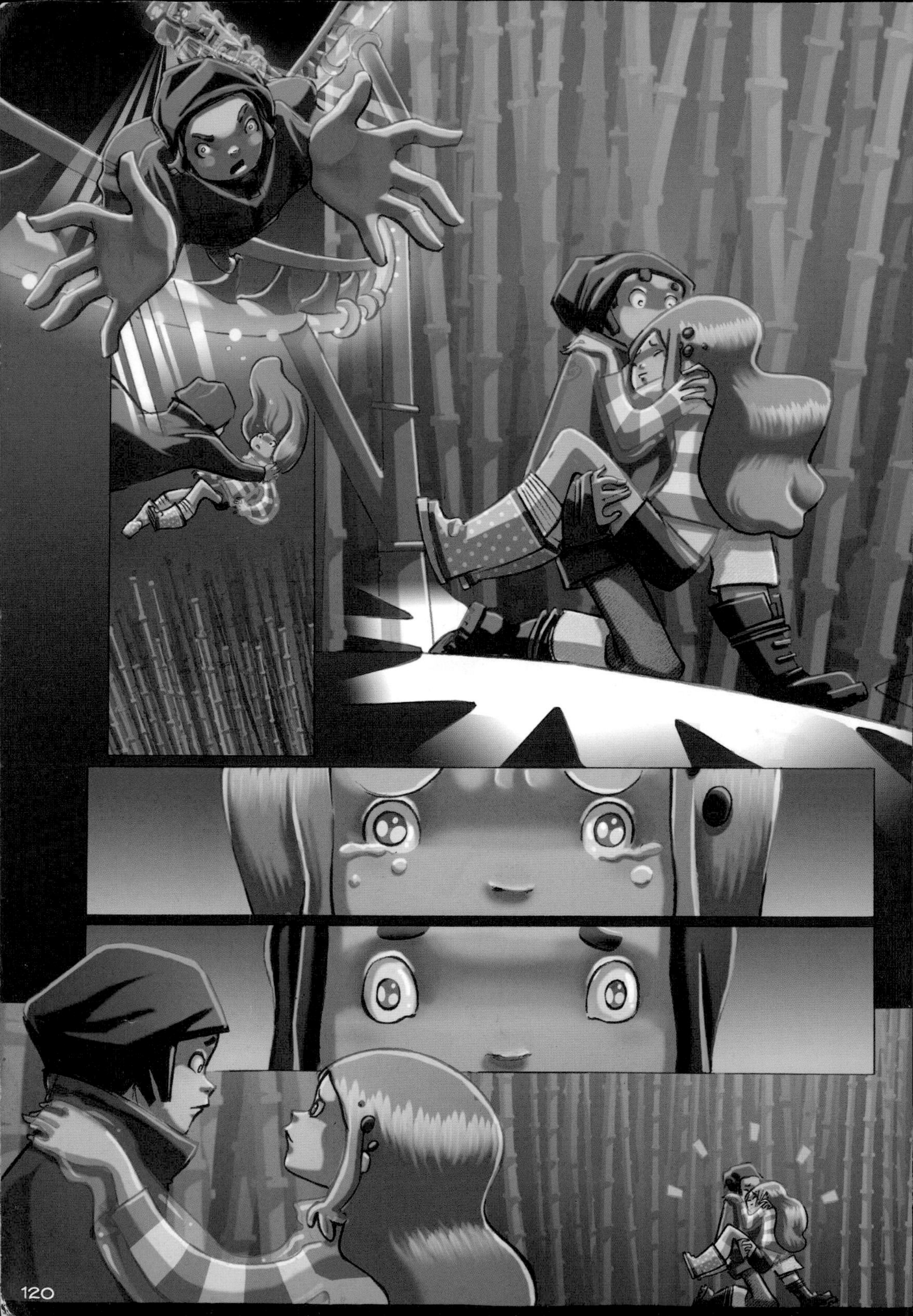

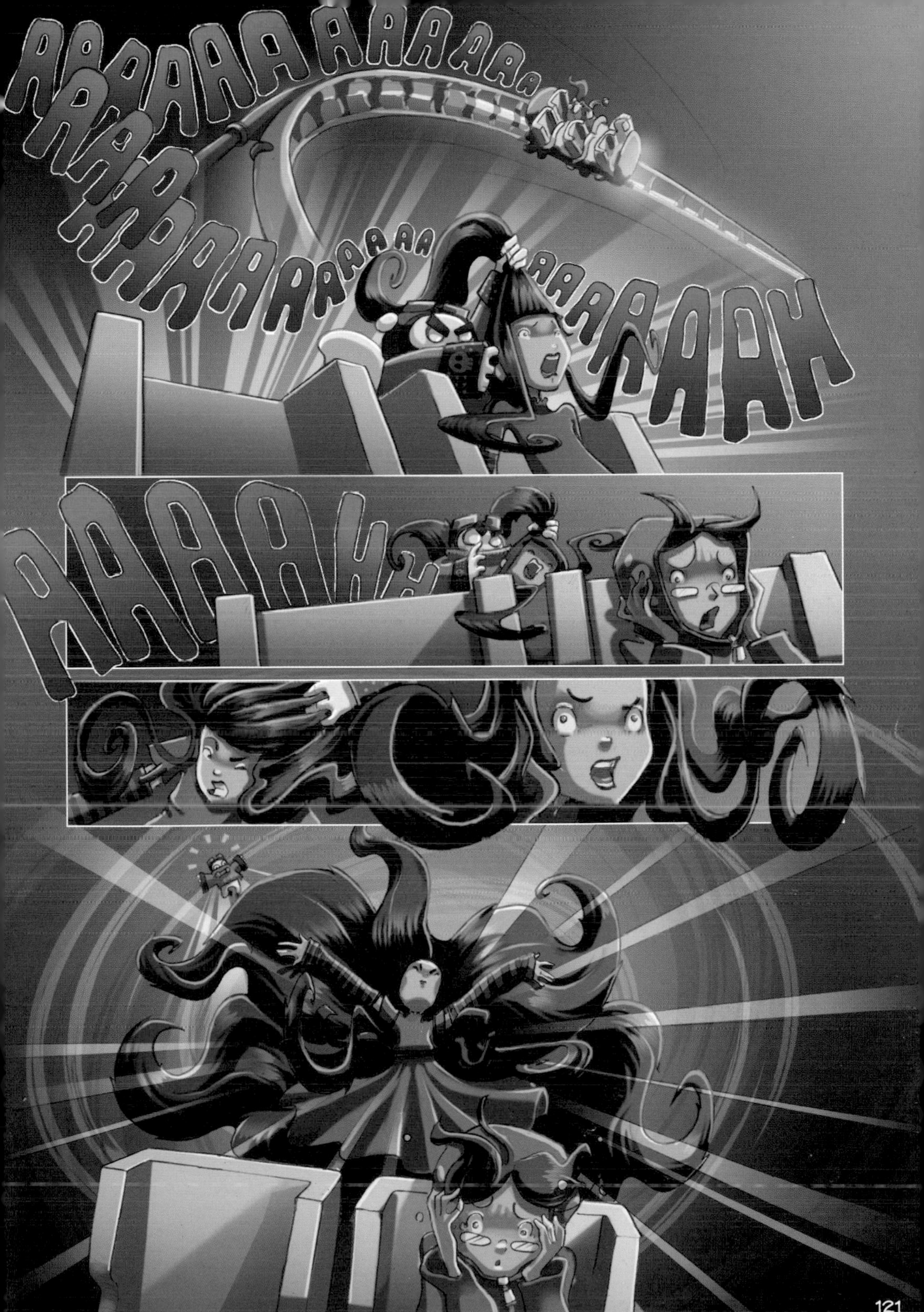
AAAAAAAAAAAAAaaa
AAAAAAAAAAAAaaaaaaa AAAAAAAAAH
AAAAAH

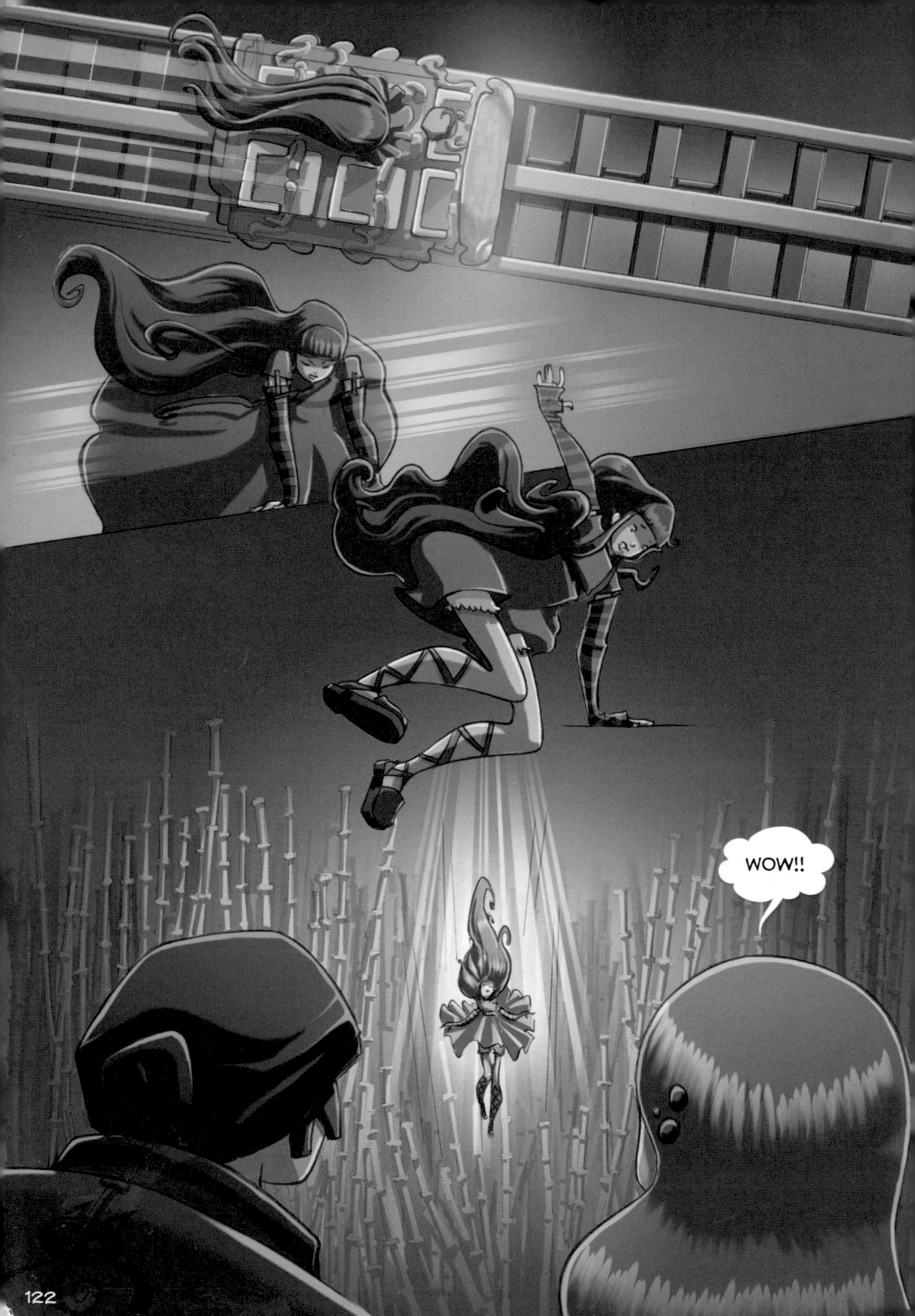
WOW!!

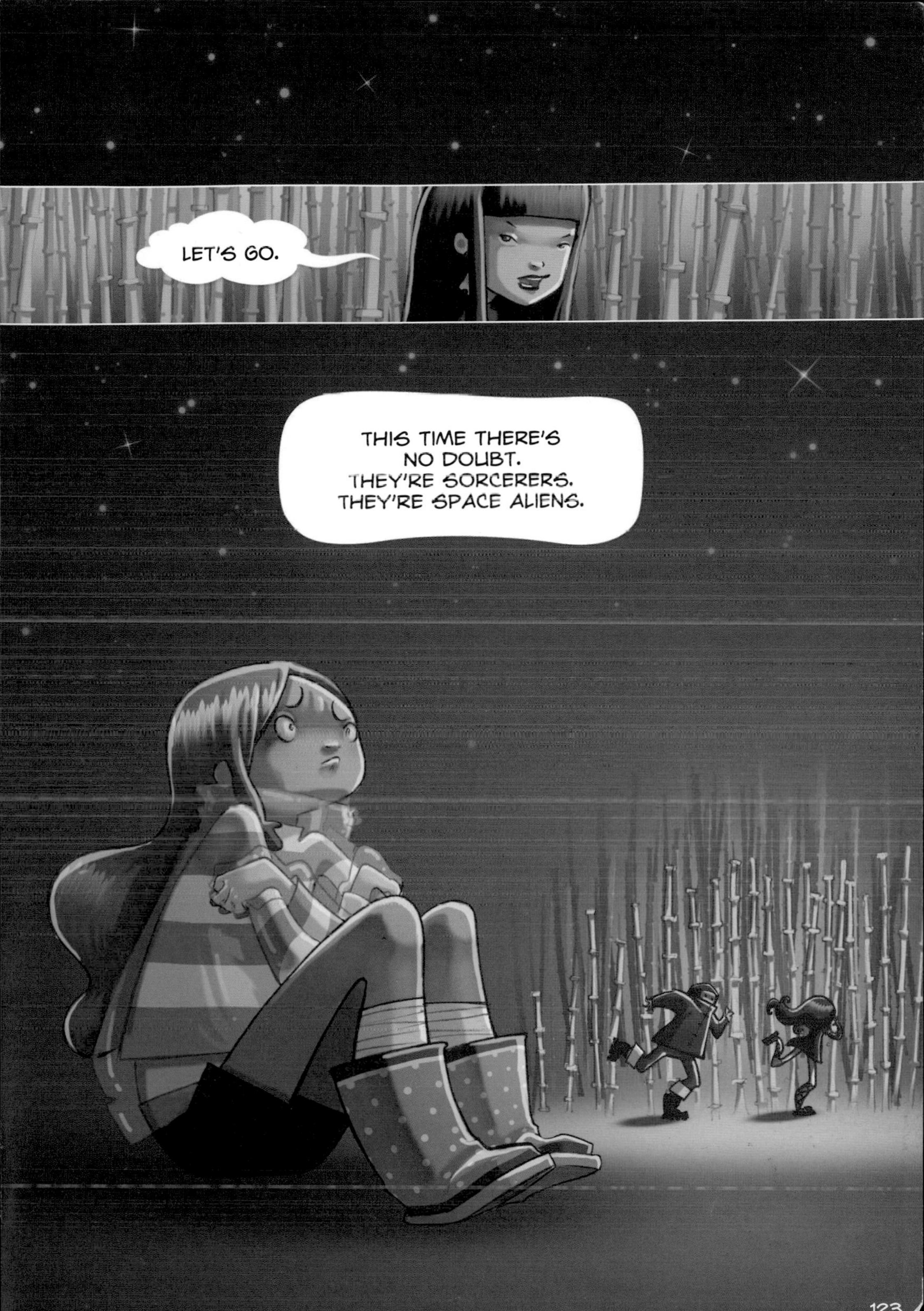
LET'S GO.
THIS TIME THERE'S NO DOUBT. THEY'RE SORCERERS. THEY'RE SPACE ALIENS.

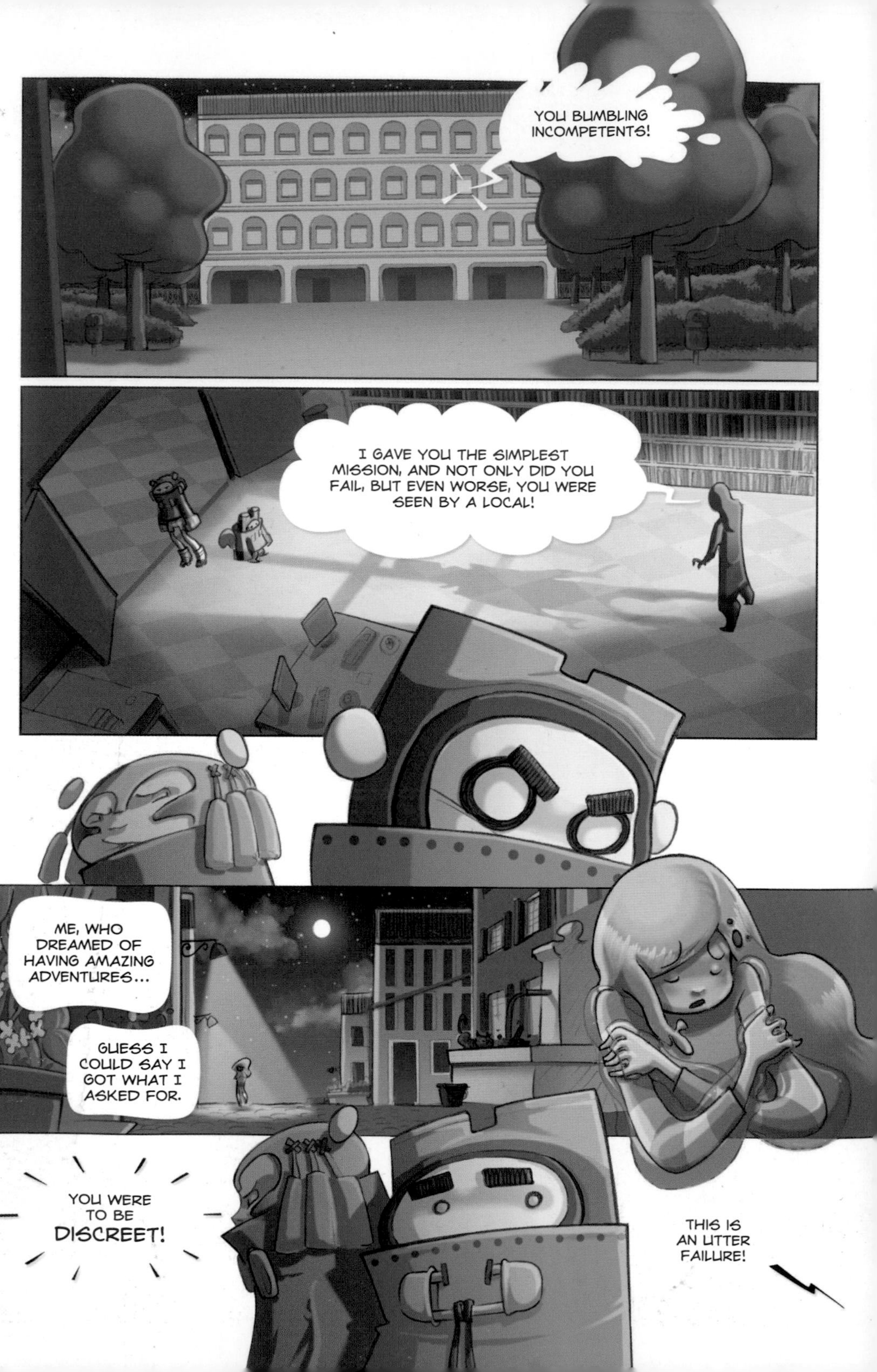
YOU BUMBLING INCOMPETENTS!
I GAVE YOU THE SIMPLEST MISSION, AND NOT ONLY DID YOU FAIL, BUT EVEN WORSE, YOU WERE SEEN BY A LOCAL!
ME, WHO DREAMED OF HAVING AMAZING ADVENTURES...
GUESS I COULD SAY I GOT WHAT I ASKED FOR.
YOU WERE TO BE DISCREET!
THIS IS AN UTTER FAILURE!

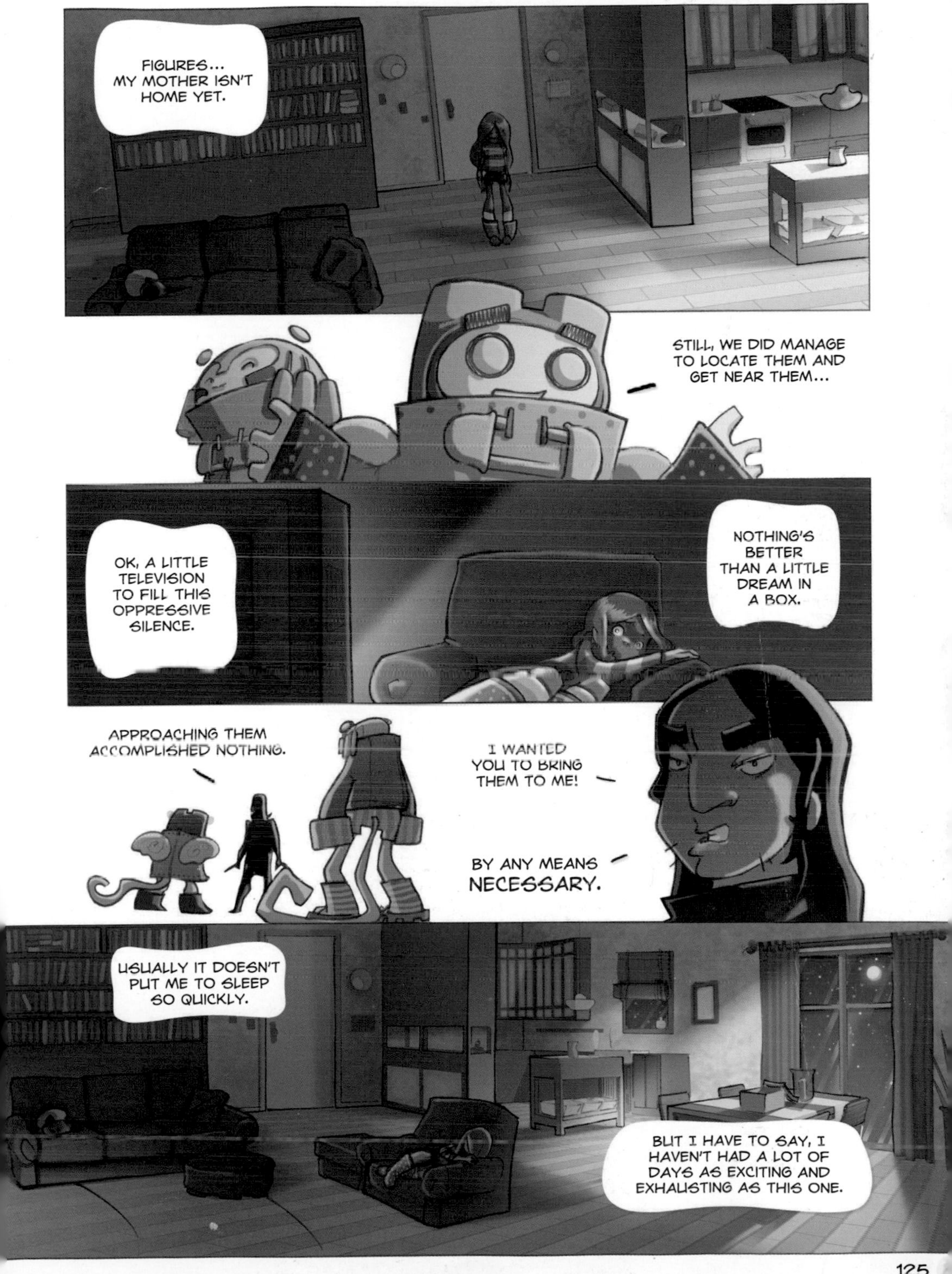

FIGURES... MY MOTHER ISN'T HOME YET.
STILL, WE DID MANAGE TO LOCATE THEM AND GET NEAR THEM...
OK, A LITTLE TELEVISION TO FILL THIS OPPRESSIVE SILENCE.
NOTHING'S BETTER THAN A LITTLE DREAM IN A BOX.
APPROACHING THEM ACCOMPLISHED NOTHING.
I WANTED YOU TO BRING THEM TO ME!
BY ANY MEANS NECESSARY.
USUALLY IT DOESN'T PUT ME TO SLEEP SO QUICKLY.
BUT I HAVE TO SAY, I HAVEN'T HAD A LOT OF DAYS AS EXCITING AND EXHAUSTING AS THIS ONE.

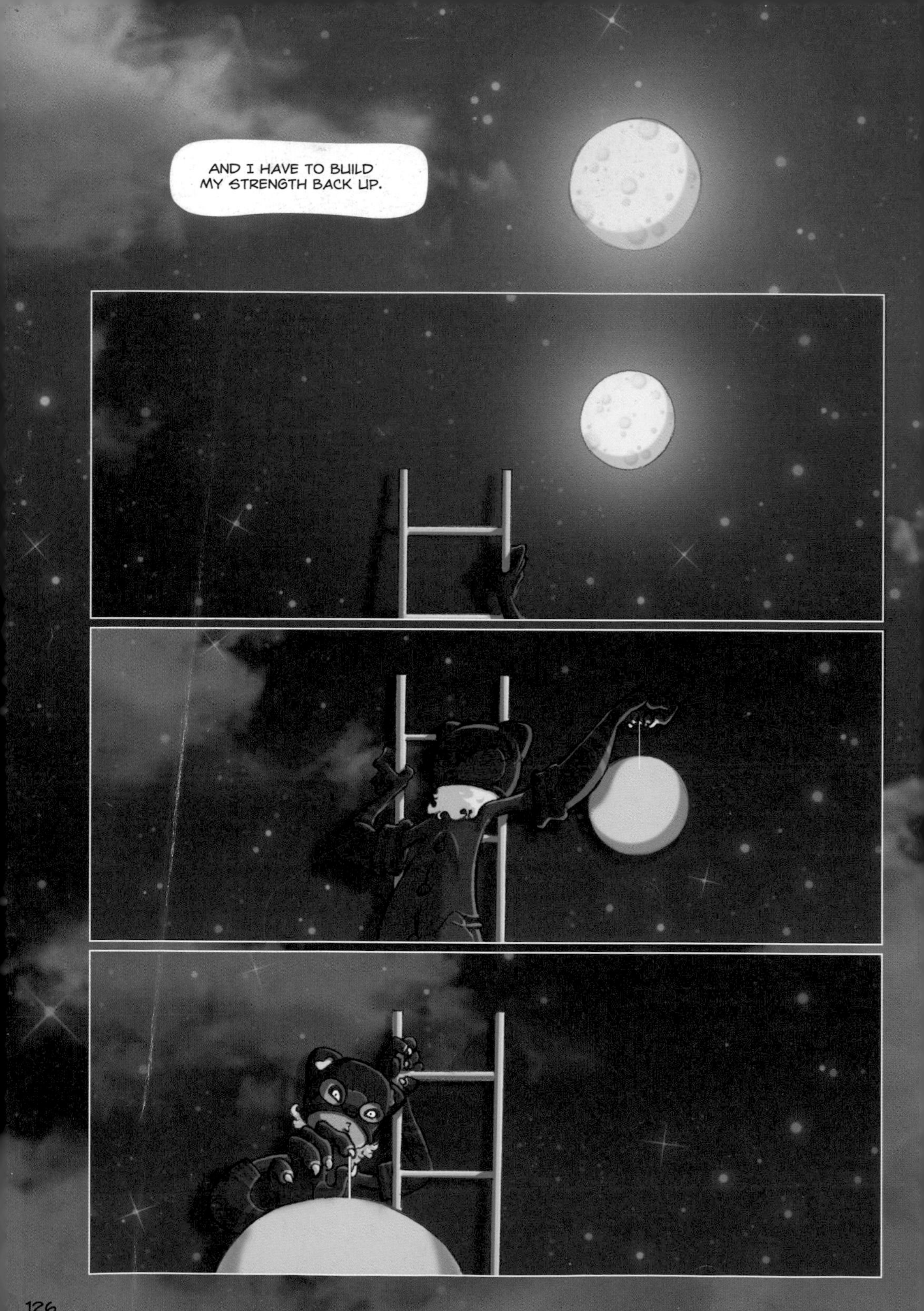
AND I HAVE TO BUILD MY STRENGTH BACK UP.

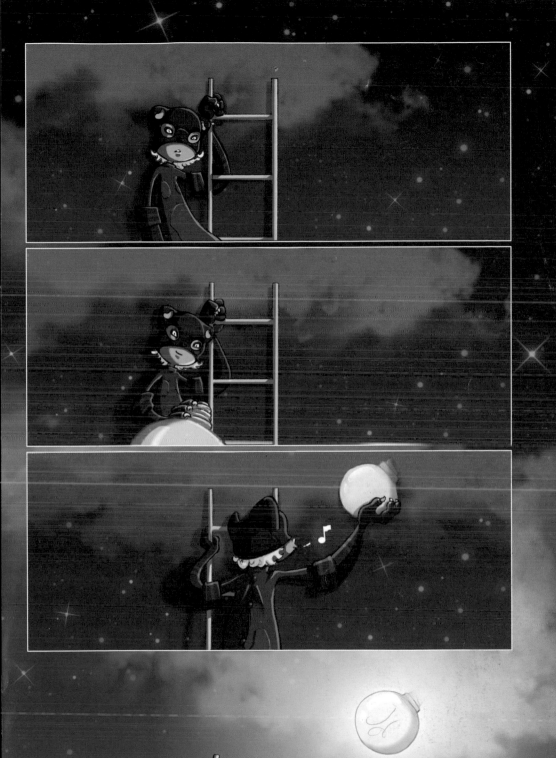

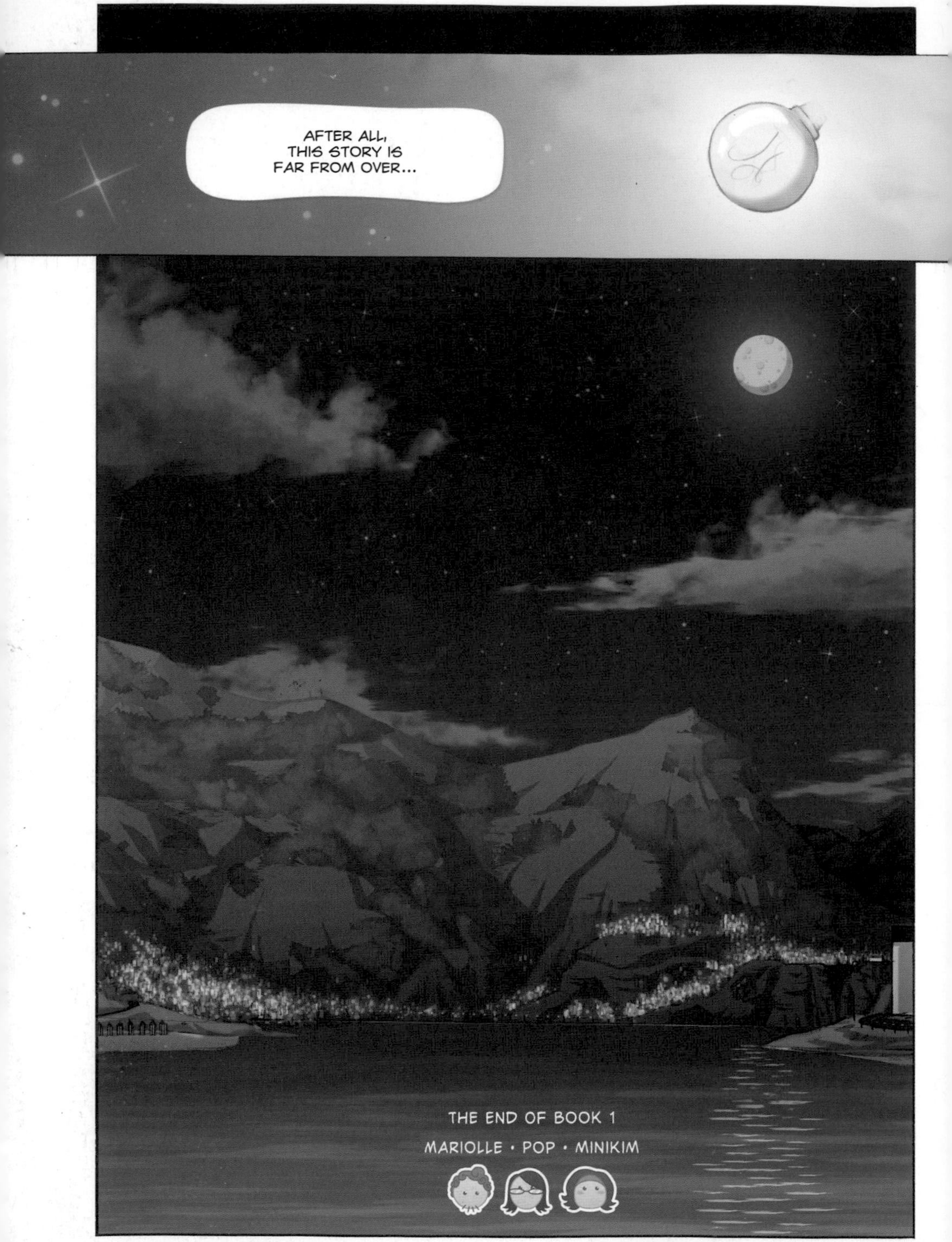
AFTER ALL,
THIS STORY IS
FAR FROM OVER...
THE END OF BOOK 1
MARIOLLE • POP • MINIKIM

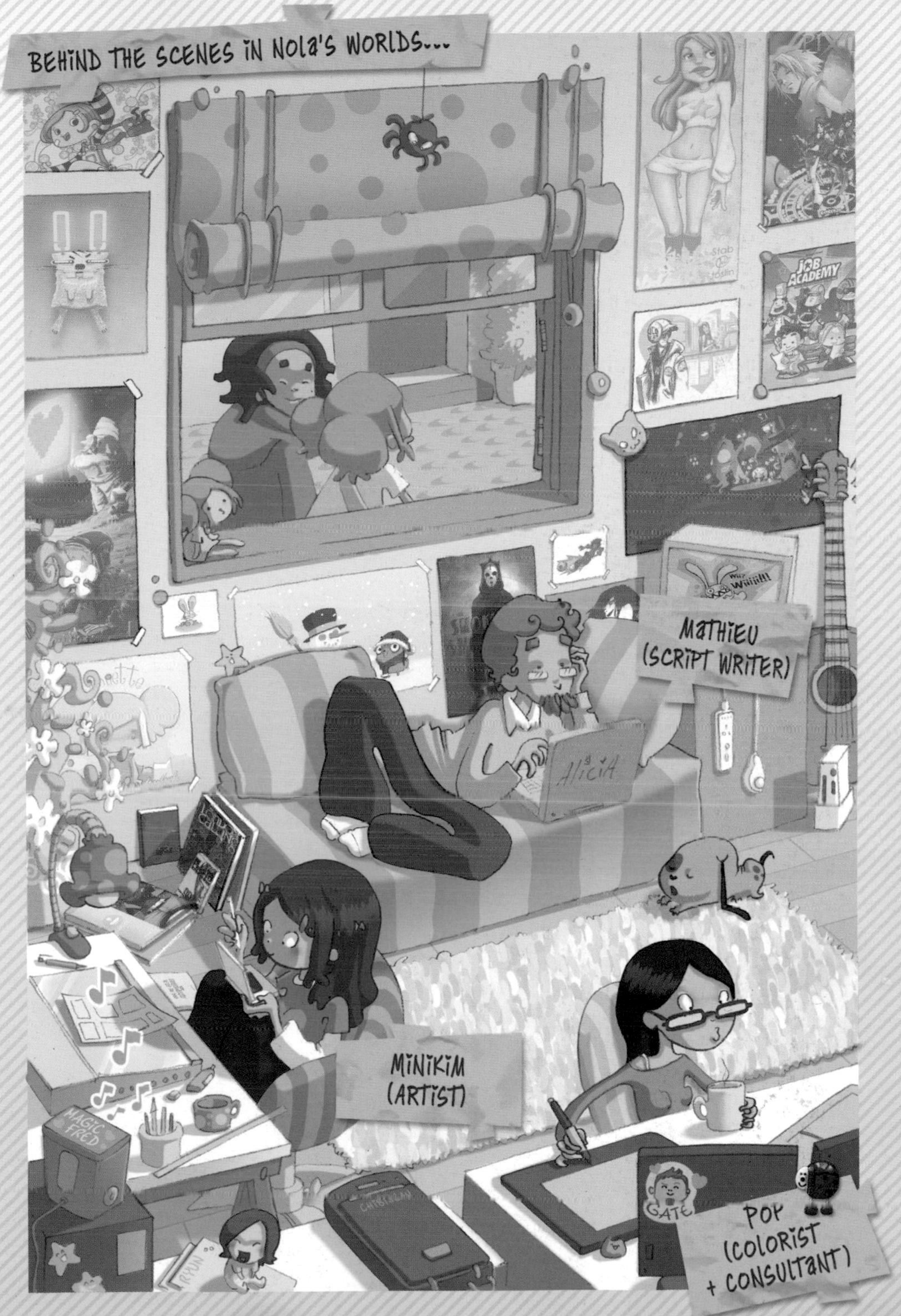
BEHIND THE SCENES IN NOLA'S WORLDS...
JOB ACADEMY
MATHIEU (SCRIPT WRITER)
ALICIA
MINIKIM (ARTIST)
MAGIC FRED
POP (COLORIST + CONSULTANT)
GATE

MATHIEU WRITES THE STORY.

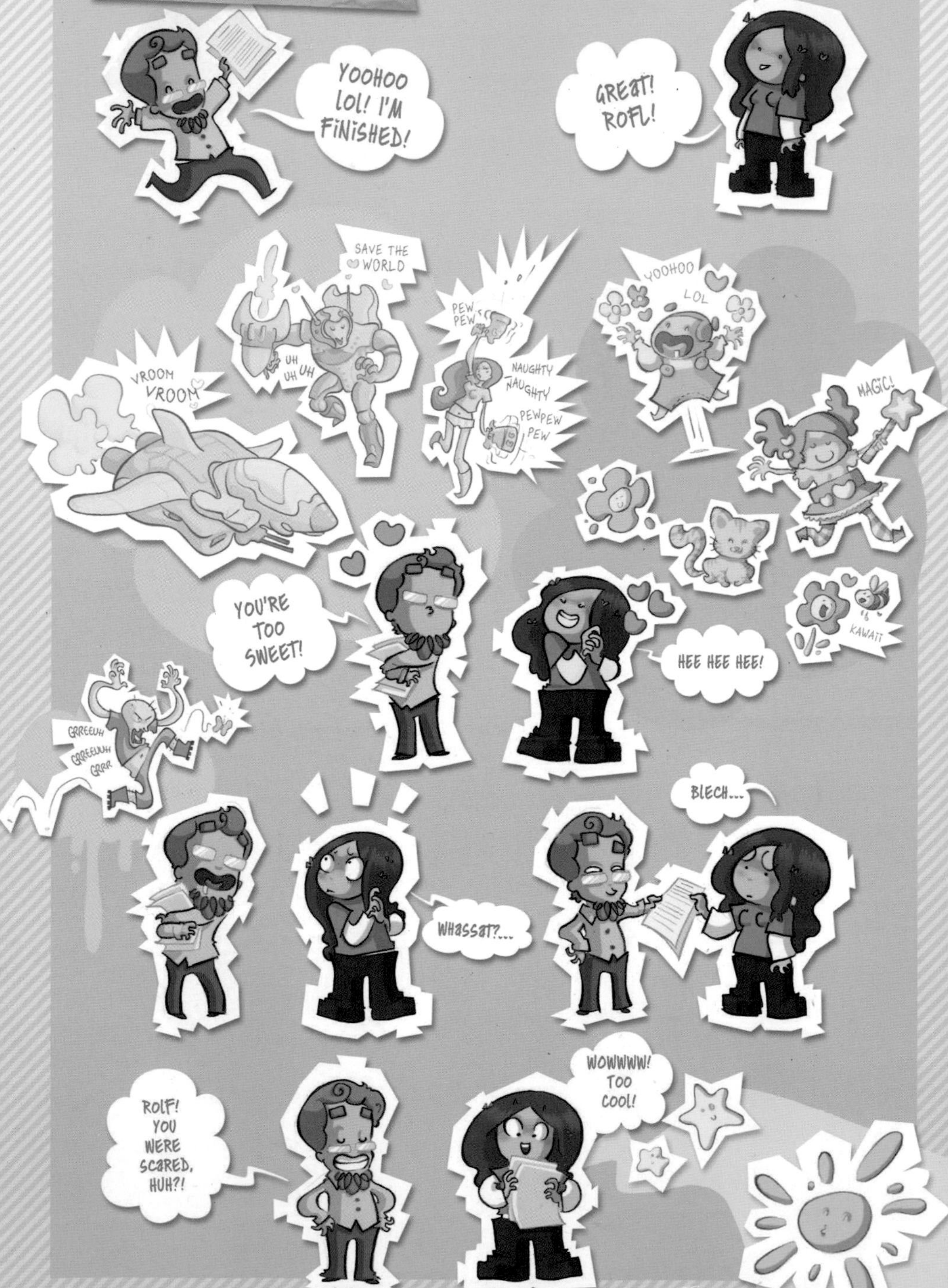
YOOHOO LOL! I'M FINISHED!
GREAT! ROFL!
SAVE THE WORLD
VROOM VROOM
UH UH UH
PEW PEW
NAUGHTY NAUGHTY
PEWPEW PEW
YOOHOO LOL
MAGIC!
KAWAII
YOU'RE TOO SWEET!
HEE HEE HEE!
GRREEUH GRREEUUH GRRR
WHASSAT?...
BLECH...
ROLF! YOU WERE SCARED, HUH?!
WOWWWW! TOO COOL!

AFTER MATHIEU WRITES THE STORY,

KIM DESIGNS THE CHARACTERS AND SETTINGS.

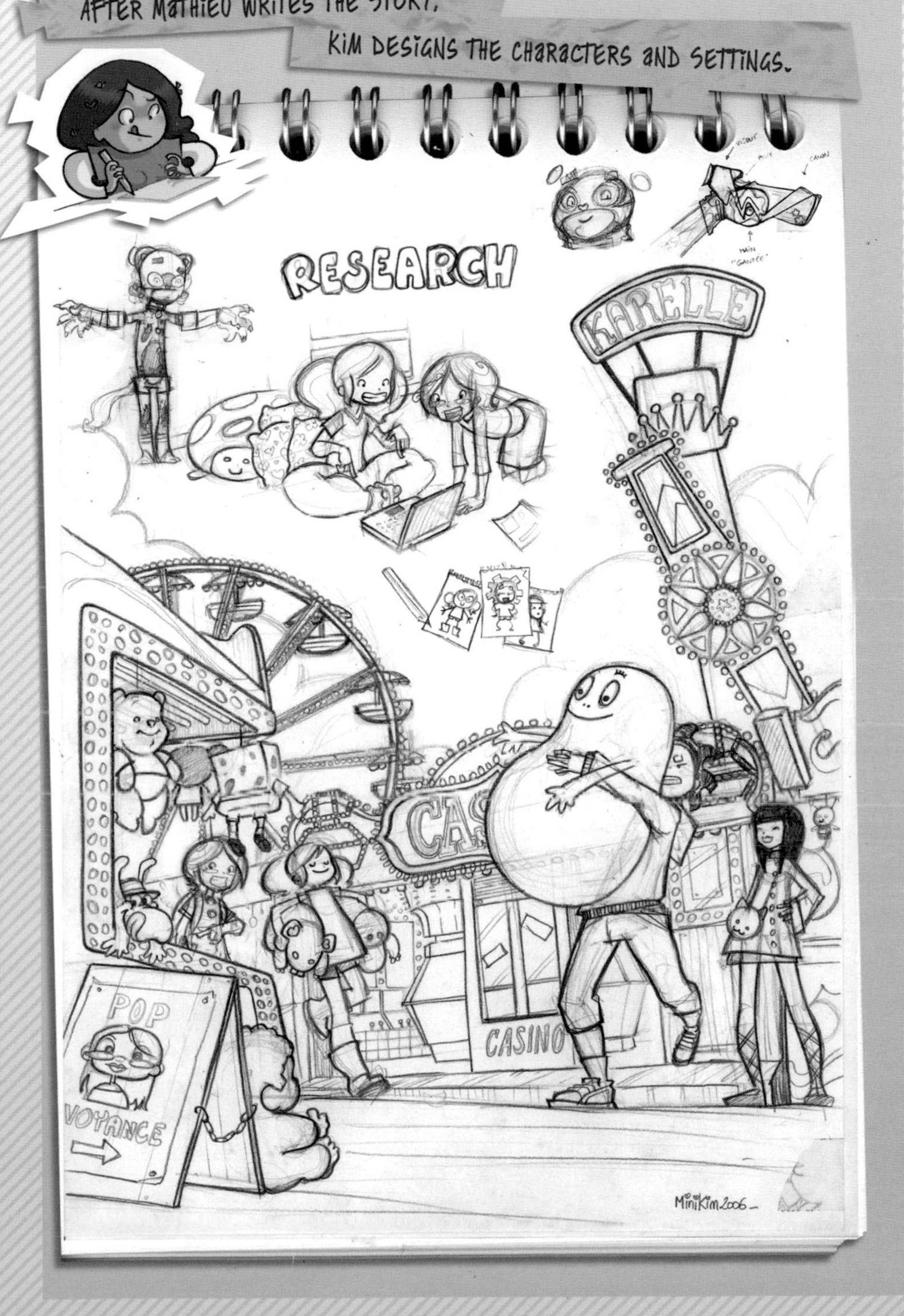
RESEARCH
KARELLE
CASINO
POP
VOYANCE
MiniKim2006

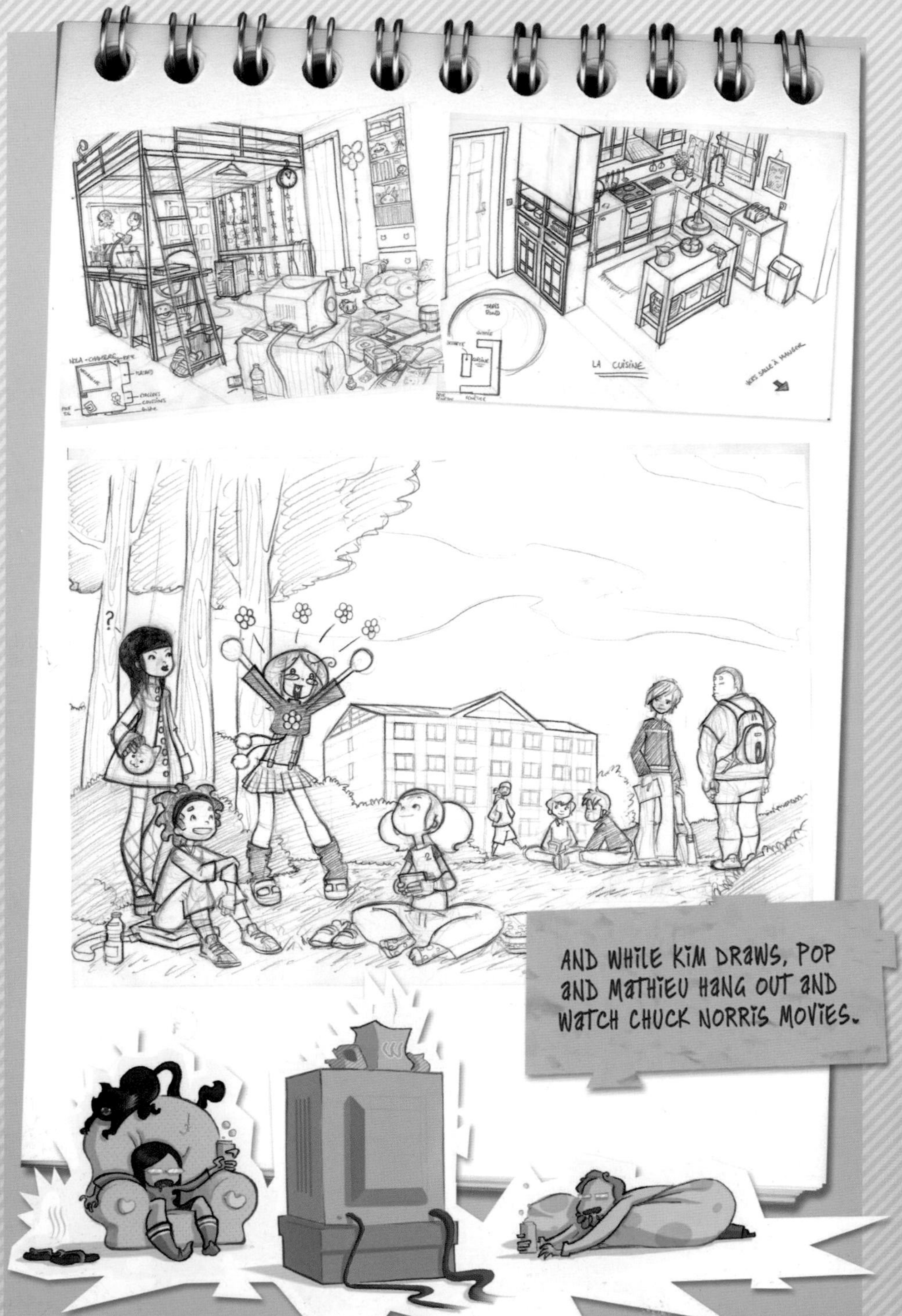
LA CUISINE
AND WHILE KIM DRAWS, POP AND MATHIEU HANG OUT AND WATCH CHUCK NORRIS MOVIES.

THEN KIM DRAWS EACH PAGE ON A SHEET OF A4 PAPER (21 CM X 29.7 CM),

WHICH IS EXAMINED MINUTELY BY POP.

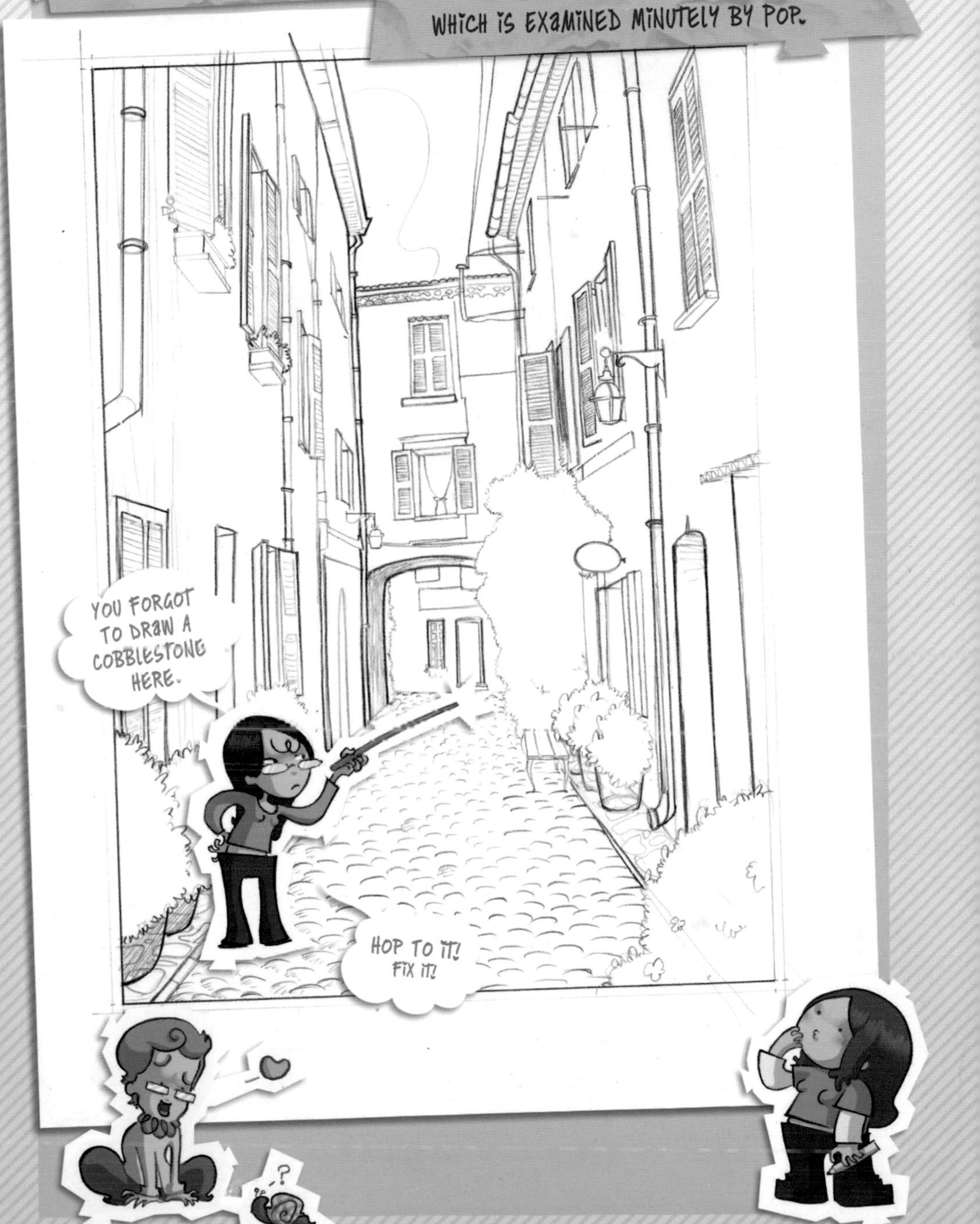

YOU FORGOT TO DRAW A COBBLESTONE HERE.
HOP TO IT! FIX IT!

EACH PAGE IS THEN CLEANED UP

WITH THE HELP OF A LIGHT TABLE AND COMPUTER SOFTWARE.

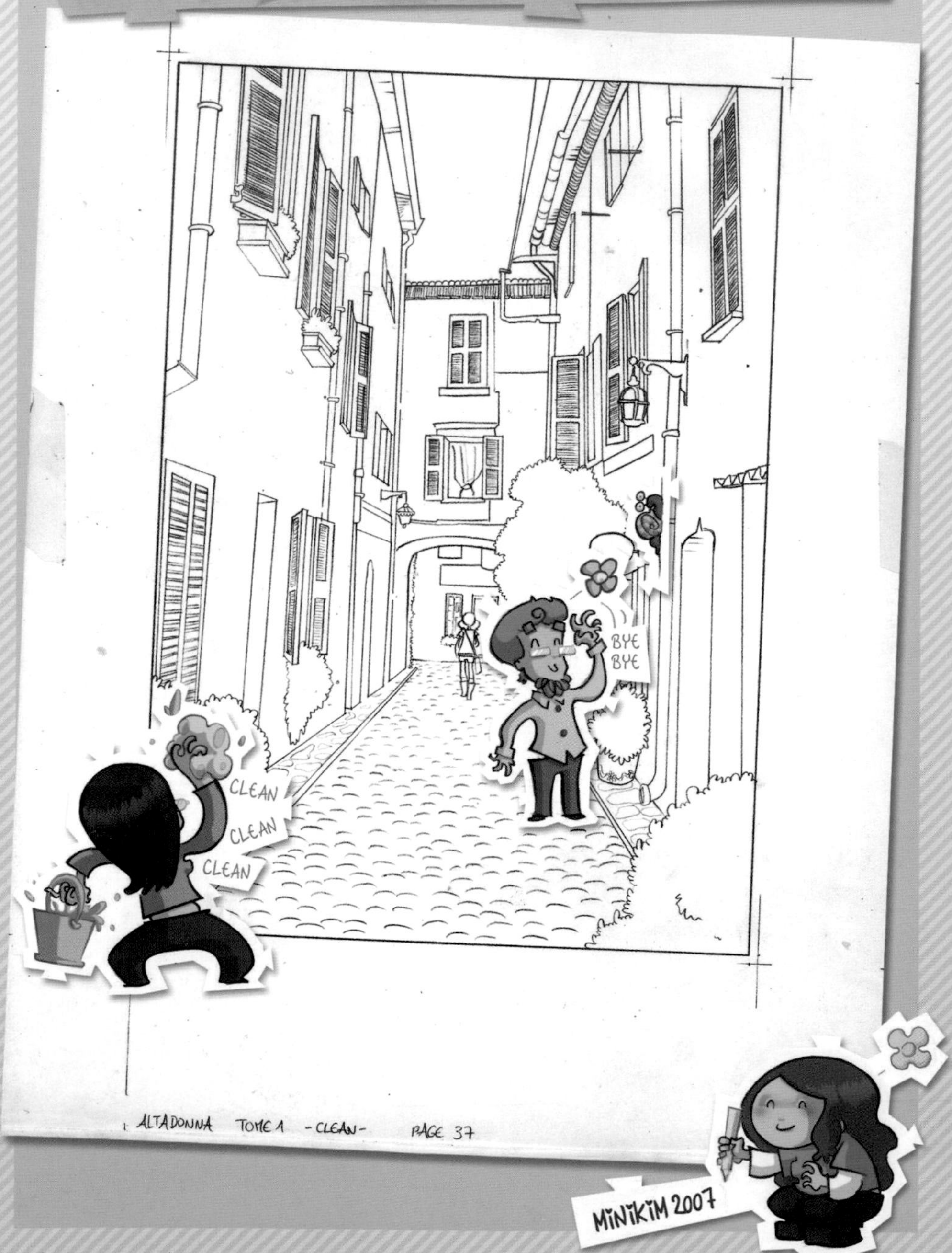
BYE BYE
CLEAN
CLEAN
CLEAN
ALTADONNA TOME 1 -CLEAN- PAGE 37
MINIKIM 2007

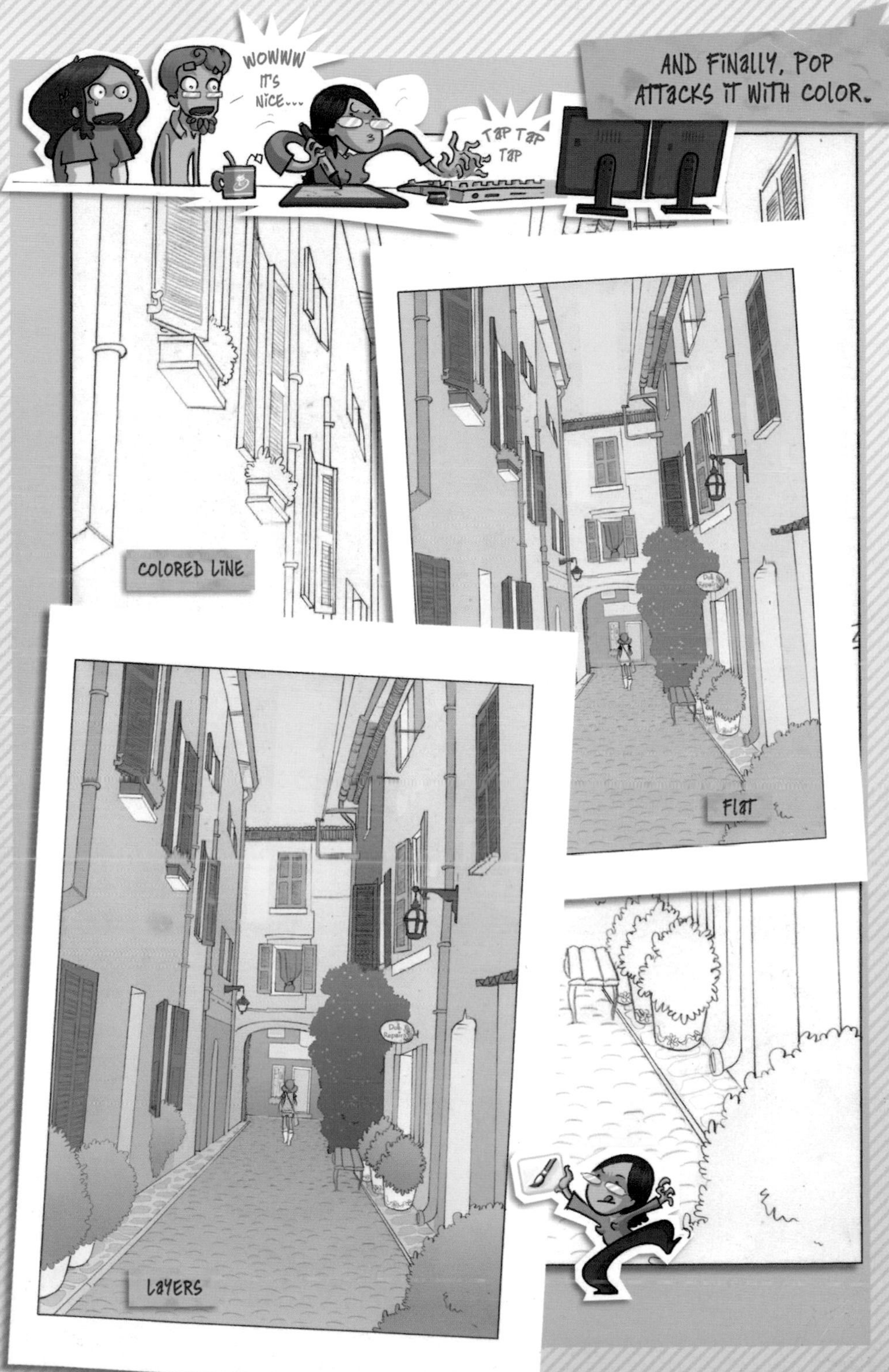

WOWWW IT'S NICE...
TAP TAP TAP
AND FINALLY, POP ATTACKS IT WITH COLOR.
COLORED LINE
FLAT
LAYERS

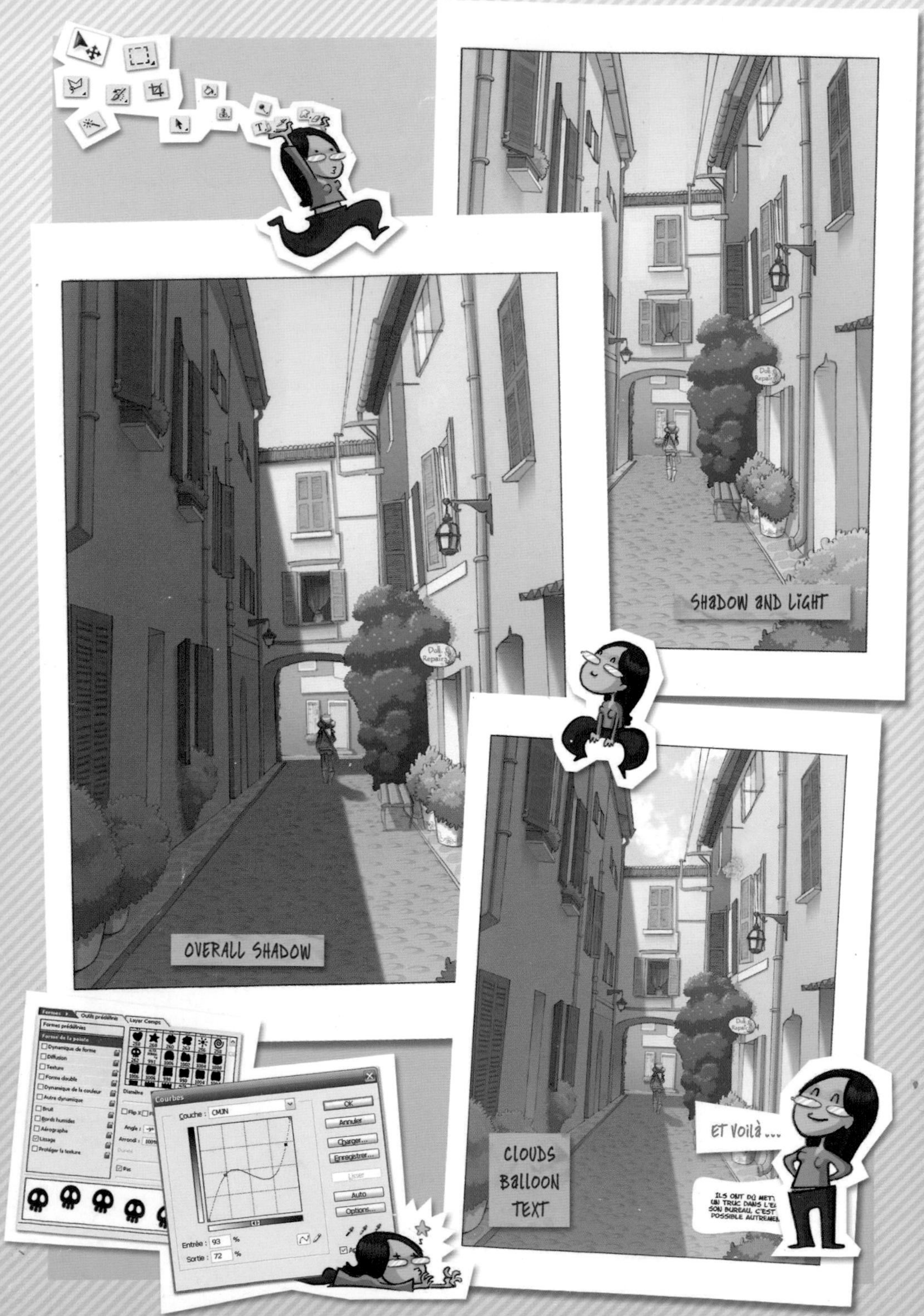
OVERALL SHADOW
SHADOW AND LIGHT
CLOUDS BALLOON TEXT
Doll Repairs
ET VOILÀ ...
Formes
Outils prédéfinis
Layer Comps
Formes prédéfinies
Forme de la pointe
Dynamique de forme
Diffusion
Texture
Forme double
Dynamique de la couleur
Autre dynamique
Bruit
Bords humides
Aérographe
Lissage
Protéger la texture
Courbes
Couche : CMJN
OK
Annuler
Charger...
Enregistrer...
Lisser
Auto
Options...
Entrée : 93 %
Sortie : 72 %